THE SUMMER WE READ GATSBY

DANIELLE GANEK is the author of the critically praised *Lulu Meets God and Doubts Him*. She lives with her husband and three children in New York City and is currently working on her third novel.

Praise for *The Summer We Read Gatsby*

"You can hear the waves crashing and ice cubes tinkling as [these sisters] reunite with lost loves and try to mend their pasts."
—*Glamour*

"A smart, entertaining romp."
—*People*

"For the beach bag: Apply sunscreen before you lose yourself."
—*Marie Claire*

"A fully engrossing page-turner filled with delightful characters and sumptuous details about one perfect July in the Hamptons. Like summer itself, this bewitching novel will leave you half in love and yearning for more."
—Elin Hilderbrand, author of *Barefoot*

"Entertaining . . . unalike half sisters Cassie and Peck Moriarty inherit their aunt's Southampton cottage and along with it a potent secret, some swoony romantic prospects, and several friends even Fitzgerald would have relished."
—*Town & Country*

"Fantastic."
—*Design Baby*

"A sophisticated comedy of manners."
—*O* Magazine's Summer Reading List

"[The] kind of book that invites sunscreen stains . . . A tale of two half sisters' summer of cocktails and cupcakes, theme parties and chiffon dresses—with a Jackson Pollock painting and a twinklingly handsome bachelor architect thrown in for good measure."
—Vogue.com's Summer's Hottest Beach Reads

"At the top of our must-read list."
—Tory's Blog

"If oddball families make you smile . . . dip into this frothy comedy about estranged sisters who reunite at the Hamptons home of their recently deceased eccentric aunt."   —*Real Simple*

"Fun, witty, and surprisingly moving."   —*Publishers Weekly*

"A plucky homage to Fitzgerald's masterpiece."
                                —*The New York Times Book Review*

"Friendships and romances rekindle, sisters grow close, objects disappear, mysteries are solved, and what is truly of value eventually becomes apparent in this charming, entertaining, and brightly written summer read."   —*Booklist*

"An excellent read for the approaching summer months—Ganek has a gift for writing light stories that are still smart without falling into the trap of snarky, cutesy, or saccharine sweet. Add to the mix a quirky cast of characters, a bit of mystery, and a dash of romance. This combination of elements may not be rare, but it is rare to find them done well."   —Lit Chick

"A pleasant escape with a satisfying conclusion."   —*Woman's Day*

Praise for *Lulu Meets God and Doubts Him*

"Its author has a savvy, satirical eye, a terrific title, and an insider's knowledge of the New York art gallery world."
                            —Janet Maslin, *CBS Sunday Morning*

"Danielle Ganek captures the absurdity of the New York art scene with wide and witty brushstrokes."   —*Vanity Fair*

"Lulu of a novel . . . Ganek's fascination with artists naturally informs her tongue-in-cheek novel." —*USA Today*

"[T]he painting remains the book's true center. Ms. Ganek allows this picture to mean different things to different people. She measures both their aesthetic wisdom and their avarice according to the ways they try to snag it. The various maneuvers that give each character just deserts make this a glossy, amusing story that still finds time to wonder, in all seriousness, how, why, and whether the art world differentiates between trash and treasure."

—*The New York Times*

"Danielle Ganek's novel has the art world asking who is who."
—*The New York Times* (Style Section)

"An amusing, suspenseful novel that delights . . . a page-turner set against a refreshingly unique backdrop." —*People*

"Innocent at heart but smart and savvy from experience, she provides a refreshingly candid insider's take on the moneyed New York art world." —*The Boston Globe*

"Slather on the sunscreen and settle in for the beach read of the summer. . . . Ganek's delightful tale has 'big screen' written all over it."
—*San Francisco Chronicle*

Also by Danielle Ganek

Lulu Meets God and Doubts Him

The Summer
We Read Gatsby

A Novel

Danielle Ganek

A PLUME BOOK

PLUME
Published by the Penguin Group
Penguin Group (USA) Inc., 375 Hudson Street, New York, New York 10014, U.S.A. • Penguin
Group (Canada), 90 Eglinton Avenue East, Suite 700, Toronto, Ontario, Canada M4P 2Y3 (a division
of Pearson Penguin Canada Inc.) • Penguin Books Ltd., 80 Strand, London WC2R 0RL, England
• Penguin Ireland, 25 St. Stephen's Green, Dublin 2, Ireland (a division of Penguin Books Ltd.) •
Penguin Group (Australia), 250 Camberwell Road, Camberwell, Victoria 3124, Australia (a division
of Pearson Australia Group Pty. Ltd.) • Penguin Books India Pvt. Ltd., 11 Community Centre,
Panchsheel Park, New Delhi – 110 017, India • Penguin Group (NZ), 67 Apollo Drive, Rosedale,
North Shore 0632, New Zealand (a division of Pearson New Zealand Ltd.) • Penguin Books (South
Africa) (Pty.) Ltd., 24 Sturdee Avenue, Rosebank, Johannesburg 2196, South Africa

Penguin Books Ltd., Registered Offices: 80 Strand, London WC2R 0RL, England

Published by Plume, a member of Penguin Group (USA) Inc. Previously published in a Viking
edition.

First Plume Printing, June 2011

10 9 8 7 6 5 4 3 2 1

Ⓟ REGISTERED TRADEMARK—MARCA REGISTRADA

The Library of Congress has catalogued the Viking edition as follows:

Ganek, Danielle.
    The summer we read Gatsby : a novel / Danielle Ganek.
        p. cm.
    ISBN 978-0-670-02178-9 (hc.)
    ISBN 978-0-452-29705-0 (pbk.)
    1. Sisters—Fiction. 2. Hamptons (N.Y.)—Social life and customs—Fiction. 3. Rich people—
New York (State)—Hamptons—Fiction. I. Title.
    PS3607.A45S86 2010
    813'.6—dc22   2009049273

Printed in the United States of America

PUBLISHER'S NOTE
This is a work of fiction. Names, characters, places, and incidents are either the product of the author's
imagination or are used fictitiously, and any resemblance to actual persons, living or dead, business
establishments, events, or locales is entirely coincidental.

For Harry,
who just read Gatsby for the first time

The Summer
We Read Gatsby

1

Summer 2008

Hats, like first husbands in my experience, are usually a mistake. But the invitation was specific. And demanding. A GATSBY party. Wear white. And below that, in imploring cursive: "Hats for the Ladies."

It's still unclear to me how *hats* were involved in Fitzgerald's story—only a few are mentioned in the novel—or, frankly, why any adult above the age of twenty would care to attend this sort of *theme* party. I'm also still not sure that this part of the story—how Miles Noble's first party at the house it took five years to design and build came to be themed around this book he'd once given my sister—was ever fully explained, but as Peck kept pointing out, I was a foreigner, so what the hell did I know?

Like many of her observations, this one wasn't entirely accurate. Peck, short for Pecksland—that's the sort of mother she has—is my half sister. We shared the same father, although he died when I was three and she was seven, after he'd left her mother for mine. I'm as American as she is, with the same navy blue passport. It's just that I never lived in the States and, according to her, I don't know *anybody*, or any of the sorts of people she would have liked me to know: American celebrities, fashion designers, New York socialites, people who could get a table at a place called the Waverly Inn, those sorts.

I didn't own any hats of the kind I imagined Daisy Buchanan might have worn, but on this, as on so many things, Peck was adamant. She not only insisted (read: begged, pleaded, and threatened to kick me out of the house) that I accompany her to Miles Noble's party, but also that I follow the oddly specific sartorial directions. She was often adamant, often about absurd things, but particularly about hats. On this, there'd been no room for argument. She hadn't seen Miles in seven years and she needed someone—me—by her side for this encounter.

I'd only been in Southampton for three days and I was in no mood for a party. Even one hosted, as Peck kept dramatically exclaiming, by the first and only man she'd ever loved. It was the Fourth of July, a holiday about which I'd always been reverent, but at that point in the summer I was still jaundiced and cynical, a divorced twenty-eight-year-old aspiring writer whose creative ambitions had led only to a dead-end job as a translator at a lifestyle magazine for tourists in Switzerland. And my only blood relative, aside from the half sister I hardly knew, had only been gone a couple of months. I was far more saddened by Lydia's death than I might have expected, especially as I hadn't seen my aunt in a few years. I was a weepy, confused mess and was finding it hard to be there, in her house, without her. So at first I politely declined Peck's invitation to join her.

But being polite and declining invitations do not agree with my glamorously eccentric half sister, and since I was at the very beginning of what was supposed to be a month of sisterly togetherness at the house we'd jointly inherited from Aunt Lydia, I reluctantly agreed to go with her. In the interest of getting along, I pulled the only dress I'd brought with me from my suitcase of jeans and T-shirts and borrowed a hat from the strange assortment Aunt Lydia had left in the house, unwisely choosing a drooping off-white bowler that made my head itch and kept falling over my eyes as Peck inexpertly maneuvered our aunt's ancient station wagon down the driveway.

"There's a situation," she announced as she pulled into the sun-dappled street, spraying gravel like she was commandeering a getaway car. This is a standard expression from Peck, who tends to speak in proclamations and for whom life is one long series of *situations*. A situation could be anything from the mysteriously locked safe in Aunt Lydia's closet that we had not been able to open to the guy wearing nothing but wet tighty-whitey BVDs we'd witnessed just that morning slowly pedaling his bicycle home from the beach. (Or the situation could be *me*.)

"The *situation*," Peck explained, in the aggrieved tone of an irrelevant monarch, "is that you and I can't *agree* on *anything*."

This was true. I was trying, I really was. But to say it wasn't going well between Peck and me would be an oversimplification. The first three days had been, well, strained. Inheritances will do that, people tell me. Our circumstances weren't necessarily unusual: a beloved elderly aunt bequeathing a small second home to two nieces who must come together to settle the estate. Except the two nieces, half sisters raised an ocean apart by two utterly different women who'd both loved the same man, had a *complicated* relationship. And it was a house in the Hamptons. Southampton, to be specific. (Apparently there are nuances I couldn't possibly understand, being a *foreigner*.) Also, as Peck kept telling me, nobody calls it "the Hamptons."

Certain types of New Yorkers, I was to learn, and style-obsessed Peck, to her delight, was now one of *these* New Yorkers, go to the Country on weekends and in the summers. To them "the Country" refers to anyplace outside Manhattan, which is "the City." The

City is where you live during the week. On the weekends, you go to the Country. Even suburbs like Larchmont and Scarsdale are the Country to such city people, as are Southampton, East Hampton, and Westhampton. These were the sorts of distinctions about which my sister was appalled to find I didn't already know.

"Literally." Peck often started a sentence that way. Lit-*tra*-ly. It was a verbal tic and could be contagious. She sped up and then slammed on the brakes as she cursed the driver ahead of us. "I don't see how we could be related. You have no sense of *priorities*."

This was a theme she kept revisiting. Peck felt vehemently that we should ignore Lydia's wishes—"It's not like she would *know*"—and keep the house we'd inherited. In her view, to trade the house for money was like looking a gift horse in the mouth and, therefore, terrible manners. I was far less prone to vehemence, but on this Lydia's mandate for us had been clear. And I had absolutely no interest in keeping what would only be a sad reminder that all of them, my father, my mother, and my aunt, all the members of that generation of Moriartys, were gone. Only Peck's mother was still around, and she was living in Palm Springs, "where she belongs," as Peck, who adored her mother, put it.

In her opinion, I should have immediately jumped to the obvious solution, one that involved my moving to New York, where *everybody* lives, allowing us to keep the house in Southampton for shared weekends and summers. Or I should go back to Switzerland, where, last she checked, the Hampton Jitney—an evocative name for what was nothing more than a big green bus that took people from Manhattan to the villages of the Hamptons and back—did not make any stops, and simply leave the house in Southampton to her. She didn't see why she should be forced to sell just because I was so determined to be, in her view, *difficult*.

"Lydia made it pretty clear in the will she didn't expect us to keep it," I said. "I'd like to honor her wishes." Whenever I pointed out that Peck couldn't afford to keep the house, that *we* couldn't afford to keep the house—even together, according to the lawyers, we couldn't afford to pay the taxes, let alone for any of the maintenance on the place—she would sigh dramatically and change the subject. "You know what your problem is?" she would ask, and then pause, as if awaiting a response. "You're afraid to *live.*"

Now she made a sound like a harrumph. "Were you always so obedient?"

"I suppose so," I said.

She looked over at me for far longer than seemed comfortable, considering that we were now going sixty in a thirty-five-mile-an-hour zone. "See, that's the thing with you. You've got to come out of your shell. Life is just too goddamned short for that kind of attitude."

That morning, I'd made things worse, voicing the perhaps too caustic opinion that she was only interested in seeing Miles Noble again because she'd recently discovered that he'd become such a financial success that he'd built himself an enormous house—a place that grew larger, "twenty thousand square feet," "thirty thousand square feet, at least," every time I heard Peck express her enthusiasm about seeing it—in Bridgehampton.

Pointing out that my half sister seemed more intrigued with the idea of this extravagant evidence of wealth than she was with the man himself was not something that needed to be said, I'll admit. But she had been going on and on endlessly about that very subject—"Literally? I can't believe he's so . . . successful"—since I'd arrived, so I wasn't exactly being the contrarian. I was simply trying to get out of putting on a dress and a hat and going with her.

Since then, she'd been even more impatient with me, and she made another noise when I clutched the armrest as she swerved to avoid a woman walking three Labradors. *"Jesus Christ,"* I muttered, as we then narrowly missed a Range Rover headed in the opposite direction.

"Don't be so *nervous*," Peck said in a tone that had grown increasingly peevish all day. She'd always seemed irritated by me, but since my arrival in Southampton she'd added a dash of what I could only interpret as disappointment. "I'm the one who should be nervous. I'm going to see Miles Noble again for the first time since he broke my heart clean in two."

I opened the window. Air rushed in, smelling intoxicatingly of salt and honeysuckle, and something else too, something like ambition. I breathed in deeply.

"Watch the hair," Peck warned. She had fantastic hair, a red-gold cascade she liked to wear fluffed as big as possible around her face. "Otherwise I look like a pinhead," she'd say, in the self-deprecating manner specific to the truly vain.

A Philip Treacy hat—I knew it was Philip Treacy because she kept telling me, dropping the name as though it might mean something to me—was pinned precariously into her curls, and she had on a low-cut vintage flapper dress. It was white, of course, and showed off her spectacular cleavage—she referred to her breasts as "the twins"—to advantage. "God, I look a wreck," she complained, although of course she didn't at all. She'd made an effort and she looked magnificent, regal and cool and stylish at the same time.

"Look at my nails," she cried out, flashing a hand in front of my face. "I've bitten them all down to the quick with nerves. And of course this dress is wrong. All wrong."

Peck is what she likes to call a Fashionina. "I coined that term," she'd explain, whether you cared for an explanation or not. "Everyone calls people like me Fashionistas. But the *Fashionina* is an entirely different creature." According to Peck, a Fashionina is more elegant than a Fashionista; a Fashionina knows about taste and style, whereas a Fashionista is all about trends. She described her fashion sense as "rock 'n' roll Auntie Mame." She took such things seriously, as befitted a fashion diva, and over the years her style had evolved into full-fledged glamour with a vintage 1930s flair. It was ill-mannered, she liked to tell me, not to make an effort.

Of *my* dress—a long white cotton thing—she'd sniffed, "Hippie chic." And then, "You really should do something with your hair," because I'd emerged from a shower with it wet and hanging down my back. I was sure I was the one who looked "a wreck." I felt haggard and exhausted and my nails too were bitten to the quick. "Actually don't." She'd reconsidered. "I'm just jealous. I've always been *insanely* jealous of you. I wish I could waltz down here with no makeup, in an old nightie and with stringy wet hair, and look like that."

It was the kind of thing she said but didn't really mean. Or meant only halfheartedly. She may have carried a tiny bit of residual resentment of the fact that our father left her mother (and her) for mine (and, a few months later, me). But our dad had now been dead for twenty-five years, and she wasn't jealous of me at all. After all, as she'd pointed out more than a few times in the past few days, there wasn't any reason for anyone to be jealous of me. I had a boring job in a boring country that wasn't New York. (Switzerland is a place she and other people often confuse with Sweden.) Peck, on the other hand, was an actor. (She was one of *those* theater people, the ones who tell you about their craft and never, ever stop believing in themselves.) And she lived in Manhattan, or "the greatest city in the world," as she usually put it. (Yes, she was one of *those* New Yorkers.)

"Maybe you shouldn't read too much into this party," I cautioned as we passed the field where I remembered picking strawberries with Aunt Lydia the first time I visited Southampton. I was trying to be conciliatory, but like many of my attempts at communicating with Peck it came out all wrong. She'd read Miles Noble's calligraphed invitation as a summons, a call to destiny from her past. I had a tendency to be more cautious about people and their intentions. Far too cautious, she would tell me.

"Maybe it's just a theme," I went on. "You know, white dresses, green lawns, finger bowls of champagne that change the scene before your eyes into something significant, elemental, and profound." I was paraphrasing from the novel because that was the sort of annoying thing I did when I was nervous, but she didn't seem to notice. "*Gatsby* is that kind of book."

To this she sputtered, "Don't tell *me* what kind of book it is. You hadn't even *read The Great Gatsby* until *I* gave it to you."

This was true. I was twenty-one that summer I read *Gatsby* for the first time. It was 2001, and I'd arrived to spend what would then be my third summer at Aunt Lydia's house with the older half sister who intimidated me. Twenty-one is late to encounter the story of James Gatz and his love for the elusive Daisy, but I'd spent a peripatetic childhood in Europe, and this classic American novel had not been on the curriculum at any of the schools my mother had found for me.

I would have missed many of the American classics had it not been for my aunt Lydia, an English teacher at an all-boys academy, Saint Something's, in Manhattan. Lydia was the first person to encourage me to write. "Start early," she'd advised. "Get a first novel under your belt now." I was nine years old, spending my first summer with her in Southampton. After that, every year she would send the summer reading list she always gave her class, and a box of books. Occasionally she visited and brought the books and the list in person. I got used to cataloguing my summers according to the books she gave me. There was the Summer We Read *Nancy Drew*, the Summer We Read *The Catcher in the Rye*, the Summer We Read Edith Wharton, and the Summer We Read *Catch-22*.

The summer of 2001 became the Summer We Read *Gatsby*. My aunt had assumed I'd already read it, and because she taught the book during the school year, it didn't appear on the reading lists she gave her class. It was Peck who gave me the book. That summer, she introduced me to many things besides F. Scott Fitzgerald: the dressing drink, a topspin forehand, thong underwear, proper smoke-ring technique, and Woody Allen. Her introduction to Woody Allen took the form of *Annie Hall* and *Manhattan*, not literally Mr. Allen, but it was powerful all the same.

Peck was twenty-five then, already plump and gravel-voiced, theatrically and obsessively recovering from what she called "the denouement of the greatest love story ever told." Her recovery took the form of chain-smoking, devouring cupcakes, and mooning about pretending to read the copy of *The Great Gatsby* that Miles Noble had given her when they first met. "I'm *obsessed*," she would tell me, waving her paperback. "I'm absolutely mad for this book. You know, a literary fetish is the new black."

Miles had read everything Fitzgerald ever wrote, he told her. "Like the Dylan song," I said when she repeated this detail, telling the story of how they met. She didn't get the reference. "Bob Dylan?" she'd muttered irritably. "What's he got to do with the price of tea in China?"

Her first words to me that summer of 2001 were "I hate you," but she'd delivered them in a cheerful enough manner, which was confusing to the pale and fragile student I was then, still grieving my mother's death, overwhelmed at the random nature of life's iro-nies. She'd just finished at NYU—she hadn't graduated, she'd sim-ply *finished*—and was planning to become famous, and she held the page of her book with one finger and gazed at me with curios-ity. "Just kidding," she said a few seconds later. "It's just that you're *so* freaking skinny. And you look just like Daddy."

Daddy? He'd been dead for eighteen years. But I did resemble our father, or at least the few photos of him I'd seen. I had his dark wavy hair and brown eyes and I was angular, like him, while Peck took after her mother, with freckled Irish skin that burned easily and wide-set blue eyes.

Miles Noble looked like Jim Morrison, according to Peck. He was brilliant, sexy, the funniest guy she'd ever known. His name had come to be a sort of shorthand for the perfect guy, an inside joke for half sisters who grew up separated by an ocean, without much in the way of inside material. When Jean-Paul, the now-ex-husband my friends referred to as "that awful Jean-Paul"—as though that were his full name, That-Awful-Jean-Paul—turned out to be so, well, awful, Peck said to me, "He was never your Miles Noble, was he?"

Men were always falling in love with Peck, or so she would tell me. And she did have a regal air that seemed to bring out the passion in even the mousiest little creatures. But inevitably she'd come up with several reasons to be disappointed. A passion for cats, for example. Or ordering a salad for dinner. Or the wrong sorts of shoes. "Tasseled loafers," she would whisper into the phone, as if such a thing were so awful it couldn't be voiced too loudly. It explained everything. Afterward, she'd always add, "Well, he was no Miles Noble."

"For someone who wants to be a writer, you don't seem to understand about this book," she complained now as she slammed on the brakes at a red light. We were on Route 27, the traffic-snagged highway that runs all the way along Long Island to Montauk, making our way from Southampton to Bridgehampton. "You, of all people, should know when a book had this kind of significance, a person doesn't just randomly send an invitation after *seven* years of nothing, with such a theme, if he doesn't intend it to mean something."

"True," I acknowledged. "But what does it mean?"

"It means, I suppose, that he's come to his senses and he wants me back. But it's too late for that. And you know what? You were right."

Her words surprised me. Peck was not in the habit of telling me I was right about anything.

"This morning." She gestured at me with one hand. "When you implied I was only going so I could see the house. It's true. To satisfy my curiosity." She nodded, as though she needed confirmation. "I would never go through that again, that kind of love. I wouldn't wish it on my worst enemy. I wouldn't even wish it on *you*.

"It's a sickness," she continued. "That kind of obsessive, all-consuming, intense feeling, where you can't eat and you can't sleep. And God, remember how tragic I was that summer we broke up? Moping around a whole summer, reading and rereading *The Great Gatsby*, as though it contained all the answers to the mysteries of life."

I did. It had been rather impressive, a heaving performance of grief and self-pity that I'd witnessed with a combination of awe and amusement. I had always believed such intense displays of emotion to be the stuff of books and movies and songs and therefore purely fictitious. I didn't think people could actually feel that strongly about each other and I viewed my half sister's dramatic display as characteristic hyperbole.

"So what do you think *he* wants?" I asked her, as a gut-wrenching sunset began to tinge the wide-open sky with pink, the famous "painters' light" about which Lydia had spoken so evocatively and adoringly, and we turned off the highway in the direction of the former potato fields that had been transformed over a period of five years into Miles Noble's fantasy of a country estate.

"He wants what every man wants when he's built a house. He wants to fill it," she said. We fell in behind a long line of cars snaking toward the driveway that would lead to the house.

"He's been living in Hong Kong and Dubai," she went on, her syllables rounded and carefully defined. "An international man of mystery, from the sound of it. Now he's come back home to roost. There's an apartment in New York too, I hear. A penthouse, all raw and ready to be designed. What he *wants* is a wife."

I'd always admired the way Peck could speak with such author-ity about the unknown wishes of others. She delivered her opinions as though she'd received some divine wisdom that told her she was right, despite any evidence or logic to the contrary.

She tapped her fingers on top of the steering wheel in time to the music, the Grateful Dead's "Eyes of the World," from a CD I'd brought along. "I wonder what he looks like now."

Miles Noble lived, for just a summer, in what could only be de-scribed, in Fitzgerald's words, as *an incoherent failure of a house*. It was the biggest thing I'd ever seen. Also the ugliest. There were small windows in strange places and a huge arched door and two turretlike structures, one at each end, giving it the feel of a mad castle, and not in a good way. As we followed the line of cars down the driveway toward a gaggle of valet parkers, we both gazed up at the house before us in awe. The front of the house was lined with purple and pink hydrangeas and far too many wood chips, a whole garden store's worth of bright reddish things. It rose awkwardly out of its landscaped acres of lawn like an ungainly pubescent girl uncomfortable with her sudden size and lack of beauty.

"Isn't this fantastic?" Peck asked breathlessly.

I glanced over at her, assuming she was being sarcastic. I was about to say something about how I'd never seen anything more hideous when I realized her awe at the sight of the house before us was not the same as mine. There was reverence in her eyes.

"It sure is big," I said.

She nodded. "Forty thousand square feet, at least. Indoor and outdoor pools. The gardens are modeled after a place in Ireland."

We stepped out of the car and a valet parker handed Peck a ticket. Then we were greeted at a long table by five or six very at-tractive women in tiny black dresses. Peck took my arm in excite-ment as she stated regally, "Pecksland Moriarty. And guest."

We made our way behind other white-clad arrivals along a path, lined with hurricane lanterns, that led to the back of the house. "I can't believe Miles lives here," Peck whispered to me, still holding on to my arm. "It's out of a movie, isn't it?"

"*The Shining?*" I whispered back, but she was too excited to realize what I meant.

"*Everybody's* here," she said as we came around the corner to a vast terrace where a sea of people were already gathered. *Everybody* was obediently wearing white. And hats. Some of the people were smart and elegant. And some were hard and bored. On them, the white dresses and the dinner jackets appeared cheap. But, I couldn't help noticing, they were, for the most part, an extraordinarily attractive group of people. So this is the Hamptons, I thought, as I allowed myself to be pulled along into the fray with my sister at my side.

"Look at that," I said to her, pointing at the lights that spelled out three letters on the bottom of the swimming pool. "What does that say? MAN?"

"Those are his *initials*," Peck exclaimed. "Miles Adam Noble. That's cool."

"Very existential," I remarked as we headed to one of several lit-up bars set up on the grass. Everything was blazing with lights, from the monogram in the pool, which was now changing colors, to the trees hung with lanterns and the tables set with candles. Even the flagpole in one corner of the back lawn was surrounded by at least four or five lights, shining upward from the base at the American flag flapping in the breeze.

As we waited for a couple in matching white tuxedos and fedoras to select something from the many choices of cocktails, Peck shook an American Spirit from a pack she carried in the tiny white box she was using as a purse. She smoked the elegant, old-fashioned way that glamorous women used to smoke, her right elbow in her left hand and the long fingers of her right hand lined up flat against her face. She'd take a deep drag and then fling her right hand with its cigarette all the way out to the side.

The His-and-Hers pair in the tuxes turned and waved their hands in front of their faces, ostentatiously fanning away her smoke. "How *rude*," Peck exclaimed as they quickly moved away from us. She blew a stream of smoke at their retreating backs.

She ordered two dirty martinis—and when I interrupted to change mine to a Coke, she exclaimed, "What are you, the mayor of Sobertown?" Peck turned back to the bartender, a pretty older man, one of those character-actor types in a white dinner jacket and bow tie, and clarified. "Make hers a double."

The bartender gave her a blank look as he poured the vodka. There were small signs on the bar indicating that the bar was "sponsored" by this particular brand.

"She's a *divorcée*," Peck felt compelled to explain. She pronounced the word as though she were speaking French, with a rolling *r* and the emphasis on the last syllable—*de-vorr-SAY*.

He handed us each a martini speared with three massive olives and winked at me as Peck clinked her glass against mine. "Big and stiff," she proclaimed, making sure the bartender and everyone else in our midst could hear her. "Just the way I like them."

She introduced me to *everyone*, her arm encircling my waist as she showed me off. She bounced from cluster to cluster, sharing an entertaining tidbit of gossip about some person or a sharp observation about another. They were all immediately friendly to me, including me in the small talk that seemed to flow effortlessly from their mouths. Some of the guests whispered in judgment at the lavishness of the party, even as they fanned out to the tins of caviar on ice and mounds of Kumamoto oysters and what looked like sculptures of fresh shrimp on skewers, and lined up for the Nobu chef rolling sushi and the Chinese man in an extra-tall hat wrapping Peking duck in pancakes. There were tiny little cheeseburgers dripping juices and ketchup onto white silk and little slivers of *toro*, a fatty tuna so fresh it tasted like it had been caught that afternoon. There was foie gras on toast and smoked salmon with crème fraîche and a man in a white suit and a sombrero at a table with hundreds of avocados, mixing guacamole to order.

Peck didn't seem nervous at all, despite her professed anxiety about seeing Miles Noble again, and she drew admiration, particularly from the male guests, some of whom couldn't help but stare adoringly at her magnificently cleavaged chest as she spoke.

"This is my half sister," she'd say proudly, as though this, a half of a sister, were a thing so special only she was fortunate enough to have one. "This is Stella Blue."

Technically this was true. My parents had named me after the Grateful Dead song. (That's the sort of mother *I* had.) Stella Blue Cassandra Olivia Moriarty. Flows daintily off the tongue, doesn't it? The Dead played "Stella Blue" the night I was born, or that was the story as told by my mother, the queen of the unreliable narrators. Her tales were always entertaining and always embellished. They just weren't always true.

They'd added the Cassandra Olivia because they wanted me to have options. I exercised those options at the age of four and encouraged everyone to call me Cassie. But Peck could never resist an opportunity to remind me of my hippie roots. To her, I was Stella Blue. Or just Stella. Often, she'd give it the full dramatic Marlon Brando delivery: STELLAAAH! Especially when calling on the phone from overseas.

She wasn't the only one who refused to call me Cassie. There was also That-Awful-Jean-Paul. He'd always opted for Cassandra and sometimes Cassandra Olivia because That-Awful-Jean-Paul was Swiss and didn't believe in nicknames or names that Deadhead mothers pulled from songs.

I became a Deadhead myself when my mother took me to see

them in Germany. I was ten years old. And a few years later, I found a Web site that posted song lists from every show the Dead ever played. The shows were listed by year and I did find one in Hartford, Connecticut, on the date I was born. They played "Peggy-O." And "Althea." Both of which could inspire the naming of a female child, I suppose. But "Stella Blue" was not played that night.

When I asked my mother about the discrepancy in her story, she said, "We take creative license with the fictional narratives that become our memories. Anthologized, these are the tales that become the story of your life." Right. That was the kind of thing she would say, a too-broad elaboration of one of the many life philosophies she'd cobbled together on her spiritual quest, one that did nothing to alleviate how the slight falsities in her tales bothered me. But when I expressed my distaste for the name my mother always said the same thing: "It could've been worse. They could've played '*Bertha*.'"

Peck and I were sucked into the crowd, greeting what seemed an endless stream of the same anxious men and gregarious women. There was kissing and squealing and handshaking and we were pulled along by the riptide of her acquaintances. We were on our second round of martinis and Miles Noble had yet to make an appearance when Peck launched into the story of how they met, for the benefit of a small crowd of listeners. Later I would look back at this moment as the beginning of what I would come to think of as a sort of awakening in me, the first in a series of shifts that led me to want to write a different story for myself.

"The first time I laid eyes on Miles Noble," she began, "I was about to be kissed." I'd always known Peck could weave a good tale but now, as she entranced us with her words, I recognized that I could learn from her. She paused before delivering the next line. "By someone else." Another pause. "And I knew. Immediately, I knew. It was the *coup de foudre*." She pronounced the words *coup de foudre* in a thick French accent, her words now rehearsed and perfectly enunciated, as though she'd performed this script a thousand times, and gotten the timing and pronunciation and the blocking just right.

"He wore a crisp white shirt, and he looked just like Jim Morrison. He had this thick wavy hair you could just run your hands through. And he was sinewy, with dark skin that would turn bronze in the sun. God, he was good-looking. But it was more than that. He had that thing, charisma, or whatever it is, that just draws you in. And after I was finished being kissed, by a freshman boy whose insignificant name I never retained, I saw that he was waiting for me. It was one of those parties where there's a keg of beer and too many poets and actors in desperate need of haircuts. I said, 'Do I know you?' And he replied, 'I've known you all my life.'"

This was the point in the story when she let out a small, stylish laugh and lit up one of her cigarettes.

As she exhaled a long, slow plume of smoke, I eyed the crowd, looking for Finn Killian. Peck had mentioned that this friend of Lydia's, an architect who'd lived in the studio above the garage that summer I was twenty-one, might be there that night. We thought we would ask him if he knew how we might open the locked safe in Lydia's closet. I hadn't seen him since that summer right after my mother died, when I'd moved through a fog of grief. I hardly remembered him. He'd seemed a distant presence, appearing on weekends and then trying annoyingly to engage me in conversation when I was busy pretending I was Hunter S. Thompson, teaching myself to write by typing out all of *Gatsby*. (I'd read this somewhere, that Thompson had learned to write by copying *Gatsby* over and over again, and it was the kind of thing I had to try, if only because it seemed an awfully easy way to go about becoming a writer.)

I didn't like Finn that summer. I remembered that he seemed so much older than Peck and me. He had a beard and talked about wine. Later, I'd come to know him better as a character in Lydia's many letters, always written in her distinctive Catholic schoolgirl cursive on crisp white stationery with a purple border and purple tissue in the envelopes. In them, she described Finn, this architect who was becoming a close friend, as wry. A quality that is uniquely underrated, she wrote.

He was very tall; that much I recalled. He played the guitar, knew more about the Grateful Dead than I did, and always seemed to be going on about a cabernet that was astute or a Sancerre that was crisp. He called me "kid," which I didn't think was necessary. And he had a *beard*. Need I say more? What made men think women liked it when they grew that pubic-type hair on their faces? Did I mention that my ex-husband Jean-Paul grew a beard the last year of our ill-fated marriage? I later figured out this was right around the time he started the affair with the buxom office manager. He said he liked the way it—the facial hair—defined his *chin*.

I realized as I scanned the crowd looking for a tall guy with a beard that I didn't have a very good memory of what Finn Killian looked like. Still, I said to myself, I would know him when I saw him.

"Pay attention," Peck admonished me before she continued her story, through another exhale. "The room fell away. All those earnest college students, still so full of their *potential*, and we talked all night. Oh, I don't remember what we said, but our eyes were glued to each other the entire time and when it was light out we walked the streets, all the way to the Hudson River and then north. There was a slight breeze and the smell of salt air."

Here she paused. "That's *him*?" she exclaimed.

I assumed this was simply an expression of how she felt that evening, walking up the West Side with a good-looking older guy, already successful compared to the college boys she'd been hanging out with. But Peck grabbed my arm with one hand and gestured with the other one, jabbing the cigarette toward the person who'd appeared on a balcony above us.

Later in life, had he lived, Jim Morrison himself wouldn't have looked like Jim Morrison. But Miles Noble was, well, *ugly*. That sounds meaner than I'd like, but there is no other way to say it. He looked exactly like a frog. Everything about him except, unfortunately, his hair, was thicker than in the photograph Peck had made me look at four times just that morning.

He stood on the balcony surveying the lavish and increasingly loud party sprawling over the back terrace and lawn. He sported a white Nehru-style jacket, like something designed for a maître d' at a hip Asian restaurant. Was that supposed to be a cool look? Or was he a fashion victim? I was in no position to judge, having been married to a European who wore brown socks with his man-sandals, but even I knew this guy was trying too hard.

The small crowd that had gathered around Peck followed her gesture and we all looked up at the man on the balcony. He didn't appear to notice.

"I don't think this was a very good idea." Peck put the cigarette out on the bottom of her shoe and then tossed it into the flower bed. "We should just go the fuck home now." But she threw back her shoulders and marched into the house as Miles Noble left the balcony above us. Our group dispersed as performers on stilts passed around test tubes of shots. I stood briefly alone at one end of the wide stone terrace with a fountain in the center, a shallow limestone pool with spewing cherubs and enormous dancing fish spraying water through thick unsightly lips.

As I finished my drink and contemplated another, I was approached by what I took to be a typically good-looking and boyish American with the healthy-looking carriage of a former athlete and the knowing and charismatic smile of the charmer who is certain he will be well received.

I was determined to be uninterested. But I felt his presence as something of a shock, an immediate and intense physical chemistry I'd never experienced before. My determination, in the face of the very strong drinks to which I was entirely unaccustomed, immediately fizzled as his eyes—the palest light brown, the color of caramels—fixed on mine and locked in.

He wore his white dinner jacket as though he'd been born in it, and he said he was sorry for my loss. He didn't introduce himself but he'd known Aunt Lydia well, from the sound of it, and he expressed his sadness that she was gone. He had slightly long hair, lightened by the sun, that fell over his forehead and curled up where it met the collar of his shirt. But his presence was that of a courtly, well-mannered athlete, one to whom life had been kind. He carried himself with supreme confidence, only slightly bordering on arrogance, and he struck me as someone who'd always been cool, like he'd had one of those American boyhoods during which he'd always sat with the other sports stars at the right lunch table.

I'd always been too cynical to believe in love at first sight, or the *"coup de foudre,"* as Peck would carefully pronounce it. Besides, I was wearing that ridiculous hat. But when he looked at me, something clicked into place in a way that I'd never experienced before. It took my breath away.

He had two martinis in his hand and eventually he held one out to me. "Drink?"

I think my mouth gaped open like a fish's for a few seconds as I sought air. But then I helped myself to another martini, which I definitely did not need, and said, in a flirtatious tone that was totally uncharacteristic of me, "You're very dexterous."

"Dexterous, huh?" He smiled, intelligent eyes crinkling. He held the other glass up in a gesture of greeting. "Are you flirting with me?"

"I never flirt." This was true. That-Awful-Jean-Paul was hardly the flirtatious type. His idea of words as foreplay had been "I'll pay for lunch." Of course, he said them in French. But flirting was not something I knew how to do. I was much more inclined to make sarcastic remarks that were usually misinterpreted.

This fellow, on the other hand, was clearly used to having people flirt with him. Most women would find a guy with a smile like his irresistibly attractive. But, I told myself in the stern tone that had become a habit, there must definitely be some kind of rule— like waiting an hour after lunch to swim—about waiting at least two years after a divorce before flirting with anyone.

"Really?" He sounded genuinely surprised. "I figured you as quite the subtle expert."

I found myself saying something like, "If I were inclined to flirt, which I'm not, I certainly wouldn't opt for such an obvious choice." As I said, I wasn't good at it.

He wasn't beaten down the way men in their thirties could start to look, as they gave up their youthful dreams and settled into the reality of adult expectations. Not like my ex-husband, for whom life had been a series of disappointments, all someone else's fault. "I'm an obvious choice, am I?" he asked, a smile playing at his lips. He had the loose confidence I'd always associated with people who grow up with many siblings, and he grinned at me like he knew exactly what I was thinking.

I took a sip of the drink he'd handed me, feeling wildly out of control, the alcohol taking hold. I was nodding and grinning and probably even blushing as I realized I was speaking words that did not seem to belong to me.

"What's so *obvious* about me?" He had a unique voice, deep and raspy like sandpaper, and I felt it in my chest. It made me want to think of things for him to say, just so I could hear what they sounded like coming out of his mouth.

Another sip of the martini. "Well, for one thing, you're overtly charming. Clearly something of a ladies' man. So, an obvious choice for someone inclined to flirt. If I were that kind of person."

Suddenly there was an explosion and I jumped. "What was that?"

He pointed to a riot of color in the sky. "Fireworks."

People stopped talking and dancing and mingling and gazed upward, childlike glee on their faces. The handsome stranger whose name I never got and I watched together, standing side by side with our faces tilted to the sky.

We spent the rest of the evening together on the terrace. I couldn't help thinking of Jordan Baker's line from *Gatsby*, about liking large parties for their intimacy. He was extremely funny. Humor had always been important to me. My mother was quite the wit and she always said she fell in love with my father because he made her laugh. "Find someone who can make you laugh," she'd advised me, as though it were that simple, as though comedians were just lurking about on the street corners waiting to meet young women and dazzle them with their funny lines. Instead I somehow ended up with Jean-Paul, whose ability to make me laugh existed only when I would repeat his more outlandishly selfish words to my friends, turning them into amusing anecdotes.

I hadn't laughed as much as usual in the past year, but that night I made up for it, cackling like a hyena at this odd, funny man whose name I never got. Later, when it should have been time to find Peck and head home, there was a commotion. I heard splashing and a familiar guffawing and I turned. Peck was dancing in the fountain. She had Miles Noble's Nehru jacket draped around her shoulders and she was kicking up shapely legs, doing the cancan and spraying a crowd of clapping spectators with the drops of water that flew off her feet.

"That's my sister," I said, as it dawned on me—slowly, the way things will *dawn*, after several martinis—that this was going to be a very strange summer.

2

It wasn't just the pounding head, the sour stomach, and the paper-dry mouth that greeted me in the morning. There was also the attendant shame, the worst part of any hangover. I was in the bedroom I occupied every time I'd visited my aunt, wrapped in the white popcorn bedspread, wishing I could temporarily be put into a coma so I wouldn't have to try to unglue my eyes. I vowed never to drink again.

Lydia's house—I'll always think of it as Lydia's house, although it was now half *my* house—was what is generally referred to in real-estate circles as a *teardown*, a crumbling, shingled place that listed far to one side like an aging dowager at a cocktail party that's gone on far too long. It was redeemed by its location in Southampton, a proper seaside town of manicured meadows that was part of the string of towns that stretch along the south fork of Long Island and make up "the Hamptons." The house was in the desirable area "south of the highway," close to the much larger and more elegant summer homes tucked behind the hedgerows that stand sentry along wide streets leading to the ocean. It was accessorized by a sagging wraparound porch that was far too wide and high for the scale of the little place. Legend always had it that Aunt Lydia won the house playing backgammon. According to my mother, my father, who was Lydia's younger brother, never believed that version of the tale.

But Lydia, a renowned beauty with prematurely white hair, had always preferred a more engaging story to one that was true, and in her telling she won the house on back-to-back rolls of double sixes. In her version, the man from whom she won the house—one of her many lovers, she'd always implied—disappeared into the ocean one night and was never seen again, except when he appeared in the form of the friendly ghost who was known to move things around and finish backgammon games left unattended. She'd liked the ghost story so much she'd allowed it to be included in a book entitled *Spirits of the East End*, a copy of which still sat on the coffee table in the living room.

My bedroom, which Lydia had called the "white room" to differentiate it from the room Peck had always taken, which was the "pink room," contained a wrought-iron double bed and two pieces of white painted furniture. There was a chest of drawers and a little desk at which Lydia had suggested I would write my "opus." My room was minimalist and spare and had windows that looked out to the scraggly, weed-infested front lawn and a crumbling tennis court. Peck's on the other hand was wallpapered in a lavish floral and featured a canopy bed with a pink quilted spread. Hers faced the wilted garden at the back of the house.

A knock forced my heavy eyelids open. "Room service," Peck called from the hallway. When I didn't answer, she swung open the door to my bedroom, brandishing a Bloody Mary, complete with tall celery frond, and her dog, a sanctimonious mutt with a pug face and a big-city attitude. In one hand she held the drink. The other hand was tucked under the dog, who was frowning at me most disapprovingly.

I was the dog's "godmother," if such a designation can be applied to a four-legged friend, and as such, I'd been offered naming rights when she acquired the little fellow. To be funny, because I, sadly, had always been one of *those* people, too eager for a laugh, I'd suggested Trimalchio. This was after the ostentatiously nouveau riche vulgarian in *Satyricon* that F. Scott Fitzgerald had used as the inspiration for the character of Jay Gatsby. One of the suggested titles for the book was *Trimalchio in West Egg*, and once I finished *Gatsby*, Lydia had given me a copy of *Trimalchio*, the first version of the book that Fitzgerald revised into *The Great Gatsby*. I never thought Peck would actually take the name for her dog. But she loved it.

Now she sashayed—Pecksland Moriarty was born to *sashay*—into my bedroom, in a silk paisley men's robe with a velvet collar, like she'd raided Hugh Hefner's closet at the Playboy Mansion, and dropped Trimalchio, who was now approaching late middle age in dog years, unceremoniously onto the floor, from where he gazed up at me in jaded fashion. That dog could really work an attitude.

Peck sipped the Bloody Mary that I'd assumed was intended for me and gave me her own disapproving frown. She never had much patience for hangovers, not being especially susceptible to them, although she did fancy herself an expert in the art of the cure. "Did you know the Bloody Mary was invented at the Ritz in Paris for Hemingway when he was married to his fourth wife, Mary? She didn't like him to drink so the bartender invented this"—she stirred the drink with the celery stalk—"the odorless cocktail. He drank it and the next day, when the bartender asked him how it went, he said, 'Bloody Mary never smelt a thing.'" She took another sip. "The eleven o'clock Bloody is a time-honored tradition here at Fool's House."

Of course the house had a name. Apparently all the best ones do. Lydia had named hers after the Jasper Johns painting. This was a gray painting featuring items from the artist's studio: a broom with a wooden handle hanging by a hinge, a cup dangling from a hook, a stretcher, and a towel. Fool's House was what Johns called that place where the art came to him. Peck always referred to the house by its full name, *Fool's House,* just as she always referred to herself as Pecksland, and to anyone named Kathy as Katherine, or Lizzie as Elizabeth. Peck prided herself on being well-mannered, often to the point of rudeness.

We were an artistic and literary family, the name of the house implied, with its whiff of the bohemian Hamptons and all the creative souls who'd sought refuge and inspiration in the romantic landscape's vast ocean and sky and wide, pale beaches. The ramshackle little farmhouse with its wide porch was not the sort of place one would expect to find in this part of Southampton. Or not anymore. Most of the smaller mildewed places had been torn down and replaced by oversized ones. But Lydia had made Fool's House the center of the universe for a merry band of artistic souls, none of whom, to her surprise, ever became famous.

Fool's House was *known,* my aunt would always tell us, for its creative energy, although the people who'd supposedly been inspired by it were mostly ones nobody ever heard of. "Dick Montpelier wrote all of *Fire at Sunset* here and John Tallucci finished the last twenty chapters of *Mister Nowhere* on my porch," Aunt Lydia used to love to tell anyone who'd listen. "Oh, and Rusty Cohen and his muse, Esme, they lived in the studio for a summer while he painted all six of his masterpieces."

Lydia couldn't make art, she always said, so she supported it. She viewed herself as a patroness and a collector, although her taste ran to things that were produced in her presence rather than great works of art that, on a schoolteacher's salary, she could hardly afford to buy at auction. I was not exactly a connoisseur, and I wrestled with paints and canvas and words on my own enough to know how hard it is to get any sort of beauty out of them, but the stuff that cluttered every nook and cranny of Fool's House was some of the ugliest art I've ever seen.

Every wall was covered in bad paintings, hung salon-style, three and four high, mostly abstracts or thick oily seascapes and watery sunsets with too-round balls of orange and yellow at their centers. Lydia had never been able to find a cheap poster of the Jasper Johns painting entitled *Fool's House*, but she did hang a reproduction, now torn and peeling, of his best-known work, *Flag*, in the dining room, where a warped round table surrounded by mismatched chairs had been the site of many raucous meals.

Above the mantel in the living room, enjoying pride of place, was an abstract piece, all dabs and dribbles of brown, black, and silver paint. Neither Peck nor I had ever asked about it and Lydia herself had never brought it up. There were also many framed photographs of the sharp-cheekboned Lydia at various stages of gray with assorted friends and lovers, images of her with groups of people at the many parties she hosted over the years. There were pictures of Peck and me, school photos sent by our mothers and snapshots of us, separately, with Aunt Lydia in Paris, or at the Coliseum in Rome, and together, from the summers we'd spent at Fool's House.

Peck handed over the Bloody Mary with ceremonial seriousness. I took a medicinal sip as my prim conscience—that petulant voice of reason—suggested that more alcohol was the last thing I needed. Trimalchio eyeballed me in his judgmental way.

"Southampton has always been known as a cure-all," she intoned, like a tour guide. "You're going to enjoy the health benefits of being by the sea. The ocean air will fix what ails you."

"I have a hangover, not a disease," I protested, taking a sip as the previous evening's activities came back to me. I'd never even asked his name, the handsome stranger with whom I'd so uncharacteristically spent most of the night flirting and acting silly.

"Sea air has the same components as lithium," she announced. "That's why you feel so good at the beach." She stared me down in a knowing fashion before continuing. "You're ailing, Stella. Anyone can see that."

"I just drank too much," I said in protest, not wishing to be analyzed. I knew she was right. I'd arrived at Fool's House in a terrible state, seized with grief but also with the sense of opportunity. I'd been simply marking time, plodding along in detached and restless fashion, when the news of Lydia's death dealt me a jolt. I took another sip of the Bloody Mary.

"Or someone slipped me something," I added as she watched me, waiting for me to praise the drink. "Was it Ecstasy? Ludes? A roofie cocktail?"

Peck grinned, passing me two Tylenol she'd been holding in her other hand. She had a pack of cigarettes in the pocket of her robe and she pulled it out, lighting one of her American Spirits with a silver lighter. "So," she said, blowing smoke directly at me. For someone who was obsessed with manners, she was cavalier about cigarette smoke and old-fashioned in her view of smoking as a glamorous pastime. "There's a bit of a situation."

Trimalchio gave me a pissy look, as if he didn't think I fully understood the severity of what Peck was saying to me. We have a situation, you hear? A *situation*.

"What now?" I asked, rubbing my still-throbbing temples.

"You really were *overserved*, weren't you?" Her opinion of me seemed to have been raised thirty notches by my louche behavior of the previous night. I murmured my assent as she continued.

"The *situation* is this." She spoke as if the words had been scripted for her. In italics. Life for Peck was not a dress rehearsal. "He. Never. READ. It." She paused, waiting for my reaction.

"Never read what?"

Peck rolled her eyes at my obtuseness. "*Gatsby*," she said, one hand on her hip. "Miles Noble never fucking read it. Didn't even know Gatsby dies at the end." She stared down at me as if this were somehow my fault before explaining.

Apparently the Gatsby theme had been concocted by a party planner with an unlimited budget and little guidance from a single male host with a new house he wanted to show off. The event co-ordinators hired to pull off the extravaganza had invited everyone on Miles Noble's contact list as well as adding a few names of their own to yield the list of the five-hundred-something people who had ended up at his house that night. "He didn't even know I was going to be there," Peck said now. "I shocked the pants off him. And he didn't remember giving me the book." She seemed almost amused rather than saddened or offended by this unexpected revelation that her preconceptions of the evening had been so off base.

"How could he not remember?" I asked.

"Because, Stella," she said, gesturing with her cigarette. "He's an *idiot*." She paused. "Not only that, I'm afraid he's got horrible *taste*."

"You said the house was fantastic," I reminded her.

She shook her head and then presented a revised version of the prior evening. "God, no. I never would have said that. The man is downright vulgar. I mean, a monogrammed pool? Could we be any tackier?"

"I thought you liked it." I knew there was no point in even say-ing it, though. Peck now believed her sensitive taste buds had been offended and she would not acknowledge that she'd initially been impressed with Miles Noble's obviously lavish spending.

"The thing I can't figure out," she went on, "is how, and more importantly *why*, he could spend all that time with me back then talking about this damn book."

I nodded. I felt a pang of sadness for her, recalling that summer we spent together right after they broke up, when there'd been so many tears that the pages of her paperback stiffened. Even if some of them were crocodile tears, she'd experienced pain. "I'm sorry, Peck," I said, handing her the Bloody Mary.

"Don't be," she said, after a long sip. "Let it be a life lesson. We never know how big a role we play in someone else's drama." She paused, allowing her words to hang in the air like an edict. "Here I had built up this whole story about the two of us and our great love, and somehow I believed his version of the story would be the same. But, of course, that's not how life works."

"He must have been happy to see you," I said.

She shrugged. "I guess he was. He kept saying, 'You look fantastic.' Over and over again. And, of course, I couldn't say, 'So do you.' So I asked him to show me around. He has a lot of art. A Jackson Pollock, a Warhol, an Ed Ruscha, stuff like that. No Jasper Johns, though. I told him about Lydia and how she came up with the name for Fool's House. He was very interested in all that. Especially her *collection*. Said he wanted to come see *my* house. So I invited him to the party." I remembered through my haze that we were to host our first party of the summer that very night.

Lydia had always held a party when she arrived in Southampton. (The first party of the summer was called the Fool's Welcome, while the last one would be, for obvious reasons, the Fool's Farewell.) On this, her will was more than clear: Lydia wanted us to spend at least one summer month living together in the house while we settled her estate and sold the house, and she fully expected us to continue all the traditions during this time.

Aunt Lydia had died in Paris. This was a detail in the story of her death she would have enjoyed, that it happened in her favorite city. Paris had been Lydia's "spiritual home" and a constant conversational reference point. If something was expensive, for example, "you could spend a week in Paris for less," and if she wanted to describe something she didn't like, it was, "Well, it's not Paris in the spring, that's all I can say." As sad as I was that this dear, funny woman was gone, I was happy to know she would have appreciated the way her story had ended. She died in an out-of-the-way tea shop on the Left Bank she always said was worth the detour. And I'm sure it was, unless you were Lydia and you keeled over at your table while finishing a pot of Darjeeling and were pronounced dead at the scene. Or *morte* at the scene. I'm not sure it was worth that much of a detour, although she'd always said the napoleon there was unparalleled. I knew she would have said she left this world as she lived in it, enjoying every single second as much as she could.

Her will had been crafted in the same elaborate language she'd used in the letters I'd saved all my life. Lydia liked flowery words. She wrote that she "bequeathed" her house and all its contents to Peck and me, her "beloved" nieces. She was quite specific in her direction that we spend a month in Southampton together, "should the timing of my passing allow for a summer vacation," while we prepared to sell the house and that we use the proceeds from the sale to check off items on what she called "Lydia's list."

Lydia's list was a roster of things she wanted us to do while we were still young enough to enjoy them: travel to every continent, have an affair with a man who spoke no English, read the classics, play backgammon for money, skinny-dip in the ocean, that sort of thing. Very *Bucket List*, but hers had been composed in 1999, when she'd had a cancer scare, and mostly included things she herself had already done.

In her will, which had not been changed since 1999, she also expressed her "fervent desire" that Peck and I seek a "thing of utmost value" from within this cherished place she was leaving us. She gave no clues as to what this *thing* might be. We'd never discussed the will with her, although over the years she'd occasionally mention that she would be leaving the house to us. She didn't own her apartment in New York, so this was her only real estate. We'd never had any conversations with her about anything valuable that she might have owned, nor was there anything in her letters about a piece of jewelry, perhaps, or one of the many paintings covering the walls of her house, that might be considered a thing of value. There was only a safe.

"A goddamned locked safe," as Peck put it. The safe was old and squat, an industrial-looking thing tucked into a corner of her closet, behind masses of mothball-and-lavender-scented clothes. There was the traditional dial at the front and a large wheel that would turn to open the door only with the correct combination of numbers. Simple enough. Except we didn't have the code. There'd been no mention of a combination to the safe in the will, or any indication of what it might contain, other than, possibly, "a thing of utmost value," and the lawyers didn't know anything about it, least of all how to get it open. In our first three days at the house we had not come up with any combination of numbers that might have opened it. We tried the obvious ones—her birth date, the date she bought the house—but the safe remained obstinately locked.

There were, besides the safe, paintings and books and papers and collections of things—an entire lifetime's worth of things—to figure out, divide up, give away, or sell. We couldn't agree on any of it, partly because we were total and utter opposites and didn't, by nature, agree on anything, and partly because we did not see eye to eye on what to do with the house itself.

The one thing we could agree on, at this stage, was that the Fool's Welcome had to go on, and we'd planned it for that evening, our first Saturday night in the house.

"Is he coming?" I asked Peck. I wasn't surprised to hear that she'd invited Miles Noble to the party. She'd invited everyone she knew and many she didn't know. She was the kind of person who made anywhere she was seem like the only place to be, and she made an invitation to the Fool's Welcome sound like a most desirable summons.

"Of course he is," she said, irritable that I even had to ask. "*Everyone's* coming."

From downstairs, suddenly, there was laughter and the clanging of pots and pans. "What's going on down there?"

"The Girls are here for breakfast." Peck always referred to all her friends as the Girls. They were always the Girls and they always only had one collective opinion. As in "The Girls say we should do everything we can to keep Fool's House." Or "The Girls think there's a locksmith in town who can crack safes." The Girls were all generally, and surprisingly, single, although they were all remarkably attractive and effervescent, and intensely groomed, with shiny, well-cut hair, manicured nails and toes, and interesting jobs in creative fields, particularly fashion. Only Peck didn't have a proper job, since she was the actor in the group and not expected to have full-time employment.

"Finn Killian's cooking omelets," Peck added, as she stood and extended a hand to help me out of bed.

"Finn Killian's here?" I suddenly remembered Lydia mentioning Finn and his omelets in one of her letters. "Why is he making omelets?"

"He's *famous* for his omelets," she announced, somewhat irritably, as if this were a detail one was expected to know. "He used to make them for Lydia all the time."

"He came over here to make us breakfast? I thought you said he was going to be at the party last night."

She made a face. "He *was* there last night. Didn't you see him? He came over this morning to help with the safe. But then the Girls remembered about the omelets and pressed him into service." Peck sucked down the rest of the Bloody Mary as she headed for the door in a rustle of silk. "You might want to think about a *shower*. You look like you've been on a bender."

Ten minutes later I came down the stairs, looking, I'm fairly certain, like a drowned mole, all wet hair and pasty skin and red-rimmed eyes, to find the tiny kitchen full of people who all seemed to be talking at once. Peck, Finn, and several of the Girls—Lucy, one named Elizabeth everyone except Peck called Betts, and another one whose name I kept thinking was Sandra—were all offering their opinions on how to get the safe open.

When I paused in the doorway, they all stopped and stared.

Finn Killian had his back to me, at the stove. When the loud talking ceased, he turned and I caught my breath. Wait. *This* was Finn Killian? It was the good-looking guy with the big grin from the night before. How was that possible? I remembered him as old and kind of ornery. Misanthropic, that was the word that always came to mind. But surely I would have remembered those caramel eyes and that voice. And where was the beard?

His hair was wet and he had an omelet pan in one hand. He smiled at me as though we were the only ones in the room. "You didn't recognize me, did you?" he said, in a knowing, teasingly arrogant way. Instantly I hated him. He'd obviously enjoyed keeping me in the dark all evening about his identity when it was clear I had not remembered him. Cut me some slack, I wanted to say, it had been seven years. And that was the year my mother had died, when I'd been blind with grief. But I didn't say anything. How could I hate someone I found so physically attractive? It was infuriatingly confusing.

It was also annoying that he appeared so crisp and refreshed, as though he'd slept ten hours and then already gone for both a jog and a dip in the ocean, which was probably the case. He was one of those people who always looked, and smelled, like he'd just gotten out of the shower.

"How do you *feel?*" he asked in a tone that indicated that he knew exactly how awful I was feeling and that he found it totally amusing. God, he was arrogant. I remembered now why I didn't like him that first summer we met.

"She needs to go to the Sip 'n Soda for a cheeseburger and a lime rickey," Peck said to him. "That's how she feels. And the onion rings. Best hangover cure there is."

"No, no. Sweat it out," one of the Girls, the tall one named Lucy, suggested. "A four-mile run. That'll cure you."

The sporty one called Betts shook her head. "The hair of the dog that bit you. That's the only solution."

Trimalchio let out a huffy little noise as though he found the talk of dog hair offensive. Peck opened a bakery box. She insisted on keeping a kitchen well-stocked with cupcakes. Cupcakes were what she considered *staples*. "Here's a hangover cure for you. A sugar rush." They all laughed as if this was very funny.

The kitchen at Fool's House had not been renovated. Ever. It still had a fat retro refrigerator and enamel cabinets that had probably been installed in the forties, before Lydia acquired the place. It was a sunny, cheerful space, however, despite the dingy linoleum floor, and that morning it was filled with light. Light and noise. They were *loud*, this bunch.

Finn poured milk into a cup of coffee and slid it toward me. I could hardly look at him. "Thanks," I said. It came out as a whisper.

"Give Stella Blue that omelet," Peck directed him. "*That* will cure what ails her."

"I thought your name was Cassie," the one whose name was not Sandra said to me. She was a petite and pretty Indian woman with a soft British accent.

Finn held out the omelet pan to Peck. "You know what the thing is?" he asked her. It was obvious he was enjoying being the male at the center of all these women's attention. "About omelets?"

He moved with an athlete's lanky smoothness. I assumed the pan contained an omelet for me. I was about to say thank you when he flipped the pan with his wrist and the omelet flew into the air, landing with a neat smack in the sink behind him.

"Hey," I protested. "I would've eaten that."

He took up a fork and pointed into the sink with it. "It was ice cold. And here's the thing about omelets." He lifted the rubbery omelet from the sink and dangled it in the air from the fork in front of Peck. "You can't reheat an omelet."

"Are you trying to make a point about our earlier conversation?" she asked, holding back a laugh. "You're quite the expert on Miles Noble, I must say." She turned to the Girls, who all spoke up in agreement. "You're quite the expert on everything, my friend."

He shrugged in a cheerful way. "Just some friendly advice."

"About omelets? I can't reheat Miles Noble? Is that what you're trying to tell me?" She laughed, gesticulating with her arms. "Well, let me tell *you* something. I think you *can* reheat an omelet. You can reheat it and make it better. But I don't have any intention of experimenting. That egg's gone bad for me." She paused, suddenly thoughtful. "I mean, the level of deception that went into this charade of his, it's not to be believed. This is a guy who stayed up all night talking to me about a book he never read. Does that sound like someone who should be reheated?"

The Girls all chimed in at once—"But you invited him to your party!"—as Finn slid a fresh omelet from the other pan on the stove onto a plate and handed it to me. I put my fork into the center and a delicious ooze of thick melted cheese poured out.

"I was just being *neighborly*," Peck explained with an earnestness that belied her words. "I'm very charitable that way. You know that about me. He said he wanted to see our house. So naturally I told him to come see it."

"Everybody out here always wants to see people's houses," Lucy said. "Isn't that right, Finn? Aren't you always showing people your house?"

"I'm an architect," he pointed out with a smile, as though that explained it. I wondered if he was one of those tedious creative types who always had to be right, fussing about the light fixtures on a site or rejecting ten different stones for an office lobby. My dislike for him intensified. At the same time I couldn't help but smile almost automatically in response.

"That's just it," Peck exclaimed. "Miles Noble just wants to make sure his is still the biggest. I may have neglected to mention that Fool's House could fit in his dining room. I think he heard Southampton and inheritance and came to his own conclusions. He was always a terrible *snob*."

"You'll be sleeping with him within the week," Betts predicted, and the others concurred with concern.

Peck shrugged. "Did you not *see* him? Besides, he has absolutely no taste at all. He could be the tackiest man in America. And now that I think about it, there was always something vaguely *criminal* about him." She said all this as though none of it were that bad.

The Girls murmured their dissent until Peck interrupted them to suggest an outing to the beach. "Let's slather ourselves with Bain de Soleil and get savage tans. My skin is the color of tofu."

I pointed out that we'd planned to spend the day getting organized. I'd already started going through Lydia's things and I wanted Peck to join me so we could make some decisions. We'd also talked about finding the code to the safe, hiring a real estate broker, and getting ready for that evening's party, although the only item on that list in which Peck was interested was the party. She'd managed to wriggle away from any discussion of selling the house or even deciding what to do with all the stuff in it. Now she turned to the rest of them. "*See* what I'm dealing with?" She wagged her finger between us. "It is absolutely perplexing to me that we could possibly be related."

"I'm as *perplexed* as you are," I said with a smile.

"We should do a DNA test," she continued. It was not the first time she'd brought up the subject. "I don't see how the same father could produce two such different daughters. How do we know your mother didn't meet some other hippies at one of those Grateful Dead shows? Maybe your real father is still out there, playing hacky sack at a Phish concert, lamenting the day Jerry died." She laughed at herself. I'd heard this from her before and didn't take it seriously.

"Let's roll," she said to the Girls. "The ocean beckons. Let's buy surfboards."

"Call a locksmith about the safe," Lucy suggested as she headed for the door. She worked in fashion and was also apparently a genius at figuring things out, according to Peck. "Isn't that what they're supposed to do? Open locks?"

"There must be a code somewhere," said Betts, helping herself to another cupcake for the road.

"What year was *Fool's House* painted?" Finn asked me. "I mean the Jasper Johns." The one whose name I suddenly recalled was Sasha stopped in the doorway to coo approvingly at him. "Oooh. Good idea."

And then they were gone, out to the garage to gather the rusty beach chairs and striped umbrella for the beach. Finn and I were alone in the kitchen. I finished the omelet as he watched me, wearing the knowing smile I remembered from the previous night. Now it irritated me, smacking as it did of superiority.

"What happened to the beard?" I asked him.

He leaned across the counter toward me, his skin a rich, golden tan that caught the light nicely. "Beard?" he repeated, laughing. "What beard?"

"I remembered you differently." I knew I sounded rude, but it was true. I'd filed him away in my brain as an avuncular older friend of my gray-haired aunt, not this young, good-looking guy with the sexy voice who was annoyingly confident. "You kept calling me kid, like you were ancient. And you had that *beard*."

"I've never had a beard," he insisted as he turned to rinse the pan in the sink. Fool's House did not come equipped with such modern conveniences as a dishwasher. "You must be thinking of another guy."

He'd had a beard, I swear. That was how I'd always told it, in my head. "It's been seven years," I pointed out grumpily. "Maybe you did have a beard, and you just don't remember. Maybe you're having a memory lapse?"

"Because I'm so *ancient*?" He laughed. "I remember everything about that summer." And he stopped washing the pan and turned around.

"You could've introduced yourself," I continued, wishing I didn't sound quite so petulant. He seemed to bring out the worst in me. "You didn't have to let me embarrass myself. I don't normally . . ." Here my voice trailed off.

"Don't normally what?" he interjected. "Guzzle martinis and throw yourself at strange men?"

"I certainly didn't throw myself anywhere," I protested. "And I was actually looking for you," I tried to explain, unintentionally making it sound like a romantic statement. The man flustered me. "I thought you might know something about Lydia's safe. And since that's apparently why you're here, why don't you make yourself useful?"

"Okay," he said. "I'll try. But she never mentioned it to me. I don't even know where it is. Will you show me?"

We were headed upstairs to the safe when Peck bounded back into the kitchen like one of Charlie's Angels, two hands up in the air, holding what looked, surprisingly, like a gun.

"Look what I found," she cried out, pointing at us a dainty pearl-handled revolver, the kind generally thought of as a ladies' gun, at least in movies and television shows. It was the sort of prop an elegant female spy might keep tucked into an evening clutch, but still, I imagined, it could get the job done.

"Is that real?" I asked, slightly nervous. Peck was not someone I wanted to see with a gun in hand. "Where did you find it?"

"That was Lydia's?" Finn looked surprised. "You need a license to keep a gun."

She blew on the end of it and posed for us. "I always wondered what it felt like to hold one of these things. It's so light. Hard to imagine it could do any damage at all."

"Where was it?" Finn asked her.

"I'm not so sure I should tell you," she said coyly. I shot her a look. "I was looking for the beach towels."

Finn reached for it. "It's not loaded, is it? I don't see Lydia keeping a loaded gun sitting around."

Peck pointed the gun at the screen door to the back porch. "How do I check?" She was about to pull the trigger—"I bet it *is* loaded"—when a slouching figure appeared through the mesh.

The visitor was the inhabitant of the studio above the garage, the last in a long line of creative people Lydia called the Fool-in-Residence. They would live—as Finn Killian had done the summer we met him—rent-free, for a period of time that was usually no longer than three or maybe four months, in exchange for what Lydia called "creating and maintaining an artistic environment." Finn had actually moved in as a friend of the family when the artist who was supposed to come that summer had landed in a prison in Thailand.

The current fellow went by the name of Biggsy. "Biggsy what?" we'd asked, naturally.

"Just Biggsy." He drove a motorcycle and had moved in at the beginning of the previous September, when, according to Lydia, the prior occupant of the studio, a photographer whose oeuvre consisted entirely of black-and-white self-portraits ("Remarkable hubris," she'd written in one of her letters), had moved out. Lydia had mentioned there was someone new, but nothing more. Peck and I had both assumed, if we'd given it any thought at all, that he'd moved out, as they all had, at some point during the desolate cold months when Fool's House was practically unlivable. There was no instruction in Lydia's will as to how we should handle such a person upon her death, and we were shocked to find him at the house when we arrived.

He was astonishingly good-looking, with the pronounced cheekbones and clear skin of those boys in the Abercrombie ads. He had very light skin that looked almost luminescent and his hair was the kind of streaky blond women spend hours at the salon trying to achieve. He was always wearing some sort of costume. That morning, it was a top hat and a seersucker suit, sized for a boy, so the ankle-length pants sat high over laced-up boots. His wrists were exposed by the too-short sleeves on the jacket, and the shirt underneath was buttoned tightly around his neck, although he wore no tie. His hair under the hat was disheveled, but looked like he'd used a hair product to get it that way.

Just Biggsy had shown absolutely no inclination to move out. When we arrived he'd greeted us with rum punches and hot hand towels and then helped us with our bags. Later he went to the grocery store, mowed the lawn, and mopped the kitchen floor. He had been careful, in the early stages of our acquaintance, to ingratiate himself with Peck and me, and after a few days he simply seemed to belong there. He was smart enough to know exactly how to do so, presenting himself as loving custodian to Lydia Moriarty's legacy and as all-purpose household help.

"He's like a *butler*," Peck had declared giddily. "Only free."

"Knock knock," he muttered now, as though he could hardly summon the strength to speak or actually lift his hand to knock. He slumped against the doorframe, looking ill as Peck still pointed the gun in his direction. "Don't shoot me. Please."

Trimalchio scampered over to greet him, uncharacteristically spry. "Dude." The Fool-in-Residence reached down to pet the dog weakly, as though he couldn't stand straight.

"Come in, come in," Peck and I said at the same time. "What's wrong?"

Peck was still pointing the gun in his direction as she waved him in.

"Is that thing loaded?" Biggsy asked. His eyeballs danced in his sockets and he looked alarmingly sick.

"Of course it is," she said. "So you, young man, had better behave."

Biggsy swung the screen door wide and stumbled into the kitchen, clutching his stomach. "I don't feel so good."

I motioned for him to sit on one of the stools at the counter, but he shook his head—too ill to sit. He was hunched over with both arms wrapped around his stomach, and he paused before us. Peck and I both froze as Biggsy sank to his knees on the floor, still clutching his middle. I was surprised to see Finn roll his eyes, completely unsympathetic to the young artist who appeared to be about to throw up.

"I'm going to—"

I was concerned, assuming he was a salmonella victim or that there was some terrible stomach flu going around. Peck was more of an alarmist, screaming, "Stella! Do something."

And then with a loud groan he threw up. A puddle of beige-and-pink chunky vomit splattered the floor.

Peck put the gun on the counter and pulled out her cell phone. "I'm calling 911."

Biggsy rolled over onto his side and held up a hand. "Wait." He lolled on one shoulder, looking down at the puddle of puke he'd deposited on our floor. "I feel better now." Peck clicked the phone shut. "I'm so sorry," he said, running one hand through his disheveled hair. "So sorry. I made such a mess. I'll clean it up."

We were all three staring down at him as he flashed us an insouciant grin and pulled a fork from the chest pocket of his jacket. He propped himself up on one elbow and held up the fork as we watched, completely bewildered. Then he lowered the fork to the pile of vomit on the floor, scooped up a big bite of it, and shoveled it into his mouth.

Peck and I exploded in disgust. "What the hell?"

"Are you crazy?"

That's when he burst out laughing. He laughed so hard he started to choke on what was in his mouth. "Dudes," he managed to squeak out, sitting up and doubling over in spasms of hysterical guffaws. "You shoulda seen your faces."

At first we didn't know how to react. We both just stood there, frozen, as he laughed at us. He took a deep breath and was able to contain himself enough to speak. "That was one of Lydia's favorites."

"You just made yourself throw up?" I stared down at the very believable vomit on our floor. "And then ate it? Are you crazy?"

"Literally? I almost threw up myself," Peck exclaimed. I could hear her already turning this into an anecdote, shaping the story in her mind in order to repeat it.

Finn looked unimpressed, as if he'd seen the vomit trick before, while he rinsed out the bowl he'd used for the eggs. Biggsy pulled aside his jacket and shirt to reveal what looked like a hot water bottle with a tube that he'd snaked up through the top of his shirt. "Cream of mushroom soup." He sat back on his heels and nodded, a proud grin lighting up his face. "Among other things."

Trimalchio nuzzled up next to him, licking his face.

"Trimalchio likes you, Fool," Peck said to him. She seemed to have made a decision about the young artist. She always had a weakness for a pretty face. "And he doesn't like anyone."

The dog looked up at her in agreement. True, not *anyone*, his expression indicated.

"He does like soup, though," I said, watching Trimalchio move on to the mess on the floor, lapping at it eagerly.

"Let's go, kid," Finn said to me. "Show me the safe."

"Safe?" Biggsy glanced over at him. "What safe?"

As Finn followed me up the stairs I could hear Peck telling the Fool-in-Residence about Aunt Lydia and the wording of the will, in which she spoke of finding a thing of utmost value. It occurred to me that it was bad form to talk about this with too many people. But it was only a brief flash of a thought, surprise that my half sister with her obsession with manners would speak so loosely about something that should be kept private, and then it was gone.

3

That night, as was tradition, we held the Fool's Welcome. Our first party on the porch started as a summer vacation does, giddily hopeful. The early part of the evening, with its fragrant, darkening air, held such expectation, like the beginning of summer: this is going to be *fun*.

First, there were dressing drinks. "It's important to mark these moments in life," Peck said as I joined her in the living room, where a brass bar cart had occupied its spot in the corner since Lydia had moved in to Fool's House. For a few seconds I wondered what Lydia would be wearing for the party that evening, before I remembered in a rush of emotion that stung my eyes with tears that she would not be joining us. God, I would miss her. "Record this moment," she might have told me. "Paint it with your words." She loved to give me writing advice, little tidbits that were like expressions of fondness, coming from her. "Writing is rewriting," she would say.

Marking a moment, in Peck's parlance, meant drinking a cocktail, so she was mixing up a batch of her "famous" Southsides, a minty concoction meant to be consumed while we dressed for the evening. "I coined that term, the dressing drink," she said. "It's the cornerstone of a civilized life.

"Isn't this so *Something's Gotta Give?*" Peck asked as she held up a silver cocktail shaker like it was a trophy. This was part of her continued attempt to convince me we could keep the place. She was referring to the movie with Jack Nicholson and Diane Keaton in which a particularly spectacular beach home stirred house lust in its audience. The dank little Fool's House resembled that light and airy—and large—house only in theory. Yes, they were both shingled and in Southampton. But Diane Keaton's was on the ocean and surely didn't smell like mildew. Fool's House was close to town and reeked like an old shower curtain. Diane Keaton's house didn't have a pair of mannequin legs in one corner with silver platform shoes on the feet, or stacks of needlepoint pillows with sayings on them—*A laugh a day keeps the doctor away*, that sort of thing. It also didn't have a floor covered in a blue-green-and-yellow floral rug so loud it could be heard as far away as Montauk. It wasn't filled with stuffed sofas and chairs and lamps collected at the estate sales where Lydia went in search of treasures in other people's junk. And I don't believe it had a tiny closet tucked under the stairs, perfect for hide-and-seek or building forts, that was now jammed so full of old coats and pillows and boxes of things that it could not be opened.

Our house had a doll called the Pink Lady. It was a relic of an earlier era at Fool's House, before it had a name, when perhaps there was a young girl occupying the bedroom that was now mine, with its view of the tiny garden in the back. The doll had bald patches and hair that was supposed to be red but had faded to a punk shade of pink. She was missing an eye and wore an old-fashioned smock that had once been pink but was now a dirty mauve color. The Pink Lady was creepy, but she'd become the house mascot and sat on the edge of the second-floor landing looking down at the living room. There was a cocktail of the same name, and Lydia had been known to invite friends to parties allegedly given by the doll at which only these horrible concoctions—something involving gin and grenadine and raw egg created during the Prohibition days—would be served.

The *Something's Gotta Give* house didn't have a leaking roof, a gas stove that looked and smelled like it was going to combust any minute, or a raging ant *situation*. But there was a certain zany joy to Fool's House that the perfectly decorated movie set lacked, and I did love it, although I knew it was wise to keep my feelings in check. This was to be a brief summer fling, that was it.

"More like *Grey Gardens*," I said. "Without the cats."

There *was* something of Edie Beale's uncensored dramatics to my half sister. When she was thirteen she'd been in a car accident that nearly killed her. She hovered near death—at least that's the way she liked to tell it; "I hovered near death, for months, I tell you, *months*!"—and then, slowly, she recuperated. She missed almost her entire eighth-grade year, spending weeks and weeks of bed rest with old movies on television and gothic romances to read, followed by many more weeks of physical therapy. Like a color photograph coming into focus, she grew bolder and brighter and more intensely saturated as she grew stronger. This process had continued until she evolved, as an adult, into a full-fledged *character* who prided herself on being an eccentric.

"Mum saw that play." Her mother was "Mum." Not "Mom," or "my mother," or even "*my* mum." Just *Mum*. As though she were a universal British parent. But Peck was not British and, thankfully, Mum was not anyone else's mother.

Mary-Alice O'Sullivan was a reasonably attractive Irish housekeeper with red hair hired to clean my dad's apartment twice a week, back in the seventies, when he was a bachelor artist. According to *my* mother, who told the version she'd heard from Lydia, Mary-Alice had parlayed that assignment into a lukewarm love affair, and then into marriage the old-fashioned way, through pregnancy. They were both Catholic and my father had remained unmarried into his late thirties—"There were rumors he was gay, of course," my mother told it—so it wasn't too much of a challenge, and Peck was born six months after the wedding. It was the late seventies in New York and even if anyone had been interested enough to do the math, nobody cared.

Once she was Mrs. George Moriarty she poured all her ambitions into her daughter. She called her Pecksland, a name she insisted had somehow been passed down through her family of potato farmers, and filled Peck's head with fanciful notions about the proper way to live a well-mannered life. She bought her daughter clothes that were too expensive, fostering her love of fashion, and insisted on lessons in diction, piano, and acting. She fueled Peck's fantasies about the life she would go on to lead, as a star of the stage or perhaps a fashion icon.

While Peck was still a baby my father had gotten more interested in music, letting his hair grow and staying out late at concerts. He met my mother, a Smith College graduate working on a PhD in philosophy she never finished, at a Grateful Dead show in Virginia. She was only twenty-two and, to hear Lydia tell it, extremely beautiful, with long streaked hair down her back. My mother told me they fell instantly and passionately in love, and that it was a love so deep and true they were powerless to ignore it, despite the fact that my father was married with a young daughter. The intensity of their love allowed them to rationalize what happened afterward, when George behaved badly, abandoning his wife and child to follow the Dead with my mother, never looking back.

Lydia was the one who used those words, *behaved badly*. My mother always told it as a straightforward love story, as though it was destiny that they should be together, previous wife and child or not. She'd leave out any judgment, or guilt, at their behavior. When she told the story, she used a lightly ironic tone, as though she herself were distanced from the emotions she described, as though God or some higher power had been at work and to refuse to go along with it would have been foolish. "Once in a while," my mother would say, quoting "Scarlet Begonias," "you get shown the light."

It hadn't been easy for Mary-Alice once my mother diverted her husband's attentions. She was a single working mother—she'd gone back to school and become a nurse—but there were arrangements where she traded housekeeping and other services for things like singing lessons for her daughter, and there'd been scholarships, too, although those were harder to come by as Peck grew older and less interested in academic success. Peck had always taken small jobs to help out, babysitting and that sort of thing, but I knew it had been hard for her, growing up on the Upper East Side of Manhattan without money.

But Peck never complained. She'd simply convinced herself that the upbringing her mother had struggled to give her (the 10021 zip code, the girls' school, the many private lessons) was not a facsimile of a privileged existence (a one-bedroom rental on First Avenue, scholarships, and bartered agreements) but the real thing. She believed she was extraordinary and that her background, as she chose to view it, was exactly the way a young woman who would go on to be a woman of style and creative substance would have been raised.

I wouldn't call her pretentious, though some people, without understanding the nuances of her performance, might use such a word, thinking she was putting on airs. But she really wasn't. She was always open about her mother and her background, and appreciative of the sacrifices "Mum" had made for her. She wasn't a snob, either. But she was a Method actor and she'd immersed herself so thoroughly into the role in which she'd cast herself that she knew no other reality.

If you asked her about this, as I once had, trying to reconcile the interpretations of the story of her life into one cohesive narrative I could understand, she would feign ignorance. But Peck was more astute than that, and I believed her refusal to grasp what I meant resided in a decision she'd made early on, that envy was far more palatable than pity. She viewed herself as a character and her upbringing as backstory. "If you need a *subject*," she would say, impatient that I'd yet to write anything resembling a novel, "why not *me*?" And then she would add, "I'd write it myself, but who has the time?"

From the bar cart Peck now chose two glasses and, with great flourish, poured the drinks into the glasses, garnishing them with two quarters of lime speared with plastic toothpicks from a collection in a small silver jar. The toothpicks had little figures on the end that were supposed to look like jesters, the kind of gift I suppose one would give to a person who named her home Fool's House.

The lemons and limes for the bar cart had been sliced by Just Biggsy. That afternoon he'd cut *panini* in the shape of hearts. He rolled chopped beef into meatballs and cut phyllo dough, sliced carrots, and shaved thin sections from the salmon that Peck had brought home from the market. He worked efficiently, his hands moving quickly, and he knew where everything was. I'd expected some jockeying for position within the house between Peck and me, without Lydia to mediate. But there were advantages to taking up temporary residence with a woman who envisioned herself as one television gig and a jail sentence away from being the next Martha Stewart; Peck was constantly preparing food and drinks and trying new recipes. And Biggsy, who was gracious and proper and deferential and treated us exactly as a long-serving butler would his royal charges, helped enormously. In those first days at Fool's House the handsome young artist proved himself indispensable.

The friction between my sister and me didn't have its source in the upkeep of our shared house, although Peck could be ill-tempered when I wasn't as quick with the compliments as she'd have liked. What we didn't agree on was the future of the house. Peck kept dropping hints about expensive renovations we might undertake and how she wanted to turn Fool's House into an artistic and literary retreat. She called me a "stick-in-the-mud" and a "nervous Nellie" when I pointed out that neither of us was in possession of money for such a plan. She even said, "Shut your piehole" when I suggested we schedule a meeting with a real estate broker.

Now Peck lifted her glass and clinked mine. She'd gotten some of the recipes for the food for the Fool's Welcome from a magazine article entitled, with absolutely no irony, "The Perfect Hamptons Party." The instructions on how to host such an event were accompanied by heavily styled photographs of carefully cast models posing as guests, looking maniacally happy as they lifted their glasses in a fictional toast to the "chef," a stout woman in a red taffeta dress.

"I wonder how they got the corn cakes to look like that," Peck had mused, staring at the image in the magazine. There was something in her voice, a poignant note. She knew, didn't she, that those freakishly grinning people toasting the model-slash-real-woman hired for the photo shoot to pose as the chef were all on the job, paid to sit around the table and raise their glasses over and over again as the light changed and the stylist angled the pasta salad just so? But she'd studied the aspirational glossy pages carefully and with yearning, as though they contained the exact formula for success.

My half sister was quite thrilled with her own social daring. She'd invited a hundred people at least, some of whom she'd never actually met. "This is how it's done out here," she informed me, when I'd wondered at the wisdom of inviting people who didn't know her.

Peck said things like this with total seriousness, to the point where you would start to wonder if you weren't actually the one who didn't make sense. "Isn't that a bit, well, *arriviste*?" I wondered aloud, speaking her language.

She waved away my suggestion with her cocktail, spilling some of it on her wrist. "You'll thank me. Later, when you get invited to everything, you'll be grateful."

"I'm only going to be here a few weeks," I reminded her. "I don't need to get invited to *anything*."

She frowned at me. "Could you be any more *boring*? Besides, I have a feeling you're going to be here a lot longer than a few weeks."

"Are you kidding?" I said. "It was hard enough to take this much time off as it was."

"This place grows on people." She waved her cocktail at me. "Drink up."

I'd been looking at the painting above the fireplace mantel, with its swirling movement and heavy layers of paint. "That one's growing on me," I said, gesturing toward it with the still-full drink in my hand. I had no intention of waking up with another hangover like the one I'd suffered through that morning.

If I thought Peck wouldn't notice, however, I was wrong. "Would you please just drink the damn thing?" she grumbled.

I ignored her and gestured at the painting. "Do we have any idea who painted it?"

"Listen to you. Aunt Lydia's body is hardly cool and already you're trying to make a play for her stuff?"

I explained that I wasn't making a play for it, just expressing my interest, and she put her drink down on the bar cart and pulled a chair over toward the fireplace. She stood on the chair to reach the canvas and pulled it down off the flimsy hook on which it had rested for years. She stepped down from the chair and flipped the painting over so we could look at the back. There, on the stretcher, scrawled in black marker, were the almost illegible words. She read them aloud. "'For L.M. From J.P.'"

"Who's J.P.?" I said.

She shrugged, gazing down at the canvas she held out in front of her with two hands. "The artist, I guess. Probably one of her friends. Or a Fool-in-Residence."

She hung the painting back on its hook and took up her drink. "Let's get dressed."

I got up to my room to find Biggsy with a camera in my closet—a small walk-in crowded with Lydia's overflow and other items I hadn't yet gone through. "Oh, hi," he said, as casually as if it were perfectly normal for him to be there.

"How did you get in here?" I hadn't noticed him going up the stairs.

"I'm working on a new series," he said, as if that explained it. He spoke earnestly, fixing his strikingly blue eyes on mine. "I hope you don't mind. I'm shooting people's closets. There's an air of mystery, and also of history, to them."

"Mystery *and* history?" I repeated.

"I'm using black-and-white film, very grainy," he continued. "So there's a sense of a long-buried memory, of the past, of encounters not quite remembered."

He hadn't moved yet, but I held the door to the closet open for him. "I have to get dressed for the party."

"Sorry," he said, slipping past me with his camera held high. He smelled distinctly of patchouli. "You're very pretty, you know."

I knew he was trying to win points with me, and it worked; the compliment distracted me from being bothered by his presence in my closet. I took a shower and got dressed for the party, sticking to jeans, because as my sister put it, I was "afraid to stick my neck out, playing the role of the foreign observer rather than participating in life." Peck could sometimes be astute, but I wore my jeans anyway. Mostly because I hadn't packed much besides the dress I'd already worn to the Gatsby party the night before. I wasn't in the habit of going to parties at all, let alone on back-to-back evenings.

When I finished putting on makeup (lip gloss), I went to Peck's room, where it looked like she'd tried on and discarded every single piece of clothing in the very extensive wardrobe she'd brought with her to Fool's House, in three enormous vintage Louis Vuitton steamer trunks, no less. Apparently she'd also poured herself a re-fill of the dressing drink in the process and was parading around in nothing but a mesh thong with "the twins" on full display as she held up different options for me to judge. "Come on," she complained, when I told her they all looked fine. She fluffed out her hair and sprayed it with a product called, no kidding, Big Hair. "Offer a critique. This is what sisters do for each other. Haven't you always wanted a sister?"

It was true, I had always wanted a sister. I'd kept a picture of the two of us from our first summer at Fool's House, when I was nine and she was twelve, on my bedside table growing up, and went through a phase of talking about my half sister so often that my best friend at the time asked me to stop. So I did as Peck asked, offering a critique of the long orange dress and encouraging her to go with a short feathered number she swore was vintage Halston, "though the tag fell out," and ignored her as she made a face when I refused to make more of an effort than my jeans and a gauzy top.

It did feel sisterly, our squabbling, and I found it enjoyable. I'd grown up in a quiet house, although there were often guests, and I spent a lot of time alone in my room reading. There was often music, bootleg Dead tapes and Bruce Springsteen and the Rolling Stones, but the homes—apartments, mostly—I'd shared with my mother had been peaceful and orderly. This was something I remembered from our summers at Fool's House together, that it was fun to hang out in each other's bedrooms, even if we weren't getting along. In fact, in some ways I liked it even more when we were arguing, like real sisters.

"You know what I *want*?" Peck was one of those people who always asked if you knew what they wanted. She'd call me up at odd hours, when I hadn't heard from her in months, forgetting, or ignoring, the time difference, to tell me she was craving truffles or "one of those dear little chicken pot pies." Or she'd announce that what she wanted more than anything in life was to have an audience with the pope. Or to host a dinner where she invited only comedians, twelve of them around the table, and let them duke it out. "More than anything? I want to be on the Best-Dressed List in *Vanity Fair* magazine," she announced, as we made our way out to the porch.

The porch was the best feature of the house, a wide, welcoming space both contemplative and gregarious that wrapped around the entire lopsided place, accessorizing it in overly grand style. One side of the porch we had draped in an enormous American flag, because that's what Lydia had always done. At the other end was the warped wooden table where meals were taken on nice summer days. Now it was piled high with food.

Hamilton Frayn, aka Sir Ham, as Lydia liked to call him, was our first guest. He was my aunt's best friend but anyone who referred to him that way, as simply a *friend*, was always quickly corrected. "He's *family*," Lydia would say. "Anyone who thinks you can't choose your family never had a friend like Hamilton Frayn."

Hamilton was gay and British and had spent thirty years of summers and weekends in a lavishly styled shingled house next to Lydia's. He was a decorator—or an interior designer, as I'd been corrected—and his place was an advertisement for a Hamptons lifestyle that seemed otherwise to exist only in magazine spreads, all plump white cushions and pale green throw blankets tossed over fat chaises, books left spread-eagled on round tables set with glistening glasses of lemonade a shade or two paler than the casually draped cashmere.

Hamilton had organized Lydia's funeral in Paris, which Peck and I had both attended, and a memorial service a few weeks later in Southampton for her many friends, but he'd been doing an installation at a client's house in Nantucket and I hadn't seen him since I arrived in Southampton. We gave each other a big hug and I thanked him for coming to the party.

"Darling, I go to *everything*. I'd go to the opening of an envelope," he said. He had an awful lot of white hair combed into an elaborate sweep on either side of his face, and eyebrows so extravagant they looked like pets. He wore his customary uniform of an unsummery tweed blazer, as though he were out in the chilly English countryside after a foxhunt and not at a casual summer party on Long Island. He also carried a fan that he waved at his face all evening, despite refusing to take off the jacket, even after I suggested it twice.

"How's your *writing*?" he asked, sounding exactly like Lydia. Hamilton was amiably ill-tempered and could be hilariously bitchy, but he always seemed to have a soft spot for Peck and me. "Your aunt always encouraged you to write."

"She encouraged *everyone* to write," I pointed out. This made him laugh.

"Of course she did," he said. "But I hope you're not letting that dissuade you. She'd be ever so disappointed."

"You know what she used to love to say to me?" I asked him. " 'There are three rules for writing the novel. Unfortunately no one knows what they are.' That was one of her favorite bits of writing advice. But she was actually a pretty good teacher. She used to make her students read a passage from a great work and then write their own piece, using a similar technique, with a similar tone and mood, whether it was a third-person omniscient narrator, or first person. She did the same to me."

"She told me you had talent, for whatever that's worth," he said. "Talent is one of those elusive concepts that is so maddening to understand. Anyway, it's what you do with talent that counts."

I fixed Hamilton a drink from the bar cart we had wheeled out onto the porch. We had picked four bottles of expensive aged scotch, he was pleased to see. "I'm a terrible snob about the stuff," he said.

When we'd gone out to stock up on provisions for the evening, Peck had smacked my wallet out of my hand when I attempted to pay. "Your mussels are no good here," Peck had said to me, as though she were the duchess of Fool's House buying out the entire liquor store. "Mussels" was one of her oft-used euphemisms for money, a word she went out of her way not to use. "I know you're *concerned*," she said, implying that I was being tiresome about money again, the way I was when I tried to talk about selling Fool's House because we couldn't afford to keep it.

Actually, I wasn't concerned. It was more that I was curious. Peck, who had no steady source of income, had always spent like she had stores of wealth at her disposal. She wouldn't talk about the stuff—she carried herself as though she were embarrassed at having inherited a trust fund and thus could afford to find it rude to even discuss the topic—but she was the type who would pay more for things if she could, priding herself on her taste for the expensive.

She never actually said the word *money* if she could help it, although once, the last summer we'd spent together, I heard her saying to someone on the phone, in a weary tone, as if she were exhausted by the intricate management of a complicated inheritance, "Family and money, those are two words that should never go together." I don't know what she was talking about then, probably something to do with a family drama pertaining to the person on the other end of the line, but there was that subtle implication, a tiny spray of words that formed a slightly questionable impression. She prided herself mostly on her exquisite taste, and when it came to entertaining, she was quick to let me know, she was an expert.

"Maybe in Switzerland you can get away with a bottle of cheap red and a pot of *fondue*." She pronounced *fondue* as if she'd grown up in a chalet on an Alpine ridge. "But in Southampton? There's no point in having a party unless you're going to do it right."

This was her usual tone with me, peeved and impatient with my lack of either enthusiasm or understanding about the way things worked in this world into which she'd imagined she'd been born. I was the naïve newcomer and she was the native, and any time I presumed to behave otherwise—like when I suggested that nobody would ever open the bottle of Midori liqueur she felt was necessary for our "full bar"—it irked her. "After all," she kept pointing out, "you don't know *anyone*."

Hamilton accepted the scotch gratefully. "Lydia would have adored this party. You girls have done a wonderful job. The Fool's Welcome. The unofficial start to summer."

Like most of our guests throughout the time we lived at Fool's House that summer, he had an opinion about what we should do with the house we'd inherited: sell it, keep it, renovate it, rent it out. At the time I thought this was a very American thing to do, to offer an unsolicited and strongly felt opinion about something as personal as a home. But I've since come to realize that this is not an American quality so much as a New York one, and that the suggestions were meant to be helpful.

Hamilton kindly suggested we not feel guilty about selling Fool's House. "If you can," he added. "Price it to get out quickly. That's exactly the way Lydia would have wanted it."

"But that's not good for the value of *your* home," I pointed out. "If we sell it too cheap, just to get rid of it, won't that make all the houses along here less valuable?"

"Darling, don't you worry about me. You couldn't buy a hamburger at the 21 Club for what I spent on my place when I bought it. It was the *seventies*." He grinned, as though remembering a particularly wild decade. "I have a broker for you. Laurie Poplin. She's good. A little tall, if you know what I mean, but she can sell houses."

"Tall?" I repeated.

"Tall women are always so keen on making one aware of their height, no?"

I nodded, and then told him we still hadn't been able to open the safe. That morning, with Finn, we'd tried all different dates pertaining to Jasper Johns's paintings but we hadn't been able to open the door. I also went through more of Lydia's papers on the cluttered desk but hadn't been able to find anything having to do with the safe, which remained firmly closed.

"I don't know why she had a safe. She never even locked her doors." He rattled the ice cubes in his drink and his eyes clouded, as though he were remembering a specific moment with Lydia. After a pause, he added, "What would she have kept in there?"

"Jewelry?" I guessed.

He shook his head. "You saw the stuff lying all over the house. All costume, the bigger and more fun the better. She wasn't the diamonds and emeralds type, was she?"

"What do you think she meant when she said she wanted us to find a thing of utmost value?"

Hamilton took an appreciative sip of his drink and said, "The thing she wanted you to find and the contents of the safe may not be the same. What she *valued* were not material things, remember?"

Peck had been fussing with the food and she came over to wrap her arms around Hamilton. "Thank God you're here," she said to him. "My sister is driving me *mad*."

"Oh dear," he said, raising his elaborate eyebrows comically in my direction.

"She's already divvying everything up," Peck complained. "Wants to just clear it all out, sell the house, and go on back where she came from, as if this place never even existed."

"That's really not true," I protested. "I'm just trying to do what Lydia told us to in her will."

Hamilton glanced from one to the other of us. "At least there are two of your father's paintings. One for each of you."

He was right. Two of the paintings hanging in the hallway had been painted by my father. They were both abstract landscapes, Lydia had explained to us the first time Peck and I stayed with her, although it was hard for either of us to see anything resembling the dunes and sky that Lydia insisted were miraculously conveyed in the murky colors. My mother had always called my father a genius. "Your father, the brilliant artist," she would say, when she spoke about him, which was rare. It was my introduction to sarcasm, but it wasn't until many years later, when sarcasm became my native tongue, that I recognized it. At the time I read into the resentment in her tone—"the brilliant artist"—her desire to have kept hold of him, rather than any commentary on his actual output. I thought she was alluding to the time and attention he'd put into his work, rather than into their short-lived marriage.

She'd kept several of my father's paintings, large, murky abstracts that moved with us from Rome to Belgium and then to Switzerland. I hung them in the tiny apartment I shared with Jean-Paul after she died, and then in the tinier one I moved into when our marriage reached its inevitable end. I'd never had much of an opinion about whether they were "good" or not. They were art and they were my dad's and they had sentimental value, if nothing else.

And even though I would go on to speak fluent sarcasm and therefore should have understood my mother perfectly well, I'd always continued to believe my father had at least some talent. He did sell some of his paintings. There had been a gallery in SoHo that represented him and I remember seeing a picture of my father and my much younger mother at an opening.

Aunt Lydia, on the other hand, infused no irony into the word *brilliant* when applied to her brother. She had a fondness for such terms as *masterpiece*, *stunning*, or even *genius*. When she used the same words as my mother to refer to him—"your father, the brilliant artist"—she meant them literally. But the two paintings in the hallway were not any better than the ones I had at home.

Peck didn't have any of his paintings. "You can keep them both, if you like," I said to her now.

She made a face. "I think they should stay right here at Fool's House, where they belong," she said, giving Hamilton a pointed look. "Anyway, Mum always told me our father was never a good artist. What he had was charisma. Which apparently I inherited in spades." She patted me on the shoulder, indicating her sympathy that I, unfortunately, had not inherited any such qualities.

As the early guests made their way up to the porch, I was distracted by the sight of a figure moving slowly across the driveway from the garage. From my perspective it resembled an old-time traveling peddler, laden with items of odd, protruding shapes for sale. As he drew closer, though, I could see that it was Biggsy, with camera, lights, and cables draped over his shoulder, like a one-man Scorsese film crew, looking to set up a shot. He wore another variation of the shrunken suit, this one in a vivid shade of crushed purple velvet, had tied a floppy silk bow at his neck, and wore his magician's hat at a jaunty angle. None of the other guests seemed at all fazed at the elaborately dressed person in their midst. In fact, they hardly seemed to notice him, which struck me as very blasé.

Only Hamilton had a comment about the costumed figure. "He's still here, is he?" He pointed. "I thought he moved out over the winter."

I noted the shift in his tone. "Biggsy? There doesn't seem to be any point in forcing him to move out now when he's going to have go as soon as we sell the place anyway."

"I wouldn't trust him as far as I could throw him," Hamilton said, as we watched the young artist set up his equipment. "I always told Lydia that. Though I do so enjoy the sight of a handsome chap dressed for a party."

"Why wouldn't you trust him?" I was surprised. Peck and I had both become somewhat enamored of the eager young artist in the four days we'd been at Fool's House, or at least enamored of the idea of him. And he'd been so helpful.

Hamilton looked alarmed at the question. "Oh darling. Gone soft on the fellow already, have you?"

"He's been cooking and cleaning since we got here," I explained. "He mows the lawn, he chops the lemons, he helps with the laundry. Oh, and he pretends to throw up. Then he eats it. Which I hear is one of Lydia's favorites."

"Yes, I've seen that performance." Hamilton shrugged, his eyebrows dancing up and down.

Peck was standing right near Biggsy, as though she were the director and he the cameraman, and I went over to see what was going on. "What's he doing?" I asked her as the porch began to fill with chattering people, with more filing up the driveway in colorfully dressed packs, but none of them seemed at all bothered by Biggsy's camerawork.

"I don't know," she said. "And I don't care. He says it's art."

She was puzzled by my lack of a cocktail in hand and immediately set about rectifying the situation by walking over to the bar cart and pouring me a Southside. "I've just had a text from him."

"Who?" I asked, still watching Biggsy.

She paused, with a cigarette halfway to her lips, incredulous. "Barack Obama." She lit the American Spirit and blew organic smoke at me in a perfect ring. "Who do you think? Miles Noble. Have you not been listening to a word I've said?"

I wouldn't have been entirely shocked to learn she *had* extended an invitation to the presidential hopeful. She'd invited several high-profile people—social figures and a celebrity whom she'd spotted at the Golden Pear—in the hopes that they would come. And some of them had come, I was surprised to note. The porch was now full of people, with more gathered in clumps on the lawn, where we'd set votive candles on the tables Lydia kept in the garage just for parties.

In the mix—Peck prided herself on her mix—were beautiful pencil-thin women, like the Girls, as glossy and groomed as movie stars at awards shows, and homely ones in elaborate summer outfits who looked as if they'd been forced to develop their personalities. There were the sad young men, of course, and lots of good-looking ones and flamboyant gay ones wearing summer sweaters in sorbet colors. There were a few hipsters, artistic types in un-Southampton black leather, and one or two stodgy older women in very Southampton pearl chokers. There were Europeans with their cigarettes and their accents and their combination of disdain and awe for American summer traditions. There were writers and artists, and a couple of Russians. A movie star made an appearance. Someone brought a hip-hop mogul. There were chignons and dreadlocks and a particular kind of blonde that seemed to exist only here in Southampton.

It was quite a mix. What they all had in common, though, was that they all appeared to adore Peck. She was clever and witty, playing the role of the eccentric hostess—madcap heiress coming through, folks, pay attention—as though she'd inherited it from Lydia along with the house. The ramshackle old porch was soon stuffed to the roof with people laughing raucously and dancing. They seemed unabashedly unafraid to look silly, wiggling their hips and hopping up and down to the thumping beat of a song that exhorted all of us to *Be the love generation, come on, come on, be the love generation.* This invitation—*We got to love, yeah, we got to love*—seemed to be all the encouragement some of our guests needed to throw their arms wildly in the air and push up, raising the roof.

"I've arrived," Peck kept telling people. And "*Je suis arrivée,*" because she was one of those women who insisted on "using" their French. (Never mind that her French consisted of about fourteen words, including the ability to order "*pommes frites*" at the McDonald's along the Long Island Expressway, much to the bewilderment of the pimpled young fellow attempting to help us for his minimum wage.)

"He said he wasn't sure he was going to make it," Peck said, of another text from Miles. "And of course I couldn't care less. I've got that Hamptons high."

"I thought nobody calls it that," I pointed out, as an ominous-looking black Escalade sped down the short driveway, spraying gravel. It had dark tinted windows and flashy tires and the license plate said MAN1.

"It's my drug lord." Peck threw her hands up in the air as if to say, Can this get any *better*?

And then there he was, stepping out of the backseat carefully, as though expecting to fight off the paparazzi. He had an unfortunate nose, through which he spoke. "Cute place," he said as Peck glided over to him with a queenly air, giving the impression she'd half forgotten she'd invited him, but would draw on her innate good manners to greet him as warmly as she would any guest.

"Welcome to Fool's House," she said, with just a hint of frost to her smile.

I could see this was exactly the right note to strike with someone like Miles Noble. Peck seemed to know this instinctively, the way she would always know exactly what fork to use and when to ask for a favor. He appeared slightly cowed, as though she really had descended from a long line of artistic aristocrats, as she kissed him on the cheek as casually as she had all her other guests and offered him a drink.

I was admiring the way Peck easily pulled Miles through the crowd when Finn Killian appeared before me. "Hey, kid," he said, and instantly I felt as jittery and alert as if I'd had four espressos. I'd never met anyone to whom I had such a physical response and I didn't like it, that intense butterflies-in-the-gut feeling of nerves. Had I ever felt that way about Jean-Paul?

"I brought you something," he said, handing me an envelope. "My mother let me take this for you. It was in an album of hers."

I opened the envelope to find a crinkled photograph that seemed, from the way Lydia looked and the way she was dressed, to have been taken in the eighties. It was an image of a younger and very beautiful Lydia standing in front of the fireplace in the living room at Fool's House, arm in arm with a woman I didn't recognize. She had short brown hair brushed back off her forehead and a broad smile. The two of them looked like they'd just been laughing and had composed themselves briefly for the photo. "That's my mom," Finn said, pointing at her. "Did you ever meet her? She was at the funeral in Paris."

Those few days had been a blur of tears and meeting people, hundreds of people, all of whom claimed to have been good friends of Lydia's, and I stared at the woman in the photo, wondering if I could have met her. She looked fun and sporty and exactly the sort of woman to have given birth to five boys, several of whom, I would learn, became gifted college athletes.

"I was sorry I couldn't be there," he said. "I was in Asia on a disastrous site visit. But I went to the memorial service here."

"And I was sorry I couldn't be at that one," I told him, still gazing at the kind woman who grinned up at me from the photo with her arm wound tightly around Lydia's. "I took three days off when I went to the funeral. And then I'd already asked my boss about taking this month to come here, so I couldn't exactly come twice."

He too was looking down at the picture of the two smiling women in my hand. "How *did* you manage to take a whole month off?"

I gave a little laugh, recalling the face my boss, Guy, a persnickety Belgian editor, had made when I asked him about finally using some of the eighteen weeks of vacation I'd earned since I started working at the magazine. Until Aunt Lydia's funeral, I'd only taken three days in the entire seven years I'd worked there, and that had been for my honeymoon. I told Finn about him and the month's leave he'd begrudgingly granted me when I promised to send him amusing anecdotes about the place he'd never visited called "ze Hamptons." "I suppose next you'll be wanting to write a book," he'd complained. "Like ze rest of my staff."

"Your mom looks nice," I said to Finn, gesturing at the photo.

"She *is* nice," he said. "I got lucky."

His words struck a chord in me. "My mom was nice too," I said of the strikingly clever woman I'd called at her insistence by her first name, Eleanor. She'd never finished her PhD, but she'd always seemed to know so much, especially about people, and now that Lydia too was gone, I felt the loss of my mother even more. She died too young, of a particularly virulent pancreatic cancer that was cruelly, but in some ways mercifully, swift. That was only a few months before I spent my last summer with Lydia, the summer I met Finn for the first time. By the following summer I was married.

"You must miss her a lot," he said gently, noting the shift in my mood. "I remember how tough that summer was for you."

It started to come back to me then, how kind he was. Finn was a nice guy. How had I not remembered that part? Around us, the party careened as my impression of him shifted slowly. We talked, exchanging details about our families, our jobs, our friends.

Eventually things on the porch were starting to wane. I walked with Finn off the porch and into the yard. "I used to drop in every once in a while to play backgammon with Lydia," he said before he waved good-bye, leaving me wondering if that was a warning or a promise. Was he looking for an invitation?

Hamilton was still there, and he approached me with a tiny elf of a man in a flowered tie. "I want you to meet a friend of mine. Ian. He's called Scotty, though, for obvious reasons. Just listen to him speak."

"I'm terribly anxious to be of assistance," the elfin man stated in a thick Scottish brogue, gazing adoringly at Hamilton as he shook my hand.

"Scotty's the cousin of the brother of an uncle of a baron or something like that. Which makes him rather a snob," Hamilton explained cheerfully. "He's also an appraiser at the auction house where I hung my hat in a previous life."

The little man clapped his hands together, clearly infatuated with Hamilton. "I'm not a snob at all. That's *him*. But I do still have a job, for now. They haven't kicked me out yet. I know where all the bodies are buried."

"It's amazing how far an accent can take the likes of us." Hamilton nodded at his friend. "This place is overrun with Brits all spouting nonsense that, to the American ear, sounds so much the richer and more intelligent in our dulcet tones."

"Like the Englishmen," I said. "At Gatsby's parties."

He looked surprised. "There are Englishmen in *The Great Gatsby*?"

"'Agonizingly aware of the easy money in the vicinity,'" I was then forced to explain, quoting from the book I knew almost by heart. Just that afternoon I'd sat on the porch for a bit with a hardcover that had been Lydia's. I'd opened it to the beginning, savoring the familiar opening sentence again. *In my younger and more vulnerable years my father gave me some advice that I've been turning over in my mind ever since.* I'd read to the part where Nick Carraway attends the party at Gatsby's house next door. "'Theirs for a few words in the right key.'"

"Oh, isn't that true?" Scotty cooed in an admiring tone. "Aren't you clever?"

I wasn't feeling at all clever. In fact I was feeling as embarrassed, as I usually did when these sorts of things came out of my mouth and I found myself in conversations where I was sure I sounded like a pretentious literary nut. But Hamilton made me feel better.

"Your aunt was mad for that book," he said to me, with a kindly pat on the arm, as though he knew how I felt. "Oh, did she ever love that book."

"I never understood it," Scotty stated, almost plaintively. "I suppose because I'm not an *American*."

"Or perhaps because you're not very bright," Hamilton said with a straight face.

Scotty nodded amiably at me. "I'm not. But I'm really quite good fun." He pointed at Biggsy hovering behind Miles Noble, eager for an introduction. "I know that chap. The handsome one in the costume. Do you remember, Ham? The opening where the artist was killed out in the street in front of the gallery?"

"I was with you," Hamilton reminded his friend. "He was run over by a taxi as he took a cigarette in the rain."

"Don't you remember?" Scotty exclaimed. "When we were outside and the ambulance was coming? There was someone filming the scene. And do you remember what he said when we told him to turn off the camera? He said, 'Hey, man, this is art.'"

"Empathetic young chap, isn't he?" Hamilton pointed out. "The poor man's body was still steaming under the pelting rain. It was rather astonishing."

"The piece was for sale at the Basel Art Fair later in the year," Scotty added. "But I don't suppose anyone ever bought it. In fact, I remember hearing that the artist had *died*."

"Wouldn't that have been an ironic twist of fate?" Hamilton asked. "But if he is the artist, he appears to be alive and well, doesn't he? Living the good life here in the Hamptons."

They were still chatting about Biggsy when Peck appeared at my side. "I need to talk to you," she whispered, hand cupped against my ear. "In *private*."

She pulled me around to the back side of the porch, where earlier in the evening Finn and I had been alone. "Stella," she whispered urgently. "We've been *robbed*."

4

When Peck said we'd been robbed, I assumed someone had made off with the safe in Lydia's mothball-scented closet. But the only thing missing, oddly, was the painting we'd been looking at earlier in the evening, the painting—"For L.M. From J.P."—that had hung above the mantel for as long as we could remember.

"Why would anyone take *that*?" we asked each other as, out on the front side of the porch, the party wound down to its natural end without anyone knowing something was awry. Miles Noble left without saying good-bye and we didn't tell anyone about the missing painting. It hardly seemed like something worth mentioning.

The next day, however, Peck put forth a theory over a lunch she and Biggsy had prepared from the leftover party food—pink lemonade with cucumber, ginger, and mint; tiny cornbread sandwiches with turkey and chutney; crab cakes on *ciabatta*; homemade potato chips; and a ridiculously delicious avocado and tomato salad with cilantro. The three of us gathered at the table on the porch. The sun was high over our heads in a cloudless sky and the inspiring light that had lured so many artists to this part of the world threw everything into sharp relief.

"Okay, so here's what I think," she said, once we were settled in. "It wasn't until I mentioned Lydia's paintings that Miles seemed interested in coming over here, right? And then, first thing, he asked me to give him a tour. Right in the middle of the party." She caught Biggsy's eye. "I know. *Rude*, right? But he was so into it, I couldn't say no. And then here's where it gets weird." She paused to take a bite of her crab cake sandwich, oozing with tartar sauce, and then washed it down with fresh lemonade before resuming. "He stood before that painting for a long time, much longer than he looked at any of the others. Almost as if he were trying to place it in his mind."

"I saw him!" Biggsy cried out, his eyes lighting up, immediately fueling Peck's suspicions. "You were already back outside and he went back in there by himself. Nobody else was around. He was staring up at that painting forever."

"Here's what I think," she said, leaning forward conspiratorially, even though there was nobody who could hear us. "That painting was the thing of value that Lydia was talking about. She probably didn't want anyone to know what it was because we would have gotten socked with big taxes. And maybe she didn't want to make it too complicated for us, because how do you divide a painting? Unless you sell it and share the proceeds. That would explain why she worded the will that way."

"And this Miles guy, he collects art, right?" Biggsy chimed in. "I knew he did—that's why I wanted to talk to him about my work. But he was too busy casing the joint. Didn't even hear me."

Peck gestured at him with her sandwich, sending a dollop of tartar sauce in his direction. "Literally. That's what happened. He figured out what it was and that it was worth something. Oh God," she moaned. "I just realized I *told* him. I'm such a blabbermouth, I had to go and tell him all about Aunt Lydia's will and the thing of utmost value."

"I had another theory," Biggsy said. "But now it seems silly. I think you were right. He had that horny look in his eye. He wanted that painting."

"I'm telling you, there's something shady about Miles," Peck added eagerly. This was exactly the kind of drama she would work to create when it didn't exist, and she was enjoying this immensely. "When I was young and didn't know better I found it sexy. But when you think about it, how did he make all that money? Oh, I do think he could be a thief. He had it in him."

I'd been listening rather skeptically as the two of them worked themselves into a frenzy of conviction, but I didn't really believe Miles Noble would appear, seemingly out of the blue, into Peck's life and into her aunt's house and walk away with a painting off the wall, even if it was the one I'd liked best. But I had no other explanation. "What was *your* theory?" I asked Biggsy.

He hung his head. "It's dumb now."

Of course this only made Peck and me implore him to tell us what he was thinking, and when he spoke a small smile played at his lips. His looks were distracting. His accent was flat and unplaceable—he told us he'd grown up in Utah, but then he also mentioned having lived in a trailer park in Oregon and summers in Idaho, so the exact source was unclear—and he never sounded particularly intelligent, but it was hard not to be thrown off by the fact that words were emerging at all from such a mouth. It was disconcerting, like one of those Abercrombie ads come to life.

"You know how Lydia always said there was a ghost?" he said sheepishly. Lydia had always enjoyed sharing her tales of the genial figure of the former owner of the house who made an appearance every now and then, hiding a frying pan from the kitchen on the bookshelf, or moving the items on the bar cart. "Well, I've seen it for myself."

"You thought a *ghost* took the painting." I couldn't help sounding dubious.

"He's more of a poltergeist," he said, looking to Peck for confirmation. "Sometimes he *finds* things."

"Oh! Oh! What if it's *Lydia*!" Peck interjected, looking pleased with herself. "Trying to tell us something. Communicating from beyond the grave . . ." Her voice trailed off as she contemplated this version.

"I didn't think it was Lydia," he said, in his usual serious tone. "But I did wonder about the ghost of Fool's House, the original owner. The one she won the house from in a game of backgammon?"

I lifted my hands in protest. "My mother said that story wasn't true."

"Well," he said, still speaking earnestly, "did you look in the closet under the stairs? Lydia once told me the ghost often tucked things away under there for safekeeping."

"I can't believe we're actually discussing the possibility of a friendly ghost swooping in and taking a painting off the wall," I said. "We're all adults."

"Stella's right," Peck said with a firm nod, like it was time to get back to the real situation. "If it was a ghost, it was the ghost of lovers past. Miles Noble did this. Maybe it was some sort of mating ritual, the first step in a dance of courtship. Or maybe he really believed it was something of value and he stole it. But we're going to find out."

We finished eating and cleared the plates and then Peck, who loved to talk on the phone, began making calls to people who'd been at the party. "Just wondering if you noticed anything *unusual* last night," she kept saying. "No, no, nothing serious. Just a strange occurrence that we're trying to understand. Well, I'd rather not say. I'll tell you everything when I know more."

To someone else she gave hangover advice—"I'm telling you, grease is the word. Get yourself to the Sip 'n Soda," she advocated—before hanging up. "That person was so drunk last night he thought

I was accusing him of going home with the painting himself," said Peck. "He offered to search his car and call me back."

"I think we should go see those peculiar neighbors of ours, the Samuelses," she said to me, holding her hand over the receiver after she'd placed the next call. The Samuelses lived in the oversized house to the east of Fool's House, and Peck believed they'd been spying on us from their third-floor window since we arrived. "They might have seen something. Miles sneaking out the back door with the painting under his arm?"

Bethany Samuels sold jewelry at private trunk shows in her home and her husband worked on Wall Street. We would see them, or more often hear them, going from zero to sixty in their Hummer on our quiet little street. They had two young girls who were always dressed in matching clothes, although one was huge and one was tiny and the outfits, old-fashioned smocked dresses and shoes that buttoned on the side, looked odd in such different sizes. They were often being wheeled in a stroller up and down the street by a nanny in a starched uniform, although the big one was old enough to ride a bicycle on her own.

Peck had invited them to the party only to avoid having them call the police to complain about the noise. "She's a faux-cialite," she'd said of Bethany Samuels, dismissing her. "And so pushy. Give her four minutes and she'll try to sell you a diamond ring. But we have to be neighborly."

Sure enough, Bethany Samuels had arrived at our party with postcard invitations in hand for a jewelry trunk show. "You should come. The best deals on diamonds anywhere." I don't know what she thought I would be doing buying diamonds, even at a discount, but she persisted. "Just come and check it out. No pressure. I'm not into aggressive sales. I know it's a Sunday but so many of us are golf widows I thought it would make sense. Husbands welcome but not necessary!"

"Social magicians," Peck called Bethany and her husband. It was the sort of term she'd claim to have coined. This was one I'd never heard before, so perhaps Peck did come up with it on her own. "They show up places, mostly at the parties where you have to buy a ticket. Then they can say, I was at so-and-so's house or I had dinner with so-and-so. And they create the illusion that they're social. But that's all it is, an illusion."

"If we go over there," I said, "we have to take Hamilton. When she handed me the invitation he told me to let him know if we decided to go. Said he wanted the opportunity to sneer at it from the inside."

"He's so *naughty*," Peck said, grinning and handing me the phone. "Tell him to get his white English ass over here and let's go."

The house that the Samuelses owned had replaced whatever small house had been there before it, and was too large for its lot and soulless. It was the kind of house that had been thrown up quickly and greedily, by a builder looking to cash in with no specific buyer in mind other than one with money to burn. It came with all the bells and whistles, a media room, a wine cellar, a gym, and plenty of steam showers, flat-panel televisions, and Viking appliances, but not an ounce of charm.

I'd hardly had time to hang up the phone and slip on my shoes before Hamilton was in our driveway, waving his fan at us, a pink sweater tied jauntily around his neck. "Are we really going to pay a call on our neighbors?" he called out. "I feel deliciously *sneaky*."

"Come up and try my lemonade," Peck instructed him, and then added in her usual slightly irritable tone, "It's delicious. But of course, my *sister* could never say so. God forbid she should pay me a compliment."

"I drank three glasses of the stuff," I reminded her. "I oohed and aahed over everything."

"You didn't say anything specifically about the lemonade," she quibbled. "It's disheartening, to work that hard on something and then have you gulp down three glasses and not even mention it." She sighed. "And then when you do say anything, it's just dripping in sarcasm, as if it's supposed to be funny. I'm telling you, I'm at my wit's end with you."

"Now, girls," Hamilton said, once he'd accepted a chilled glass of lemonade with ice from Peck and quickly declared it "marvelous." He gestured with his fan in the direction of our neighbors' house. "What exactly is the reason for our visit to the unsightly mass of cedar shingles on the other side of you?"

Peck quickly explained about the missing painting and Hamilton took his glass of lemonade into the house as we followed him. There we gazed up at the forlorn hook that was all that was left in the empty spot above the mantel.

"When the *Mona Lisa* was stolen from the Louvre," Hamilton said, "more people came to see the empty spot where she'd hung than had ever come to see the painting."

"This was hardly the *Mona Lisa*." Peck gestured toward the hook. "Do you know who painted it?"

Hamilton rubbed his chin. "I always wondered. She was somewhat coy about this one. One got the sense it was more *important* than any of the others. But she never said who the artist was. I'm not sure I ever asked."

I told him about the words on the back of the frame.: FOR L.M. FROM J.P. Peck shared her theory that Miles Noble had figured out what it was and taken it.

"I wish we could just ask the old girl," he said, somewhat deflated. An air of sadness seemed to have come over him suddenly. "I just don't know."

"Could this be the thing of utmost value she was talking about?" I asked him.

He shrugged. "I haven't the foggiest. We never talked about dying. I didn't know *what* was in her will. I didn't even know she had one."

"Well, there's a reason someone took this painting," Peck proclaimed with authority. "Now let's go see if we can get anything out of that nosy pipsqueak next door."

As we headed off together down our driveway on foot, Hamilton threw one arm around each of us. "I'm having a party on Tuesday. I want you both to promise to be there. I'm simply adoring having the two of you here."

"See, Stella," Peck said, peering around his girth at me. "Hamilton thinks we should stay at Fool's House."

"That's not exactly what I said and you know it," he corrected her. "If I had the money I'd buy the place and let you enjoy it. I wish I could do that. But the real estate market out here has gotten so crazy, even Lydia was thinking of selling."

We both stopped walking, shocked at what he just said. Peck looked over at me. "That's impossible."

Now it was Hamilton's turn to look surprised. "What? Of course not. We both were talking about selling. The real estate market out here has gone wild. Houses that only a few years ago were five hundred thousand are now five million. We were going to sell these two places—we thought we might get more if we sold them together, you see. And then we planned to move to Greece. Or some days it was Morocco. Then for a while we thought of Fiji, but neither of us had been there. We called it cashing in our 401(k)s."

Peck shook her head, refusing to believe him. "Lydia would never have cashed in on Fool's House. She loved this place."

"We may not have actually done it," Hamilton said as we started to walk again. "But it was highly amusing to talk about it. Now I don't know. Greece and Morocco don't sound as much fun without her." He paused for a moment, and then continued. "I'll probably just stay and complain bitterly while some young couple tears Fool's House down and puts up another of these monstrosities too big for its lot." He shuddered dramatically as we turned into our neighbors' driveway and their house came into view. "How could anyone build such an ugly thing?" he asked gleefully.

"My sister said the same thing about *Miles Noble's* house," Peck reported in the manner of a journalist who can't believe there are actually people in the world who can't see clearly, that is, the way she does. "But his is *huge*."

He tilted his head toward me conspiratorially. "More to go wrong, then."

The front door to the Samuelses' house was propped open and we followed two women in beach cover-ups through it. "Oh, it's worse than I imagined," Hamilton whispered happily as we stepped into the living room, where a riot of mismatched blue-and-white patterns caused him to recoil slightly. "Look at the toile!"

Peck admonished him with a grin. "You're so bitchy."

"I wouldn't be," he protested, "if I didn't know they spent a bloody fortune doing this up with that leech Emmet Leary. I think he picked these fabrics with his eyes closed and then laughed his little self all the way to the bank."

There were several rows of sandals and flip-flops lined up near the front door, next to a basket of patterned Chinese slippers in assorted sizes. A hand-lettered sign indicated that we were to take off our shoes and don a pair of the slippers before entering.

"Is the woman mad?" Hamilton looked to me. "I'm absolutely not taking off my shoes. What a repulsive thought."

"Me neither," Peck crowed, lifting her heel to show off a dainty sandal. "This is disgusting."

I hesitated, then slipped off my sandals.

"My sister is so *obedient*," Peck pointed out. "She can't help herself. She's like a schoolgirl, isn't she? Afraid Headmistress is going to come looking for her."

There must have been fifteen women in Bethany Samuels's coral dining room—"More toile!" Hamilton exclaimed—where ropes of diamonds and pavé bracelets and huge cocktail rings were laid out on velvet trays. The chatter was loud and excited as the women fluttered around the table, draping themselves in expensive baubles and admiring their reflections in conveniently placed hand mirrors. There was something frenetic about the way they picked at the shiny pieces before them, like birds nervously preparing their nests.

"Witness the wives," Peck intoned under her breath, in the voice of a *National Geographic* commentator. "My friend Lucinda became one of these, a 'wife of.' I watched her transformation."

There were two untouched platters of tea sandwiches on a sideboard, along with bottles of Voss water. But all the focus in the room was on the jewelry displayed on the polished dining table. There was so much of it, and the women approached the task of sorting through it with a frantic seriousness, their necks straining slightly with the effort.

Bethany, a petite blonde with flat hair that hung stiffly to her mid-back, gave us a wave as we came through the door, but she didn't interrupt what she was doing, coercing a bug-eyed customer in a beach cover-up that was too tight across the hips into dropping what sounded like sixteen thousand dollars on a pair of earrings. According to Bethany, the earrings were a "wardrobe must-have" that could be worn "for day or evening."

"You'd think they were giving the stuff away," Peck whispered to me as we stood to one side, watching the women shop. "They won't even call their husbands. They don't make this money themselves. I mean, some of them might. But not the ones I know, the ones Lucinda hangs out with. They'll drop twenty grand on stuff they don't need or even really want."

By the following summer Bethany Samuels's husband would lose his job and they'd have put that house on the market. The women she knew would no longer feel comfortable shopping in such conspicuous fashion even if they were able to. But for now, they were intent on the business at hand.

"What do you think?" the woman in the orange tunic called out to Peck, extending an arm with three bracelets on it. "Which one do you like best? Or should I get all three? They look nice together."

"All of them, definitely," Peck said, reaching into the tray of bracelets and pulling three of them onto her own arm. She held it up, admiring the way they looked on her, like she could, if she wanted, drop a few grand on some bracelets to go with what she called her "patio look," green pedal-pusher pants and a patterned halter top that vaguely resembled a tablecloth. Peck waved the arm with the bracelets on them at me. "You know, this is all discounted. And she said she would even give us a neighborhood price. Another ten percent less."

Hamilton gave her a mock-stern look. "Pecksland Moriarty." And then he leaned over to whisper, "We're not here to shop."

She shrugged and slid the bracelets off her wrist. "I'm insanely jealous right now." Slowly, she placed each one carefully back on the velvet tray as though reluctant to part with them. "Although you couldn't pay me to sleep with one of those fat losers just for the shopping privileges."

I pulled her by the arm to get her out of there before she whipped out the credit card she'd tucked into her bra, just in case, and we made our way over to Bethany. Hamilton introduced himself and explained that he was also a neighbor. "I'm an interior designer. I'd love to see what you've done with the place."

Bethany was more than happy to give him a tour. "Shop, la-dies," she told us, waving in the direction of the jewelry. "I'll be right back."

"Actually," Peck said as we followed them out of the dining room, "we wanted to ask if you noticed anything unusual at our party last night."

Hamilton gazed around in comic distaste as we moved into what was presumably a family room, decorated in primary colors that made the room look like a nursery school classroom.

"Unusual?" Bethany repeated sharply. "What do you mean?"

"Something strange happened in our house," Peck explained, deliberately sounding mysterious. "And we thought you might have seen something that would help us figure it out."

Bethany gave her a look. "Well, *what* was it?"

"Something was *stolen*," Peck intoned, cheerfully playing a role she'd seen on television. Bethany shook her head, the sheaves of hair hardly moving. She seemed unable to decide whether she wanted to be Peck's best friend or run in the other direction. Inse-cure people often had this reaction to my sister. "I went home early, remember?"

Peck, of course, wouldn't have willfully remembered anything about Bethany Samuels, but she nodded as though she had. "Maybe you saw something once you got *home*? Through the window?" Bethany Samuels was hardly the type of woman she would aspire to befriend, and it was becoming clear that Bethany was starting to think the same of her.

"We *don't*. Look. Out. The window." Bethany seemed to resent the implication in Peck's words, but she sounded guilty. Peck was probably right about her spying down on us from the third floor.

We'd moved on to the kitchen, where the walls and backsplash were covered in patterned tile of yellow and blue and green. "Emmet has outdone himself," Hamilton said to Bethany.

"Oh, do you *know* him?" she crowed, happy to ignore Peck, who was sounding more and more like an interrogator. "Isn't he genius?"

Hamilton was nodding, wearing a baffled look. "He's genius, all right."

"What was stolen?" Bethany asked me. She'd clearly decided I was the good cop to Peck's bad.

"A painting," I explained. "About two by three feet, easy enough to slip under an arm."

"It was an abstract," Peck chimed in, as though she were in the habit of talking about art. "Modern."

Bethany Samuels made a face. "I know nothing about modern art," she stated with pride, as though she'd made a decision just then and there about Peck. Peck was what she might call "out there" or "artsy," as in "not the kind of person who could help me get into a country club."

"It was the one that was hanging above the mantel," I said. "In the living room."

"I've never *gone* into the living room," she said, in pointed fashion. "I've never even been inside the house." It was hard to tell if she was offended or hurt not to have received a more intimate invitation from either Lydia or us.

When we finished up the tour Bethany tried to interest us in some "cheap and cheerful" cocktail rings before we said our goodbyes and she moved on to a much more likely customer, a very tall, very pretty woman—"Now that's a trophy wife," Peck whispered to me—in white jeans, gazing adoringly at herself in the mirror as she assessed what looked like chandeliers hanging from her ears. According to Bethany, these too were "must-haves."

"Oh, look, there's Laurie Poplin," Hamilton cried out with enthusiasm as we walked back down the Samuels driveway. He waved his fan at a horse-faced woman in a minuscule tennis skirt that highlighted a God-given gift of impossibly long, shapely legs.

Laurie Poplin was a Rockette. Or had been. She was one of those tall-drink-of-water types who'd made a living off her legs. Now she was divorced and still using the legs, selling real estate, the kind of broker who advertises with photographs of their various listings in local magazines. Her ads included an image of herself, taken a good ten years ago, in a predictably tiny baby-doll dress. The headline on her double-page spread claimed LAURIE POPLIN IS THE HAMPTONS.

"This is the real estate broker," Hamilton said as she drew closer to us.

She looked both Peck and me up and down in a competitive manner and appeared to determine she came out favorably. This decision allowed her to be friendly, and she waved one well-tended hand in our direction. Her hair was dyed an ash-blonde that might have been called "champagne," and the tapered nails were painted solid pink to match her plastic-looking pink shoes.

"Laurie Poplin is here to help," she exclaimed. We were to learn that she would often refer to herself in the third person with her full name. "If anyone can sell your place, Laurie Poplin can."

Hamilton invited Laurie to come back to Fool's House with us and take a look around, and she nodded vigorously. "I was just going to pop in here for a minute. And then I'm meeting Finn Killian. You know Finn, don't you? For tennis and then lunch."

A sudden wave of jealousy washed over me as she kept talking. What was Finn doing playing tennis and having lunch with such a woman, a woman with the plastic pink purse and shoes that matched her nail polish? "I can come back here later," she was saying, as I quickly dismissed any thoughts of Finn. I wasn't at all interested in him, I reminded myself. And even if I was, well, I wasn't. End of story.

Laurie chattered away about all the houses she'd sold recently in our neighborhood, including the one now belonging to the Samuelses, as we walked back to Fool's House, where Biggsy was diligently mopping the porch floor. Laurie extended her hand to him with a huge, ready smile that appeared to have many more large teeth than the average person's.

"Laura," Peck said, because she insisted on doing that, eliminating nicknames in an attempt to be charmingly old-fashioned. "This is Biggs. The current Fool-in-Residence."

The Rockette was grinning at Biggsy, still holding on to his hand. "It's *Laurie*, not *Laura*. And I've met *you* before." She gave him an appraising look, like a cougar eyeing her prey.

"Did we date?" He smiled charmingly back at her. He was kidding, of course, but she appeared to consider the possibility. One got the impression Laurie Poplin had been on a great many unsuccessful dates. There was something poignant about her eagerness and her plastic shoes and the truly spectacular legs, as though she thought that if only circumstances had been *slightly* different, her life might have been a success. But she lived in Southampton because it was cheaper than Manhattan and there was a decent public school for her daughter, and not, as she would go on to claim repeatedly, because she *loved* the beach. And etched on her face was the unfulfilled potential and the many small disappointments that had led her to this place where she was forced by virtue of her own personality to pretend it had all gone exactly according to plan.

"Biggsy is a piece of art," Peck called over her shoulder as she moved toward the front door ahead of the rest of us. "He's *interactive*."

Laurie was looking understandably confused as Biggsy shook his head. "I'm just an artist." He'd told us he became an artist so he wouldn't become a *criminal*. His work was about the search for identity, he said, how we find a sense of self without the benefit of context. He was most well-known in the gallery world as a video artist, he told us, although I suspected he was *well-known* in the same way that the previous inhabitants of the studio, Dick Montpelier and his unread novel and Rusty Cohen and his six nude masterpieces, were *famous*.

Peck led all of us through the house, giving Laurie Poplin the tour, while the real estate broker took notes with a dubious pursing of her pink-glossed lips. Hamilton added in a few comments of his own.

"You can't sell this house to anyone who will tear it down," Biggsy said to her as we traipsed back down to the living room, where the hook above the mantel served as a reminder of the missing painting. "Nobody appreciates architectural integrity any more."

"Lydia wanted the house sold," Hamilton added, repeating what he'd told us earlier. "She'd been wanting to sell it for the past two years."

Biggsy looked horrified. "That can't be true. She never said anything to *me*."

Laurie Poplin gave a nervous giggle and then said she had a couple who were perfect candidates to buy the house. "Old money as opposed to new," she explained, seemingly enjoying her sense of herself as astute master of social nuances. "Old money likes a place with a sense of history. They don't want to spend too much and they can't buy new. It has to have a pedigree."

We started to talk about price, which made Biggsy roll his eyes in disgust and leave the room. "Pricing should be very aggressive," Laurie said. "That's the only option, if you absolutely have to sell."

"We don't absolutely have to sell," Peck said. "Who says we *absolutely* have to sell?"

"Darling," Hamilton intoned. "You do have to sell this house. It's all right."

Laurie Poplin was used to this kind of reaction. "It's going to have to be a rock-bottom, too-good-to-be-true estate-sale price to get any action."

This prompted Peck to cry out, "What am I, an aging hooker, that I need *action?*"

"I was under the impression . . ." Laurie said, drawing on her reserves of patience. This is why estate sales were such a pain in the ass, she seemed to be thinking. "Just to clarify? That we were trying to get this done as quickly as possible. That's usually how it is when it's a question of settling an estate."

"We are," I told her. "Thank you very much."

She turned to me. "Well, this couple I have in mind, they know what they want. They're in a position to move quickly. They love the location already. Location. Location. Loca—"

"Bring them by any time," I said, interrupting her.

"Not *any* time," Peck quickly protested. "What if we're sleeping? What if we're entertaining? What if we have *gentlemen callers?*"

"They'll be out here all week," Laurie exclaimed with the glee normally associated with an Oscar nomination. There were quite a lot of teeth involved. "They're *houseguesting.*"

"Everyone has houseguests," Peck complained to me. "*We* should have houseguests."

When I didn't respond she told me what my problem was. She was fond of telling me what my problem was. "You're a terrible snob," she would say. Inevitably Trimalchio would look up at me, as he did now, as if to say, "Me too, I'm a terrible snob. Although I prefer *discerning.*"

Now, apparently, my problem was that I was immature. "Literally," she cried out. "You're a *fetus.*"

"Oh, just the opposite," Hamilton told her, coming to my defense. "Your sister is old beyond her years."

"I'm not saying it like it's a bad thing. She's charmingly naïve," Peck explained while they all listened. "But she lives in her own la-la land in her head. Look at her, all curled up inside herself like a pill bug."

"I'm right here," I reminded them.

"Well, it's true," Peck said to me. "It's time for you to grow up. You have to shed that protective layer and come out into the world. That's the only way you'll learn how it *really* works."

The Rockette must have decided she'd heard enough, for she headed off, giving us a jaunty wave—"Laurie Poplin will get it done!"—as she let the screen door slam shut behind her. *Thwap.*

5

Two days passed before Finn dropped by to play backgammon, not that I was counting. Not at all. Peck and I were busy. We spent those days arguing about what to do with the things Lydia left behind as we tried to sort through them. And I'd written a long e-mail to my editor outlining in comic detail my first few days in ze Hamptons. "Send more," he'd commanded. "This may be a column. 'My Summer Vacation.'" The locksmith we'd brought in to open the safe didn't seem like he could crack even a barn door, let alone an industrial-strength safe, but he handed us a bill anyway. Miles Noble, according to the assistant who answered his phone when Peck called him, was "unavailable," and would "return" when he was back in the country. And we'd found no clues that might explain why he or anyone else might have walked off with Lydia's brown-and-white painting.

When I came across the backgammon board tucked onto the bookshelf, Peck and I agreed to take a break from our ineffectual organization of Lydia's many belongings and play a few rounds. "I'll bring out the iced tea," she said. "You set up the board."

I'd set up the game on the table on the porch and was waiting for her with Lydia's hardcover *Gatsby* in my lap when the Fool-in-

Residence appeared from across the driveway. He had a piece of paper in his hand.

"What are you reading?" he asked, in a congenial tone. I held up the book so he could see the title.

"*The. Great. Gatsby?*" He read the words as if he'd never heard the title before, as if this were just a book, and not required reading. "Any good?"

I nodded. "Some people say it's the great American novel."

He shrugged his shoulders, indicating that what *some people* say about books didn't interest him one iota. As if books were one of those things, like buggy whips, for example, that are no longer relevant to modern living. "Don't tell me what happens at the end," he said. "I hate when people tell me what happens at the end of a book."

Peck came out to the porch with a pitcher of iced tea. "What's that?" She pointed at the piece of paper in Biggsy's hand.

He held up what looked to be a letter from Lydia, a sheet of her distinctive stationery covered, front and back, in her flowing cursive. "The nuns used to beat it into us," Lydia would tell us. "Penmanship is important."

"I thought you might want to see this," he said, holding it out.

Peck took the letter from him and started to read it aloud. "'Dearest,'" she read. "'I can't tell you how much I've enjoyed our weeks together. You are family to me, only better, for our friendship is unencumbered by the emotional baggage between blood relatives.'"

Here Biggsy interjected. "She kept talking about wanting to introduce me to you two, her nieces."

The language was unmistakably Lydia's. She mentioned a mille-feuille they must have shared somewhere and a debut novel she'd enjoyed while on the train from Hamburg. She was curious, she wrote, to know how the piece he'd shown her was received at the Basel Art Fair.

" 'They say you can't choose your family but I say you can. You find family in the people who fill your world and bring you joy,' " Peck read aloud. " 'We must redefine the word to allow our gay and lesbian friends (I'm thinking of Hamilton as I write this) to marry, and we must allow it to include the close friends who, in the absence of a traditional romantic relationship, or perhaps in addition to it, are our loved ones.' " She turned the page. "She goes on to some details about a party she was giving and she signs it, 'With fondest love, Lydia.' "

It certainly sounded exactly like Lydia. I'd received many such letters from her myself and had saved every one, often rereading them. She'd written in such a vein about Hamilton and about Finn, and also about a few of the women who had been such close friends they'd become family, but I'd never heard her speak that way about anybody by the name of Biggsy. Usually the person occupying the space above the garage only stayed for a summer and, with the exception of Finn, the son of her good friend, they were a transient bunch.

Peck and I had been the only people actually related to Lydia left in the world for the last twenty-five years. Her parents, my grandparents, were both only children. Her mother had died very young, when Lydia was twelve and her much younger brother, my father, was only a baby. Their father had done what he could to raise them, but he succumbed to lung cancer before my dad was out of college. There were no cousins, no elderly aunts or uncles, unless there were some Moriarty relatives still in Ireland.

So it had always made sense when Lydia would speak of family this way. I'd taken her advice, drawing around me a small band of female friends whom I adored at home in Lausanne. There was Kelly, the wittiest one, a half Irish and half Lebanese chef married to an American man who wanted to move back to Philadelphia. And Patrizia, my university roommate, had published several books about her family that became bestsellers in Europe, and had helped get me my job at the magazine. Tessa and Julie were both from New Zealand and had gone to hotel school. These were the women who helped me through my mother's death and my breakup with That-Awful-Jean-Paul. I missed them suddenly, with a pang, especially Kelly. She would have had something funny to say about the absurdly good-looking young artist in our midst.

Biggsy folded the letter carefully and tucked it into the side pocket of the swim trunks he was wearing. He moved deliberately, like an actor trying to get the blocking right, with the grace of someone trained to use his body expressively. "Don't you get it?"

Peck was shaking out one of her American Spirits from the pack and she lit it with a dramatic flick of a lighter shaped like a pig. She squinted at him, inhaling deeply before she asked, through the exhale, "Get *what*?"

Biggsy tilted his head in a cocky manner, holding up both arms to gesture at himself, and grinned at us the way he had after the vomit prank. "I think *I'm* the thing of value."

We must have both worn similar dubious looks because he added, "Think about it," in the huffy manner of a person handing over an untruth. "What did Lydia value more than anything? She was always talking about wanting to introduce us and—"

"She and I were like this." Peck held up two fingers to show how close she was to our aunt. "We spoke on the phone at least twice a week, we wrote letters. She even had a Facebook page. And I didn't even know you were living here. In the past all the fools stayed only in the summer. Lydia wasn't here herself all winter. There's no *heat*."

He shrugged, modest pride on his face. "I made do."

Here I interjected. "Did she even know you stayed here all win-ter? She told me when you moved in. And then she never mentioned you again." I'd been trying to recall my more recent phone conversations with my aunt, replaying her words in my mind. But I was pretty sure I was right when I said she'd never mentioned him after the first time. There'd been other things to talk about, a show at the Pompidou she was excited to see, rereading Edith Wharton, which she'd done all winter, and certain dishes she'd had in her favorite restaurants. She always wanted to know what I was reading, what I was writing, and, in the year after my divorce, naturally, what guy I was dating. On two of the three of these, my answers—nothing, nobody—usually disappointed, which often led her to say something along the lines of "You are the sole author of the story of your life, my dear. Make it a good one."

"I have no family of my own," Biggsy went on to say with a pleading look. "I was an orphan at a young age. Lydia was my family."

At the time, it did seem slightly odd that he brought out that letter when he did. We hadn't asked him to leave. Lydia was gone, and with her went the tradition of the Fool's House summer residency program, but all of it—her death, the inheritance of her house and her things, the talk of value, sharing a roof with a half sister—was new and overwhelming, and he seemed such a permanent part of the landscape, and so helpful and caring, that we didn't think to ask him to go. Free butler service is hard to turn down. And if we didn't exactly *believe* some of what he told us about his past and how he ended up there, we willingly suspended our disbelief. So his sudden presentation of this letter, after we'd been there almost a week, struck me as strange.

He must have been able to read my mind. "I just found it," he said quickly. "I was going through my things and it was at the bottom of a box. She sent it in a Christmas card. I thought you might like to see it."

"You know," I said, as Peck sat down at the other side of the backgammon table, "you're going to have to find another place to live. You might want to start getting prepared."

He nodded. "I know. I will." He looked down at his feet. "But listen, can you spread the word, among your art-collector friends? I do commissions."

"I don't have any art-collector friends," I said.

Peck looked up at him sharply. "You're talking about Miles?"

"Can you introduce me? I have an idea for a piece called *A Fool and His Money*. The fool, that's me. Or is it? That's part of the piece, which one of us is actually the fool. We trade places. The collector, or the person who buys the piece, will switch places with me, for a set amount of time, a night, a week. They go to the studio and make art. And I go live in their house, the way I do here."

"It's brilliant," Peck assessed. "It's *conceptual*."

"I like the idea of trading identity," he said, warming to his subject. "I'm very interested in the idea of appropriation."

"Appropriation?" Peck repeated with a laugh. "Isn't that just an art term for stealing?"

He pointed at her. "Bingo. I would film the whole thing, of course," he explained. "And that video becomes the piece they keep. And also any work they create on their own."

"Conceptual art is very popular these days," Peck proclaimed in that way she had of declaring things generally held to be common knowledge as though she had come up with a brilliant new idea. "And of course, Miles has very good taste. I'll see what I can do."

One of Pecksland Moriarty's great qualities was her enthusiasm. And when she fell in love—with anything, the onion rings at the Sip 'n Soda, the stray dog who became Trimalchio, the orange platform sandals in a store window—she fell instantly, and she fell hard, judgment and rational thought be damned. It was an aspect of her personality I admired, and often wished I could emulate, but one which was also cause for concern.

"Now go away and let me beat the pants off this sister of mine," she said, waving him off. Peck prided herself on her backgammon ability. My half sister was quite proud of many skills she did not actually possess. But either because of or in spite of Lydia, who was born with a talent for games such as bridge and backgammon and gin rummy, a talent she swore was hereditary and even more pronounced in our father, Peck imagined she was so good at the game she could take her backgammon prowess to Monte Carlo, where the real money was.

"You can make a cool fifty grand in a few nights in that place," she was telling me as I beat her soundly in the first game and we repositioned the pieces for another round. I wondered if Finn would show up.

We played another game and then another as Peck kept screaming and cursing and standing up dramatically as though she was just going to walk away from the table in disgust. Evidently her losses gave her pause, because she reconsidered her desire to travel to Monte Carlo to make the money to keep Fool's House and devised another plan. "Am I too old to become a hooker?"

"Now there's an idea we can use," I said, stacking up my men. "We turn Fool's House into a high-end brothel."

She pondered the idea further. "With the money we make we can renovate the house. Make it super high-end. Hamptons Hookers, what a concept. I can't believe nobody's done it yet."

"Okay, stop," I said, somewhat afraid she was considering this an actual plan. "I don't want to wake up in the middle of the night to find I'm being shopped to one of your male friends."

Peck paused, and then burst out into an exaggerated fit of laughter. "You know, you can be funny sometimes." She implied that this was a rare and unusual occurrence, preferring to think of herself as the comic one.

"Momma needs a new pair of shoes," she whispered into the

leather cup, blowing on the dice. "Momma likes Manolo, so make it a good one." She kept blowing on the dice, taking her time. "Momma needs a pair of those feathered ones with the jewels on them for evening. The flat sandals are fine for day. Or maybe the crocodile pumps."

"Just roll already," I finally had to say.

"Fuck," she screamed when it was my turn again and I rolled a neat little pair of twos to take it home.

"What's going on up there?" a raspy voice called from the driveway.

Neither of us had noticed Finn Killian pull up in his jeep with the cloth top rolled down and a surfboard hanging out the back. There was a Grateful Dead *Steal Your Face* sticker on the back of the car.

"My so-called *sister*," Peck called out with genuine resentment seeping into her words, "just beat me most ungraciously. The worst part is," she continued as he hopped up the steps to the porch, "she doesn't even care. She's *European*."

As Finn strolled over to the table, there seemed to be a bounce in his step. He appeared so affable as he glanced down at our game with curiosity, without any of the arrogance I thought I'd seen in him. How had I remembered him so differently from that first summer? Was it because I'd actually had feelings for him I didn't want to acknowledge and rejected him before he could reject me? Or was it just that I'd been in such a fog of grief over my mother's death that I hadn't been thinking straight?

He stooped over us, checking out the board. He was so tall, his legs endless in his jeans, and he wore his height with a kind of casual elegance.

"What's with the *Steal Your Face*?" I asked him, more sharply than I intended. I really wasn't good at this male-female interaction, sounding brusque when I was trying for flirtatious and charming. "Aren't you a little *old* for that sort of thing?"

Trimalchio jumped up at Finn's side and he picked the dog up, scratching his neck as Trimalchio eyed him adoringly. His hair was wet and hung over his forehead. "My godson put that on there," he said. "It's supposed to be ironic."

"So you're ironically *not* a Deadhead anymore?" I pulled the last of my men off the board, beating Peck again.

"I'll take winner," he said. "And it is he, young Connor, who is ironically *not* the Deadhead. Calls it old people's music. For aging losers like me who don't know anything about cool rock 'n' roll. Hence the sticker."

Peck relinquished her spot at the table, saying, "It's cocktail hour somewhere, isn't it?"

"I should warn you, kid." Finn took her place, sliding in across from me with Trimalchio on his lap. "I play for money."

I was putting the board back together and I didn't look up. "That's the only way."

"This was on Lydia's list," Peck called out as she headed into the house to mix up a batch of Southsides with the fresh mint Lydia had always grown off the kitchen side of the porch. "Play backgammon for money. And skinny-dip in the ocean, don't forget that one."

He rolled a one and I threw out a six, so I went first. A lucky first move for me. I quickly placed my men and it was his turn. As we talked, Finn was shocked to learn that not only had I never been to a baseball game—"Understandable," he said, "under the circumstances. Living abroad and all that"—but I'd never even watched one on TV.

"It's sacrilege," he announced. "The New York Yankees are a religion."

"So I hear." I knew Peck was a big Yankees fan because she'd had been threatening to drag me to a game while I was in the States. But she was a fan of *everything*.

"Oh God," he cried out a few seconds later, after another lucky roll of the dice for me and a terrible roll for him. He smacked himself on the forehead. I thought he was reacting to the dice, but he'd just realized that my lack of education about sports meant I also wouldn't know anything about American football. "Now *that's* a crime," he said. "You didn't watch the Giants win the Super Bowl?"

"What's the Super Bowl?" I asked, enjoying the look of mock horror that swept over his face. "I'm kidding. Of course I know what the Super Bowl is."

He mimicked me in a comic voice that was actually spot on. "*I know what the Super Bowl is.* What is it then, smarty pants?"

"It's a big football match," I said, teasing, as he groaned.

He shook his head back and forth. "Match? It's not a match. No match."

"I know," I said, neatly stacking my board. "I just said that to annoy you."

"You like that, do you? To annoy?" I'd flipped the cube, upping the financial stakes of the game, and Finn made a face as he realized I knew what I was doing. "How about some mercy? Didn't I teach you how to play this game?"

"Now who's not remembering?" I said, recalling now a few lively games on the porch, with Lydia loudly cheering for me all those years ago. "I beat the pants off you."

It was a beautiful clear afternoon that grew slightly crisp as the sun moved across the sky, and we fell into an easy sort of teasing banter.

Peck came back through the screen door with mint cocktails and fresh potato chips she'd made herself earlier in the day. "I'm famous for my Southsides. Try them, *try* them," she insisted. We paused the game to sip the drinks.

"Well?" she asked, demanding the compliment before we'd

even gotten the stuff down our throats. We both pronounced them delicious and she pulled one of the rocking chairs over to the side of the table to watch. The conversation turned, naturally, to the missing painting.

"It's the one that was in the picture of your mom and Lydia," I pointed out to him. "It was hanging there forever."

"Who do you think might have taken it?" he asked.

"We know who took it," Peck said, rocking back and forth. "It was Miles Noble, the first love, she says in a voice laden with irony." She paused to ensure that we appreciated her witty words. "All we have to do is go over there and find it. Or get him to give it back."

"Are you sure about that?" Finn asked her. "Why would this ironic first love, a guy who's apparently made a bucketload of money, come over here and steal a painting from you? It makes no sense. There were a hundred people here that night, all of whom could have taken it. How do you know *I* didn't do it, just as an example?"

She looked at him with comic suspicion. "Did you?"

"I did not." He pointed up at the garage. "But have you looked up there?"

"Biggs didn't take it," she scoffed. "He's an artist—why would he take another painter's work? Besides, if he were going to steal anything from us, he could have taken it before we arrived."

Finn shrugged. "Why don't you just take a look? Maybe there's a clue?"

"We're not going to go snooping around in his room," Peck said. She then attempted to claim Finn was being racially biased.

"Racially biased? Biggsy couldn't be more Caucasian," I pointed out.

"He's got some *Japanese*." She set her lips in a thin line, as though there were no arguing with the facts. But I was pretty certain there were no Japanese ancestors lurking in his past. Besides, there was nothing even vaguely Japanese about his blond, corn-fed looks. But this was the kind of contrarian conversation—the sky is blue, no, it's red—my sister thrived on. Eventually it was always best just to move on. "But I guess it couldn't hurt to look up there. I'm insanely curious about him."

She gestured for us to follow her. "Come on," she said. "He's not there. He took his motorcycle and said he'd be back tomorrow. I didn't ask where he was going."

I glanced at Finn and then we both stood and followed Peck.

The space above the garage had been carved into two rooms, connected by an arched opening. One side was monastic, with a neatly made up twin bed, a simple wood bedside table, and a tiny re-frigerator with one red apple sitting on top. The other side was utter chaos, a riot of colors, scraps of papers, camera equipment, and props. In the middle of the mess sat a small metal stool and a rickety worktable, nicked and covered in paint, piled high with books and pens and scanned images. Pinned to the wall above the table was a piece of handmade paper on which was written in gothic script: RUMORS OF MY DEATH HAVE BEEN GREATLY EXAGGERATED.

Finn pointed to it. "Lydia told me he started those rumors himself."

"Maybe he wanted us to think *he* was the ghost," Peck added, nodding her approval. "I really was starting to believe it. He's so pale, you know."

We looked around, searching for a potential hiding place for a framed canvas, or a clue that Biggsy might have had something to do with the missing painting, but there was nothing at all like that in either of the two rooms.

I felt slightly uneasy looking around Biggsy's private space, and there was a part of me that expected to find something. But what?

And then Peck made a discovery. From the photographs spilled on the table, she pulled out several of herself. The one she held up was slightly blurred, a still taken from video, and in it she was smiling at someone in the distance. "Do I have a stalker?" she asked, almost proudly. "I told you, it wasn't him. And I was right, see? There's nothing here. Biggs has a very pure relationship with art. He's always saying we must revere the artists who came before us."

Finn looked around and made a face. "This seems like the kind of thing I could see him having a hand in."

"You're just jealous," Peck teased as we filed back down the stairs. "He's too good-looking for his own good, that's what his problem is. Nobody trusts a guy who is that pretty."

When we got back to the porch the backgammon game we'd left there had been finished, all the red pieces stacked neatly in the slot along the side of the board. Most of the black ones on Finn's side were still out, as if he'd lost the game.

"This has to be Biggsy," I said, looking around. "He must have known we were up in his room. But where is he?"

"I told you he was a stalker," Peck said, clapping her hands. "Come out, come out, wherever you are," she called in delight. "We're not afraid of you, little ghostie boy!"

But he didn't appear. "Lydia would have enjoyed this," Peck said, pouring herself another drink. "Now, if you'll excuse me. I'm going upstairs with my dressing drink."

Finn's eyes, lit up with amusement, met mine. "Dressing drink?"

"I coined that term, you know," Peck called over her shoulder as she headed for the screen door.

"No, you didn't," Finn teased. He leaned back in his chair and I couldn't help but notice as his T-shirt rode up slightly, revealing the flat muscles of his stomach. "There were dressing drinks long before you were born."

Finn and I exchanged another glance as she left us alone on the porch, and then we focused our attentions on setting up the board for a new game. We played a few more games, but with Peck gone it seemed the spell was broken. The magic between us had gone. Or we were tired. After the easy flirting banter of earlier, we grew polite with one another.

"When do you go back?" Finn asked me, in the stiff manner of someone making small talk. He was unfailingly polite, one of those well-brought-up men who'd been trained to stand when a woman entered the room and help with coats and allow ladies to go through doors first. Usually he'd try to be funny, but he would, of course, be nice to anyone who was related to his friend Lydia. I suspected now that what I'd perceived as a spark of something chemical between us was simply good manners. He was probably charming that way with everyone he met, even men.

"Not until the end of the month," I told him, trying not to sound disappointed at the shift. I was, after all, just saying I would be leaving soon. And then I'd probably never see him again. And clearly my overactive imagination had played tricks on me, assuming he'd come over here for a reason other than simply a passion for the game of backgammon or a sense of tradition.

Did I imagine a look of disappointment on his face? Or was he just bored, ready to move on to the rest of his evening like Peck had? "You think the house will be sold by then?"

I shook my head. "I doubt it."

Peck came down in a long pink chiffon gown that dragged on the floor as she swung open the screen door and posed for us. "*Vanity Fair*, get a load of this one."

"Great dress," Finn said to her.

"Isn't it?" She looked down at herself with pride. "But I don't think it's right for one of Hamilton's Tuesday night suppers. I'm going back to try again."

Finn looked questioningly at me as she headed off. "*Vanity Fair*?"

"She seems to think she should be on their Best-Dressed List," I explained as I stood and stacked the chip bowl on the drinks tray.

"Can I help you bring this stuff in?" he asked, picking up our glasses. This aspect of him seemed uniquely American, a healthy ego and brash confidence lurking under the manners. I'd had a few boyfriends (an Italian, two Australians, a Swede who lied about everything) before Jean-Paul, none of them American. Finn Killian was so different from all of them. He insisted on paying me the five dollars he owed me for the game and then he held the door for me. "Sorry," he said as his elbow grazed my arm slightly. "Let me get that."

We brought the dishes into the kitchen. I ran the water in the sink to rinse the glasses. He was behind me and I felt his presence like an electric jolt, as though there were a force field between us. For a fleeting few seconds I thought—okay, I hoped—he might spin me around and kiss me.

I waited for it. I tensed as I heard him move behind me. But then he sounded farther away and I turned to see he was at the door.

"See you around, kid."

6

It was all gay, all British on Hamilton's festively lit patio when we arrived next door that evening. (Note that I said British, not English,
so as not to offend Scotty, the proud Scotsman.) The men were tan
and close-shaven, and all looked like they'd just been styled for a magazine spread in white pants and perfectly draped blazers. Their shirts
were pink, pale blue, and bright orange. Some wore fitted T-shirts.
They all looked fantastic, every one of them groomed and impossibly
elegant, even the ones who weren't as thin. I was totally underdressed
in my jeans and top. My wedge sandals now felt clunky and unstylish.
I should have listened to Peck, who'd shuddered dramatically at the
sight of my shoes when I came into her room earlier in the evening.

"When you socialize with gay men, Stella, you have to make
an effort," she'd said, gesturing with her lipstick. She herself had
settled on a set of pink-and-green hostess pajamas a stylish housewife in the seventies might have worn to a key party. She'd teased
half her hair and pinned it up in the front and applied false eyelashes and glittery green eye shadow. Very Fashionina. "They de-
spise wedges, by the way," she'd added with grandiose authority.

"Finally," Hamilton exclaimed. "Some female company. Look
at you." He nodded approvingly as Peck spun around so he could
get the full effect.

"I'm sorry about my sister," Peck said, handing him a bottle of the scotch he liked tied with a ribbon. "She thought you really meant *casual* casual. Not Southampton casual."

He ushered us into the center of the patio, where we were swept up in a sea of hugs and cologne. They were so American, all those pink-cheeked men, welcoming and open and sophisticated, but not like any I'd either imagined or known. They weren't like the tourists I occasionally ran across in Lausanne, coming out of the McDonald's across the street from the train station, or waiting for the bus at the Place Saint-Sulpice, loudly and heavily exclaiming about the famous Swiss punctuality. And they weren't like the expats either, the ones who'd made their permanent home overseas for so long they were only half American, the other half nothing, a shifting desert of acquired characteristics.

"These boys were all friends of Lydia's," Hamilton explained to me. "She was quite the fag hag, you know. Oh, don't look so shocked. She loved when we called her that. She was a crusader for gay rights. Wanted all of us to be able to marry. I said, 'Darling, what do I want to get married for? If I wanted a sexless relationship, I'd be better off marrying *you*.'"

I laughed while Peck wandered off and found a shy young man in a flowered shirt who, she was thrilled to learn, was interviewing for an internship at *Vanity Fair* magazine.

Hamilton steered me toward the bar, where a man who looked like an aging soap opera actor was fixing cocktails. "Are you having fun in Southampton?" he asked, handing me a glass of wine. "Lydia would have wanted you to enjoy this while you're here. You should go to the beach. There aren't any beaches more beautiful in all the world."

"That's what Lydia always said. She would tell me to take my notebook and try to capture the way it felt to breathe the ocean air. And then she would add, 'But description can only get you so far.

Plot is a verb. Don't you forget it.' I've been trying to write about my time here. There seems to be so much to figure out."

"You're a clever girl. Don't worry," Hamilton said as the party grew louder around us. "Just relax and let the circus unfold around you."

"Is that what you do?" I asked.

"Darling," he said. "I *am* the circus."

I asked him what he thought of Peck's theory that Miles Noble had taken the painting from above the mantel.

"I suppose *anything's* possible," he said, indicating with his eyebrows that he didn't really buy it. "I've heard the fellow's house is absolutely dreadful. And he went through four or five architects and designers. He has awful taste. Perhaps he's also a thief."

"Peck thinks it could be some sort of courtship dance," I added. "But she hasn't heard from him."

"Good heavens," he said. "That's complicated. I wish I had more to tell you about that painting. Lydia didn't go on about her things the way people do now. We weren't all giving each other *tours* of the house and explaining every piece of art and furniture. We just *lived*, you know. Lived in the spaces of our homes and enjoyed each other's company. The only one she really talked about was her dead brother, the brilliant artist."

Someone dimmed the lights on the patio and the crowd seemed to grow more jovial. A platter of brownies was passed around. I was about to take one when Hamilton put a hand on my arm. "Maybe you'd better not."

"I'm addicted to sweets," I said, helping myself to a small one. "It's one of my many vices." I popped the brownie into my mouth.

He smiled. "These are special. If you know what I mean."

The chocolate, rich and gooey, was already dissolving in my mouth when I realized what he meant. They were pot brownies. "Oh well," I said. "When in Rome."

"Lydia was a bit of a pothead," he explained with a grin. "She liked it for its *medicinal* qualities."

"There were a lot of things I didn't know about my aunt," I said. "Or about any of my family." They were all gone now. Every one of them. Only Peck and I were left.

Hamilton was chewing thoughtfully on a brownie of his own. "She was extraordinarily generous, not just with money, but with her time and her energy. I always told her to be more careful about allowing these ghastly people to live with her. I gave her a gun, you know."

"We didn't know," I said. "Until Peck found it."

"I want you to be careful of that gorgeous young thing living above the garage," he said. "Lydia knew I wasn't keen on any of them. Except our man Finn, of course. But he was different. A family friend. The rest of them . . . not much talent there . . ." His voice trailed off.

"I wish she were here to explain it all," I said. I missed my aunt terribly. "Some good characters here," she would have whispered in my ear. "Listen to them talk. Write them into a novel." Missing her—that physical ache in the heart that made it feel as if it could sometimes break in two—dredged up the feelings of loss over my mother from which I'd thought I'd recovered. And layered into the emotional cocktail that had me feeling like one big nerve ending were, I was starting to suspect, some deeply suppressed sentiments relating to the early loss of my father. All this, I told myself, explained why I felt like I was going mad that first week at Fool's House, alternately too quick to laugh or cry.

"Lydia cultivated a daffy persona," he said with a smile. "But she was a very intelligent woman. I suspect she's enjoying all this attention from the grave."

The night had grown cool, but it was warm under the canopy hung with sparkling lights that covered the patio, where quick-witted men made saucy remarks and we ate perfectly tiny bite-size morsels of delicious food, lamb lollipops and miniature bacon-lettuce-and-tomato tarts. A few other women joined the colorful swirl. I noticed Laurie Poplin towering over the rest of them. She was coming directly toward me, elbowing poor little Scotty out of the way in her eagerness to get to me, grinning like she was bursting with something to tell. She was wearing a pink-and-white dress that barely covered her ass. Okay, I thought grumpily, we get it: you've got legs. No need to shop in the children's department to make sure we all see them.

"Hey," she called as she got closer, awkwardly throwing one arm around my shoulder in a half hug. I got the impression she didn't want to say my name, either because she couldn't remember it or because she didn't know whether to call me Cassie, or Stella, as Peck did. Hamilton left us to check on the music.

"I remembered where I met that boy at your house before." She was a bit of a sprayer, one of those unfortunate people who gather saliva in the corners of their mouths when they get excited.

I took a step back to avoid being showered. I was starting to feel stoned and the too-tall Rockette loomed over me, making me dizzy. "Biggsy?"

She nodded with great enthusiasm, the cords in her neck even more pronounced by such vigorous extension. "He wasn't Biggsy then. He was Jonathan something or other. He lived in the pool house."

I was trying to follow what she was saying while also backing away from her, but she kept getting closer. "Whose pool house?"

"I'm about to tell you," she said. She could afford to be coy, now that she had my attention. "It was an estate sale. An old woman, real Waspy and elegant. The house had been in the family forever. You know the type?" She paused, as though she wasn't sure, since I was so *foreign,* that I would understand.

I assured her I was able to extrapolate, given our location.

"She lived there totally alone all summer, except for this guy in the pool house," she continued. "Not even the staff lived in; they all just came during the day. She was isolated. The family was gone, all except this grandson in Los Angeles, a hipster filmmaker." She paused again, to be sure I was following her.

I nodded. Hipster. Filmmaker. Got it.

"One morning the housekeeper arrived to find the newspapers still in the driveway. And she knew something was up. The old lady always read the papers first thing in the morning." Another nod kept her going. "She died under mysterious circumstances. An overdose of her regular medication, they thought. The police investigated. But nobody pressed charges and nothing conclusive was found. The thing is, this guy, Jonathan, the one who's living at your place now? He wouldn't leave. He moved into the main house—this was a major property, and I'd arrive for a showing and find him swanning about in a silk bathrobe, like the lord of the manor. It was creepy." She stopped. "Sorry. He's not related to you or anything, is he?"

I assured her he was not, as far as we knew.

"So, the kid who inherited the place, the grandson, he never came to see it. Just wanted it sold. The housekeepers moved on to other jobs. But nobody made the guy leave. He stayed there all summer. It was so weird. Finally the house got sold."

"And then he left?"

She nodded impatiently, as though frustrated with my lack of attention. "We heard he'd *died*. I never saw him again. Until he re-surfaced at your aunt's place, having been there with another older woman who lived alone. Who is now . . . *dead*."

"Aunt Lydia died in Paris," I said. "It was a heart attack."

"All I'm saying . . ." Her voice trailed off. "Well, you have to admit, it's strange, that's all. Especially when he was rumored to be dead himself. I heard he was hit by a car."

"Where did you hear that?" I asked. "Why did everyone think he was dead?"

She shrugged. "I don't know. But you can imagine my surprise when there he was. Just like a ghost." She looked around, her neck craning as she sized up the crowd. "So," she continued. "I heard you saw Finn today."

I nodded, picking up the proprietary tone in her voice.

"Played a little 'gammon, huh?" She waved her glass at me. "Did he win? He always beats me when we play, he's just *too* good. You know he has a regular game with Jack Louis? The big IPO guy? That one never wants to pay his debts, either. Finn and I are having dinner tomorrow night. Maybe we'll shake the dice a bit first. Or after—"

I interrupted her. "Excuse me," I said, holding up my empty water glass. In my pot-addled state I didn't feel the need to hear any more about Finn from her. I got it: they were together. She seemed intent on making that clear. And that was totally fine with me. Why wouldn't it be? I wasn't interested in him. I couldn't be. I had too much to do and only three more weeks to do it in. "I'm going to get some water," I said, moving away from her. "But you're going to show the house, right?"

"Well, yes—" she was saying as I headed on toward the bar, where Peck was still entertaining three of the original admiring group of men that had surrounded her at the beginning of the evening, still audibly declaring her "fabulous" and "a piece of work."

"Stella!" she cried out. "I'm sharing my tale of irony." She pulled me close and continued speaking to the group with me at her side. "So here I'm thinking he's throwing this Gatsby theme party for me. It seemed pretty specific, right? The book had become this symbol, I thought, of our love. We were *madly* in love, you know. For almost five years of my life."

Every time I heard Peck tell the story of her love affair with Miles, the length of time they'd been together expanded. She was almost twenty-one when she met him. He was twenty-six or so, she'd told me. Within months they'd talked about getting married. But she had to finish school, she still thought. Later, after she'd dropped out and kept busy with acting class and auditions, he moved in with her for a while. They broke up after he went to Hong Kong and told her he'd met someone else. She lied and told him she'd met someone else too. She was twenty-five. So it was three years, to my calculations. But somehow in the telling it had become three and a half and then four and now five years of her life.

"This wasn't some drunken one-night stand or anything," she explained. I'd heard her use these exact words so many times. "For all these years I've told myself the same story. I once knew this great love. We can only go through that one time in our lives. Believe me, I would never do it again."

She was in full performance mode, pausing to assess her audience's attention to her tale before she continued. "I was, of course, curious. He *gave* me *The Great Gatsby*, you see. Everyone's favorite book. Right, Stella? Ask my sister." She gestured toward me like Vanna White on *Wheel of Fortune*. "I gave *her* the book and she spent the whole summer copying it down." Her eyes glittered, as though she too had partaken of the brownies. "Anyway," she continued breathlessly, "you can see why I might have made certain assumptions."

"A Gatsby white party to woo you back after seven years. That's *so* romantic," one of them said, sighing. He wore orange corduroy pants that he kept pulling at, as though they were too tight.

"That's the thing," she cried out, in preparation for delivering her punch line with a leading lady's flair and comic timing. I could learn a thing or two about telling a story from my sister. "It wasn't at all romantic. Because he didn't even *remember* giving it to me."

Scotty was on her other side and patted her shoulder. "Maybe he was just saying that. Maybe he got flustered when he saw you again. And he lied."

I thought there might be some truth to Scotty's version. It did seem too big a coincidence that Miles Noble's first contact with Peck after seven years should be a Gatsby theme party invitation. But my sister shook her head. "He hadn't even *read* it."

There were big reactions all around. "That's terrible," said the one in the corduroy. He had perfectly feathered hair, like Jon Bon Jovi, one of Peck's favorite singers.

"How rude," exclaimed the third man. He wore stylish tortoise-shell glasses he kept putting on and taking off.

The sensitive Scotty made a compassionate face. "Unrequited love," he said sympathetically. All night, I'd noticed, he'd been gazing adoringly in Hamilton's direction while the older man ignored him. "The cruelest of life's ironies."

"It *was* rude," Peck was saying, talking over him in response to the man with the glasses. "He has terrible manners. And now I find myself questioning what I always thought to be the defining story of my life. If I could believe myself in love with someone who could lie like that, to the point where he didn't even read the book that became such a symbol of our relationship, then what else could I believe?"

She looked genuinely distraught, near tears. We were all riveted. But then a rueful smile indicated the shift to come. "Then he shows up at the Fool's Welcome. And steals one of the paintings right off the wall!" She paused and looked around at each of us in turn, sharing her incredulity. "Was he sending a signal? I'm obviously no good at interpreting, since I thought the invitation to the party was a message, and that turned out to be dead wrong."

They murmured their assent. "He's definitely sending a message," said the one in the corduroy. "He wants you to come after him."

"Or is he just a thief?" she asked rhetorically. "Did he think it was worth something? What do I do?"

"Show up at his house," the one in the glasses suggested. "Wearing nothing but a trench coat. And stilettos. Seduce him and make him tell you everything."

"Invite him to lunch," said the one in corduroy. "With some fabulous people. And then *ignore* him. You'll drive him mad. He'll be forced to confess."

The glasses-wearer shook his head. He was heavyset, with a shock of gray hair. "Did you know?" he asked. "There's an F. Scott Fitzgerald suite at the Ritz in Paris. Suggest that he take you there, to make up for it. And then ask for the painting back."

Scotty rubbed his chin. "I don't think he took your painting. If he came to your house, what he wants is *you*."

Peck caught my eye. "He's our suspect, I'm telling you. I know it. I'm starting to find it a little bit sexy. Very Jennifer Lopez and George Clooney, you know? In that movie where she's locked in the trunk with him?"

Scotty put an arm around her waist. "Just let him see you in this outfit with those false eyelashes, working those shoes, and he'll fall even more head over heels. You're *fantastic*."

Peck wore a look of total glee as she basked in their attention. "Literally?" she cried out. "I've already forgotten about him. Miles who? I'm in love with all of you."

She glanced around at them. "But isn't it a funny coincidence? That he would hire an event planner who would suggest a Gatsby theme party? How could I ever have been in love with someone with such a lack of taste. I mean, aren't theme parties totally gauche?"

This was greeted with a chorus of noes. A theme party was fine, as long as it was sophisticated. "Fitzgerald will always be immensely stylish," Corduroy added with a benevolent nod.

All of a sudden, it hit me, in a pot-induced flash of clarity, the kind of thing that often is later revealed to be ridiculous: I knew the combination to Lydia's safe.

7

To spend one's childhood abroad as an American is to grow up with a permanent sense of yearning. There's a place far away that is ours but it only seems knowable through movies, books, and the occasional television program dubbed in German or French or Italian.

I fetishized certain aspects of what I perceived as typical American life. I read obsessively, studying American novels as if they were textbooks, the keys to understanding a country I could know only through words. I specialized in stories about suburban teenage angst. And although I've since somewhat lost my taste for it, I adored root beer. As it was not a beverage option at the local café, it became an exotic treat that I was first introduced to at the home of an American friend, the daughter of a businessman who was transferred every two years. Her mother made us root beer floats, with big globs of vanilla ice cream in the glasses of root beer she poured from cans brought over after one of the visits back to the States they called "home leaves." I had a thing for Kraft macaroni and cheese too, which horrified my mother, a whole grain and fresh vegetable lover. She couldn't understand why the fake orange and chemical taste made me feel American. I didn't understand it either.

But my mother had rejected her country without regret, turning her back, she always implied, on the pain she'd known there—like mine, her father had died young, and her mother never recovered, fading away in a haze of alcohol and grief—and the inescapable sadness of the loss of her husband, my father. It made sense to me, her wanting to stay in Europe and not go back. But I wanted to go, and so, every third summer or so, while Eleanor would go on a mission to Nepal or Thailand or Namibia, I went to stay with Lydia at Fool's House, where I would drink soda by the six-pack, a habit my aunt willingly indulged. I stopped drinking root beer the summer Peck made me try a real beer—I was fifteen and of legal age to drink beer in Europe, as she pointed out, appalled that I'd never tasted the stuff.

I still had a thing for Tootsie Rolls, and when I got back to Fool's House that night, with a case of pot-induced munchies, I ate through the fresh stash I'd picked up at the supermarket that afternoon before sitting down at my computer to test my instinct about the combination to Lydia's safe. I was pretty sure I'd guessed correctly, recalling the long, languid conversations about Fitzgerald and Edith Wharton with Lydia on the porch. This would be after what Lydia would call "reading hour," a spell of time, usually more like two or three hours at a stretch, after lunch, when we would take seats in the rocking chairs on the porch with our books and read happily. After reading hour, there'd often be writing hour, when Lydia would suggest a quick exercise, "just for fun, for the pleasure of the creative endeavor."

Peck usually skipped reading hour, and always passed on the writing exercises, scheduling a tennis game or heading back to the beach to work on her tan. But I enjoyed sitting there with a good book and only the chirping of birds to break the quiet. Lydia felt strongly about the writer she called Scott, as though she'd known him, and she would often read me a line or two that she found particularly evocative.

I Googled F. Scott Fitzgerald. He was born on September 24, 1896. Finn had been right, I suspected, in his hunch that Lydia would choose such a number, a date relating to one of her favorite artists, as the combination for a safe, and we'd tried the dates that Jasper Johns painted *Fool's House* (1962) and *Flag* (1954) and even his birth date (May 15, 1930) to no avail. But we hadn't tried the birth date of one of her favorite writers. And this suddenly seemed very Lydia.

I kneeled before the safe on the floor of her closet, the overpowering scent of mothballs tickling my nose. I turned the dial, first one direction to 9, then counterclockwise to 24, and back around to 96. Nothing happened. I sat back on my heels, wondering if I'd been mistaken. I tried again, this time turning the dial several times before stopping at the 9. I tried 9, 24, 18, 96. But that didn't work. I started to think I'd been wrong, that only someone who'd eaten a pot brownie would come up with such an idea. And with such conviction. But then I gave it another try, leaving off the 18, but spinning the dial twice past 0 first, and the safe door clicked open.

I pulled it toward me. I was about to look inside when it hit me: I should wait and do this with my sister. Even though I was almost certain she wouldn't have waited for me—Peck has the patience of a sugar-addled toddler—if she'd been the one to figure out the combination, I knew I had to wait for her. It took all the willpower I had to close the safe back up again without looking inside it. Peck deserved to be part of the discovery process. Plus, she would throw a major hissy fit if she was left out of anything.

I let my imagination run wild, conceiving all sorts of scenarios: in the safe was a huge diamond, or a million dollars, or how about a signed first-edition *Great Gatsby*—wasn't such a thing the most rare of collectible books? Or would it be a certificate of authenticity, or some other official piece of paper that might indicate that the painting now missing from our wall was actually some rare and valuable thing, desired by museums and art collectors who would pay up for such a piece? Or it could be nothing. I had to keep my expectations in check.

I shut the door. I left the safe locked and wandered through the house, gazing in fascination at the paintings on the walls, most of which didn't look nearly as bad now. I was stoned. In fact, some of them looked pretty good. Even the two painted by my father no longer seemed so amateurish. I decided I would ask Peck if I could keep the one that had more pinks and purple, if she would agree to take the orange one.

I flipped through some of the books on the shelves, and stared at the photographs in silver frames that populated every free surface. There were images of Peck as a child in her school uniform and a few of me and my mother, her long hair always blowing, in India and South Africa, and, later, with Lydia on top of a mountain in Switzerland on one of her visits. I particularly loved the ones of Lydia and my father when they were younger, wearing bell-bottomed pants and shirts with big flowers on them in sixties fashion. I stared at my father's face, the dark eyes, short, straight nose, and full mouth that I'd inherited.

Peck didn't come home while I was still awake and eventually I dozed off with the light on in the bedroom. I don't know what time Peck came in, but I woke in the morning to the loud rumble of thunder and rain pouring off the porch eaves. Fool's House felt like flimsy protection against such a force of nature, the sky a mood-altering gray that wrapped the tiny house in a thick blanket of fog. The moisture seeped in everywhere and while Peck slept in, I strategically placed buckets under the places where the roof leaked.

It was hardly cold but the dark morning called for a fire and I piled up the wood in the fireplace to build a big blaze that radiated heat and filled the room with the smell of wood smoke and the glow of dancing flames. Even the cheap-looking art, not quite as fascinating as the night before, looked charming in the mellow lamplight. I waited for Peck in the living room with a pot of coffee and cupcakes for breakfast.

My curiosity about the contents of the safe was an itch I was dying to scratch. I suppose I could have woken my sister; she would be annoyed that I hadn't. But there was something about the calm of the dark morning I wasn't in a hurry to disrupt.

The quiet disappeared soon enough, though, when Pecksland Moriarty came down the stairs in a gold lamé dressing gown. This was the sort of attire she assumed most of the world would find to-tally normal but also unique and cool. She expected to be lauded for such style and when she came down the stairs with enormous dark glasses covering her eyes, moaning dramatically, she posed with an unlit cigarette held elegantly in a tilted wrist, waiting for me to remark on her "look." I was reading *The New York Times* and did not offer a comment. This made her sigh and exclaim, "Good God, those boys can party."

"I thought you didn't get hangovers," I said, pouring her a cup of coffee from the pot at my side.

She lifted her sunglasses to squint in irritated fashion at me. "Isn't that exactly the point I'm making? I don't. *Normally.*"

She made her way gingerly to the sofa, easing herself down onto the cushions. "Literally? Half the time you don't listen to a word I say. You have ADD, Stella. And when you were hungover, I gave you a Bloody Mary, not some mangy little cup of coffee that's going to do nothing for me."

"Would you like a Bloody Mary?" I handed her the box of cupcakes.

She sighed. "No." She took the box and helped herself to one of the cupcakes. "The clean living starts today."

I waited until the sugar kicked in before telling her. As I suspected, she was annoyed I hadn't woken her sooner. And annoyed too that she hadn't been the one to figure it out. "I'm the one with the Fitzgerald thing," she complained. "You've totally copied me. As usual." She made a face indicating her impatience with me, looking me over as if seeking something else she could claim I'd copied from her. Finding nothing, she continued. "I suppose you think a literary obsession is extremely chic? Even, as in my case, when it's predicated on falsehood?"

She paused, frowning at me, then stood. "Well, what are we waiting for?" She headed for the stairs, lamé rustling, holding the unlit cigarette in the air in one hand and the coffee in the other. "Are you telling me the truth? You didn't even peek?"

"Wouldn't you have waited for me?" I asked as I followed her.

She moved more quickly than one would expect from someone with a hangover. "No way," she cried out as she scampered up the stairs ahead of me, spilling coffee.

We knelt in front of the safe together and she clutched my hand in hers. "Oh God, I'm nervous," she cried, at her most theatrical. "What if it's empty?"

"I had that thought," I started to say.

Peck interrupted me, shaking her head. "Of course you did. You're so *negative*. Let's think big, let's think positive. Now open the damn thing already."

The combination, 9, 24, 96, worked again, and the safe clicked open. We looked at each other with great anticipation before pulling open the door. Not all that surprisingly, the safe contained no big stash of money, no pile of jewels, and no first edition of *Gatsby* or any other collectible book. In fact, it almost appeared empty, although a closer look revealed a few of the usual papers: Lydia's birth certificate, her Social Security card, and then what appeared to be a packet of letters, tied up with a neat ribbon.

Peck sat back on her heels. "I'm so *greedy*," she exclaimed, laughing a little. "Expecting the thing to be full of dough. Or no, that's not it. Actually, I expected a *surprise*. A surprise of utmost *value*."

I sat back too. "I don't know why, but I had this idea we might find a first-edition *Great Gatsby* hardcover with a dust jacket. Signed, maybe."

"What would that be worth?" Peck asked, scoffing. "Nothing. Maybe a few grand?"

"Signed?" I reached for the packet of letters and untied the ribbon. "Those things are worth a lot to some people."

"I can't imagine anyone would spend much for an old book," Peck was saying as I gazed down at the letters in my hand. In the upper-right-hand corner of each of the envelopes, all the same pale blue tissue paper, was an address on East 51 Street, with no name, written in a neat print.

I held them up to Peck. "What do you think these are?"

She frowned, disappointment on her face. "Whatever they are, they're not the thing of value. I just don't know why Lydia had to be so *confusing*. I'm sure she's up there chuckling away at us."

I handed one of the envelopes to her, took one for myself, and we began to read. All the letters were, in neat little block print, addressed to *Dearest Lydia* from someone named Julian, who signed off each of them as *Forever Yours, Julian*, or, *Impatiently and Infatuatedly Awaiting Your Response, Julian*. And, more than once, *Desperately Yours, Julian*. They were in no chronological order and seemed to span a period of years in which Julian, married to someone by the name of Rita, claimed to be madly and irrevocably in love with Lydia.

"Julian?" I asked as Peck and I each read through the dense and perfectly formed words crammed onto the tissue-thin pages. Some of the letters were three or four pages long, filled on both sides with intense and overwrought proclamations of love. "I don't remember Lydia ever mentioning that name."

Peck didn't look up from her reading. "It's him. The ghost of Fool's House."

This Julian fellow was the original owner of Fool's House. And yes, they'd played backgammon together. But Lydia didn't win the house from him that way. She bought it from him, paying off her debt over a period of about a decade, from the sound of it, with money she'd carefully saved and invested wisely. He made it sound as if he had given her a very good price on it because he wanted her to have it, for it to be a place where they could be together and be free. They'd been friends up to that point, but then they fell in love. Or he did.

"Listen to him, he was absolutely *insane* for her." Peck read some of the words aloud. " 'I can't eat. Or if I do, I taste nothing. I can't sleep. Or if I do, I'm tormented by dreams of you until I awake in a sweat, imagining you with someone else.' " As we read on, it became evident that Lydia was not waiting around for her married lover to be available while his wife wasn't paying attention. Lydia had other company. A lot of company, from the sound of it. Not to mention some of those young artists and writers who took up residence above her garage each summer.

"What a naughty thing she was," Peck said, in an admiring tone. "Can you imagine having her as a teacher?"

"If he was so in love with her, why didn't he leave his wife?" I asked, as I read on. "And why did Lydia never mention him?"

"The wife might have had the money," Peck said, flipping ahead. "Were there any kids?"

"Listen to this," I said, reading aloud. " 'Did you ever find the silver cocktail shaker that belonged to Grandma Nonah?' Who was Grandma Nonah? Her grandmother? Or his?"

Peck looked up. "I think we might have had a Nonah somewhere in the family. Is that the cocktail shaker on the bar cart? Or another one?"

I read on. "'I suspect the ghost of Fool's House,' he writes. 'You know I have always told you the house is haunted but in the most amiable way. Our specter would enjoy a cocktail or two, of that I'm certain.'"

"I thought *he* was the ghost," Peck complained. She slumped back on her heels again. "Now we find out there was another ghost? A previous one? Was he one of her lovers too? God, this is all so confusing. How come we know so little about our ancestors? And I'm afraid Aunt Lydia was rather a slut."

"Shut your piehole," I said, borrowing one of her expressions. "Lydia was not a slut. She embraced life." I was never a believer in ghosts and always assumed Lydia's tales of her haunted house were, as they say, strictly for entertainment purposes. "Maybe in her mind her ghost was Julian. And his was a different, earlier version."

We went back to our reading, handing over each letter as we finished it, reading aloud the bits that we couldn't resist sharing. "'I will never forget the image of you in that white dress with your feet on the porch railing as you squinted at the words on the page, bringing them to life for me the way you must have done for your students,'" Peck intoned, giving dramatic voice to Julian's words. "'I'm now convinced all of them, and their fathers too, must have been in love with you and I am madly envious of the hours they would have spent watching you move before them, your hair all done up in a bun. I certainly hope you never wore a sleeveless dress such as that one when you taught a class of teenaged boys, for they would have been helpless to concentrate in the face of the vision of your slender, shapely arms. Lydia, you have the most beautiful arms.'"

"He sounds a bit crazed," I said.

"She did have beautiful arms, though," Peck added. "You have the same ones, Stella. I've always been madly envious that you got the Moriarty arms." Arms were the kind of feature about which Peck would profess envy while making it clear that she didn't actually feel at all strongly about them, not when she knew full well that boobs such as hers were far more likely to make other women jealous.

Then I came to a letter in which Julian mentioned—in the same flowery language Lydia had always favored—the "darling niece" who was living with her. " 'Darling niece,' " I read aloud with a jolt. "Is he talking about you or me?"

This darling niece, according to the letter, had lived with Aunt Lydia from the sound of it, and as I read on, it became evident that it was I who had spent a full year with her when I was two, while Eleanor followed the Grateful Dead to Europe and didn't return.

This came as a shock. It was a version of the story I'd never heard or even suspected. I'd always been told by my mother, and by Lydia too, that the reason my mother never wanted to come back to the United States was because it was too painful for her after my father died. I always understood that she'd left with me *after* he was killed. They were deeply in love, I was told, and this great passion was the rationale for his behaving callously toward his first wife. But from Julian's allusions, it seemed my mother had already moved on almost a year before my father's accident, a year that I apparently spent living with Lydia, first in Southampton, right there at Fool's House, and then in New York when the summer ended and it was time for Lydia to go back to teaching. Presumably my father lived with us too, or stayed at Fool's House that summer, although Julian didn't mention him.

I felt slightly dizzy, reading that letter, and I handed it to Peck before leaning back against the door to regain my equilibrium. My mother's few stories rushed through my brain, a torrent of words always delivered, as I remembered them, in the slightly ironic tone that allowed her to keep her distance and turn them into anecdotes. She'd take on a conspiratorial tone, as though sharing a confidence. But then she'd end up revealing so little. I knew next to nothing about any of them, not my father, not her parents, or his. "It could have been worse," I could hear her saying, with a laugh ready to burst forth each time. "They could have played 'Bertha.'"

Peck read through the letter quickly and then looked up at me, her eyes shining with tears. "You didn't know." It wasn't a question but a statement of fact. She gave me a look of frank sympathy.

"Did you?" I asked.

She shook her head. "I didn't realize she left you here. Mum did tell me about your parents as a cautionary tale. She told me they fell out of love and that your mother went to Europe to get away from a needy husband who quickly grew too demanding. Mum wanted me to know the truth, that no matter how much in love you think you are, it fades. Inevitably it fades, even the grandest of loves." She paused, as though thinking of her own situation. "I was only seven when he died, so it was later, of course, when she told me this as a warning. By the time I started to get to know you, there didn't seem to be any reason to share this information."

"I wish I'd known," I said simply.

"What difference did it make if they were still in love or not when he died?" She reached out and patted my knee with one hand. "You couldn't change the ending of that story."

"I called my mother the queen of the unreliable narrators," I said, as the rush of words in my brain abated.

"I thought *I* was the queen of the unreliable narrators," Peck said, only half kidding.

"I suppose we all are," I said. "That's what I'm starting to realize. We all tell our stories the way we want to. And sometimes those stories have nothing to do with reality."

Peck was clutching a handful of letters and she shook them in my face. "That's *exactly* what happened with me and Miles. I got stuck in my version of the story. And I could never move on. I believed this fiction about the one true love. That's a bullshit story if there ever was one. Why is the whole world obsessed with this myth of true love?"

I nodded. "I've wondered that. Even as I read these letters, they sound like fiction to me."

"That's because you've never been in love," she said matter-of-factly. I must have given her a look, because she added, "Don't get your panties in a wad. You know it's true. You got married because you thought it was time and you didn't want to be alone. You told yourself a romantic story—talk about an unreliable narrator—and you wanted to believe it. Of course you did. You're a writer, aren't you?" Peck shrugged. "We're all storytellers. We choose to tell ourselves the kind of tale we want to hear."

I took up another of the letters, ready to continue. "I don't remember Lydia ever mentioning that I'd lived with her. Not even after my mother died."

"She probably didn't want to hurt your feelings," Peck said gently. "It didn't mean your mother didn't love you. She must have been going through a lot."

According to Julian, who, in some of the letters, seemed to be writing from a kind of sanitarium or rehab center where telephone privileges were limited, Lydia used me, the darling niece, as an excuse not to see him. He complained that she was always giving him the brush-off, that he'd opened his heart to her and she'd tossed it into the wastebasket, much as he predicted she would toss his letters into it after reading them.

Then we came to another revelation: Lydia had been married. It was a brief alliance, no more than a year from the sound of it, with a younger man she met at the school where she worked. He was the father of one of the students, and his first wife had died in a fire. She married him to spite Julian, or that's what Julian seemed to want to believe. The marriage fizzled in a short time, and when they were divorced, Lydia surprised Julian, who was himself still married, even more by not rushing to be with him again.

"Wow," I said, after I read through to the end of the letter for Peck's benefit. "Another thing she never told us. Lying by omission."

"Doesn't this sound like That-Awful-Jean-Paul? The first husband who didn't work out?" Peck glanced over at me. "Everyone makes mistakes. Even Lydia."

"We talked so often when I was going through my divorce," I said, thinking about the phone conversations with Lydia. "I can't believe she wouldn't have mentioned this then. She was so sympathetic. And encouraging. I kept wanting to believe there could be a happy ending. And she'd say, 'Sometimes you have to scrap your first draft and start over.'"

When we'd finished reading all the letters, I gently placed the stack back into the safe, leaving the door open. "Seems kind of anticlimactic, doesn't it?" I said. "An affair with a married man? That was the big secret hidden in the safe?"

"I know," Peck said. "Kind of trite for someone with Lydia's imagination. The cheating husband, the tiny cottage by the beach where the lonely mistress would wait for him to be free, feeling justified when her attentions were drawn to other company."

"I was expecting something more dramatic," I said.

"Stella," Peck intoned, "I go through *life* expecting something more dramatic. That's *my* downfall. And yours is that you don't expect *enough*."

We sat there for a while, crouched on the floor near the open closet door in Lydia's cluttered bedroom, filled with things we needed to make decisions about. Most of it would go to charity—

there was a thrift shop affiliated with the school where she had taught for so many years—but what of the rest? The strange thing was, I kept feeling like Lydia would be home soon, so we could ask her about it. That's what went through my mind: we can ask Lydia when she gets home. My brain had played the same tricks on me when my mother died.

Peck suddenly jumped up. "Literally, if I don't get some grease in me I'm going to pass out. Let's get out of here."

Later, after we'd stuffed ourselves on eggs and bacon, we sat quietly on the porch together. The rain had stopped but the sky was still a cozy pale gray. Peck lit a cigarette and when she put the pack down on the table I took one for myself. She would never comment on such a decision. She wouldn't welcome it too exuberantly, the way some smokers would, making you want to quit right away before the thing was even lit. She wouldn't raise her eyebrows in question or nod knowingly or look shocked or do anything to acknowledge the cigarette in the hand of a nonsmoker. I loved this about her.

I inhaled deeply, enjoying a newfound feeling of closeness between my sister and me that was almost tangible. We fell into a companionable silence, rocking back and forth in the old chairs, looking out at the small raggedy lawn and the tennis court, smoking. Something had shifted between us.

"Our family was fucked up," she said, after a while.

"All families are fucked up." I took comfort in that knowledge, and in the obvious but suddenly poignant realization that my sister and I were each other's family, fucked up or not. She was all I had. "I'm named after a Grateful Dead song they didn't play the night I was born. For all I know, they weren't even at the show. Maybe he didn't even *like* the Dead!"

"Oh, he loved the Dead all right," Peck said. "It was when he started getting into music that everything went south with Mum.

She was *never* going to go to a Dead show with him. She blamed the music. All of a sudden her husband grew his hair long and started playing the guitar and claiming his great lament was that he hadn't gone to Woodstock. She didn't know who he was."

"That's pretty funny," I said. "Because my mother said he was very square. But she said it like it wasn't a bad thing."

After a pause Peck waved her cigarette in my direction. "Did I ever tell you about *my* first Dead show?"

I nodded.

"It was the last show Jerry ever played," she intoned, beginning the story as she'd always told it. I remembered that she'd begun with this erroneous detail the last time I'd heard it. "I was—"

"It wasn't," I interrupted. "The last show was in Chicago. You saw them at the Meadowlands."

She sighed, a deep and distraught expulsion of heavy breath, as though the weight of my interruption was more than she could bear. "Okay. It was the last show Jerry ever played . . . at the Meadowlands. God, Stella, no wonder you're divorced."

"Ouch. Was that necessary?" I asked her with a laugh, but she'd taken another breath and moved on with her tale.

"It was 1995. Bob Dylan opened for the Dead."

The words that constructed the story of her first and only Dead show washed over me with soothing familiarity. When she was through we fell silent again, basking in the calm of the early afternoon on the porch. All the emotional turmoil I'd lived with since my mother died and the divorce and then Lydia's death seemed to drift away.

After a few minutes of quiet, Peck spoke again, this time sounding just like Lydia. "There's a great tradition of writers out here, you know."

I nodded. This had been a favorite topic of Lydia's, the writers and the artists on the East End, and I knew what Peck was trying to do by bringing it up. The legacy of the arts was what drew Lydia out here in the first place, she always said, long before it was considered "a playground for the haves and the have-mores," and Peck sounded like she was hoping she could use it to draw me out there too, intimating that I would finally become a writer, if only I stayed. If only we could keep Fool's House.

"Truman Capote lived in Sagaponack," she added, after a pause. "John Steinbeck was in Sag Harbor. There were so many artists, photographers, even theater people. That was when this was a place for true eccentrics." Clearly she placed herself, as Aunt Lydia always had, in this category. And I do believe considering yourself an eccentric is the first step toward becoming one. "Willem de Kooning lived out in Springs," she continued wistfully, as though she were speaking of old personal friends of hers. "That's also where Jackson Pollock lived. And where he died."

"Did you ever notice how Lydia always mentioned Pollock when she talked about Dad's car accident?" I said, remembering. "She always added, 'Like Jackson Pollock,' when she'd say he died in a car accident. And then she'd say, 'He was forty-four years old, exactly the same age as Pollock was when he died.'"

"I know. What was she implying?" Peck lit another cigarette with the one she'd just finished. "That he had talent to match? Ha."

"I wanted to believe it was true, speaking of fictions we tell ourselves," I said. "All evidence to the contrary. Lydia wanted to believe it too. She always said he hung out at De Kooning's studio, remember? As though he were one of them."

Peck nodded, exhaling thoughtfully. "In her mind, he was. She had such reverence for artists. What did she say? There was nobody more poignant than a failed artist?"

"Hitler was a failed artist," I pointed out. I'd known my share of them, even married one. Jean-Paul had never gotten over the fact that he'd inherited no musical talent whatsoever, despite his determination to become a guitarist.

"I am too," she said softly. "I might as well face it."

I looked at her sharply. I'd never heard her question herself. She took a drag from the cigarette in her hand, elbow clasped elegantly at her waist, and then her eyes met mine. "All these years I've been telling myself I was destined for extraordinary things, to be an acclaimed actress, a movie star, a *legend*." She smiled. "I told myself I was unique, that what Miles and I had was this rare, literary sort of love, and that it was indicative of this rare, literary sort of life. I believed myself a *student* of the theater, rather than just a wannabe." She paused, looking up at the night sky. "There comes a point in life, I guess, when you can't keep believing your own tales."

When Peck's cigarette was down to the filter she stubbed it out and continued, as though she'd been thinking about her old friends. "All the writers used to go to Bobby Van's in Bridgehampton. They'd get drunk there after a hard day's work. That was before the paparazzi were out here and the celebs. Before the tacky nightclubs and the promotional parties and those awful reality housewives." She paused, as though recalling it. "The artists' and writers' softball game had real artists and real writers back in those days."

You'd have believed she was there. Like we always believed Aunt Lydia.

8

The next day I was on the living room floor surrounded by paper when the phone rang. Aunt Lydia had not only saved her love letters from the passionately devoted Julian, but also, apparently, every piece of correspondence she'd ever received, including, for some reason, hundreds and hundreds of Christmas cards, some crinkled and faded with age, others more recent and crisp, with marketing-brochure-style photos of families or just their children, wearing Santa hats and gap-toothed grins, or on safari in Africa in matching khaki shorts.

There were so many of them, all those families with at least two children, sometimes as many as five, smiling for the camera. I tried to imagine what those families were like and what kinds of houses they lived in—in some I could see a fireplace or a bit of staircase in the photo and could extrapolate. I found them fascinating, these mini promotional pitches for each family. Some of the parents seemed to go out of their way to create a specific mood, while others just seemed to have grabbed any old photo, even ones where all the eyes were red and devilish from the flashbulb. I sorted through the deep container filled with cards and photos, unsure what I was looking for, or what I should be doing with them. They were worth nothing, obviously. But I couldn't imagine throwing them away when Lydia had carefully stored them over so many years.

Peck had started out that morning helping me, but her curiosity waned early and she'd wandered off after dumping out the contents of one of the desk drawers all over the floor to make us coffee. "Stella. The phone," she commanded from the kitchen at the first ring of the old black rotary that sat on a side table in the living room.

Peck and I had differing opinions on telephone behavior in general. She was, and still is, one of those people who are so afraid to miss anything that they jump to answer a ringing phone no matter what they might be doing, eating dinner, watching a play, riding a bicycle. She would even answer the phone in the middle of sex, a disconcerting habit I'd experienced from the other end a couple of times, calling from Lausanne and reaching her at eleven in the morning New York time.

Lydia's land line was not a phone number I'd put into circulation as a way for anyone to reach me. Peck, on the other hand, had passed along the phone number to every single person she knew. She explained this by saying it was because her cell phone service was erratic in that area of Southampton, but then admitted to me she loved the 283 exchange, which indicated to anyone who cared about such snobbish things that the number in question had been in Southampton for some time.

"Stellaaah!" came the reproachful cry from the kitchen when Peck realized I hadn't immediately jumped up to answer the call. "Get the *phone*."

I did and was pleasantly surprised to hear Finn's voice on the other end of the line. "Hey, kid," he said with no introduction. "Aren't there a few more things we need to cross off Lydia's list?" I sat on the sofa and cradled the phone to my ear as I could hear Peck shouting from the kitchen, "Who *is* it?"

"What did you have in mind?" I asked. "You thinking of having an affair with a man who speaks no English?"

"Ha." His gravelly voice vibrated through the receiver. "I slept with a girl in Abu Dhabi once who could only say, 'Yes, please.' Does that count?"

"Aren't you quite the player?" I said. "And you seem determined to have me know this about you."

"You intimidate me, kid." He used a teasing tone that indicated that he couldn't actually be intimidated by anything. "I'm trying to show off, sorry."

"No problem," I said. "I'm sufficiently impressed. Abu Dhabi?"

"Okay," he said. "That wasn't true. But I've never skinny-dipped in the ocean."

"You?" I feigned shock. "Mister Surfer Dude?"

He laughed. "I know. It's embarrassing. I've got to do something about it."

"And I take it you want *me* to help you with this?" Somehow I was able to fall into a joking banter. Was I flirting?

"Well, I can't go alone," he said. "Aren't you the one the list was for? Peck can't possibly need to do that one. She'd skinny-dip in the Four Seasons Pool Room if she thought anyone was watching."

"What's the Four Seasons Pool Room?" I normally couldn't stand to talk on the phone, but I could have stayed on with him all day.

Peck had appeared in the living room with flour all over her face and hands. "Who *is* it?" she whispered insistently when she saw me curled up happily on the sofa with the receiver.

"The Four Seasons is a restaurant in the Seagram Building," Finn was saying as I put my hand over the receiver and mouthed, "Finn Killian."

"It was designed by Mies van der Rohe and Philip Johnson in the late fifties," he continued as Peck widened her eyes in excitement and then joined me on the sofa, sitting practically on top of me so she could hear what he was saying. "It was the first building of its kind, a gorgeous bronze, the best example of curtain-wall architecture ever. It's really special. And the restaurant? Some people think it's pretentious. But it's such a beautifully designed space, I just really appreciate it as an architect."

"I've heard about it," I said. "But I don't think I've ever seen it. We didn't go to New York much when I came out here."

Peck leaned even closer. "What? Where?"

"The Grill Room is the power-lunch scene. That's what people think of when they think of the Four Seasons," Finn was saying as Peck was getting increasingly frustrated that she didn't know what was going on. "What does he *want*?" she asked in an insistent whisper.

I wasn't sure what he wanted—to go skinny-dipping?—but he seemed to be enjoying telling me about the Four Seasons. "You walk through the Grill Room to the Pool Room, which is where I like to sit. It has this square marble pool in the center and these trees that change with the seasons. It's considered Siberia for the power lunchers but it's really pretty."

"Sounds cool," I said. "But are you sure you're not a power-luncher?"

At the mention of power lunching Peck was apoplectic with curiosity. "Who? Who's a power-luncher? Are you talking about Miles?"

Finn let out a laugh. "I get *hired* by the power-lunchers. But the Pool Room *is* cool. I've always thought it was very romantic. But I've only ever gone there with other architects. It's that kind of space. We all get horny over Mies van der Rohe; we can't help ourselves." He paused. "I'd like to take you there. If you'd like to go to

New York one night. It's kind of a landmark. A little touristy, people like to complain about the food, of course, but worth going once at least, just to see it."

He was rambling. Was he nervous? He always seemed so comfortable in his skin, confident to the point of arrogance. But now he was going on as if he thought he needed to talk me into this idea, as if he were just doing his civic duty, encouraging me to sightsee while I was there. "I'd love to go to the city," I said, as my cheeks burned with pleasure.

"The city?" Peck repeated, hardly whispering now. "You're going to the city?"

He paused again but it wasn't awkward, just careful. "I was going to invite you to dinner tonight . . . I mean, that's why I called, to ask you. I thought you might need a break from your sister. What is she doing, trying to rip the phone from your hand to listen in?"

That was exactly what she was doing. "I thought you were inviting me skinny-dipping."

"Skinny-dipping?" Peck repeated, with a comically leering face. "I love skinny-dipping."

He laughed. "Well, dinner first. I was thinking in town. But now I'm suggesting we drive into the city for dinner at the Four Seasons. Are you up for that?"

I was. "I'll pick you up at five-thirty," he said. "It'll take about two hours to drive. Oh, and men have to wear a jacket. It's a little pretentious, sorry. But I hope you'll like it."

"I'll be ready," I said. We almost hung up several times after that but we kept talking. Peck seemed to think she'd gotten the gist of the conversation—skinny-dipping—and realized she was going to have to wait until I got off the phone to hear any more details, so she wandered back to the kitchen to whatever baking project she'd begun earlier. I told Finn about the combination to the safe and the letters we'd found inside. He was easy to talk to, asking questions about the content of the letters and how I felt about what I learned from them. We talked for another hour, my ear aching from holding the phone to it for so long.

When I finally got off the phone, Peck, as expected, went into a tailspin of excitement at the news that I would be going to the city for dinner with Finn. She screamed, jumping up and down, like a beauty pageant contestant.

"The Four Seasons!" she exclaimed breathlessly, and then immediately shifted into a more serious mood. "Oh, I wonder where they'll put you. It's very important to get a good table."

"We're sitting in the Pool Room," I explained.

"Of course," she said dismissively. "*Nobody* sits in the Grill Room for dinner. Besides, the Pool Room is *romantic*. But you have to get one of the tables next to the pool." She brushed the flour from her hands and headed immediately for the stairs. "Now, what are we going to wear?"

"*We?*" I said, laughing, as I followed her up the stairs. "*We* are not going to the Four Seasons, last I checked."

"It's the royal we," she said, amiably poking fun at herself. "And I can't help it, I'm excited. My baby's growing up. You're coming out of your *shell*, Stella."

"It's just dinner," I said. "With someone I *never* liked."

"Well," she said, already searching my closet, "he always liked you."

"No, he didn't," I quickly corrected her. "He was just being polite."

Peck inspected and dismissed everything she found in my closet. The only dress, the long white one I'd worn to Miles Noble's party, Peck deemed entirely unsuitable for dinner at the Four Seasons. She was taking the question of what to wear on this occasion very seriously and, for a change, I appreciated her laserlike focus on my wardrobe.

"No, no. It's all wrong," she said sternly. "The Four Seasons is very linear. It's about the architecture."

"That's why Finn wants to take me there." I was enjoying the sisterly concern. "Mies van der Rohe makes him horny."

She gave me a brisk nod. "I get it. There are these *magnificent* draped chain curtains on the windows." Pecksland Moriarty is one of the only people I know who can pull off using the word *magnificent* in everyday conversation. "It's very modern. You have to wear something modern. I would say black, but it's still a date. We want you to look soft and pretty. I'm thinking pale gray."

"I don't have any pale gray," I pointed out. My wardrobe was still very collegiate, jeans and loose tops, a few sweaters. I'd brought a couple of skirts, but they were casual.

"You don't have *anything*," she assessed, making a face. "But we're not going to fix that situation in time for dinner. And I've got the perfect solution."

She left me with the pile of discarded clothes and came back thirty seconds later holding a simple gray dress with a gathered waist and a swingy skirt on a hanger. "Vintage Valentino," she said. "I bought it because it was so cheap and practically unworn. I don't know how I thought I was going to starve myself into it but I figured it was collectible at that price. Anyway, I want you to have it."

"Oh no," I protested automatically, even as I was hoping it would fit me. "I couldn't."

She stared at me in disbelief. "You are, without a doubt, the most ridiculous person I've ever met. What the hell am *I* going to do with a dress that just sits there reproachfully in my closet, reminding me that eating dessert at every meal does not a size zero make? *Literally,* you'd be doing me a *favor.*"

The dress fit perfectly, as though it were tailored expressly for me. I twirled in front of the mirror. "I'm so proud of myself," Peck said. "Look at you. Now, what about the hair? You're a pinhead."

She sat me down in her room and took a curling iron to my long, stick-straight hair. "I spoke to Miles Noble," she announced, as she frowned at the limp lock of hair she was attempting to "volumize." "He told me he *enjoyed* seeing my aunt's house and her art collection. Can you believe that? It's like he wants me to know he took the painting, right? Then he said I should come over to see *his* collection sometime. He's taunting me, I know it."

"Did you ask him about the missing painting?" I asked as she pulled on my hair. "Ow."

"Of course I didn't *ask* him about it. I don't want him to know I'm onto him yet. Maybe I'm supposed to go over there and take something of his, you know?"

"I don't think so," I said.

She frowned at me, but whether that was because she didn't like my not agreeing with her or because my hair was a *situation* was unclear. "Well, we're going over there tomorrow. You're coming with me. And no advance warning either: we're just going to stop by. Like we're in the neighborhood."

"Why don't you just tell him you want to come by?" I asked. "He invited you to see his collection. Why would we *be* in that neighborhood?"

She stood back, admiring her handiwork. "Never underestimate the element of surprise, Stella."

While I was waiting for Finn to pick me up, I sent a group e-mail to Kelly, Patrizia, Tessa, and Julie to tell them about my date with Finn and almost immediately received four responses in quick succession, all sent "Reply All." Kelly, married to an American, had a lot of advice about keeping things simple and upbeat. "American men are refreshingly straightforward and optimistic," she wrote.

"Yes, but he's an architect!" was the immediate message from Tessa, whose fiancé was a famous French architect based in San Francisco with whom Tessa had been arguing, almost since they met, about where to live. "They make everything complicated, often more than it needs to be. They can't help it." And then she sent a follow-up e-mail almost immediately. "And they're arrogant," she added. Julie, who was a hopeless romantic, waxed on about destiny and one door opening when another closes, and Patrizia simply shared a bit of gossip about my editor, whom she'd spotted having lunch in an out-of-the-way café with an Italian publisher. I missed them, I realized as I attempted to describe Finn's smile without sounding like a total sap. But even as I typed my words I recognized that our lives and our friendships were starting to shift. Kelly and Tessa were both leaning toward moving to the United States, although Tessa claimed she would go "kicking and screaming." Patrizia had started to speak fondly of "going home," feeling the eventual pull of many an expat. Julie had always planned to go back to New Zealand before she got too settled in Lausanne, although she'd lived in Switzerland for almost twelve years.

I'd just closed up my laptop when Peck shouted up the stairs, "Finn's here."

My heart actually skipped a beat as I grabbed my purse and hurried down. Peck was on the porch with a cigarette, her elbow clasped at her waist, as though she were the one waiting to be picked up for dinner. "A crisp white shirt," she murmured as he stepped out of the car, wearing a navy blue jacket that set off his slight tan nicely. "Finn, you clean up well," she called out as he came toward us.

"You look really pretty, kid," he said to me as I walked down the porch steps, his eyes wide in surprise.

He walked me around to the passenger side of the jeep and opened the door for me. The Grateful Dead was on the stereo.

"Stella Blue." "This was never one of my favorite songs," I told him, suddenly nervous. It hit me that it wasn't a very good idea to go on a two-hour car ride on what was essentially a first date. What if we ran out of things to talk about and then had to sit through a long fancy dinner in silence?

"Not mine either," he said, looking at me for a beat before he closed my door and came around, giving Peck a jaunty wave before he slid in next to me. Well, that was rude, I thought.

He pulled out of the driveway and we were quiet, listening to the music. *It seems like all this life / Was just a dream.* It occurred to me as he didn't speak that I must have misinterpreted his invitation, reading romantic intentions into the talk of skinny-dipping and dinner in the Pool Room. He was obviously just being polite, taking out the family friend, the visitor from abroad, out of allegiance to Lydia. I replayed our conversation on the phone to see if I'd missed some signal, but Peck had been distracting me, and the nuances of whether the invitation was for a date or just a friendly outing escaped me as I tried to recall his words. It didn't matter; the situation was now more than clear and it annoyed me that I'd been fooled.

"Rough day at the office?" I asked, slightly sarcastic. I felt silly now, in my borrowed finery with my expectations sitting heavily on my chest. And what had happened to his sense of humor? He was practically sullen.

He nodded distractedly. "Sort of. I've got a couple of difficult clients right now."

After that we talked, but our conversation was stilted and I grew increasingly annoyed with him. He made no effort to be funny and entertaining. Instead he appeared tired and it seemed suddenly ridiculous to be driving to dinner hours away with someone who didn't even seem to like me. And then the voice in my head kicked in, reminding me that even if there had been romantic intentions on his part, there would have been no point in reciprocating when I had so much to do and would soon be leaving this place behind.

It was time, I told myself when we fell into another silence, to go back home and focus on the career I'd allowed to languish. In an e-mail just that day, my editor had expressed an interest in giving me more actual writing projects, rather than only translations, and I'd enjoyed thinking about turning the e-mails I'd sent him into a column. I'd been jotting down notes since I arrived in Southampton and I was excited about getting back to writing. Perhaps after tonight I could write a column about uncomfortable dates.

"Tell me about your writing," Finn said then, as if he could read my mind.

"There's not much to tell," I said. I'd never been comfortable talking about myself or about my yearning to write.

"When I first wanted to be an architect," he went on, "I used to believe that my first efforts at designing something had to be perfect. When those first sketches weren't good—of course they weren't, they were supposed to be rough—I thought that meant I wasn't supposed to be an architect. It was only later that I understood how the process works. I imagine it must be similar with writing."

I didn't realize at the time how these words would later resonate. That night I thought he was being condescending, and I grew prickly as a result. I resented my earlier excitement at the prospect of what I'd assumed—erroneously, I now believed—was a romantic dinner.

There wasn't much traffic and in no time we were standing in the plaza in front of the Seagram Building and Finn was showing me what he meant by curtain-wall architecture. He spoke as though he were addressing a class of students and my responses grew more and more sarcastic.

Then we were in the restaurant, which really was stunning,

being fawned over by a maître d' who either recognized and adored Finn or was just making him feel as if he did. He led us to a table next to the pool and presented it with a flourish, as though he knew it would please.

"Do you like it?" Finn asked me. He sounded doubtful, as though I were the sort of spoiled woman who might roll her eyes at his enthusiasm.

"It's beautiful," I said, resenting his implication. And it was, although I was confused by his behavior, especially when I saw the prices on the menu. The evening seemed awfully extravagant and yet not in the least romantic, and I couldn't understand why we were there. He ordered a bottle of wine, and then asked if red was okay. Again, the question seemed phrased for another type of woman, one who would find fault with the choice of wine, who might even send it back.

We ordered our food and then spent the rest of the evening exchanging barbed remarks. I'm not sure who exactly I thought I was channeling, but something got into me that night, and I bantered with him like it was a sport in which I excelled. I did not, however, and I suspect I simply came across as rude. For his part, he seemed to have made some sort of unfavorable decision about me. This brought out the worst in me, and after a few sips of wine, I heard myself making fun of him for being an architect, accusing him of having poor taste, although I'd never seen anything he'd designed. If I thought I was flirting I was failing miserably.

"I designed my own house," he said, and it sounded awfully pompous to me. That, I think, is when I pointed out that it was awfully presumptuous for a single man to assume a woman he might later meet would like it and want to live there, and the conversation went downhill from there.

He shrugged and took a sip of his wine. "*Everybody* likes it."

I suggested that he was arrogant, like all architects, and he pointed out that I hadn't seen his house. I said I'd never been invited and then he made fun of me for being *formal*.

"I'm not formal," I said, sounding exactly like the type of woman he seemed to think I was, one who would be jaded by the Four Seasons and send back the wine and expect an engraved invitation to show up at his house. "I'm *Swiss*." It wasn't the kind of thing I would ever say and I blamed him.

He rolled his eyes and then he reminded me I was actually an American, and I told him I didn't need reminding, and I believe the word *Eurotrash* came out of his mouth. By then I'd had a lot more of the wine than he'd had and we'd ordered coffee and dessert and I couldn't imagine that we would ever be friends again, let alone anything else, after such a disastrous dinner.

"You're quite a character, kid," he said to me in a most infuriating way.

"Just because you *are* a character," I replied, quoting a line from *Pulp Fiction*, "doesn't mean you *have* character."

"Really?" he said, making a face. "Movie dialogue, that's what we've been reduced to?"

Dessert, in the form of an enormous puff of cotton candy, was placed between us before I could answer. "You ordered this?" I asked him, annoyed that he seemed to blame me for reducing the conversation when in my view it was all his fault that things were not going well. Why had he even invited me in the first place? And why had he misled me with all that talk of skinny-dipping on the phone? And by the way, I wanted to say to him, I wasn't interested in being misled. I wasn't interested at all.

He pulled a piece and popped it into his mouth. "Try it." I did and it was delicious. The child-friendly dessert seemed to bring both of us back to our normal selves and we shared a couple of laughs as we polished it off.

The ride back to Southampton was a lot more conversational than our earlier trip, and it went quickly. We both seemed to have dropped our defenses, and we chatted easily. When we pulled into the driveway at Fool's House, nearly all the lights were off. Only the light over the front door was on, creating a welcoming glow. Finn walked me up the steps and we stood facing each other. "Thank you," I said. "I'll always remember this night."

"Me too," he said, grinning down at me as though he only half believed me.

This time I was pretty sure he was going to kiss me and I'd decided I would kiss him back, despite what I believed was my increasingly intense dislike for the man. I found myself tilting my head back slightly in anticipation. But rather than the passionate embrace I expected, he simply pecked me lightly on the cheek and said, "Good night, kid."

I felt foolish as I slipped off the slightly-too-big shoes I'd borrowed from Peck and padded through the living room. I was disappointed that Peck wasn't there and I quickly got out of the gray dress, hung it on her door, and got into my pajamas. I'd just gotten into bed with Lydia's hardcover of *The Great Gatsby* when I heard the screen door slam. A few minutes later Peck swanned into my room in a long printed caftan, a bakery box in one hand and a bottle of wine in the other. "Cupcakes and chardonnay. The perfect way to end an evening out."

I'd never been so grateful to see her. I was so happy that tears pricked at my eyes. "I'm so glad you're home."

She paused to stare at me. Trimalchio had followed her and tilted his head to stare at me with much the same expression. "What's wrong? And why are you even home? Why isn't Finn ripping that silk dress off your body and throwing you down on the bed? Why aren't you two fucking your brains out?" She put the bottle and the box on the chest of drawers and pulled a wine glass from each pocket. "But then, why aren't *I* fucking the brains out of the very good-looking guy I met tonight? He was in *mergers* and acquisitions; isn't that kinky?" She poured us each a glass of wine and sat on the edge of my bed. "What's the matter?"

"Nothing's the matter," I said, swiping at my eyes. "I'm in bed."

"I see that." She took a sip of her wine and then a bite of the cupcake. "Mmmmm. How was your date?"

"It was fine. Only it wasn't a date." The tears were still coming despite my attempt to wipe them away.

"What do you mean? Of course it was. The Four Seasons Pool Room—what else would it be?"

I shook my head, shocked to find myself practically sobbing now. "He said it himself: it's a tourist site. And I suppose I'm the tourist." I gazed up at her, my cheeks wet with tears.

"You're not a *tourist*." She looked as horrified as if I had said I was a stripper, or a terrorist. "You were born at New York Hospital."

"Well, he certainly acted like he was just showing me around, like you would a tourist. There was nothing romantic about it at all. In fact, he couldn't have been more obnoxious."

She pursed her lips thoughtfully. "He's probably feeling guarded. You didn't remember him. After he pined for you all those years."

"Pined?" I scoffed at what I suspected was just her usual hyperbole, the tears stopping now. "He didn't *pine*."

"Oh, he pined, Stella." She folded her arms and glared at me sternly. "He pined all right."

"What do you mean?" I sipped the wine she'd handed me and then took a bite of the cupcake.

"Don't play coy," she said. "It's unbecoming on you."

"I'm not being coy," I insisted. "I just didn't think he liked me that summer, that's all. We hardly talked. And after tonight it was more than obvious that he still doesn't."

"He *talked*. It was you who gave him the cold shoulder. He was mad for you. Totally smitten. Don't pretend you didn't know that."

"I had no idea," I said, warming at the thought of it: Finn Killian, smitten. With me. But then I quickly dismissed it. "Anyway, it doesn't matter now. What's the opposite of smitten? 'Cause that's what he is."

"He's probably just reeling from the cruel irony," she cried out, performing now. "You finally come back here, after breaking his heart by getting married, and you've conveniently disposed of the starter husband. He's conveniently not encumbered by any of the replacement Stellas he's tried to convince himself he should like enough to settle down with, and he's all excited. He puts on that white dinner jacket and shows up at exactly the sort of party he can't stand. And you don't even remember him."

I stared at her. "You're completely crazy, you know that? It's the Moriarty mental illness. It's gotten hold of you."

She pointed her glass insistently at me, spilling wine on my bedspread. "Not only do you not recognize him, all you do is talk about selling the house and getting the hell back home to *Switzerland*. Which puts a new twist on being geographically undesirable. So can you blame him if he's a little careful?"

"Why invite me to dinner at all, if I'm so undesirable?" I protested. "Why bother getting dressed up, driving all the way into the city, eating that fancy meal?"

"Look, Trimalchio," she said to the dog. "Stella's getting peevish."

She grinned at me. Trimalchio too seemed to be amused.

"I'm delighted to be the source of your entertainment," I groused. "But I still don't understand why Finn was so rude."

Peck gestured with her wine glass again, sloshing the chardonnay around. "He's thirty-five. We're at that age."

"We? You're not thirty-five," I pointed out grumpily.

"Women reach it by thirty. The age when it becomes imperative that we settle into a home life. And a man, when he builds himself a house without a wife already in place, immediately sets about trying to find one. That's the stage Miles Noble has reached too. So why would Finn waste his time with you?"

"That's my point," I said to her. "Why? And more important, why would I waste my time with him?"

She sat at the foot of the bed and patted my leg through the blanket. "He probably should just stick with Laurie Poplin. And you? You can stick with those Eurotrash literary types you seem to attract like bees to honey."

This caused a reaction in me, which, of course, was her intention. "Laurie Poplin? The real estate broker? Are you *crazy*?"

"What? She's nice. They've gone out a few times. She's mad about him. Thinks he's a *genius*." She was goading me. "Men like to be appreciated. And he always was a leg man."

"He was not," I said.

"How would you know? *You* didn't even remember him." She refilled our wine glasses. "All I'm saying is, you should give him another chance. I think you scared him. He was so blown away by how you looked in that dress he didn't know how to act."

"That's ridiculous," I said. "Anyway, there's no need for another chance. I probably won't see him again. And I think you're right: he should stick with the Rockette. They could have tall children together."

We stayed up until the sun rose, talking about everything and nothing. Not since university days had I spent this kind of late-night time with women, and I'd forgotten how much fun it was. I was falling in love with my eccentric half sister.

9

It was a scene straight out of Hitchcock, the wide sky filled with black birds, hovering above us like crows over a carcass. The birds were mostly of the Sikorsky variety, enormous helicopters flown by not one but two pilots, seating six or eight passengers, and they waited their turn to land on a tiny square patch of asphalt with a white painted H in the center, perched right up against the edge of Shinnecock Bay.

The small square hardly seemed big enough for the black chopper that landed in a froth of whitecaps and wind. As we watched, supposedly taking a break from a casual afternoon ride on ancient high-handled and rusted bicycles we'd found in Lydia's garage, one of the pilots came around and opened the passenger door. We weren't the only gawkers. The helipad on a Friday afternoon appeared to attract an audience. There were four or five cars of spectators in the parking lot and more than a few cyclists and walkers and older women with strollers watching the choppers maneuver into a landing. A black Mercedes with tinted windows rolled forward to pick up a dapper bald gentleman in a blue blazer emerging from the helicopter with a vase containing a fresh white flower arrangement in his hands and an attaché over his shoulder.

Behind him was an elegant woman in white holding a brown-paper-wrapped parcel under one arm and a purse on the other. She wore a straw hat she had to hold awkwardly to her head as she hurried to the waiting car, while the little man in a suit and a red tie who'd picked them up passed her to unload the rest of their things. The rest of their things included bags of groceries, a big red cooler, garment bags, golf clubs, endless small shopping bags, and four enormous matching suitcases that must have been heavy, for the little man could hardly drag them. They were the Hamptons version of the Beverly Hillbillies, and it took a very long time for them to get all their belongings loaded into the car. You could almost hear the people in the sky cursing down at them.

"Now that?" Peck shouted at me over the whir of the helicopter as she gestured toward the people overstaying their welcome on the helipad. "That's bad manners."

Finally the parade of weekend necessities was over and that bird was free to soar back up, allowing another one to buzz down. The landing looked terribly precarious, the copter tipping from side to side before touching down in a rush of wind and noise and rippling waves. This one took less time to unload, spilling out four golfers and their bags of clubs, each with one small overnight bag. These four didn't have a ride, a fact that seemed to incense each of them, and they stood in the middle of the parking lot with the bags all around them, all four of them in the same pose, clutching one ear and screaming into the cell phones that were smacked up against the other.

"Are you sure this is a good idea?" I shouted at Peck as we waited for the helicopter that would dispense Miles Noble. "Some people don't like surprises."

"We're not surprising anyone. We're simply out for our afternoon bicycle ride. If we *happen* to bump into someone we know, well, that's normal. Everyone is always bumping into people at the helipad."

Three more helicopters landed and took off before Miles

emerged from one of them with a phone to his ear. He wore a striped dress shirt with the tails loose over jeans. Just as Peck was about to sail forward on her bike to greet him, he turned and gave a hand to a woman stepping out behind him. She was tall and gorgeous and preposterously chic.

"Fuck," Peck mouthed in my direction. "Let's just go." She looked around frantically. The only way out of the parking lot was in the direction of Miles and his lady friend, who were headed straight toward us as they made their way to an idling car, this one with the license plate MAN3.

"Pecksland Moriarty," he called out by way of greeting, as if he had been expecting to encounter her there, on her bicycle. The helicopter took off in a rush of gravel behind him and he had to shout to be heard. "Waiting for me?"

"I've been waiting for you for seven years, buddy," Peck cried out in a jocular tone as the helicopter flew away.

The girl—she looked familiar, as if maybe we'd seen her in a Ralph Lauren ad—at his side was checking her BlackBerry, a device my Belgian boss always referred to as "ze Crackleberry," and seemed unfazed by this revelation. Miles too appeared unfazed. "Hey, I thought you were going to stop by," he said, still talking loudly to be heard. "Why don't you come now?"

The woman with Miles went around to the other side of the car and hopped into the backseat without saying hello as Peck explained that we were just out for a ride but we were also checking on the helicopter arrival of some friends.

"Really? *Who*?" Miles asked Peck.

"Houseguests," she answered quickly, shouting over the noise. "My friend Nacho. Do you know him?"

"The polo player?"

She smiled indulgently. "Another Nacho. And two of his friends."

"There's another Nacho?" he asked, glancing down at the BlackBerry that appeared fused to his hand.

"This place is *infested* with them." At that moment, I adored my half sister. She seemed so brave, her spine erect, shoulders thrust back like an army cadet's, chest magnificently on display, as she leaned against the old bicycle. Her acting skills might not be developed enough for a career in the movies, but they certainly could be put to enough good use in her everyday life. I could see Miles being drawn in by her. "They're *wild*, those Argentines."

"Well, if you want to come by now, I'll be home in a little while." He looked almost childishly disappointed at the thought that Peck and I were going to be entertaining some crazy party boys from Argentina, but he tossed this invitation out casually.

"Maybe we will," Peck called out as another chopper hovered above us, making it difficult to hear anything.

He paused on the running board of the car, seeming reluctant to go, despite the Ralph Lauren model waiting in the backseat. "I can give you a ride right now."

Peck shook her head. "No, no. We're getting our exercise. But we'll go home and then take a drive over, ourselves."

The Escalade pulled out of the parking lot in a roar of dust and Peck turned to me, shouting, "I told you we should get some houseguests."

The fictional Miles Noble, the well-read, well-traveled, well-off version that existed in Peck's imagination, would have known there was an F. Scott Fitzgerald suite at the Ritz hotel in Paris. He would have been there. Many times. He would have sipped cocktails at the Bar Hemingway and known that it was there that the Bloody Mary was rumored to have been invented. But the real Miles Noble, Peck was surprised to learn, had never stayed at the Ritz.

She brought it up as we set out on what was to be a lengthy and detailed tour of the thirty or forty rooms in the house Miles Noble had built for himself. To hear her tell it, she'd practically grown up at the Ritz, but Miles misread his audience.

"The Ritz is for tourists," he declared, after making sure we'd been handed flutes of champagne by a man with dyed blond hair and a serious stare. And then he must have noticed that this was not what Peck wanted to hear, because he quickly added, "That's what I've heard, anyway. I usually stay at my friend Jamie's apartment."

He was wearing another version of the collarless jacket that seemed to be his signature style, and he'd gotten too much sun on his unfortunate nose, so it was peeling. He'd appeared genuinely pleased to see Peck and me at his door when we arrived and immediately suggested a tour. It was that sort of house, the kind that was built for showing. Now he looked mystified as he listened to Peck explain how writers could receive mail at the Ritz hotel, just as Scott and Zelda had when they lived there. People often looked this way around my sister. Miles stared at her as though she were speaking a language he'd never heard before.

The layout of the house was that of a traditional colonial, but one gone berserk on cheap rum and wanton sex. There was the center hall, in the colonial tradition, but this one was a soaring two-story space with an immense staircase. And then there were other halls, which seem to run in all different directions, with extra alcoves, unnecessary rooms, and odd seating arrangements popping up at strange junctures. It seemed to go on forever. Some parts of it were "upside down" to take advantage of the field views, so the kitchen and the dining room were on the second floor, and there were living rooms on every floor. The woman who'd been on the helicopter was nowhere to be seen as Miles led us through hallways that seemed to go on and on, proudly pointing out details he wanted us to notice: hand-hewn beams flown in from France; floors that were battered and treated in Tuscany; plaster walls that took thirty men more than a year to finish properly; pewter doorknobs the size of footballs.

The color scheme seemed to be "multi"—lots of purple and orange and patterned greens mixed with striped yellows—and chosen to be as jarring to the eye as possible. Really, I'd never seen anything less conducive to comfort. It was all layers upon layers of silks and velvets and mirrors and a mix of spindly coffee tables and squat chairs and expensive-looking pieces that served no purpose. The art seemed to have been chosen by four or five different people, all with competing tastes. None of it went together, or with the house. Or with Miles, who, despite the contrived clothing, was more appealing than I would have expected. He was self-deprecating in a charming way and seemed almost childishly eager to impress both Peck and me.

Peck didn't feel the need to ooh and aah. She acted like she toured forty-room palaces every other day. Somehow she managed to sound both imperious and seductive and, in a pretty sundress that highlighted her tan and her figure to great advantage, she was definitely having an effect on Miles as she chided him for not remembering that he'd given her *The Great Gatsby* in the first place.

I was surprised to see petulance used effectively—it so rarely works—but Peck was an expert at it. Miles was practically melting under her haughty glare. I felt like the third wheel as he kept gazing at her in wonder, but he made sure I was included in the conversation, touching my arm as he pointed at a detail—the bullet hinges on the doors, for example—I might not have noticed on my own.

"You were good too, like a lit major," she went on, airily amused, as though the memory was just coming back to her now in the vaguest way. "I remember staying up all night talking about that damn book."

Miles raised his shoulders to his ears with a sheepish look. "I wanted to go to bed with you, babe."

We'd been slowly moving through the house, and Peck stopped to give him an exasperated look. "That's ridiculous. It probably took you as long to read the CliffsNotes as it would have to read the whole book."

"Sorry," he said. He didn't sound sorry; he sounded like he wasn't in the habit of having to be sorry but knew it was the right thing to say. "A guy'll say anything to get a girl to go to bed with him. Haven't you heard that about us?"

"But you knew so much about it." She had her arms folded over her chest in the classic pose of a woman discontented with male behavior. "You could've written a thesis on Gatsby and the American dream."

He shrugged again, looking pleased with himself. He seemed absolutely delighted by her, as though she'd gone on to become the famous actor she'd always intended to be, and was now a celebrity who'd deigned to visit his humble abode.

"And then," she continued, as we started walking again (at the rate we were going, it would take the whole evening just to see the house), "you didn't even remember that you gave it to me." Here she looked at me. "What is it with you people and your faulty memories?"

"What people?" Miles glanced over at me for explanation.

"Stella here doesn't remember a thing," she said, gesturing at me. "Her brain is a sieve."

"Sorry," he said again. He wore a look that indicated he might once again say anything at all to get her to go to bed with him. For all his braggadocio, there was something very sweet about the way he seemed so enamored of Peck, and I couldn't help but wonder about the explanation he'd given Peck for how she ended up at his house on the Fourth of July in a white dress and a hat for a Gatsby-themed party. He had told her that both the theme and the guest list, as well as the menu, décor, and music, were the work of an overzealous party planner who took it upon herself to invite everyone in his address book. But the kind of guy who just told us he chose every single doorknob in this house of his would not have left details like the theme and the guest list for his first party at this house to chance, would he?

"Some house, huh?" he said, trying to prompt a response from Peck, who thus far had not offered one word of praise about the house. He led us into the living room—or the largest of the many rooms that might have been designed for such a purpose, *living*, which, in this extravagantly unattractive house, meant displaying far too much presumably expensive but ill-chosen furniture, art, and decorative objects. He gave Peck an eager look. In his gaze, I could see a glimmer of what she'd said about men who build their own house and then look to fill it with a wife. He was like a film producer, both auditioning and wooing a reluctant leading lady for what he believed, whether she knew it or not, would be the juiciest part of her acting career.

"It sure is big," I offered when it became clear that Peck was not going to answer him. She looked around dispassionately, as though she wasn't impressed at all. In fact, she looked slightly horrified, as if she hadn't fully realized the magnitude of the poor taste on display. Miles gave me a fleeting grin, the kind that leaves you unsure whether you'd been granted a smile at all, or just given a sneak peek at private thoughts that were meant to be hidden. Had he smiled like that at Peck when she fell in love with him the first time? Or was this a newer variation, acquired later, along with the money and the other things?

"Thirty fucking thousand square feet," he bragged, like he just couldn't help himself. I wished he wouldn't. He seemed determined to get Peck to comment on the house, but for some reason, perhaps because she knew it would have an effect, she seemed equally determined not to. "Not counting the indoor pool."

He had his BlackBerry in his hand and it vibrated now. He stopped in the hallway to take the call and we stopped too as he dismissed the business at hand with a few quick noes and then, "I gotta go."

He really does look like a frog, I thought as his eyes moved up and then down Peck's body in a distinctly appraising manner, lingering on the twins. She preened slightly under his gaze. Once he was off the phone, he steered us in front of a painting that hung above the sofa with one hand at Peck's lower back and the other at mine. "This is a Jackson Pollock," he intoned with a preacher's reverence as we stared at the painting, lit from above with its own brass picture light. "This is a Pollock?" I asked, surprised. I'd been expecting the recognizable Jackson Pollock, he of the wild splatters of color, the paintings for which he'd become known as Action Jackson. This painting was quieter, an abstract in browns and earth tones, but without the splatters and the energy.

"An early one," Miles explained.

Peck pulled out severe black glasses I'd never seen her use, and was quite sure she didn't actually need, and perched them on her nose so she could get a better look. I would have laughed at her but she looked so grave and humorless, like a serious art historian, as she inspected the painting that it kept me from even cracking a smile. "Is it *signed*?"

He nodded. "Pollock always signed his work."

"Tell that to the lady who bought one for five bucks at a thrift shop and then decided it must have been worth fifty million, if it was real." She was still squinting up at the painting from behind the glasses. "They made a movie about it. Nobody would authenticate it for her and she got really mad."

"I hope this one's real," Miles said. "If it's not, I got hosed."

She examined him over the frames of the glasses on her nose and paused. Her expression softened and I watched as her entire demeanor shifted and she offered up her first smile since we walked through his door. "I doubt that."

He returned the smile with one that lingered and they gazed at each other, almost in wonder, for a few seconds. I turned away, staring more closely at the painting so as not to appear to be staring at them. I was trying to figure out a way to leave them alone and was about to suggest that I take a walk outside when Peck tapped me on the arm.

"What does this look like?" she asked, in the manner of a teacher with an unprepared student. She'd taken off the glasses and was gesturing with them toward the painting.

"I'm not sure," I said. "I might have slept through that class."

"It looks like ours," she replied briskly. "The *missing* one." She turned to Miles. "So." She gave me a conspiratorial glance as she took his arm. "Where is it, the other one?"

"What other one?" He looked confused again, like he was having trouble aligning the woman in his memory with this person who kept shape-shifting in front of him. "I still haven't paid for this one."

At this she gave me a meaningful stare, as though this were a clue.

"Come on, Miles, we know you did it," she said softly, the way a hostage negotiator might begin a dialogue. "You know we know. But nobody else has to know. You can just return it, no questions asked. Nobody gets hurt." She paused, taking in his look of utter shock. "Don't do that. Don't play coy," she said, using words I'd heard from her more than once. "It's unbecoming. Let's just cut to the chase here. Is it a game of seduction? A cat and mouse thing? Should I be casing the joint for a reciprocal take?"

"I have no idea what you're talking about," he said, sounding totally confused. I believed him. He seemed much more the type to have overpaid for a painting at auction, only to find out it was actually not authenticated, or to have bought one that was considered by all experts to be the worst of its kind, than to have stolen anything. "What is it you think I did?"

Peck smiled and held up a hand. "You took the painting that was hanging above the mantel at Fool's House."

"What painting?" he interrupted her, and then she spoke over him: "That's exactly what we're trying to ascertain."

It then dawned on Miles what Peck was insinuating. "You think I *took* a painting from your house?" He sounded hurt and incredulous.

I intervened. "No, no," I said quickly. "My sister was just wondering if you might know how we could try to get more information. The painting above the mantel went missing that night and we're trying to figure out what happened to it. And what it was. We were wondering if you saw anybody do anything strange that night."

"I'll tell you what I saw," he said to me. "That weird kid in the suit sniffed her shoe." He jerked his thumb in Peck's direction.

"Biggs?" She made a face, like she wasn't going to believe anything negative about our artist in residence. "He *likes* me. But he told us you were staring at our painting all night, like you were planning to do something with it."

"That guy kept following me around. He was trying to sell me something. He wanted to come live in my house and teach me how to paint or something. I finally had to ask him to get me a drink, just to get rid of him. That's why I got out of there—he wouldn't leave me alone. There's something not right with that dude."

"He's an *artist*," Peck said. It seemed pretty evident to me that Miles had not taken our painting, but Peck seemed determined to continue believing that he had.

"If you think anyone took anything from your house that night, I'd check *him* out," he said. "That guy's loco."

"You think Biggs took our painting?" Peck looked to me for confirmation. "Why would he do that?"

"It has the ring of truth," I said, suddenly thinking Miles might be right as I replayed Biggsy's words and actions in the hours following the theft at the party. He'd been so quick to focus blame on Miles, and Peck had been so willing to go along with that theory, that we hadn't even considered the possibility that he might have had something to do with it. "He's always talking about the ghost. Maybe it's one of his pranks."

"Who was the artist of this missing painting?" Miles asked. An obvious question to which we still did not have the answer.

"We don't know," Peck explained. "It wasn't signed. On the back it just said, 'For L.M. From J.P.'" She turned to me breathlessly and grabbed my arm. "Oh my God. J.P. Jackson Pollock? Is that possible? We had a Jackson Pollock?"

I shook my head slowly. "I doubt that."

But Peck was already squirming in excitement. "Think about it. It looks like this, doesn't it? And he lived out here. She *revered* him. Maybe she met him and he gave it to her. Or she bought it from him, way back when. When did he die?"

"She would have been too young, I think," I said. "And if she'd met him for a split second, or even attended the same party as him, believe me, we would have heard about it."

Peck was nodding her head. "Literally. She would've taken out an ad. She adored him. Almost as much as she loved Fitzgerald."

"And if it was a Jackson Pollock, even a bad one, wouldn't it be worth a lot, millions of dollars?" I said, looking to Miles for confirmation.

He nodded. "He never sold a painting for more than eight thousand dollars when he was alive. But now? Well, they're hard to get."

"She wouldn't just leave something like that hanging there with no indication of what it was," I said. "And only a vaguely worded suggestion in her will."

Peck was still nodding in agreement. "Unless . . . *this* is the thing of utmost value she wanted us to find."

"You think your aunt left you a Jackson Pollock and didn't tell you?" Miles said in surprise. "And then it was stolen?"

"Possibly by the *butler*," Peck cried out, with an appreciative laugh for the increasingly zany nature of the tale. "The butler did it! Or it really was a ghost. Or, how about this? The butler is the ghost. Fool's House *is* haunted, you know." She pointed at Miles. "I came here today believing *you* had stolen this painting off our wall. But now I realize *he* took it. And then led me, led us, my sister and me, to believe it was you. That's crazy."

He grinned at her before offering his arm again. "*You're* crazy," he said as they moved ahead of me, arm in arm. "Shall we continue the tour? We can chase down your Pollock later."

He sounded doubtful that the painting in question could turn out to be a Jackson Pollock. I too had my doubts, but Peck and Miles had moved on to the hall and I followed them, keeping my thoughts to myself.

"I'm pretty pissed off at that foot fetishist in the costume, trying to lay the blame on me," Miles was saying to Peck. "I'm going to go after his ass."

"Tough guy," Peck cooed at him. She'd dropped the disdainful air and was now openly flirtatious. "Aren't you going to show us your bedroom?"

I was about to suggest that I wanted to see the garden and would meet them outside when Miles turned to me. "Come on, Stella. First the bedrooms, then the indoor pool."

The master bedroom was predictably and absurdly huge, deco-rated like a fantasy version of an old men's club, all mahogany trim and green felt with a "manly" brown rug and heavy drapes. The bed was so far from the television he'd need binoculars to watch it. And the fireplace was big enough that he could roast a goat over the gas flames if he wanted to.

Miles picked up a remote control. "Check this out." He directed it at the electronic shades and pressed a few buttons, but nothing happened. Then he pointed it at the fireplace with its elaborately carved mantel. "Where the hell's the music?" he wanted to know, jabbing at other buttons on the remote control in his hand. He kept trying to get the fire to start, directing the remote at the fireplace with increasing vigor. The fire sparked but wouldn't light, no matter how many times he tried. And then it still wouldn't light, but it wouldn't stop sparking either. All of a sudden the shades went down, but just as quickly they sprang back up, and kept up that rhythm, moving fiercely up and down on the windows with a loud electronic moan. He must have found the radio button when he was trying to make the shades stop jumping and the fake fire stop sparking but instead of music a sports radio station broadcasting what sounded like a baseball game came on at full blast. It was very Meat Loaf and "Paradise by the Dashboard Light," the announcers describing a play at home plate.

All Peck and I could do was watch as he jabbed the remote into the air. "I. Hate. This. Fucking. System."

I tried to excuse myself to leave them alone in the bedroom. "I'll just go back downstairs and—" but Peck wouldn't hear of it and Miles was sufficiently cowed by his equipment malfunction to scoot us out of the bedroom as quickly as possible.

"Someone else can deal with this," Miles said, tossing the remote control on the bed. "I have to show you the pool," he repeated, as though the tour had a set route, like one of those Disney rides where you can't get off until the end.

"Yes, Stella," Peck said with a grin. "He means the *indoor* pool."

The indoor pool was in a faux grotto, with little alcoves dotted around the walls in which candles were placed. There were hundreds of them and they were all lit, flickering and reflected in the pool water. There were thick white towels rolled up on double-wide terry-cloth-covered lounges and slippers wrapped in plastic waiting to be used, like at a hotel spa.

"Isn't this something?" Miles asked Peck. No longer haughty, she now responded with the sort of indulgent smile one would give a child at Christmas. "It sure is. If I were you, I'd never leave."

"More champagne," he called out, refilling our now-empty glasses from a bottle sitting on ice.

"How did *that* get there?" Peck asked him.

"The butler did it," he said, in a jokey announcer's voice. He clinked her glass with his. "To reconnecting."

She smiled at him and then at me. "To reconnecting."

Miles turned to clink his glass against the one in my hand. "You never forget your first love," he said to me, briefly fixing his light green eyes on mine before glancing back at Peck. "You two should stay for dinner. I've got a few people coming over and my houseguests will be arriving any minute now."

He spoke as casually as he could, but he seemed to really want her to stay. I got the sense that he'd given some thought to both his words and his delivery, as though he'd been waiting for this moment.

"We're on our way somewhere," Peck said quickly. "In fact, we have to go, Stella. We're going to be late."

"You can stay," I told Peck. "I'll pick you up later."

"My driver can take you home," Miles added.

Peck shook her head. "Nope. We made a commitment."

"Let me guess," Miles teased jealously. "You have to meet your friend Nacho?"

For a brief second I thought Peck might have forgotten her earlier explanation for our presence at the helipad, but she caught herself in time. "Girls like us book up early," she replied. "And we don't play social opportunist."

"Well, how about tomorrow night then?" he asked. "A casual barbecue here, a few friends. Some of them I think you know."

"Who?" she asked sharply. "Whom do I know?"

He smiled. "Marni and Gordon Little?"

"Marni Flock?" Peck looked incredulous. "I knew her back in the day. We used to see each other on auditions. She's *married?*"

He looked pleased that he could offer enticement in the form of a mutual friend to get her to say yes. "She said she was excited to see you."

Peck made a bitchy face. "I'll bet she was, if she's got a ring on her bony finger. She was always so competitive. Anyway, we've got a few things tomorrow night." She looked over at me. "But maybe we can stop by."

"Come early," he said, smiling lazily at her. When he looked at her that way, I could see it, whatever it was that had grabbed hold of her so many years ago. "Before your other stuff," he added as an afterthought, as though it didn't matter whether the "things" she had were real or not, as though whatever they were, they weren't nearly as sexy as what he was offering. "We're going to catch the sunset."

He walked us out to Lydia's ancient station wagon. Just as Peck was about to get into the car, he pulled her toward him, put both hands on her face, and kissed her on the lips. I slid into the passenger seat to give them a little privacy.

The combination of the kiss and the notion that the missing painting might be the thing of utmost value Lydia mentioned in her will—a Jackson Pollock—launched Peck into a state of such overt excitement she could hardly drive. The transformation from her earlier haughtiness to this subsequent giddiness was almost alarming, and I offered to take the wheel. She couldn't stop talking, interrupting herself with giggles as we sailed along the back roads, past the farm stands with their homemade pies and the neatly groomed horse farms.

"Biggsy must not have known at first," I said, getting caught up in the excitement. "Or he probably would have taken it before we got here. It was only when we mentioned the thing of utmost value that he would have started trying to figure out what it was."

"And that was right before the party," Peck reminded me, almost bouncing in her seat.

"Once he figured it out, he must have planned to take it, knowing there'd be a hundred potential suspects in the house that night," I said, thinking aloud. When we were standing in front of the Pollock at Miles's house I hadn't been immediately inclined to go along with Peck's theory. It seemed so far-fetched. But she was one of the most persuasive people I'd ever met, and by the time we were almost home I was almost convinced we must have inherited a piece of American art history.

"And then I, idiotically, helped him out by assuming it was Miles," Peck added, shaking her head. "All he had to do was suggest that I was right and off I went. He must have been *thrilled*." She pulled into our street. "It's not the money I'm thinking of," she added in that grand manner people have of revealing exactly what they're thinking by stating what it is that they are *not* thinking. "It's the idea that this could be an undocumented Jackson Pollock. Think of what that would mean."

When we pulled into our driveway, Biggsy's motorcycle was not in its usual spot next to the garage. "Thank God," Peck exclaimed. "I have no idea what to say to him."

"Nothing for now," I said. "Let's find out more before we do or say anything. Let him think we're still enamored of him."

She'd stopped the car in front of the house and now she looked over at me. "You're more sly than you let on."

I grinned at her. "I suppose I am."

She gestured with her chin through the windshield at the crooked little house, bathed in the purple-pinkish glow of the setting sun. In that light, the house was at its most fetching: the shabby could be seen as chic, and the peeling paint and the splintered wood were less evident. The hydrangeas were in full midsummer bloom, plump in their lavender and blue, and on the second floor one of the two small windows had its shade pulled, so it looked like the house was winking at us.

"I love this house so fucking much," Peck said. It sounded like an accusation. "This is, *literally*, my favorite place on this earth. They'll have to carry me out of here in a wooden box. Like they did Lydia."

"Lydia died in Paris," I reminded her as I got out of the car and swung the door shut behind me, leaving her there in the driver's seat, gazing up at the house. In the morning Laurie Poplin was bringing her clients to look at the house, and I understood what Peck was trying to express. But selling Fool's House was a decision about which we did not seem to have a choice. I didn't want to sell it either. I was loving the feeling I had there of being connected to my aunt and, indirectly, to my father and the rest of the family Peck and I had never known. I loved the feeling of legacy and tradition, and I loved the light in the garden and the ocean air and reading on the porch. But we could not afford to keep the house. I hated being thrust in the role of the practical one.

As I walked slowly toward the house, lost in thought, I tripped and fell backward, my feet pulled completely out from under me. I landed awkwardly, smacking my wrist to the gravel, and then the back of my head. The wind was knocked out of me and I lay there as pain shot up my arm. I noticed a few swift-moving clouds passing as I looked up, stunned.

Then Biggsy was above me. "I'm so sorry. I don't know how that happened. I just—" I caught the slightest note of insincerity in his voice but I couldn't breathe, let alone formulate a response. "Are you okay?" he was saying, doing a very good imitation of looking worried, when I got some air into my lungs and could sit up slightly.

Peck ran from the car doing her best Brando. "STELLAAAH!"

"Can you hear me?" Biggsy kept saying, but I couldn't answer him. I couldn't talk, although I was able to take another shallow breath. I smelled his patchouli scent.

"What did you do to her?" Peck roared at him, fierce as a mother lion. It made me smile, and they both noticed. "Oh, look, she's fine," she said, kneeling down next to me. "You're *fine*, right, Stella?"

"You're okay?" Biggsy said, his voice dripping with concern. He had on long board shorts with a buttoned-up dress shirt and the top hat he liked to wear, but from my point of view, on the ground in pain, he'd lost the quirkiness that had made him likeable and easy to envision inviting into one's home. Now I was certain he'd stolen the painting. And I suspected he'd tripped me on purpose.

"I'm really sorry," he said, as though I'd spoken my thoughts. "It was this cable." He held up the cord that had pulled my feet out from under me as I walked. "I'm shooting some footage for a piece. I was plugged into the garage and I pulled the camera out into the lawn."

His eyes darted nervously in my direction, his amiable façade starting to crack, as though something rotten inside were going to begin oozing out.

"I don't believe you," I said to him. "I don't think we can believe anything you say."

He looked shocked, and there was an undertone of anger in his voice when he spoke. "What are you talking about? I would never hurt you guys. You're like my family."

I took the advice I'd given Peck earlier not to say anything further just then, and I assured them both I was fine as they helped me up onto the porch.

10

My second Saturday at Fool's House brought an East End morning so crisp it could wipe your brain clean. My wrist was still sore and there was a bump on the back of my head, but Peck was right about ocean air curing what ails. Only a few tiny puffs of cloud danced across the blue sky as I took Trimalchio past the tall privet hedges and down to the most gorgeously wide-open stretch of pale sand that was usually unpopulated in the earlier hours of the day. We went for a long walk and by the end of it I felt completely fine. When we returned to Fool's House, Peck was sitting on the front steps with three of the Girls, Lucy, Betts, and the one whose name was not Sandra but Sasha. They were waiting for me.

"It's an intervention," Peck called out, waving as we came up the driveway. "The Fashioninas are here." The three of them had the manners to look slightly sheepish as my sister explained that they were there to help with the *situation*. The situation, apparently, was me.

"It's a *fashion* intervention," Lucy offered with an apologetic shrug, as though the circumstances needed clarification. Lucy is one of those women who are always wearing *exactly* what you wished you were wearing, if only you owned it. Today it was a perfect little dress, just simple white cotton, but she'd paired it with a chunky beaded necklace and great shoes, and she looked fantastic. "Not an intervention, just . . . we want to help. Helpful suggestions. Don't call it an intervention, Peck. It sounds so drastic."

"It *is* drastic," Peck said with a laugh.

"We're here to take you shopping," Betts added. She was more casually dressed, in long white shorts and a tank top but with cool sandals and a delicate gold chain around her neck. Her clothes flattered her muscled body and she also looked exactly how you might hope to look on a beautiful summer day. Sasha too, in fitted white jeans and a sleeveless navy top that highlighted slim arms, was chic and simply right. "And to lunch," she added softly. "It's just meant to be fun."

I was suddenly conscious of what I'd thrown on for the walk— now-sweaty gym shorts and the old T-shirt that said MAJORCA across the front in faded letters. I'd never been all that interested in clothes, though I had moments like every woman when I hated everything in my closet. But I'd been so busy at work—we were a lean staff of expats, and we put in long hours at the magazine— and then taking a class in the evening and trying to make time to write on my own that I never really gave it much thought.

"It's time, Stella. You're a late bloomer, we know that, but you've done it. You've arrived. And . . ." Peck paused for dramatic effect, gesturing at her friends. "You need a new wardrobe." She herself looked like a fifties housewife gone wild in a vintage floral-print dress she'd paired with boots, a denim vest, and dark glasses covering her eyes. Somehow it worked. She had that gift. "And it's totally on me," she added. "So don't freak out. You already wore the only thing I own that would fit you and you can't go to Miles Noble's barbecue in that one old hippie dress you brought with you."

"I wasn't planning on going," I said. "I don't want to be the third wheel again."

She glared at me. "You're *going*. I need you to go with me. But not looking like that."

"Why don't we take a peek at your closet," Lucy suggested, in the gentle tone of a legal mediator. She spoke like Peck, in the perfectly enunciated syllables of well-traveled American girls who spent semesters abroad. "That's usually a good place to start."

"I'm living out of a suitcase," I protested. "It's okay. Really. I appreciate the thought. But there's no need—we're showing the house today. And I don't—"

"Come on," Betts interjected in a soothing voice. "It'll be fun. We can go to the Sip 'n Soda for a cheeseburger first."

Peck stood and dusted off the back of her dress. "I won't take no for an answer," she told me. "Let's buy at least one dress for you to wear tonight. Something very chic and beachy, nothing too-too."

We all traipsed upstairs to the bedroom where the clothes I'd brought with me were hanging forlornly in the closet. "See," Peck exclaimed, quickly rifling through the hangers. "Nothing."

Lucy nodded her approval. "I have the perfect thing in mind," she said. "Pale green chiffon, but not mother-of-the-bride. Just pretty and casual. It will go great with your eyes."

They all murmured in assent. "Pale green is perfect for you," Sasha said to me in an encouraging voice, as though pale green were something one needed to be smooth-talked into accepting.

"And shoes," Peck added. "Shoes are key."

It was decided that the Girls would go ahead to town and Peck and I would meet them once I'd had a chance to shower, leaving the house empty for Laurie to show. But I was still drying off when Peck came bounding back into my room without knocking. "There's a bit of a *situation*," she announced.

I assumed she was talking again about the old pair of brown wedge sandals I always wore with my Levi's. Or maybe it was the

Levi's, faded over years of washing and sagging at the knees, but so comfortable. But she was referring to something going on outside and told me to get dressed quickly.

It was a *situation* all right. In our front yard was a presumably straight American man in his late fifties, with the requisite paunch and gray hair brushed conservatively over a balding spot, wearing a coral cashmere sweater and trousers the bright orange-pink color of a flamingo. His wife wore cashmere too. Hers was camel and it matched, exactly, her camel trousers. She had a blonde helmet, held firmly in place with at least a can of environmentally irresponsible hairspray and gold "daytime" earrings.

The cashmere couple was with Laurie Poplin on the muddy stretch of lawn that separated the tennis court from the driveway, and they all appeared to be yelling at Biggsy. The Fool-in-Residence had a rusty ball machine out on the far end of the court and it was now firing tennis balls at a mad rate in every direction, including at the visitors on the lawn. He was attempting to stop the machine by kicking it. His strategy was not working. But that didn't keep him from continuing to pretend, gently pushing at the wayward appliance with his feet, encased in flimsy canvas sneakers. He had on a tennis sweater with navy and maroon stripes at the V-neck and the sort of white trousers Bill Tilden would have sported at Wimbledon. He looked to be trying to contain his laughter.

There were round patches of dirt on the knees of Mrs. Cashmere's neatly pressed camel trousers and she did not look pleased. In fact, she looked like she wanted to smack someone.

"He angled the thing right at her wide camel ass," Peck informed me in a hushed voice as I headed down the porch steps with her. She too seemed hardly able to contain her laughter. "And, oh God, did he make contact. Right in the sweet spot. It wasn't pretty."

"He did it on purpose?" I asked. It suddenly occurred to me that this fellow in our midst could be more dangerous than we thought.

"Of course not," she said to me, with a grin. Her hair glinted in the sunlight as she hunched over slightly to keep herself from breaking into a laughing fit. "That machine is an antique. It's obviously broken."

Tennis balls were shooting everywhere—with good speed; he must have set the thing on "fast"—as Coral Cashmere continued to lace into Biggsy. Laurie threw in a few choices words of her own as well. We heard "irresponsible" and "unacceptable" and "could have lost an eye."

"I don't know how you lose an eye on your ass," Peck pointed out in a whisper as we drew closer. "But that guy's ugly mad."

Biggsy had managed to turn the ball machine off, probably just by turning the switch. I didn't believe for a second that the machine was faulty. Neither did the man in coral cashmere, and he continued to berate the artist. Biggsy came up off the tennis court with his racquet in his hand as we approached the unhappy threesome on the patchy lawn. There was a strange gleam in his eye and, he suddenly called to mind guys I'd met before, that global breed of tortured artistic souls, so desperate to separate themselves from the rest of us. I'd seen them in the parks in Zurich where heroin needles littered the ground, lurking about galleries in Berlin wearing pencil-leg pants, and on trains in Austria with Eurail passes and an attitude. They survived, somehow, feeding off others, without shame or the compulsion to achieve. He was one of them, I could see now; only his extreme good looks and cultivated oddballness made him stand apart.

Biggsy apologized, swearing he had no idea what had happened to the ball machine. He wore a look of false sincerity as he hunched his shoulders up around his ears in his best version of a suitably humbled and embarrassed accident-causer. He was a good performer, so his attempt at looking contrite appeared authentic enough. I could see the man in the coral sweater wanting to believe he was telling the truth. But the charms of Fool's House appeared to be eluding the couple, as they stared up at our rickety little place with obvious distaste.

Laurie followed them into the house, gushing about a genius architect by the name of Finn Killian to whom she would recommend they speak about a possible renovation. "He would know exactly how to retain the old Southampton charm of this place while giving you the modern conveniences you need." She spoke about him in a proprietary fashion I didn't care for, and I wondered, for about the thousandth time, if Finn could possibly be involved with her.

Laurie made it sound as though she and Finn were a couple, which irritated me far more than it should have. She also made it sound like he was more talented than God, but even the promise of such a divine connection didn't appear to be enough to win over the couple who would thereafter be known as the Cashmeres. They went back out to their car, a Volvo with a Princeton sticker on the back. Biggsy's plan to annoy and disturb had worked.

"Not to worry," our real estate broker said as they pulled off. "Laurie Poplin is on this. But next time, make sure your houseguest stays out of the way."

"He's not a houseguest," Peck explained patiently. "He's the Fool-in-Residence. You need to understand the difference, if you're to understand this house. We have an artistic legacy to preserve. We can't dump the house on just anyone who comes along."

"Peck, we're not exactly in a position to be selective," I pointed out. "Last I looked nobody was lining up to hand us a check."

Laurie nodded, like she was taking it all in. "A house out here is an identity. Most buyers have yearned for this for a long time. There's almost an expectation that they *deserve* it. But it has to be the right kind of place. A house that reflects how seriously they take themselves. That couple? They're not interested in artistic legacy. But someone else will be. And Laurie Poplin will find that someone for you."

Before we headed into town to meet the Girls we told Biggsy to clean up the tennis balls.

"Any more of these *situations* and my baby sister's going to kick you the hell out of here on your ass," Peck called down to the tennis court, where he was bouncing one of the balls on an old wooden racquet.

The hedgerow was a blur of green as Peck sped into town. "We're going to have to ask him to leave," I said, gripping the armrest as we took the turn around the pond a lot faster than seemed safe.

Peck glanced over at my white-knuckled grip and made a face. "We can't let him go until we get the painting back. What if it really is a Jackson Pollock?"

Our research the night before had proved inconclusive. We'd Googled images of Jackson Pollock's work when we got home from Miles's house and compared them to the painting in the background of the photograph Finn had given me. There certainly seemed to be a resemblance between some of them, but it was hard to tell anything more than that.

"I'm not so sure," I said, repeating my words of the previous night.

"If we can sell it we might be able to keep Fool's House," she mused thoughtfully.

"Lydia never expected us to keep Fool's House," I reminded her.

"Lydia never expected to die when she did either," she said softly, which quieted us both into contemplation until we reached town.

The parking lot behind picturesque Main Street, with its policemen ready to give tickets at the slightest infraction, was almost full, but we found a spot and pulled in next to an enormous man who glared at us from behind the wheel of what looked like a toy car.

"Don't tell the girls about the painting," Peck said as we strolled through town.

I was surprised at this. She was one of the earliest Twitter users, the type of person who would tell her friends, and anyone else who would listen, every detail of her life. "Why not?"

"We shouldn't speak about an ongoing investigation," she said, only half joking. "And they're always so opinionated."

We spent the rest of the day wrapped in a warm blanket of gossip, laughter, and fashion. I'd been sorely missing the group of friends I'd left behind in Lausanne—we'd been e-mailing back and forth, which wasn't the same—but the Girls were very good company and Peck was at her imperious best. I never realized how much I would love having a sister. We had cheeseburgers and onion rings at the luncheonette and Peck ordered a lime rickey. I tried a root beer float for the first time in years. "Remember how you used to be obsessed with that stuff?" Peck cried out before turning to the others to explain. "When we were little we'd come out to stay at Fool's House, and the first thing she'd do when she got there was go to the fridge and get herself a can of root beer. Lydia bought it by the case and she'd guzzle it down all day long. Never gained a pound either, which really pissed me off."

I grinned at her, enjoying the memory. "Then you made me drink a real beer and I lost my taste for it."

"I should hope so. You were, like, twenty."

"I was fifteen," I pointed out.

"Exactly my point," she said. "You were far too old not to know how to drink."

Real estate was, as usual, a major topic of conversation. The Girls, none of whom actually owned any real estate, had opinions about it nonetheless, which they were more than willing to share at high volume. Apparently they had opinions about me as well, and Peck presented their thoughts as a collective conclusion, as in "The Girls agree with me that you should move to the city."

"Everyone should live in New York at least once," Sasha said, nodding at me.

"We know *everyone* in the magazine business," Lucy exclaimed. "We can easily get you a job."

"Once you live in New York," Betts added, "you'll never live anywhere else."

"That's what happens to us New Yorkers," Lucy said, scraping clean a bowl that had contained a triple order of fresh peach ice cream. "We can't move. That's why we're all single."

"It's true," Sasha added. "I let the love of my life leave because he moved to Düsseldorf."

"And how about me with Miles?" Peck chimed in. "I let him go off to Hong Kong. He broke my heart clean in two."

Betts waved her spoon in my direction. "Shut up, all of you, you're scaring her. Now she'll never want to come, or she might end up like us. We're spinsters. All we care about is our careers and each other."

"She's not single, she's a divorcée." Peck could never say the word without the French accent, just as she could never refer to a Target store as anything but *Tar-jay*.

Betts shook her head. "Divorcées are leathery blondes on bar stools sucking down Absolut Bay Breezes. We're all simply single. As in free."

"I'm single and *happy* that way," I clarified.

"We are too," Sasha said, nodding in approval. "We don't rely on *men* for happiness. Your girlfriends become your family."

"God, listen to you. I'm going to throw up," Peck interjected. "Besides, Stella's gone on a couple of dates with Finn."

"One date," I said. "More of a business dinner."

"I thought he was seeing that tall woman." Lucy looked to the others for confirmation. "The former Rockette we met at Christian's party?" She glanced at me and must have caught the alarmed look on my face. "Sorry. I didn't mean that the way it sounded. It's probably not even true."

"No, it probably is," I said. "It's okay. I couldn't be less interested. He's not my type, anyway."

Peck was staring at me. "Well, you're *his* type."

"You're everybody's type," Sasha said, patting my hand. "Smart, funny, *natural*. Forget about him."

I did try—Finn who?—as we made our way down Main Street to deal with the fashion situation. But I couldn't get the image of him out of my mind, first imagining I saw him on the corner, when we waited for the light to change, and then again across the street.

"Lucy's the ultimate *Fashionina*," Peck said more than once as we headed into one of the boutiques lining Main Street. Whatever she was, Lucy was good at it. The pale green chiffon dress she'd found was pretty and perfect and they found another dress for me that I also really liked. The second dress was black and too expensive, but it fit like it'd been made for me and I figured it was practical, as I could wear it anywhere. When I went to pay, Peck intervened.

"No, no," she insisted, waving away my wallet. "This is on me."

"I have money," I said. I didn't make much at the magazine but I hadn't bought clothes in a long time. I took out my credit card.

"Listen to her, Miss Moneybags," Peck cried out. "I want to buy this for you. It's a *present*."

The Girls were watching us. "You don't have to buy me a present," I said, trying to keep my voice low.

"But I want to," she said, making no effort to keep her own voice down. "It's what big sisters do." She grabbed the pile on the counter, adding a beautiful subdued yellow dress she'd picked out for herself to wear that night, and thrust it at the saleswoman with her credit card. "Besides, when we sell our Jackson Pollock we'll be rolling in it, Stella." She whispered this last statement so the others wouldn't hear her.

11

"Hey," Miles called out to the group that was already gathered on what he called the observation deck, on the third floor of his house. "This is Pecksland Moriarty. The actress," he said, appealing to her vanity. "And her sister, Cassie," he added, gesturing at me. "From Switzerland."

"I didn't know *you* knew Miles Noble," one of the women cried out to Peck. She couldn't have weighed more than ninety pounds, and she had on her tiny elfin hand a diamond so big it looked like she could hardly lift it to wave at us. She had ironed hair that looked like a wig, extensively highlighted with honey tones, and she was almost but not quite pretty in a carefully cultivated way.

Miles grabbed Peck around the waist. "She knew me before I was Miles Noble." He seemed to want to present her in a certain light, as though he wanted to convince her and the others that she was special to him. Something in the way he pulled her toward him made me certain the invitation to his Gatsby party had not actually been the casual result of a thorough event-planning team.

"We were college sweethearts," he was saying. "Well, *she* was in college. At NYU. I was poor and struggling, trying to make my way in the world. When she left me, I was such a mess I had to go all the way to the Far East."

Peck made no attempt to correct this version of things. In fact, I could see her revising her own story on the spot. "Marni," she cried out. "I heard you were going to be here. Miles said you were excited to see me."

Marni looked startled to be reminded that Miles had told her Peck would be there, while a red-haired guy in a red shirt, whose name I was told was Ollie, bowed comically in my direction.

"I thought your name was Stella," he sang out. "I met you at the Gatsby party. I was the one in the white dinner jacket." He laughed at himself. He vaguely resembled Conan O'Brien. "This is my wife, Heather. We don't live here. We're permanent houseguests."

His bottom-heavy wife sat in a lotus position on one of the director's chairs positioned around the teak deck and she didn't move to greet us as she spoke. "As long as you bring a nice gift and send flowers and a note afterward, you could spend the whole summer houseguesting."

"But you must handwrite the note," Ollie continued, holding up one hand like he was writing in the air. He had the air of an entertainer who knows he is expected to sing for his supper. "You can't let the girl in the flower shop scribble something. And wine is always appreciated. We're fond of the full bagel and smoked salmon breakfast from Russ and Daughters, aren't we, honey?"

"I'm writing a book," Heather announced airily to nobody in particular. "*Houseguesting in the Hamptons.*"

Miles had helped himself to two of the canapés on a tray and held them out to us. He introduced us to a few of the others—Marni was apparently the very recent third wife, as he whispered bitchily to us, of an older man who grunted at us—but not to three women clustered off to one side in cocktail dresses and inordinately high heels who looked like they'd wandered in from another party. The woman who'd ridden the helicopter with Miles was not among them.

"They have four kids," Miles said of the houseguesting couple, through a mouthful of caviar on a slice of potato. He accidentally dribbled some of the caviar onto his shirt and then scraped it up with his finger and popped it into his mouth, leaving a little grease spot. He tossed three more of them into his mouth in quick succession.

Ollie looked up from his BlackBerry. "Four kids, four dogs, four nannies."

"Four is the new three," his wife added.

"I thought everyone was having five now," Peck tossed out, which didn't seem to please Ollie's wife at all. Clearly four children was an accomplishment. Having four children trumped couples with three or two and especially oddballs with just an "only." Four was status. Or it was, until all those damn people started having five.

Marni chimed in with "I have two stepchildren," but that didn't seem to count to Heather Bosley, because she turned her back and didn't respond.

"He's a major art collector," Miles informed us about Marni's husband, Gordon, the grunter who had lifted a weak hand in greeting. One didn't get the sense that charm was the reason Marni had married him. He appeared seasick, slumped in his seat with one hand on his stomach. Marriage obviously agreed with him.

"We're the newlyweds," Marni explained while her new husband, jowly with a beefy belly, rubbed his concave chest. He looked surprisingly morose for someone who'd just tied the knot and was, theoretically, still on his honeymoon.

"You should see his Pollocks," Miles added.

"And books," the older man said, shrugging his shoulders. "First editions."

"I keep trying to tell him he should collect jewelry!" Marni tossed out, laughing at herself. She was the only one. "But he doesn't listen to me. Is that my fate as a married woman? Everyone keeps telling me husbands don't listen to their wives."

Her husband ignored her. He seemed to be regretting the rash decision that had led him to leave his second wife—of fourteen years, I would later learn from Peck—for this much younger woman.

"Ask him about *your* painting," Miles prompted Peck. "He knows a lot about Jackson Pollock. He's the one who told me to buy mine."

"Weren't you looking to buy another one?" Gordon Little asked Miles. He spoke in a monotone. "I heard you've been sniffing around."

Miles held up a finger to shush him. "Don't say that in front of these two. They thought I stole one from them."

Gordon stared at him as though he wasn't sure if he was supposed to believe Miles wasn't the thief. "We weren't going to tell anyone about that," Peck told him in a dramatic stage whisper that made Gordon perk up with interest.

"About what?" he asked Peck.

She sighed, as though her hand were being forced, and then went on to explain about the house we'd inherited and the now-missing painting inscribed "For L.M. From J.P." on the back, leaving out the part where she had suspected Miles of taking it the night of the party.

"It's unauthenticated?" Gordon asked, sounding slightly more interested. "Not signed, obviously?"

"Except for his initials on the back," Peck was quick to add.

He pursed his lips together and looked at Miles. "You think it's an early one? Like yours?"

"I never saw it," Miles said, his interest picking up. "But it could be, couldn't it?

"Do you have that picture with you?" Peck looked at me but I hadn't brought the photo of Lydia and the painting with me. "The only image we have shows the painting in the background. It was there above the mantel for as long as I can remember."

"You think your aunt *knew* Jackson Pollock?" Gordon asked us.

I shook my head. "That part doesn't make sense. She would have been a child when he died."

He went on to ask a lot of questions about Lydia and her art collection in his disgruntled fashion while the others gossiped and Ollie leaned over to engage me in our own conversation. He asked the question that always drove all the Europeans into fits. "What do you do?" That-Awful-Jean-Paul in particular always used to complain about it, perhaps because he'd never had a suitable answer.

I told him I was writing a novel—there was no need to mention that I'd been starting this book since I finished college and it currently existed only in the notes I'd been jotting down that summer—and he went on to reveal, eagerly and apropos of nothing, that he'd gone to Harvard.

The three women off to the side never sat with us or greeted us as the sun set. They stood together as the rest of us chatted, and then, as if on cue, they all filed up and kissed Miles on each cheek, one after the other, saying good-bye. "Behave," he yelled after them as they clomped down the steps in their very high statement shoes.

Peck was still talking about Jackson Pollock and our missing painting with Gordon Little. "I'll check in with some dealers too," he offered as his wife listened carefully, eyes darting between Peck and her husband, who seemed to be directing his words at Peck's *twins.* "If there's a possible Jackson Pollock out there, I'm sure someone will know about it."

Ollie said, for my ears only, "I studied art history at Harvard."

Marni did not seem at all pleased that her husband was expressing so much interest in our painting, but it was time to eat and

Miles and the unpleasant blond butler ushered us down the two flights of stairs. Dinner was served by a whole slew of black-clad waiters—all men, all very young and all very, very good-looking, as though a casting agent had been involved. "Eye candy," Marni declared them as we made our way onto the wide patio at the back of the house. "Like you, honey," she said to her portly husband. You're *my* eye candy." He seemed to believe that she found him pleasing to the eye as he nodded in agreement.

We were warmed by four standing heaters, the kind I'd only ever seen at outdoor restaurants, and we were individually offered cashmere blankets in assorted colors that hung over the back of our chairs to fight the slight summer chill.

Peck, whether because she was simply doing what came naturally to her, or because she sensed she was *auditioning*, took on the role of the cohost, helping Miles direct his guests to their seats, making sure that the wine was served, and suggesting the good-looking men offer the choice of both flat and sparkling water. She encouraged Miles to dim the two enormous lanterns filled with lightbulbs that hung off the back of the house and cast the terrace in too-bright near-daylight and asked the blond butler to bring out more candles.

Miles looked enthralled by her involvement. "I told you, lots and lots of candles," he called out after the man hurrying into the house.

We were all sitting by then, and we pulled the blankets around our shoulders and started the first course, smoked salmon with caviar and sour cream on potato pancake as big as Frisbees.

Heather, mother of four, an identity she continually tossed into the conversation, much the way her husband seemed fond of adding a dash of *Harvard*, was suddenly chatty. She used the word *heinous* often, and incorrectly, about a dress on someone named Serena, about the breath on a bond salesman she'd been forced to talk to, and about the night of sleep she'd gotten without the benefit of the white noise machine she relied on. She was an expert on everything, it seemed. Most especially she was a parenting know-it-all. As none of the rest of us except Gordon and his grown-up kids had any children, it seemed an odd conversational tack. And yet on she went, offering her opinion about bedtimes, mealtimes, and naptimes and getting into the best nursery schools. "It was brutal this year, especially for boys," she informed us, as though we'd been requesting the inside scoop. In particular she was fanatical, she said, about *reading*. "You have to read to them from the instant they come out of the womb. And then you have to continue to do it every night."

On this, I agreed. But nobody else could get in a word. Miles ignored her, carrying on his own conversation with Gordon, while the rest of us learned about something called Ferberizing, which seemed to involve letting a baby cry him- or herself to sleep or something equally depressing.

Gordon was sitting next to me, glumly picking at a hard roll. "So, what kind of books do you collect?" I asked him when Miles turned his attention back to Peck, and Marni was telling the others they were shopping for a new house. Gordon had seemed to droop visibly at the idea of spending money—"I mean, has anyone *looked* at the Dow lately?" I heard someone saying—but as I expected, the question about the books invigorated him noticeably. He tilted his head, as though he were about to tell me something in confidence. "Mostly I buy first editions of novels I've enjoyed reading." He spoke softly so I had to lean in to hear him. "I have a first edition of *To Kill a Mockingbird*: that's probably my most valuable piece. I have an inscribed *Catch-22*. A whole series of Agatha Christies. I like detective novels—those are fun to own."

His whole demeanor shifted when he talked about his books. I got the sense he enjoyed this version of himself, the sort of quirky intellectual who might troll antiquarian book fairs looking for treasures for his bookshelf, rather than the version Marni seemed interested in promoting, the rich man with his toys.

"Is there one book you wish you could own?" I asked him.

He nodded, accustomed to the question. "A first-edition *Great Gatsby*. Signed. With a dust jacket. That's the holy grail of book collecting, in my mind."

I thought of the hardcover I'd found at Fool's House. It wasn't signed but it had a dust jacket, and I'd wondered about it, having heard somewhere that such details were important to collectors of books. "Is that hard to find?"

"Almost impossible," he said with a grin that indicated he knew the market for such things very well. "It would cost in the neighborhood of a hundred grand or more. That's if you can get one. They just don't come up." He went on to tell me about the mistakes that would indicate a first-edition *Gatsby* to a rare books dealer or collector. "The mistakes get corrected in later editions. That's why they're important. And a dust jacket, that's extremely rare. The first-edition game is all about the dust jackets." He was getting himself all worked up, saliva gathering in the corners of his mouth. I wondered if he'd ever discussed *The Great Gatsby* with his new wife. "In 1925, when the book was published, dust jackets were simply wrapping paper. They were tossed in the garbage when the person received the book. There was a mistake on the original dust jacket, a lowercase *j* where it should have been uppercase. That's one of the things that would mark something as a first edition." I made a mental note to check Lydia's copy of *Gatsby* I'd been reading.

The smoked salmon was followed by thick grilled steaks with vegetables and risotto with truffle oil and French fries. Even the competitively thin Marni, who apparently never ate—"I never eat!" she exclaimed more than once—popped a few fries in her mouth.

Peck ate as she always did, with gusto, and I followed her lead. That-Awful-Jean-Paul had turned out to be fussy about food, a bait and switch that took me entirely by surprise after a whirlwind courtship during which he professed to be a foodie and took me to some terrific restaurants. Then, after we were married, he allowed me to see the real him, a neurotic eater with incessant stomach ailments—ulcers, intestinal diseases, and fictional-sounding diagnoses that grew increasingly closer to cancer the more he repeated them—who hated to spend money on restaurant food.

Marni was on my other side, and when Gordon turned back to Miles I asked his new wife if they lived nearby. That seemed to be her cue to tell me all about her newly acquired stuff—the house "down the road" they were going to sell for a better house with water views, a place on the Intercoastal in Palm Beach, an apartment overlooking Central Park, the plane, a boat, even the new watch her husband had just bought her that afternoon, which she extended a skinny wrist to display.

I heard Finn Killian's name from the other side of me, in a conversation between Miles and Ollie, and I strained to hear what they were saying about him. From what I could glean, Miles was advising Ollie, the Harvarditis victim, on how to deal with architects. "No architects," Ollie kept repeating. "No work. If we buy anything, it will be ready to move into and cheap."

"Don't you say that word," his wife teased. "Cheap is not in my vocabulary."

"Oh God," Marni squealed. She seemed to be getting drunk, although I hadn't seen anything pass her lips other than the few French fries and a sip or two of water. "Me too. Don't utter that word in my presence!"

"Just buy her a house," Miles said to Heather's husband. "Buy her anything she wants. It's cheaper than divorce. Take your lessons from Gordon."

Heather flashed him an uncertain smile and Marni made a face. It was hard to tell if Miles was kidding.

"I don't want anything fancy," Heather continued defensively. "A country house," she clarified. As in "We desperately *need* a country house." They wanted something with *charm*, she went on to explain, as if charm were a totally unique and esoteric thing to want, as if they were the only people ever to use that word, as if nobody out here knew what she knew about the subject. They wanted a place that would reflect who they were as a family. A farmhouse or something like that, she said. It didn't have to be big; Heather didn't want to lose her kids, as she apparently kept doing in Miles Noble's palace. And no pool; she wanted to be able to sleep and not worry that one of them was going to drown. But it had to have *charm*. "I'm a deeply creative person," she said earnestly. "I have to be inspired by my environment."

Her husband kept insisting they were simple people; they just wanted to be home with their kids and not participate in the social scene. They weren't trying to make new friends, since they didn't even have time to see the ones they had. And they weren't trying to make a statement, like *some* people. He seemed convinced. "We don't need his and hers marble bidets and a screening room—"

"—of course we don't. We can come here when we want to see a movie," his wife interjected. "Right, Miles?"

A joint was making the rounds. Heather took a deep drag and tried to launch a discussion about kids and drugs. "You have to talk to them about pot."

"Sure, you do," Ollie called out. "They have all the best sources."

"I have a house for you." Up to that point I hadn't talked much except to ask questions of the Littles on either side of me, and they all stopped to listen. "We're selling exactly the house you just described."

I must have done a pretty good job talking them into Fool's House, a place that was all about creativity and *charm*, as I told them, because by the time dessert was served—individual chocolate soufflés with enormous dollops of fresh whipped cream—they were practically ready to make me an offer. I described the supposedly famous creative energy of the place, the light on the lawn, the crumbling tennis court, and, of course, the gregarious porch. "It's not just any house, Fool's House," I heard myself saying. "Not just a structure with rooms in which to sleep and bathe, but a lifestyle, an identity, a destination."

They ate it up. It was a strange feeling, to be in possession of something to sell. I'd never thought of myself as a salesperson. At the magazine, the editorial team and the sales staff were kept totally separate, and the sales people always seemed so *other* to me. But that night, I enjoyed the experience, spinning a tale I knew they wanted to hear. It wasn't difficult to make Fool's House sound appealing. I'd grown to love the place.

"My sister fancies herself a writer," Peck called out to them in warning. "She tends to *embellish*." But she didn't seem to mind the sales angle and even added in a bit about Lydia's ghost and the unfinished backgammon game we'd returned to the porch to find played to an end.

"When can we come see it?" Harvarditis wanted to know.

"Maybe *we* should look at it," Marni added. "We need a new house."

Heather glared at her as her husband seemed to grow nervous at the thought of buying a house. "I don't know," he muttered. "Is this a time to buy? Or should we rent? What do you think, Miles? You seem to have the Midas touch."

The whole table of people looked to Miles for a decree on the economy. Miles propped his feet on the table, taking a deep drag of the joint. He seemed used to being asked the question. He was a rich man, after all, the sort of alpha male who was in the habit of giving his opinion. "Don't think you're going to steal their house on the cheap. Real estate out here is gold. I had an offer on this place just the other day that would make your ass squinch."

This made Harvarditis laugh so hard he kept gasping for breath and banging on the table. He laughed for what seemed like hours, and eventually the dessert wine was finished, after-dinner cigarettes had been smoked, and it was time to go home. We all got up at the same time and headed into the house.

Peck pulled me aside as we stepped through the door, allowing the others to move on to the front of the house without us. "I've made a *decision*," she whispered urgently. "I'm going to *stay*."

"Maybe you shouldn't rush into anything," I suggested. "I thought you were never going to fall in love again."

"I'm not talking about falling in *love*," she said with a coy smile. "I have no intention of doing that again. But at the same time, you can't fight destiny. I'm talking about *marriage*."

"Marriage?" I repeated, somewhat incredulously. "Why all of a sudden are you, of all people, interested in *marriage*?"

"What does that mean, *me, of all people*? I never said I didn't want to get married. That was *you*." Her voice had gotten louder, like she wasn't afraid of anyone overhearing her. "Anyway, I've called Finn to pick you up."

"You did what?" I stared at her. "I don't need Finn to pick me up. He's not a chauffeur."

"He was out here anyway, at a client's house for dinner just down the road," she was quick to say. And then she launched into one of her observations, intended to distract me from what she'd done. "People are always having him for dinner. He's what's known as the extra man. He's tall, he went to Princeton, he has a job. That's enough to get a guy in this town invited anywhere. It's one of the great injustices of our social system." She paused and then added, with a mischievous smile, "I wanted him to see you in that dress."

"You're crazy." I was half dismayed and actually half pleased that she'd summoned Finn on my behalf.

She grinned. "Runs in the family. Based on how quickly Finn agreed to drive over here, he certainly didn't mind."

"What about Laurie?"

"The praying mantis?" she scoffed. "Not likely."

"Who's a praying mantis?" Miles wanted to know as he came up behind Peck and threw one arm casually around her shoulders.

"Nobody you'd care to know." She smiled at him. "My sister's getting a ride home. She's going to look after Trimalchio."

"And I'm going to look after you," he said, kissing her on the ear. She leaned back, tilting her head.

They walked me out to the front of the house and Miles patted my shoulder. "Behave," he said, as though I were one of those three girls who'd graced his deck with their miniskirted presence earlier in the evening, the kind who had a tendency to get naughty.

"*Namaste*," Peck whispered as she wrapped her arms around me, enveloping me in a cloud of Jo Malone fragrance and hair.

12

When Finn's jeep pulled into the courtyard, the muscles in my stomach clenched involuntarily from nerves. I stood and took a deep calming breath, telling myself it was just a ride home and to stop being such a ninny. For some reason this was the word that popped into my head—*ninny*. It wasn't one I'd ever spoken aloud. Finn stepped out of the car as I moved from the stone bench where I'd been sitting toward the passenger side. He caught my wrist to stop me. "Don't you look nice."

I was tempted to dismiss the compliment in my usual fashion. Instead I simply said, "Thank you." And then I added, channeling some of Peck's regal graciousness, "Thanks for coming to pick me up. I didn't know Peck was going to impose on you like that."

He gave me a funny look as he opened the passenger door and helped me in. "I was happy to do it." He went around to the driver's side and I caught a whiff of his now-familiar soapy scent as he slid in next to me. I wished he didn't have such an effect on me.

"Is this Brett Dennen?" I thought I was being so casual, chatting about the music, but my mouth was dry and my voice cracked slightly. "I thought I was the only one who knew about Brett Dennen."

He laughed. The planes of his face, in profile, caught the moonlight, and I was struck, not for the first time, by how much I liked his looks. He wasn't classically handsome in a way that was too pretty or called attention to itself, but his face in profile, with its straight nose and strong jaw, was striking. He looked, well, nice, but I guessed there must be something wrong with him, some dark secret, a syndrome whose symptoms wouldn't manifest themselves until one had known him awhile.

"So," I said, as nonchalantly as I could, once we'd been driving for a while. "You and Laurie Poplin are an item?"

He looked over at me in surprise. "An *item*," he repeated with a laugh. "Is that what you kids are calling it these days?"

"You know what I mean, Killian." I was trying for the bantering tone that had come naturally at first, but my words sounded too weighted, like I was interrogating him.

Finn, on the other hand, seemed able to banter just fine. "I don't have any idea what you mean," he said with another laugh. "Laurie Poplin is selling one of my houses. Is that what an item is?"

"You know what an item is." I wanted to be offhanded and clever but it all came out too heavy. "She says you're a *genius*."

"I get that a lot," he said, grinning. "Don't you?"

"No," I said. "Nobody has ever called me a genius."

He smiled. "Your aunt Lydia did. But what about you? No cozy male friends waiting for you back in Lausanne? Any Swiss boyfriends?"

"Not Swiss," I said, thinking of Maurizio, the Italian friend of Patrizia's who'd invited me to dinner a few times, and Lorenzo, the new salesman at the magazine who'd been making eyes at me at our last meeting. "Italian."

"*Italian?* You have an Italian boyfriend?" He looked over at me again with a disgruntled air. I was almost certain he was just being charming. This is the way he was with everyone he met, I suspected. He was a guy who was used to being popular. Peck had just told me that he was often the "extra man," invited to social engagements precisely because he was *available*. His charm had a practiced air that didn't detract from its effectiveness.

I shook my head in my own attempt at charm, trying to add a little laugh, but it came out more like a cough. "I wouldn't call any of them boyfriends."

"*Them*?" he repeated, mock horrified. "There's more than one?"

"From what Peck tells me, Laurie Poplin is not the only woman in your life either," I pointed out. "You're quite the ladies' man, I hear."

He looked over at me. "Are you kidding? No, sadly, there are no ladies in my life at this moment. Besides, Laurie's got loftier goals than a poor architect for hire. Miles Noble is more her speed. She told me she's heard he's a *leg* man."

"Funny," I said. "That's what Peck said about you."

"I *am* a leg man." He was still looking in my direction even though he was driving, and a small smile played at his lips. "But I'm also a foot and elbow and hollow of the neck man. I'm especially a funny bone man. I'm known for that."

"I've heard that about you."

He was taking the back roads and he asked, "Would you mind if we stop at my house before I drive you home? It's on the way. Sort of."

"I'd like to see it," I said, curious about his taste.

As he drove I told him we now thought he might have been right about our Fool-in-Residence and the missing painting. "It could be one of his pranks," I said. "Like he's planning a big reveal or something any day now. But we also think the painting might actually be something. Or Peck thinks so. I'm not sure. The initials on the back were J.P. And it resembles an early Jackson Pollock."

He looked understandably incredulous. "You think Lydia had a Jackson Pollock?"

I shook my head, now unsure. "It was just a thought. We have to get the painting back before we can figure it out."

"There's no way Lydia Moriarty owned a Jackson Pollock and never told any of us," he said. "J.P. couldn't be Jackson Pollock. She never met him."

"How do you know?" I asked him.

"You think she would have been able to keep it a secret if she had? How often did she tell you about the time she met De Kooning?"

He had a point. She'd loved to tell the story of how she met the famous artist through my father. "About a hundred times."

"But now that you mention it, I do remember Biggsy telling me he was obsessed with Jackson Pollock. It's one of the reasons he came out here in the first place. He went to visit the Pollock-Krasner House and he had to stay in the area."

"Pollock-Krasner House? You mean where they lived?"

He nodded. "In Springs. It's a museum now. You can tour the house and his studio. But he died in the fifties. Lydia would have been a kid. I don't see how she could have met him and had him inscribe a painting to her when she was eight or nine years old and never told us."

"I guess you're right," I said. "But it has to be something, doesn't it? Why else would anyone have taken it? Did your mother tell you anything about it when she gave you that picture?"

He shook his head. "No, but why don't we ask her? Come for Sunday dinner tomorrow on Shelter Island. You can meet the whole Killian clan."

"All four brothers?"

"And all their wives and kids. And dogs. There are twenty of us," he said. "Ten kids ranging in age from fourteen to two. My mom's the matriarch, the only sane one at the center of the vortex. You'll love her." He turned onto a narrow dirt road lined with trees. "This is my place."

I don't know what I expected; he was an architect, after all. But I hadn't given much thought to the type of house he would have created for himself. Everyone I knew lived in small rented apartments or, in the case of my editor, the top half of a house he shared with his elderly mother. I was the first of my friends to own even part of a house, and that was only due to the very generous, if mysterious, Aunt Lydia. Jean-Paul and I had shared an apartment belonging to his brother, which my ex-husband kept for himself after we split up. I didn't know anyone—except Miles Noble—who lived in a house of their own design. Finn's house was beautiful, a converted barn he'd spent three years redesigning, keeping only the old planks of wood, dark with the patina of age. The front of the house retained the original barn shape. The back, though, was open, like a dollhouse, all clad in glass, with sliding doors framed in bronze. From the front door you could see out the back.

"I had no idea you were this talented," I said to him in genuine surprise as he led me in.

The first floor was an open plan with a dining area containing a long rippled table that could seat twenty and a living area with deep-cushioned sofas. The floors were bare and gleaming and there was a wall of bookshelves, stacked neatly with books, constructed from the same dark, aged wood as the floor. Everything was orderly, from the dishes on the shelves above the sink to the pens, papers, tape dispenser, stapler, and other items lined up on the desk. I guess the impossible neatness and order shouldn't have surprised me. He was an architect, after all. But I'd never been in a man's home that looked like this, not that I'd been in so many men's homes at all, really.

This one was so well thought out that every sight line offered something else that was visually arresting, and I wandered through the space in awe. The energy of the house was happy, as though many generations of children had been born under its roof, though it was technically only a few years old. I couldn't imagine anyone possessing such a gift, one that allowed them to create a home like this.

"When my dad died," he said softly, "I gave my brother Seamus the lease on my apartment and moved out here full-time. I built this place with my father in mind. And I had to stay. I wanted to get away from the world. I've lived here for three years."

"I wouldn't want to leave here either," I said, gazing about with admiration and wonder.

"I hardly did. After this summer, though, my brother's moving to the suburbs. His wife is pregnant again with another boy."

"So you'll get back your old apartment?"

He nodded. "I think I'll split my time. I like to work out here. I've got an office upstairs."

The staircase to the second floor had a hand-crafted bronze railing Finn had designed himself. I knew this only because I asked him, but he did look pleased that I was so enthralled with the place. In fact, I was so busy admiring all of it, I missed a step going up and tripped over my feet.

"Am I making you nervous?" He laughed as he pulled me up, holding my hand lightly in his bigger one.

"Yes," I said, telling the truth. He *was* making me nervous. He was so obviously talented, and despite my earlier conviction that there must something wrong with him that would explain why he was still single at his age, I couldn't help being drawn to him. Our eyes met and we paused there, on the stairs. The physical tension between us was palpable and I strained toward him, half expecting that he would wrap his arms around me and put his lips to mine. Why else would he have invited me to his house? After a beat or two, though, he looked away and continued up the stairs with my hand in his. I was confused, not just by his behavior, but by my own. I kept telling myself I wasn't ready to get involved with any-

one at all, let alone someone who lived on the other side of the
ocean from me. And yet there I was mooning up at him like a teen-
ager in lust. Meanwhile, he didn't seem to even notice. Was my
imagination vivid enough to conjure up this kind of attraction? I
hadn't thought so, but perhaps I'd been more effective at getting
my creative juices flowing than I believed.

Upstairs, he showed me his bedroom quickly—the bed with a
simple metal frame piled high with crisp white pillows, linen curtains framing the window, a comfortable leather chair, a fireplace
with a box of firewood, again, all of it so *neat*—and then the second
bedroom and another room for music. This one was filled with
vintage guitars, hanging from special clamps on the wall. "Check
this out," he said, pulling a banjo down from its spot. "This was
Jerry's."

"Jerry Garcia? How did you get his banjo?"

He shrugged, holding it out so I could see it. "It was for sale.
He'd given it to his driver, or so they told me."

I took the banjo. It was heavier than I expected it to be, with a
faded Grateful Dead sticker on one side. It didn't have strings, so it
couldn't be played. "*Why* do you have this?"

"I'm a geek," he said. "A fan. It's probably not even real. I mean,
I have a letter authenticating it. The guy who had it got from the
driver, or so he said. But it could just as easily be worth *nothing*."

I gestured toward the guitars. "Play something for me."

"It's been a while," he said, but he pulled an old Les Paul from
the wall and took a pick from a bowl he kept on a small table.
There was a low sofa along one of the walls and we sat there. He
propped one foot on the table and cradled the guitar in his lap.
"How's this?" He picked out a few chords and I recognized the
tune. A Bruce Springsteen song.

He sang the beginning of the song in his unique, raspy voice.

"We'll walk together, side by side." He had a really good singing voice, perfectly pitched, but with a hoarseness that made each word so sexy. It was one of those God-given talents that always fascinate me in their foreignness—the ability to carry a tune.

"You're good," I told him when he stopped. I could have listened to him play all night. "Really good."

"Thanks." He stood and held the guitar at his side, looking down at me, his eyes locked on mine. My heart flipped over. Now he was going to kiss me, that was obvious. And I was going to kiss him back. That was obvious too. But then he held out a hand to help me up. "I'd better get you home," he said, pulling me to stand.

"Home?" I didn't want to go anywhere, let alone home, wherever that was. My life in Switzerland seemed small and far away at that moment.

I started to head to the door. "You're right. It's late. I have to check on the dog. And who knows what Biggsy's been up to in our absence?" I was determined not to let him know that I was disappointed, so I kept talking as he followed me back out to his car. "I met a guy tonight who collects first editions of books. Do you know that a first-edition *Gatsby* with a dust jacket is the holy grail for book collectors? I've been reading Lydia's copy, an old hardcover with its dust jacket." I was babbling, but he nodded as though I were making sense and we slid into our seats in the jeep for the short ride to Fool's House.

"Do you want to come in?" I asked at the door. I was just being polite, I told myself. His actions up to now had made it clear we would not be having a physical relationship and that was absolutely fine with me. It was much better not to be distracted by him for the rest of my stay. I decided I would go with him the next day to visit his mother, only to ask her about the painting, and then I would put him out of my mind until my flight home, at which point it would be easy, I imagined—out of sight, out of mind—to forget all about him

He paused. "I do. I really do. But you'd better rest up for tomorrow. The Killians can be intense. If you have a lacrosse stick, you might want to bring it."

"A lacrosse stick?" I laughed, holding the screen door open. "What would *I* be doing with a lacrosse stick?"

He shrugged. "My sisters-in-law will have extras. They always do." He looked around. "Are you sure you're going to be okay here alone?"

Biggsy's motorcycle was not in its usual spot, so he obviously wasn't around, but I assured Finn I'd be fine.

"I changed my mind," he said suddenly, sliding past me into the house as Trimalchio wandered lazily in from the kitchen to greet us. "I'm coming in. In fact, I'm staying the night."

"That's really not necessary," I protested.

He held up one hand. "I insist. I'll sleep on the sofa."

"I'd really prefer it if you didn't," I replied in a sharp tone. "There's no need for misplaced chivalry." I'd moved toward the coffee table in the living room, where I remembered leaving Lydia's copy of *The Great Gatsby* after I'd spent a little time reading that afternoon on the porch.

Finn ignored my sharp tone. "I don't trust that guy," he was saying, gesturing through the screen door toward the garage. "You told me you thought he tripped you on purpose, didn't you?"

"I'm a big girl," I said, glancing over at the bookshelf. Perhaps I'd moved the book and didn't remember. Or had Peck put it back on the shelf in an effort to tidy up? I was distracted and annoyed that he was foiling my plan to ignore him. I don't need you to stay up on guard watch all night."

"It'll just be tonight. While Peck's out," he said, looking around as though assessing potential danger "The guy's unstable. Who knows what else he might do?"

"I think he took my book, actually. Well, Lydia's book."

"The *Gatsby*?" He'd slipped off his shoes and was lying back on the couch like he was settling in for the night. Trimalchio, who'd gotten into the habit of sleeping at the foot of my bed, had hopped up next to him and curled into a ball. "That clinches it. I'm staying. I want to be here when he comes back.

I gave him an extra blanket from the closet under the stairs and got us each a glass of water before heading up to my own room, feeling very self-conscious. I thought there was no way I'd be able to fall asleep with Finn downstairs, but after a quick check of the rooms upstairs to look for the missing book, I got into bed. Within minutes I must have slept, and I didn't stir until the light streaming through my window indicated that it was already late morning.

I wandered downstairs and followed the smell of coffee and bacon into the kitchen. There I found Finn in the exact position as the last time he was at Fool's House in the morning, at the stove making omelets. "Good morning," he sang out, as if it were totally normal that the two of us should be alone together on a Sunday morning. And it actually felt kind of ordinary. I thought I would have been caught up in the strangeness of having the morning-after without the night-before, but I'd slept so well I felt as relaxed as I'd been all summer. "Breakfast on the porch in three minutes. The newspaper and coffee are already out there."

I made my way out to the porch, where Finn had set the table with Lydia's linens and put out fresh-squeezed juices and glasses, a bowl of cut-up fruit, a pitcher of milk, and the sugar bowl, as well as the pot of coffee. I poured myself a cup and hugged it in two hands as Martin Sexton—another musician Finn and I had discovered we both liked—was on the stereo singing fittingly about feeling happy on a Sunday morning.

He came out a few minutes later with a platter piled high with eggs, bacon, and pancakes. "Dig in," he said, depositing the platter in front of me. "I'll just grab the syrup." Then we sat on the porch with the newspaper, like an old married couple, eating and reading aloud to each other certain odd details of stories we found interesting. Finn was a politics junkie and had a lot to share about the race for president. Now, looking back, I realize something shifted between us that morning. But at the time I was only struck by the recognition that I was happy, just like the song that played like a sound track in the background. Happy wasn't a state with which I'd been familiar, not in a long time, but it felt great.

Lydia would have gotten a big kick out of this, I thought to myself as I poured us each another cup of coffee from the pot. I could almost picture her grinning with delight as she gazed down from the heavens at Finn and me around the table. There was one rainy afternoon that last summer I was there, the summer I met Finn for the first time, that now popped into sharp relief in my memory. I was in the same bedroom—"the white room"—I always occupied when I visited Fool's House, curled up with *The Beautiful and Damned*, which I went on to read after finishing *Gatsby*, when I heard her call for me from downstairs. Finn was taking his godson to Montauk, she yelled up the stairs, and she thought I might go with them. She'd been trying to push us together all summer, I remembered now. I didn't want to go anywhere and I kept myself very still that afternoon on my bed, not answering, hoping she would think I'd gone out on my own, although I'd spent most of my time that summer reading, either on the porch or at the beach or in my room. She must have known I was in the house. It was pouring down rain, so I was obviously not at the beach. But I heard her tell him I'd probably gone to the market with Peck. He must have known that wasn't true, because Peck and I didn't willingly

go very many places together that summer, but he left. And I remember feeling disappointed all of sudden that he was gone.

I was reading the Style section when I looked up to see Hamilton and Scotty making their way up the driveway, loaded down
with newspapers and shopping bags and a to-go carton containing
four paper cups of coffee.

"We come bearing news," Scotty called out. At least I think
that's what he said. His Scottish brogue was so thick it wasn't always easy to decipher his words.

"Literally," Hamilton added, holding up a stack of newspapers.
"We've brought every paper. Even the *Financial Times*. I love their
weekend section."

As they drew closer they assessed the scene before them: both of
us with tousled hair, at the table with the Sunday *New York Times*
spread all over it, and remnants of breakfast. "Look how cozy,"
Hamilton intoned with approval. "Finn and our Cassie on a Sunday morning."

"It's not what you think," I was quick to say. "Finn stayed on the
sofa."

They both stared down at us with suspicion. "Right," Hamilton
said, clearly not believing me. "Well, we're obviously interrupting,
so we'll just go in and find Peck."

"Peck's not here," I said. "And you're not interrupting anything
at all. We're finished. Please join us."

Scotty looked to Hamilton for guidance on whether to sit or
not. "We brought breakfast," he added. After a pause Hamilton
held up the bag he was holding. "Fresh croissants," he said, pulling
out one of the chairs. "And cinnamon buns. One of the great seduc-
tions of American life."

"I've never had one," Scotty explained as he took a seat, once
Hamilton had indicated that they should. He piled the newspapers

on top of the one we'd already been reading and handed us each a paper cup of coffee. "Hamilton took me to a place called Ye Olde Bake Shop. Isn't that charming?"

"Where's Lady Pecksland?" Hamilton wanted to know.

I repeated that she wasn't home but I didn't offer any more information than that. This, of course, would never work with Hamilton, who liked to know *everything* and wasn't ever too British to ask.

"Not home on a Sunday morning?" He raised his eyebrows in comic fashion. "Well, we know she's not at church."

"She's at a friend's house," I said, trying to be discreet. That morning Peck had updated me via text messages that began WARNING: MAY CONTAIN TMI. (TMI = Too Much Information.) On this, she was absolutely correct. I really did not need to hear how many times Miles Noble was able to get it up in the hot tub. Much as I suspected, they *had* watched from behind a curtain hanging in a second-floor window until Finn picked me up. Then Miles suggested a swim in the indoor pool, which was lit with all those candles. When the houseguests attempted to join them, he suggested they swim in the outdoor pool if they were so inclined, and asked them not to disturb their host and Peck when they left in the morning.

"A friend, you say?" He'd opened the bag of cinnamon buns and passed them around. Scotty was holding one delicately, eyeing it as if he couldn't figure out what to do with it. Finn took one too, always polite. I shook my head but Hamilton rattled the bag at me impatiently. "I didn't figure you for one of those tedious New York women who are perpetually on a *diet*."

"I'm not," I said. "But I just ate eggs, bacon, and three pancakes."

He reached into the bag and took out a cinnamon bun and handed it to me. "Don't postpone joy. It's one of my mottoes. Now, what *friend* is this of whom you speak? Might he be the friend in possession of the ugliest house in the Hamptons?"

Finn was grinning. "He *might*."

"If you must know," I said, in my best mocking imitation of prim, "it's Miles Noble. And yes, she stayed the night."

"We may never see her again," Hamilton said, grinning at me and indicating the cinnamon bun in my hand. "Now take a bite. You'll be most grateful you did."

I did as I was told. "So, what's the news?"

"You tell me," Hamilton said. He hadn't been surprised to learn that the code to Lydia's safe was F. Scott Fitzgerald's birth date and he also hadn't been surprised to learn that the only thing contained in the safe was a stack of love letters. He had been shocked to learn, however, that Lydia had been secretly married. "I'm still disappointed that all we've had so far is the grand news of a wedding. It's so . . . pedestrian," he commented now, making a face as he chewed his cinnamon bun. "I would have expected something more dramatic. A love child, perhaps. Or an identical twin separated at birth."

"You said you had news," I reminded him. "Was it about Biggsy? That's why Finn stayed here last night. He thinks he's dangerous."

Hamilton nodded. "Finn's right. And you'd do well to listen to him. The boy is trouble. Too bloody good-looking. Those sorts of looks warp the senses."

"He's not *that* good-looking," Scotty said, through a mouthful of his second cinnamon bun. "I don't think he's at all right in the head. And there's nothing attractive about that."

"You're a jealous little fellow, aren't you?" Hamilton fussed at him. "Now, here's what we've learned. Someone—and we suspect it was him—has been texting Giles from a cell phone with a Utah area code about selling a Jackson Pollock. I've decided we need a plan. First we have to confirm that Biggsy or Jonathan or whatever his name is does, in fact, have the painting. I suspect that he does. Then, second, we will get it back."

"Then, third, we'll get rid of him," Scotty added.

Hamilton smiled in my direction. "We? *We* have to get rid of him?"

"I think he also took Lydia's copy of *Gatsby*," I told them.

"Well, we'll get that back too," Hamilton said, very matter-of-factly. "Now, here's what I propose. And I offer my services willingly. I can get the young man to tell me if he has the painting."

"How do you propose to do that?" I asked, noting the way Scotty looked at Hamilton sideways, as though he'd had a little experience with Hamilton's plans and wasn't so pleased with the direction this was going.

"The old-fashioned art of seduction, my dear," Hamilton said with a smile. "I'll take one for the team, as you Americans might say."

"What makes you think he'll allow himself to be seduced by you?" I said, half laughing. "He's *straight*."

"Straight to the next man," Hamilton scoffed. "That chap will play it any way he can."

"He had pictures of Peck in his studio," I pointed out. "I think he likes women."

"He has pictures of *everyone*," Scotty added, speaking up suddenly. "And their houses. The insides of their closets. He told me all about it. He fancies himself the next Great American Artist, if you know what I mean."

"So what will you do after you seduce him?" I asked Hamilton.

He looked at me as though the answer were obvious. "If he has the painting, I'll play the patron, of course, and offer to help him sell it. I'll arrange a meeting with the potential client, have him bring the work, and then we'll grab it. You and Peck will be there and then you'll kick him out."

"Sounds too simple," I said.

"The best plans are always simple." He grinned at me and then pointed at the garage, where there was no sign of Biggsy's motorcycle near the door. "Is he up there?"

I shook my head no.

"He'll be back," Finn said.

Hamilton nodded, picking up his *Financial Times*. "Let me know when he returns. We'll set our plan in motion." He gestured at the rest of the breakfast items. "We'll leave the rest of this for you adorable creatures. Let's go, Scotty. We must give the lovebirds back their Sunday."

Finn and I hung out on the porch for a few hours after they left, then he went home to shower and change. When he picked me up that afternoon to go to Shelter Island neither Biggsy nor Peck had returned to Fool's House.

"You're not going to spend every night on the couch until he comes back," I said, once we'd settled easily into our usual spots in the jeep, as comfortable and relaxed as if we'd been doing so for years. "Besides, Peck will have to come back eventually. She doesn't go anywhere without an extensive wardrobe."

"From what you told me, she didn't need much in the way of clothing," he pointed out.

"She's into dressing gowns and gold lamé and sunglasses that match. She buys vintage ballgowns and faux fur stoles. She actually wears hats. At some point she's going to need a look."

For the rest of the ride he gave me the color on the family I was about to meet: his mother, Pat, and the four brothers, Seamus, Ryan, Liam, and Dean, and their wives, Marty, Lisa, Diana, and Tina. We took the five-minute ferry ride to Shelter Island and made our way to the battered old wooden house that Finn's family had owned for many years.

The house was simple and well-tended, with a gently sloping

back lawn that ran down to the water. On the lawn two extra-long picnic tables draped with red-white-and-blue-patterned tablecloths were set for the early dinner we were to enjoy with the family. There were stars-and-stripes napkins and cups and a big sheet cake decorated as the American flag with strawberries and blueberries and whipped cream.

"My mother must have gotten a discount on the red, white, and blue decorations after the Fourth of July," Finn said with a laugh as he led me down to the dock, where most of the family was gathered, watching the younger children paddle about in the water and some older ones maneuver a canoe. They were all big, or so it seemed to me, enormously tall and muscled, even the women. As we approached I assumed Finn's mother must have been inside, but then a figure that I'd taken for one of the teenagers, in loose shorts and a T-shirt, turned and greeted us with a wave and a shout. She was petite and brown from the sun, with her hair brushed casually off her forehead, and she wrapped her arms around me in the tightest hug and wouldn't let go.

"I'm Pat. I adored your aunt," she said, grinning warmly at me. The lines around her faded blue eyes were the only indicator of her age, as everything else about her was youthful in the most natural way. "I think I'm going to adore you too."

I fell in love that day. Not necessarily with Finn—that would come later—but with the whole boisterous lot of them. They were loud and friendly and opinionated and fun, the athletic brothers with their sporty wives and photogenic children, and they included me in their table discussions as readily as if I'd been there many times. They asked a lot of questions about Switzerland—"Do you have a cuckoo clock?" one of the smaller boys wanted to know— and about Lydia and Fool's House. Pat was more than eager to talk about her friend. I'd brought the photo of the two of them that Finn had given me, and I pulled it out after the cake had been devoured and the kids had run off to catch fireflies and throw lacrosse balls with their dads while their moms cleared the dishes.

"She *loved* that painting," she said when I explained that it was missing and asked if she knew who the artist had been. "But she was so secretive. I remember I asked her about it once and she went all mysterious. Wouldn't tell me who painted it or where she got it."

"Do you think it could have been a Jackson Pollock?"

At first she shook her head. "Oh no. She would have told me that. She was mad for Pollock." But then she changed her mind. "But come to think of it, anything's possible. She did have a strange attachment to that painting." She took another small bite of cake and chewed thoughtfully. "I suppose it could have been. She may have had her reasons for not wanting to tell anyone. Maybe she didn't want it to get stolen. She never locked her doors."

"In her will she told Cassie and Peck that she hoped they would find 'a thing of utmost value' in the house," Finn explained. "And then they'd only been in the house a few days when that painting disappeared off the wall during a party."

"Well, she did like to talk that way," Pat said, considering the idea. "We used to poke fun at her. But it would make sense, I suppose, if she did have a Jackson Pollock she wanted you to have but didn't want to say what it was. Perhaps for the taxes. She did like to be cryptic too. She was always trying to get us to answer her riddles."

"And there was an old hardcover *Great Gatsby* too," I added. "With a dust jacket."

"I didn't know anything about that," she said. "But with Lydia there was always another story to everything. First there'd be one tale, and then another. Or there'd be a practical joke involved, so the first tale was the setup for the prank. I never knew what to believe with her. It sure made it fun to be her friend, though."

We chatted for a long time as the sky grew dark and thousands of stars erupted in the inky blackness. The children were carted off after giving "Nanny" a good-night kiss, and the brothers and their wives all hugged me and Finn.

When it was just the three of us the talk turned to selling Fool's House.

"Have you buried a statue of Saint Joseph in the front yard?" she asked.

"Oh, Mom," Finn groaned. "Don't start with that stuff."

"It works," she said to him. To me she added, "Buy a statue of Saint Joseph and then bury it near the front door. I know it sounds silly. I don't usually go in for mumbo jumbo. But I've seen amazing things come from this. That is, if you really want to sell it."

"I don't want to. But we have to sell it," I said, despite the second thoughts I'd been having about letting go of Lydia's house.

Eventually Finn said it was time for him to take me home, as he had an early flight to Colorado to check on a job site, and we said good-bye to his mother. She wrapped both her arms tightly around me for the second time and said, "I'm *thrilled* to know you."

"Well, she convinced me," Finn said as we drove back to the ferry. "I'm starting to think that *was* a Pollock."

"If it is and Biggsy took it, do you think he plans to sell it or keep it for himself?"

He shrugged. "Who knows? Hamilton better get it back soon."

"The man has a plan," I said jokingly. "Did you see the look on poor Scotty's face when he realized what Hamilton had in mind? Hamilton has no idea the guy's madly in love with him."

When he pulled up to Fool's House, the place was dark. Biggsy's motorcycle was not there and no lights were on in the house or the studio. "I'll be fine," I said as Finn hopped out of the driver's seat and came around to open my door. I'd already gotten out, though, and he stopped in front of me, blocking my path to the house. He looked down at me with an unreadable, almost pained expression.

"Thanks," I said. "I had a great day. And I fell in love with your family. Especially your mom . . ." My voice trailed off as I noticed that he was looking at me funny. "Are you okay?"

Suddenly he took my face in both his hands and pulled me toward him. He kissed me passionately, leaning me against the side of the car and pressing his whole body into mine. It's a good thing he did, because my knees went weak at the contact after the physical tension that had been building between us over the ten or so days I'd been there. I melted into him and we kissed for what seemed like a very long time.

When we came apart, I'd never wanted anyone as intensely as I wanted him. I'd never felt this way before, like I *needed* his touch.

"I'm sorry," he said. "I couldn't help myself."

"Don't apologize," I whispered. "Come inside."

He shook his head. "I'm . . . I . . . I . . . want to take things slow."

"I'm only going to be here a couple more weeks," I said.

"That's exactly what I'm afraid of," he said, and then he kissed me again, gently this time, before heading back to the driver's side of the car. "See you when I get back," he said before he slid into the jeep with no indication of when that might be.

13

I could hear the screams from the porch. By the sound of it, someone—Peck?—was inside the house upstairs being stabbed or robbed or beaten. Whatever it was, a crime was clearly taking place.

It was Tuesday morning and Peck, as far as I knew, was still at Miles Noble's. The Bosleys were coming to look at Fool's House, but they were not due for another half hour at least. I'd taken Trimalchio for a walk, and I should have backed the hell out of there and called the police when I returned to hear all that racket from inside. Instead, like a heroine in a bad movie, I ran to the kitchen and grabbed the biggest knife I could find before hurrying up the stairs. Trimalchio, trotting along at my side, didn't appear at all concerned, but he was a New Yorker and thus, jaded.

The screams were coming from Peck's room. And, as far as I could tell, from Peck herself, whose one and only line as a television actress had been a high-pitched yelp that sounded exactly like the sounds emanating through the door. She was being violently attacked, that much was evident. Was it Biggsy? I turned the knob, ready to burst in and save her—with a *knife*?—but the door was locked. Just as I was about to kick down the door like I was a character on *NYPD Blue,* I heard her say, "Fantastic." Actually, she practically screamed it. "Fan-tas-tic!" What I was hearing wasn't

attempted murder: it was the unmistakable sound of extremely rig-
orous sex.

Peck and Miles—at least I hoped that's who it was—must have
decided to slum it for some reason. I listened outside the door for
some indication that the screaming couple might be slowing down
or picking up the pace, as in reaching a climax, but this sounded
like it was going to go on for a while. What were they doing at
Fool's House when there was so much more room to roll around
over at his place? Besides, I had cleaned her room that morning, ti-
dying huge piles of clothes that covered the floor and making the
bed up with the throw pillows in anticipation of our real estate
showing.

Finally I knocked. "Sorry to interrupt," I called out.

There was no immediate answer but the screams subsided
somewhat. Then muffled voices. I knocked again as the moaning
sounded like it was picking up again. Either this was the most
mind-blowing orgasm ever or one hell of an acting job.

Finally Peck shouted, annoyed, "Okay!"

"The Bosleys are coming to look at the house," I said. "With
Laurie Poplin. You might want to get up. They'll be here soon."

When I got to the foot of the stairs, still clutching the huge
kitchen knife, I was startled to see that they were already there. A
whole family of them, peering in through the screen door at me.
Four children and their frazzled-looking parents—Heather in
stained yoga pants and those strange plastic shoes with holes in
them called Crocs, and Ollie in his Harvard crew shirt and his own
pair of purple Crocs. The two of them looked deflated, as though
their hopes—a charming and well-located house in the Hamptons
they could actually afford—had been dashed by the sight of the
rickety little shack with its sagging porch.

Ollie threw both arms in the air. "I didn't do it. Wrong guy, I
tell you, it wasn't me," he joked.

"Daaad," the older boy drawled, admonishing him. He had shoulder-length hair and wore a purple rash guard and long shorts. "Dylaan," his dad said, mimicking his tone.

"Is this a bad time?" their mother asked in a sharp tone. She held up a plate covered in tin foil as they all looked at me expectantly. "We made an appointment, remember?"

"My wife likes to be early," Ollie explained, as though this was one of many things he found impossible to understand about the woman he married.

"Of course," I said. "Come on in." I inadvertently waved with my weapon, hoping Peck and Miles were finishing up and getting dressed.

"These are for you." Heather gestured with her plate. "Health muffins. We baked them this morning."

The littlest Bosley was too afraid to come into the house. "Oh, Poppy," her mother said, glaring at the knife in my hand. "The lady was just using that for cooking. Like Mommy does all the time."

Her older daughter corrected her. "You *never* cook."

"I made the muffins," her mother reminded her, using the same petulant tone as her daughter.

I led them into the kitchen, so I could put the knife back in its drawer. "There," I said, kneeling down so I could face Poppy. "All gone." She nodded warily and allowed me to take her hand.

"Try one," Heather said of the muffins, thrusting the plate at me. "Homemade. So much better than store-bought."

"This house is small," the younger boy, whose name was Lucian, noted as Heather looked around at the worn-out kitchen with a defeated air. It seemed she'd had a much grander vision of her simple country house than ramshackle little Fool's House. They had some money, Miles would tell us later. Ollie was a scientist and smart enough to have invested a little in biotech stocks, and had been somewhat successful. But not quite enough for the lifestyle they expected they were supposed to lead in New York City: a townhouse in Brooklyn with four kids at private schools, and nannies to make sure nobody was getting neglected, and orthodontists, tutors, coaches, vacations, and, naturally, a second home.

Fool's House was the kind of place they might be able to buy, if they stretched and scraped and made do, spending vacations there instead of traveling, getting rid of a nanny or two now that their kids were a bit older. But it would never be the house of their dreams.

"Yoo-hoooooo," Laurie called in through the screen door. "You were *early*," she said to Heather in an accusatory tone. She wore a minidress, this one acid green and sleeveless to show off her bony shoulders, and she clattered in on high heels, distracted and glaring at her phone. "Did you *tell* them to come early?" she asked me, suspicious perhaps that I was going to cut her out of the deal.

I assured her I was not plotting anything and told her to go ahead and give them the grand tour. "You might want to avoid Peck's room for a while, though. She and Miles are just getting up."

"Miles Noble is here?" Laurie glanced quickly at me.

Ollie looked shocked. "What's Miles doing *here*?"

I shrugged. "He's with my sister."

Laurie shepherded the Bosley parents into the living room after giving me a nasty look and they left the children with me in the kitchen. Dylan, the older boy with the long hair, wanted to know if we had any donuts.

"We're not allowed to eat donuts," explained Clementine, the oldest. She sported a midriff-baring tank top and terry-cloth shorts so tiny they really could have been more accurately considered an undergarment. In her mouth was a purple candy pacifier that made it look like she was wearing purple lipstick. "But we eat them all the time anyway."

"Our mom's too busy to notice." Dylan looked around for the stash of sweets he seemed to know we would have.

"Stay-at-home moms are always busier than the working moms," his little brother, Lucian, informed us. He sounded like he was parroting one of his older siblings or something he'd heard on television, but he spoke with conviction. "Everyone knows that."

Clementine pulled the candy pacifier out of her mouth to explain. "The stay-at-home moms have to do all the work at the schools and the charities. But the office moms don't have to do that stuff. They feel guilty for working and come home and bake cookies with you and stuff. Stay-at-home moms, they don't have time to bake. Unless it's for a bake sale. But then we're not allowed to eat any of it."

"So, are there any donuts?" Dylan asked again. He shrugged as though he knew he might sound slightly rude, but survival depended on it.

We didn't have any donuts but there were plenty of freshly baked cupcakes, frosted in pink.

"Frosting, awesome!" declared Lucian, smiling at me as though his opinion of me had suddenly gone way up. They all seemed to view me differently now that baked goods—not rock-hard health muffins with bits of carrot and zucchini, but cupcakes, with frosting—had been provided. Little Lucian appeared to have fallen in love. He patted my hand as he stuffed half a cupcake into his mouth in one bite.

"My friend Jesse has a *Prada* mom," Poppy declared through her own enormous mouthful of vanilla cake and pink frosting, quite proud to be able to offer something to the conversation. Then she quickly shoved the rest of her cupcake into her mouth, as though she wanted to get it finished before her mom showed up and took it away from her.

"What's a Prada mom?" I asked, surprised by how much I was

enjoying their company. I could actually imagine the four of them spending their weekends and summers in this house, reading on the porch, making forts in the small closet under the stairs, learning how to play tennis on the crumbling old court.

Poppy paused, unable to answer my question. Then she spoke through a mouthful. "I don't know."

Clementine had left her candy sucker on the counter and was pulling apart the cupcake I'd given her. "It's a mom who wears cool clothes and is skinny and wears her daughter's jeans. You know, a fashion mom. As opposed to, say, the office moms who wear suits—those are called power moms. Or there's the Lilly moms."

"What's a Lilly mom?" Poppy asked the question for me.

Clementine rolled her eyes before answering, in that singsong teenage way that makes every sentence sound like a question that should be followed by a "Duh." "The proud-to-be-preppy kind. The ones who wear Lilly all the time? Lilly Pulitzer?"

"What other kinds of moms are there?" I figured I might as well do some research. I hoped to become a mom myself one day.

"Our mom's a yoga mom," Dylan said. "There's lots of those at my school."

"They make you eat *edamame*," Poppy complained. "And organic ketchup. It's disgusting."

"They don't know *anything* about fashion," Clementine added. "They try to make you buy no-brand jeans. As if."

"They're *obsessed* with summer reading," Dylan added, making it sound like a disease.

"What's wrong with summer reading?" I asked in amusement.

"Reading is *boring*," Lucian explained in a gentle manner, as though he didn't want to hurt my feelings by pointing out something so obvious.

"The woman who lived in this house was obsessed with summer reading too," I told them. "She was my aunt. Her first question would have been 'What are you reading?' and if you told her, 'Nothing,' she would have screamed in horror. Then she would have gone to the shelf in her living room and gotten a book for you and made you read it. She would always say it was the way you learn what matters in life. And then she would probably tell you to try writing one of your own. She always wanted everyone to write their stories down."

"Our mom always says she's going to write a book," Dylan said. "But she never does."

"What kind of mom are you?" Lucian looked up at me, pink frosting on his nose and in his hair and on the tips of his very long eyelashes.

"I'm not one," I said, wiping the frosting off his nose with a napkin. "Yet."

"You can babysit for us," Lucian said, gazing up at me again with those bedroom eyes. "Any time you want."

"You have a husband?" Poppy wanted to know, like a journalist firing questions at a subject.

"That's rude," Dylan told his sister. "You're a pimple."

She let out an angry whine. "I am not a pimple. You're a pimple. You're a pus pimple."

"You don't even know what a pus pimple is," Dylan pointed out. "And you have very bad manners."

"It's okay," I said, grinning. With four kids in this small house, it would never be too quiet. "What about the dads? Are there different kinds of those?"

"The dads are stressed out all the time," Clementine said.

Dylan added quickly, "The dads are the sports police."

"What's the sports police?" I asked, taking mental notes. Four kids seemed like the right number, and I found myself thinking

Finn would probably want at least that many, after having grown up with all those brothers. Then I quickly dismissed that thought: What difference did it make to me how many children Finn Killian wanted to have? "Like referees?"

"Nah, they just force you to be on all these travel teams. Even if you don't want to." Dylan folded his arms over his chest as though he had decided then and there not to be a party to any of that sports ridiculousness ever again. "Even if you suck at sports. They sign you up without asking. And then they make you go to the games and practice 'cause they say you can't let the team down. But you didn't even want to be on the stupid team."

"They're the ones who coach stuff," Clementine added for clarification. "Or get in fights on the sidelines."

"Can moms be sports police too?" I asked her.

Clementine nodded. "They're called soccer moms," she said. "They try to pretend it's just supposed to be fun. But they get really mad when—" All of a sudden she let out a loud squeal, startling all of us. "Look at him!"

She was pointing at the back door, where Trimalchio had appeared, draped in a velvet cape tipped in faux leopard. He looked ridiculous. And he knew it.

I opened the door to let him in. "Who did this to you?"

Trimalchio was a good sport, benevolently allowing himself to be caressed by four sets of sticky hands. Then Biggsy appeared behind him. He followed the dog with his video camera over his shoulder. Only he didn't realize the screen door was shut and he walked right into it, thrusting his elbow through the screen, jabbing a large hole into it.

The two younger Bosley children, Poppy and Lucian, thought the hole in the screen was the funniest thing they'd ever seen and burst out laughing, as though it was a clown act and he'd done it on purpose. Maybe he had. "Hello, Cassie," he said, all friendly. "I see you found the cupcakes I made."

"*You* made these?" I was suddenly afraid he might have slipped something into the cupcakes.

"Just trying to help out," he said, giving me a look. I wondered if he realized he'd become our number-one suspect in the mystery of the missing painting and now the case of the missing book.

"Do it again," Poppy demanded. "Again."

"Is that your dog?" The children clamored around Biggsy. "Why is he wearing a costume?" "Are you making a movie of him?"

Biggsy made a face at me, as if to say, See? *They* want me here. "Hey, kids," he said to them. "Want to be in a film?"

The younger ones immediately said yes. Clementine wanted to know if their mother needed to sign a release.

"Hey, man, this is *art*," he said, as he zoomed in on Trimalchio's patient mug.

"*They* ate the cupcakes," I said to him, in a warning tone. He was weird and probably a thief or at the very least a nuisance, but I didn't think he would actually hurt any children. They were smiling happily, rubbing sticky fingers over Trimalchio, and none of the four of them appeared to be frothing at the mouth or writhing in pain from some sneaky poisonous ingredient.

"Weren't they good? Did Miss Cassie tell you about the ghost of Fool's House?" he asked, now focusing on tiny Poppy's face, which immediately scrunched up in preparation for tears at the word *ghost*.

"What ghost?" Lucian asked in excitement.

I quickly reassured them. "It's just a story *some people* like to tell. There's no ghost."

Biggsy swung the video camera into my face. "Of course there is. He likes to play backgammon."

"I play backgammon," the older boy, Dylan, said.

"I don't want to live in a haunted house," Poppy whispered to me.

"If you leave a backgammon game unfinished, the ghost will play it out. And red will always win," Biggsy continued. "He takes paintings off walls and moves things around. He's a good ghost." Both boys deemed a ghost cool and awesome and Clementine didn't care. Even little Poppy gazed up at me with total trust, believing the ghost was just a made-up story. So if he'd been trying to scare them, he was unsuccessful.

Biggsy clapped his hands, trying another tack. "Want to look in the refrigerator?"

The three older ones nodded warily while Poppy gave me a nervous glance. "That's enough," I said. "Show's over, Fool. You can go now."

He ignored me as the children stared up at him. "For some reason, people always want to open the fridge when they look at houses," Biggsy explained to them. "We don't know why. It's just one of those nosy human things that we do. It's instinct. Or habit. So go right ahead."

Dylan hesitated for a few seconds and then pulled open the door to the refrigerator. They all examined our groceries.

Lucian was the first to notice. "What's that?" He pointed at something.

We all looked more carefully. "It's an arm," Clementine announced in a bored matter-of-fact tone, as though it were not only normal but expected to find a severed limb in the fridge. After all, wasn't that where they belonged?

"How did *that* get in there?" Biggsy directed his words at Trimalchio. The dog looked like a grand stage actor ready to take five, weary of a role he'd been playing for too long but for which he'd become famous.

In planning his little prank, intending to scare off another set of possible buyers, Biggsy had forgotten a most important rule: know your audience. The Bosley children were unfazed by the arm. Only four-year-old Poppy got excited about it, and that's because she thought it was fantastic. In fact, they all seemed to think it was great, and they grew animated at the thought of living in such a fun house.

Laurie brought Ollie and Heather back to the kitchen amid the excitement. Ollie saw a severed arm as an opportunity to demonstrate his razor-sharp wit. "This house must be cheap," he said. "It didn't cost an arm and a leg. Only an arm."

Laurie laughed as though those were the cleverest words ever uttered by a man. Clearly she must have thought the showing had gone well.

"Follow me, children," Biggsy said, leading the four of them out the back door with Trimalchio following. I was about to suggest that we go too, rather than leaving the children alone with him, when Peck came into the kitchen in a cloud of freshly applied Jo Malone. She was wearing an old-fashioned bathing suit, the full one-piece armored kind. This one was red with white polka dots and made her boobs and butt look huge. She also sported an enormous straw hat, candy-red lipstick, and very high platform espadrilles.

"Welcome to Fool's House," she cried out. "Can I offer you a Bloody Mary? How about some fresh lemonade? Or pancakes!"

"The children might like that," Heather suggested, somewhat flabbergasted by the sight of Peck in her elaborate getup, exactly the desired effect.

"Children? What children?" Peck's smile faded a bit. She didn't have much tolerance for small people who couldn't partake of her famous Southsides and had little in the way of amusing anecdotes to share.

"I would take a cappuccino," Ollie offered.

Peck made a face. I knew what she was thinking: *Some people have such bad manners.* This would be the perfect excuse for her to refuse to sell them our house, even if they did make an offer. "We do not," she enunciated, "have a cappuccino maker."

Laurie Poplin smiled coldly at Peck and said she hoped they hadn't woken her up. "It's almost *eleven*," she pointed out in a snide way that made me think Finn had been right about her feelings for Miles Noble. She glanced toward the hallway before asking the Bosleys if they wanted to go back up and see the bedroom that they'd missed.

They shook their heads. "We got the idea," Ollie said.

"We'll probably want to come back at night," Heather added.

Ollie only mentioned Harvard once. "I had a blanket just like that at Harvard," he noted with enthusiasm, of the popcorn spread that covered the bed in my room. And Heather liked the studio above the garage, which she planned to use for her pottery and yoga and, as she put it, "my writing." Their shift in attitude toward the place from the beginning of their visit until the end was palpable and Laurie Poplin bounced on the balls of her feet as she walked them to their car.

We stood on the porch watching them load the four children into the predictable hybrid. Biggsy had disappeared again, his motorcycle gone.

"I. Did. Not. Like. Those. People," Peck announced as the Bosleys pulled out of the driveway while Laurie stood there waving at them.

Laurie had just pulled away in her own car when Miles Noble came out to the porch wearing Peck's silk paisley robe. His hair stuck out from his head in tufts and his face was puffy. "What people?" He kissed her on the neck. "Hey, Stella."

"People like that don't deserve such a place." She was still glaring down the driveway. "This house is special. And those people, your houseguests, were . . . uninspired. Uninspiring."

Miles looked confused. "Which houseguests?"

"The Bosleys," I explained, trying not to notice how the sash to Peck's robe was coming loose—it was clear that Miles was not wearing anything underneath it. "We met them at your place on Saturday night. Remember? They said they wanted to look at our house?"

Miles barked out a laugh. "They did? A house they would actually *pay* for?"

"See," Peck said to me in a quick shift. "They'll never make an offer. This conversation is moot."

Miles couldn't keep his hands off her. "Moot," he said, nuzzling her ear. "I want to moot you."

"Miles," she admonished. "Get a room."

"Maybe I'll buy it," Miles said, grinning lazily. "I like it here."

Peck turned to me. "Miles and I like it better here," she said. "His house is too big."

Miles nodded somewhat sheepishly. "My house is ridiculous."

"Literally. I got *lost*," Peck explained. "For like an hour. Plus, it's horribly ugly."

"It's really ugly," Miles said to me. "I should sell it." He looked over at Peck and ran one finger along her cheek. "I'm going to sell it. I hate it. So, what's for breakfast? Where's that butler dude?"

"He's disappeared again," I said. "And I think he took Lydia's copy of *The Great Gatsby*. I can't find it anywhere."

"Did you look up there?" Peck gestured toward the garage before turning to Miles. "He's got pictures of me in his room. He's been *filming* me."

"He kissed your fucking shoe. You're hot, babe, what can I say?" Miles tied the robe more securely around his thick waist. "Now, can we get some breakfast? I'm *starving*."

"We should go up there again," Peck said to me.

Miles gave her an exasperated look and headed for the door. "If we don't get some food first, you can forget going to Paris for the weekend, babe. I'll be in a starvation-induced coma."

She grinned at me. "He's always starving. I swear, the guy is all appetite."

"Paris for the weekend?" I asked, surprised at how quickly their newly reignited love affair seemed to be progressing. She nodded. "Miles is taking me to the Ritz. We're staying in the F. Scott Fitzgerald suite."

Miles turned at the door and gave me a hangdog look. "I do what I'm told," he joked, in the manner of a man who was used to having other people do what *he* told them and couldn't quite figure out exactly how he'd gotten himself in this situation.

14

Peck had acquired, somewhere, an original Pan Am flight attendant's uniform from the seventies, and this was what she was wearing two days later when I came out on the porch to find her waiting for me. "When on a quest," she announced, handing me a cupcake, "it's important to dress appropriately." She eyed the shorts I'd pulled on quickly. "Or not."

Hamilton, never one to miss out on anything that smacked of an adventure, had orchestrated a day of what he called "sleuthing" for the three of us. I had a hunch he too would be dressed for our escapade and I wasn't wrong. He strolled up the driveway wearing a safari-style jacket with loads of pockets, as though, should the occasion arise, he might reach into them to pull out tools or other necessities. He daintily clutched a small cooler from Petrossian Caviar in one hand like a purse. With the other hand he waved his fan. "Isn't this exhilarating?" he called out to us as he approached.

Biggsy's motorcycle had not reappeared in the two days since he'd left the Bosley children outside, so Hamilton had not yet had a chance to execute the first part of the plan he'd concocted. But in the meantime we were setting out on a fact-finding mission, attempting to figure out if the painting in question could, in fact, have been painted by Jackson Pollock. I wasn't sure exactly how we were going to accomplish this but I loved the notion that we were on a quest. This kind of thing needed air, and Peck and Hamilton together were the kind of people who would breathe life into a speck of an idea until it became something entirely different, the way a kernel of corn could become popcorn when hot air was involved.

"First order of business," she stated once Hamilton had stepped up onto the porch. Peck, whose favorite show was *Law and Order*, approached the day as though she were on assignment. "We go up to the studio to look for the *Gatsby* that Stella here thinks may be a first edition." She pointed at the garage. "And we search for any other clues we might have overlooked the first time."

I led the way to the garage and up the stairs to the somewhat stuffy second-floor studio. I half expected to find the space cleared out, indicating that Biggsy had pulled up stakes and taken off with our painting, but it looked exactly the same as it had the first time we'd gone up there, Biggsy's shrunken suits and collection of hats still in the small closet, the piles of photographs and papers all over the table.

Propped up against a shelf along one wall was a large book, open to reveal an image of a painting on the well-worn page. "Check this out," I said, closing the book to note the cover. "Jackson Pollock."

"There's a *clue*." Hamilton was out of breath after the climb up the stairs. "I'd say that's a start."

I quickly flipped through the pages, many of which were marked with yellow Post-its or covered with ink where Biggsy seemed to have been making notes to himself in a scribbled handwriting that was impossible to decipher. I scanned the images to see if there were any that looked like ours, but none of them appeared to be an exact match, though there were some that seemed vaguely similar.

While I was flipping through the pages of the book that Biggsy or someone had clearly spent much time with, Peck held up a sheet of stationery that appeared to be a letter from Lydia, covered with her same round schoolgirl handwriting.

"Another letter?" I asked eagerly, closing the book and stepping closer to the page she was now inspecting with a frown. The sight of Lydia's handwriting brought a swift pang to my heart as I reached for what I believed to be another communication from the aunt we'd all adored. And then the wrench of emotion turned immediately to anger when Peck showed me that what had appeared to be Lydia's perfect penmanship was actually the same few lines written out over and over. Biggsy had copied them and then practiced them again and again to achieve the rounded letters and distinctive look of her handwriting.

"This must have been a practice sheet," Peck said, her hand shaking slightly as she held the paper for the two of us to see.

"Damn that bloody snogger," Hamilton exclaimed, now that he'd caught his breath and realized what Peck was holding in her hand.

"I knew there was something off about the way he suddenly brought out that letter," I said, now seething at the thought of Biggsy digging around Lydia's desk to steal some of her stationery and then copying out a few sentences from a letter she'd written to someone else, one of us perhaps. "It was a fake."

"A good fake," Peck pointed out, but she too looked angry. "Kid's got talent." She shook the sheet of paper as though trying to rid it of negative energy.

"The kid's a menace," I added quickly. "He's been nothing but trouble."

"Why would he create a fake letter from Lydia?" Hamilton wondered aloud. "Why go to all the trouble of perfecting her handwriting? Unless he was planning to falsify something else? A check, perhaps?"

I looked over at Peck. "We should find out if there were any checks from her account made out to him."

Peck shook her head. "I don't think that was it. I think he did it because he could. He wanted to lull us into a false sense of security. Like we're all just one big happy family. But he's going to rob us blind right under our noses and call it art."

"We're going to have to confront him," I said, sifting through piles of papers and things in search of anything that might shed some light. "He could be more dangerous than we realize. Especially because he's obviously not going to leave this place willingly."

We didn't find Lydia's copy of *The Great Gatsby* or the painting or any other clues, and eventually Hamilton suggested we move along. "I don't want to be in here when that chap comes back. He could be one of those violent types."

"If he walked in here now I'd kick him right in the balls," I said. I was angry and I meant it, but Peck burst out laughing.

"Listen to you," she exclaimed as Hamilton let out a chuckle too. "Miss Tough Guy. Didn't I say she was going to come out of her shell this summer?"

"I'm rather afraid." He made a comic face as he covered his crotch with his hands. "Balls. It sounds so . . ."

"'Kick him right in the balls,'" Peck repeated with a laugh. "I didn't even think you knew that *word*."

"What?" I said. "Balls?"

"Enough," Hamilton cried out. "You're making me want to cross my legs. And we must go."

"Okay, then." I held up the practice sheet and waved it in the air. "I'm taking this with me. We're going to have to get that guy out of here."

We filed back down the stairs behind Hamilton and came out of the gloom of the garage into clear sunshine that threw everything into sharp relief. In unison all three of us pulled our sunglasses back over our eyes to block the glaring light.

We were all in high spirits, with snacks and outfits (at least theirs) carefully considered, and a sense of infinite possibility in the air as we got into the ancient station wagon. Peck slid into the driver's seat, Hamilton took the passenger side, and I went in the back with Trimalchio on my lap. The dog, with his permanently jaded facial expression, was the only one who didn't seem caught up in the adventure, and he peered out the window like one of those tedious city people who make a big show of hating "the Hamptons," complaining about the traffic and the social anxiety and the crowds.

"I've brought sustenance," Hamilton said as he held up the cooler to show us before tucking it in between the two front seats. "But we shan't fill up. I'm taking us all to lunch."

Peck gunned the old car into reverse. "Literally to Lunch," she said over her shoulder in my direction, in the tone of the know-it-all forced to explain yet again. "It's a place out on 27 toward Montauk. It's really called the Lobster Roll, but the sign out front says Lunch and everybody just calls it that. They have the *best* lobster rolls."

Everything Peck liked was always the best. This was one of the ways she distinguished herself, by having the most discerning palate. She presented her opinions much the way an old-fashioned magazine editor like Diana Vreeland would have done.

"Pecksland, you're quite an expert on *everything*," Hamilton noted drily. It was the sort of thing only he could get away with saying to her. From him she heard it as a compliment.

We drove through Southampton on our way to East Hampton, to pay a call on an art dealer Hamilton knew who specialized in discreet private sales and who was the type of person who would know if there was an unauthenticated Jackson Pollock being shopped around and if the one we were missing was actually painted by Pollock or not. As Peck drove, Hamilton entertained us with stories of old Southampton, and how much better it used to be. This was a favorite theme, how it used to be the quietest old place where you'd just go to the beach and everyone knew one another and you'd get around on a bicycle.

"On a regular bicycle," Hamilton clarified. "Not like these idiots in spandex racing along Gin Lane like they have to get somewhere."

Peck agreed with him about old Southampton, as if she too had known it then, as if she'd grown up here. In some ways, of course, she had. We'd both visited Lydia several summers during the course of our childhoods. But to hear Peck talk, she'd spent every minute of every summer at a house in the country with a pony and a bicycle and lemonade stands at the beach. She never modified her stories in my presence and I would never correct her. I enjoyed them too much. In fact, that morning in the car, I almost believed she *had* grown up in Southampton.

"It was so much better then," she said, allowing a wistful tone to seep into her words. "Everybody knew one another. Nobody locked their doors. And the creativity in the air was so thick you could cut it with a knife." She paused to look out the window. "You'd actually see people setting up their easels on the dunes," she said in a pensive tone as she glanced out at the passing hedgerow. "Like in the days of William Merritt Chase and the Shinnecock School of Summer Art. People were painting *everywhere*. There were actors and writers and creative people doing their thing. There was all this *spontaneity*."

The privet hedges were intimidating, keeping sentry and offering total privacy for the denizens of the vast palaces, old and new, hidden behind them. We couldn't see many of the houses from the street but Hamilton had juicy tidbits of information to share with us about each one, and he made Peck take a less direct route through what is known as the "estate section" so he could point out the places in question through the car window. He'd given this subject, the houses of the Hamptons, much passionate study and could speak with authority. He knew about the old places and also about the new ones, which shingled manor had been lost in a divorce, which stucco villa had been in a family for generations, which gargantuan new construction had been built with no regard to how a family would actually inhabit the enormous space, and which tiny, older house was slated to be ripped down and replaced. He knew prices and names and secrets. He knew about the clubs and their members, and he knew about the locals too and their equally messy lives.

"Each one of these houses," Peck said as she took her eyes off the road for far longer than felt comfortable, "is the realization of someone's dream."

"Or someone else's nightmare," Hamilton added, pointing to a slightly dilapidated white place barely visible through an overgrown hedgerow. "I believe that's the place Laurie Poplin was trying to sell when she first met Biggsy, who was then Jonathan."

"Finn said Lydia met him at Schmidt's Market," I said, as Hamilton passed around tiny blinis with sour cream and smoked salmon.

"It depends on whom you ask," Hamilton said, glancing back at me. "I once heard her say he just appeared at the end of the driveway one day. She told me he answered an ad on Craigslist."

"That's so random," Peck exclaimed, narrowly missing a bald-headed man in a tiny toy sports car. That morning there seemed to be a preponderance of miniature vehicles driven by follicle-challenged men on the road as we passed the farm stands and the cornfields and the cashmere shops.

Peck changed the subject to one she'd been revisiting several times with increasing intensity: she wanted to turn Fool's House into a retreat for creative people. "Kind of like Yaddo," she explained earnestly.

"Have you ever *been* to Yaddo?" Hamilton asked her, stretching the word—*beeee-eeee-innn*—into three syllables to enunciate how preposterous he found her idea.

Peck was forced to admit that she hadn't been to Yaddo, or anywhere like it. She didn't even know exactly what Yaddo was.

"Yaddo's *enormous*," he told her. "You could only house three or four artists in Fool's House at a time. That's not at all the same."

"We can add on some rooms," she exclaimed with increasing petulance. "I just think we were meant to keep the place in the family, and I think we should find a way to do that. Now, I read something this morning on the Internet about a whole bunch of potential Jackson Pollock paintings that were discovered in a storage bin out here somewhere. But they weren't signed. And the article pointed out that he always signed his work."

"Yes. In fact he rather famously insisted that his wife, Lee Krasner, sign her work, when she never had before," Hamilton added. "Or it was a scene in the movie."

"Maybe ours was one he didn't like," Peck speculated. "And that's why he didn't sign it."

"He was known to throw canvases into the town dump," he said as we snaked slowly along Route 27 behind an endless line of sun-baked cars. "Right in East Hampton. I doubt he would have signed those."

"It did say 'From J.P.' on the back," she mused. "I wonder if someone could authenticate that."

It took a long time to get to East Hampton. The sun was high in the sky and it was hot by the time we pulled up to the neat shingled bungalow with window boxes where the art dealer—Giles Moncrief was his name—spent his weekends. Everything about the small place, including its owner, was well-tended. The paint-ings on the whitewashed walls were all small and abstract, subtle in hue. The furniture was stylish and subdued as well, and the effect was soothing. There was iced tea garnished with lemon slices in a tall pitcher and the very stylish Giles poured us each a glass.

He wore narrow gray trousers and a fitted purple shirt and he looked only at Hamilton. Like Scotty, he appeared to be infatuated with our white-haired friend. He had a *Masterpiece Theatre* accent and a thin mustache that he kept touching as he fired questions at him. "Oil on canvas? Black, white, and brown abstract, you say?" he asked with a carefully contained eagerness that seemed at odds with his sleek demeanor. "Small? And it's been missing how long?"

I'd brought the photograph Finn had given me of Lydia and his mother in front of the mantel with the picture in the background, and I pulled it out to show him the painting we were there to discuss.

Giles Moncrief sighed heavily as he held the photo as close to his eyes as he could, examining it carefully. "'For L.M. From J.P.'? That's on the back? And it disappeared when?"

He spent quite a bit of time staring at the photograph and looked a few things up on a laptop computer while we explained what little we knew of the painting that had been hanging above the mantel at Fool's House for so long, and about Biggsy, the artist whom we suspected of stealing the painting.

"He lives there, rent-free, in exchange for fake vomiting on your floor?" he asked, looking up from his computer.

"Well, it's a bit more complicated than that," I tried to say.

He nodded with an annoying smirk, but he seemed to be trying to get all the facts. "Yes, I suppose it is, as he may or may not be in possession of a painting that belongs to you that may or may not be a Jackson Pollock." He looked for confirmation to Hamilton, who was happily fanning himself and enjoying his iced tea in one of the too-small chairs.

"You've heard nothing more from him?" Hamilton asked him. "We're certain this is the fellow who texted me?"

Giles shook his head. "He hasn't responded again. Very often stolen paintings never resurface, you know."

"How d'you mean?" asked Peck, growing more British by the minute.

"People steal paintings for all sorts of reasons," he explained. "It's awfully hard for a thief to sell a high-profile piece. Certainly a potential Pollock, even one that could be impossible to authenticate, would attract a lot of attention. Not everyone wants that attention."

We talked for a while longer, but Giles could not confirm that the painting in the photograph could have been painted by Pollock. He could also not definitively say that it hadn't. But he promised to let us know if he heard anything, and we left him gazing thoughtfully up at one of the paintings on his wall, no further along in our search for information than we had been when we pulled in. "I'll text him again," he said. "I'll tell him I have someone interested."

Over lunch—the most delicious lobster rolls, as promised, at a photogenic roadside shack—Hamilton told us what he knew about the author of the love letters in Lydia's safe. "I don't know much at all. It was before my time. But she always said he was the most beautiful man. Lydia and I always did have a weakness for handsome men."

He paused to heavily salt, for the third time, his side of French fries. "I never met him. But I was under the impression from what little she told me that he was neurotic. An artist, of course. She wouldn't have been interested in him if he weren't. A hypochondriac. And his wife was worse, always nearing death and then recovering, so he couldn't leave her. He checked himself into Silver Hill every other week."

"She did eventually buy the house from him," I said.

He nodded his head. "She worked hard. In some ways, your aunt was very practical."

"Then why all this mystery around the will?" I asked in frustration.

Hamilton shrugged. "I haven't the foggiest."

"But you knew her better than anyone," Peck protested, picking the celery out of her lobster salad.

He pursed his lips together before answering. "How well can we really know another person? People can be in your lives for years—they can fill your lives. But all you really know of them are the stories they tell you. And then they die. They always leave a mystery behind."

We were quiet for a bit after that. I was thinking of Lydia, with her white hair that hung in thick waves around her shoulders, and the gypsy rings she always wore. She was always dressed for a party, even when she was tending the hydrangeas around her property, or reading on the porch. Even, I supposed, when she'd been at the front of a classroom, lecturing a roomful of boys on Gatsby's green light. She'd always carried herself very erect, a commanding presence. I remember going to meet her plane at the airport when she'd come to visit my mother and me and being surprised to see, when she emerged from baggage claim in a rush of much larger passengers, that she was actually quite small, because I always thought of her as such a big presence. She'd been a model at a time when a pretty face could earn some money, even if she wasn't that tall.

"She would tell us to make an effort to get to know each other," I said. "'You're sisters,' she would say, 'you should *know* each other.' Didn't she say that all the time?"

"She did," Peck acknowledged. "She said it all the time."

"Drove my mother crazy," I said. "She'd never admit it, but I think it bothered her. She always seemed like she wanted to forget there was a first wife and a daughter whose father had moved out."

"Mine too," Peck said with a laugh. "And she would definitely *never* admit it. She'd say, 'Of course, you're absolutely right, you *should* get to know your half sister.'" She mimicked her mother's high singsong words. "And then I'd say, 'When can we go visit my sister in Italy?' Or Belgium, or wherever you were living at the time. And she'd say, 'Not *this* summer.'"

"My mother knew yours would never let you visit us," I said, remembering now. "So she could play the laid-back one, always saying, 'Sure, no problem, we'd love to have Peck.'"

Peck nodded her head. "It's true. Mum acted like you were raised with wolves, like, in a commune or something. She always said your mother was so *alternative*. That's what she called it, like your mother was a radio station."

"And my mother always said yours was limited," I told her.

"Lydia loved both of you," Hamilton said definitively, as he paid the bill. "And she would have been so happy to see you enjoying each other the way you are this summer. This would have given her such joy."

"But we still hate each other," Peck said, startling him for a second or two before he realized she was kidding.

"Are we near Jackson Pollock's house?" I asked as we got back into the car. "Isn't Springs out this way?"

"Oh, let's go, let's go," Peck cried out. "*Inspiration.*"

"It's on Springs Fireplace Road," Hamilton said. "The Pollock-Krasner House and Study Center. I'm surprised Lydia never took you there. She certainly forced me to go more than a few times. It's quite moving, for some odd reason."

"Let's go, let's go," Peck repeated, like a child being enticed by the promise of a candy store visit, as she pulled out onto Route 27 behind a red pickup.

"I seem to remember that it is open on Thursdays, Fridays, and Saturdays in the summer months," Hamilton said. "And today's Thursday and it's July, so I think we can go without an appointment."

Hamilton directed Peck and we got lost, but eventually we pulled alongside a small, picturesque 1879 farmhouse, the home of a fisherman, we were to learn, before Jackson Pollock and his wife, Lee Krasner, bought it for five thousand dollars in 1945 with the help of a two-thousand-dollar loan from Peggy Guggenheim. The house was very close to Fireplace Road, set off by a small, scraggly hedge, and at the end of the short driveway was a sign and a wooden box containing pamphlets describing the place and its affiliation with the Stony Brook Foundation. We parked and wandered to the back of the property, where there were several outbuildings, including one that had been the original outhouse that the two artists had used for several years before they added plumbing and electricity. This was now a gift shop and information center, where we were greeted by a cheerful woman and given instructions.

I did feel a shiver of excitement as the three of us stood together briefly, gazing at the shingled studio at one end of the property. It had been moved there from its original location near the creek— the former foundation remained—where it had blocked the view of the water from the house. The property, with its almost iridescent light, was extremely serene, and we were immediately transported back to a simpler time when the isolation Pollock would have experienced here would have made it, temporarily at least, easier for him to go out to the converted barn with its northern light to work than to a bar to drink.

The house and studio were apparently left exactly as they had been when Lee Krasner died, with some of the original furniture and bits of driftwood they had collected while beachcombing. We were able to wander through the rooms she'd occupied with her brilliant but difficult husband until he died in 1956. Krasner continued to live there until she died in 1964.

"It reminds me a little of Fool's House," Peck said of the ramshackle little home, and Hamilton and I agreed that there was something of a similar feel to it, although the interior of the Pollock-Krasner House was sparse, without any of the clutter Lydia had accumulated over the years.

We entered the house through the back door directly into the kitchen, like at Fool's House, and walked slowly through the rooms on the ground floor. There was a large round table in the open dining room, where they'd apparently hosted many guests. In the living room, shelves still contained their collection of books and hundreds of old jazz records, even a hi-fi system that Pollock had installed only a year or two before he died.

On the second floor were two bedrooms. One of them had been Pollock's studio when they first moved in and then Krasner's. Later, when he died and she painted in the converted barn out back, this became something of an office. The other room was their bedroom. "They slept in twin beds," Hamilton whispered. "No wonder they had a difficult marriage. And look, there's the toilet. You can look at it, but you mustn't sit on it."

Peck, in her passion for all things vintage, crowed enthusiastically at the sight of a collection of old-fashioned suitcases lined up neatly on one side of the room and then called us over. "Check this out," she said, pointing at one that was engraved with the letters *J.P.* below the handle. "Remind you of anything?"

The house was interesting and evocative, but the real highlight of our visit was the studio, with its clear northern light, where we were instructed to take off our shoes and put on a pair of slippers from the bins near the door.

"I'd forgotten this part," Hamilton grumbled as he removed his heavy brown lace-ups.

"I wouldn't take mine off for Bethany Samuels," Peck said. "But Jackson Pollock is a different story."

The purpose of the slippers became evident when we were invited to walk across the paint-laden floor, on which Pollock had created his most important works and where his footprints remained visible. We fell silent as we padded across this vivid piece of history, as thickly layered with drips of paint and colors and as redolent with energy as one of the artist's masterpieces. "Wow," Peck intoned breathlessly as Hamilton and I followed her into the space.

A series of photos documenting the artist's work habits and methods dotted the walls, and the three of us spent some time studying them, then gazing reverently down at the floor. The experience was surprisingly moving and even the normally chatty Peck was awed into quiet while we soaked up the atmosphere in the studio. "I envisioned myself skating around like a crab, like he did when he was painting," she whispered. "But I feel like I'm in church."

We eventually retrieved our shoes and made our way out to the back lawn of the house, where there was a cluster of granite boulders on which Pollock had been photographed with his girlfriend, Ruth Kligman, on the day of the accident that killed him. Peck and I paused there while Hamilton was still chatting with the woman who ran the information desk and gift shop.

Peck pulled out a pack of American Spirits and lit one with a world-weary sigh as she rested one leg on a rock. "Sometimes I just don't know what the hell the guy in the sky is thinking." She lifted her eyes as though she might find the answer up there.

I followed her gaze upward. "You getting existential on me?"

She gave me a look of pleased surprise, as though I'd just alerted her to something nice about herself of which she hadn't been aware. "I am, aren't I? It's the salt-scrubbed air, Stella. It's giving me deep thoughts." She paused, taking a deep inhale, and then she broke into a silly voice. "Jack Handey's Deep Thoughts." She looked to see if I got the reference. I did. The summer we read *Gatsby* we also watched a lot of *Saturday Night Live* reruns.

She smoked for a while in silence as we stood looking out at the view that had inspired Pollock. "You know," she said, "I started reading *The Great Gatsby* myself the other day."

"You did?" I was surprised. Peck, for all her talk of literary fetishes, was not an avid reader.

"I read the whole thing at once. It's shorter than I remembered it. And I probably shouldn't admit this," she said, "but I always thought it was this great love story. I think I read it as a romance novel the first time. But now, when I read it again, I realized what he was saying about that kind of love. It's just a dream, right? It's not real, the way he loves that memory of Daisy, right?" She lifted her sunglasses and squinted at me. "Isn't that exactly what I did with Miles?"

I nodded. "I guess so. But you really were in love with him."

"I was," she said. "But am I now? Or is it just a dream? And think about it, Stella. Could I actually love someone with no style or taste?" She gestured at her outfit to make her point. "How is that even *possible*?"

"He can acquire taste," I suggested. "With your help. He already said he would sell that house of his."

She nodded. "But where's he going to find a buyer who wants a monogrammed pool?"

"I'm sure they can change that to something else. Or get rid of it," I said. "The point is, I think you do love the person underneath all that stuff that doesn't matter. And it's obvious that he loves you."

She put one hand on my shoulder so she could lift her foot and tap the cigarette out on the bottom of her shoe and then she gazed at me. "Hamilton was right about you. You're not immature at all. You're wise beyond your years, Stella."

"I thought I was a pill bug."

She pulled me closer to her. "You're kind of funny too. Maybe we could have an act. The Moriarty sisters."

15

Laurie Poplin was the type of person who would call every number she had listed for us six times in quick succession until she
got either of us on the other end, so she was particularly excited to
reach me on what must have been her first try. "You're *there*," she
marveled.

It was a Friday morning. Peck and I had finished organizing
the second floor, taping up the boxes labeled GIVE AWAY, and I'd
moved on to the living room, with its overflowing desk and mountains of papers that could probably all be thrown out, while Peck
packed one of her old-fashioned Vuitton steamer trunks to take to
the Ritz for the weekend with enough outfits to move permanently
to Paris. "One should always be prepared," she explained in a huff
when I commented on the size of her luggage. "I've never been to
the Ritz, so I don't know what I'm going to want to wear, do I?"

"Hello, Laurie Poplin," I said into the phone while Peck smiled
at me, noting my improved telephone response time. Her smile
quickly turned to a frown, however, when she heard me say the
name of the real estate broker she preferred to call Laura. She
hadn't liked Laurie to begin with, mostly because she wasn't going
to like anyone who had anything to do with the selling of Fool's
House, but now she had even more reason to dislike her. Laurie

had called Miles, saying she'd heard he might be putting his house on the market and wanted to offer her services. "She *heard* he might be selling his house," Peck had complained. "And I know what kind of services she thinks she can offer. They're like hookers, these women. They can just call up any old guy they want, pretending it's business, and then: watch the fuck out. It's some racket, real estate sales. It's unbelievable what women in this town will do to get a rich guy."

"I've got major news to discuss with you," Laurie was singing now through the telephone, all faux friendliness.

"Let me guess," I said. "The Bosleys want to come back to see the house."

"How did you know?" She sounded almost hurt that I'd stolen her thunder. Peck was now shaking her head vehemently and gesticulating at me.

"Just a hunch." I hadn't told Peck or Finn that I'd buried a statue of Saint Joseph under the hydrangea bush by the front door, and I was surprised at how quickly it appeared to have worked. "Is it the only thing in this neighborhood they can afford?"

"Not at all," Laurie was quick to say. "But they do love it. And here's the thing I know you and your sister will like. They don't want to change a thing."

While Laurie was talking, Peck was growing increasingly agitated at my side, mouthing, "No! No! Tell her no!"

"They're even talking about buying it furnished," Laurie continued, as proud as if she were making the offer herself.

"They're cheaper than I thought," I said. "But sure, bring them around."

"Don't sound so unimpressed," Laurie huffed. "I told you I'd get it sold. And they're talking about moving in for August. So this could go quickly."

As I had the phone to my ear, I'd been gazing out the screen door to the front lawn. Just as we were about to hang up, a rather astonishing sight appeared in my line of vision. "Bye now," Laurie Poplin was saying after arranging to bring the Bosleys back, but my jaw had dropped to my chest and I couldn't answer her. I couldn't speak because what I was seeing was Hamilton, naked except for his socks, clutching his clothes and shoes in front of his private parts, dashing through the open garage door and across the driveway toward the house, pale flesh jiggling like a bowl of Jell-O.

"Oh my God," I said, when I could say anything, the words catching in my throat, as he dropped a shoe and bent down to pick it up, then lost the bundled-up shirt. This necessitated another labored bending and retrieval, and at that I had to look away.

"I know, isn't it fantastic?" Laurie squawked into the phone as though I'd been talking to her. "I'm telling you, it only takes one—"

I interrupted her to say, "Good-bye, Laurie," and clicked the phone shut as Hamilton rushed up the porch steps. His hair was wildly disheveled and his face tomato red, in contrast to all that nakedness. "Oh dear," he said, smiling a little when he suddenly noticed me for the first time and realized I must have been standing right there, witnessing his little parade of flesh and dropped clothing.

"Okay. This—" Peck said as she noticed the commotion and came over to join me at the door. "This, I would call a situation."

Hamilton had reached the other side of the screen door by now and he peered in, clutching his clothing in strategic places. He looked not unlike Trimalchio caught sneaking a brownie. "May I come in?" he muttered. "Please?"

Peck and I grinned at each other as we stood aside so he could swing open the screen door. "Are you coming from the garage?" I asked him. "Did you *sleep* with Biggsy?"

A soulful expression came over his face as he shook his head.

"No. No, I couldn't do it. I thought I could, he's so beautiful. And he was game, I tell you." He dropped a shoe, but fortunately he didn't bother to pick it up. "Especially when I told him I would help him sell the painting. He has it, by the way. Much as we suspected."

"So you were successful," I said in an encouraging voice. "But you didn't sleep with him after all? I thought that was part of the plan."

He shook his head back and forth, as though he couldn't quite believe himself. "No. I thought about that silly little Scotsman and I realized I love *him*. I don't know if he feels the same for me, but I owe it to myself to find out."

"Are you kidding?" Peck looked over at me in amusement. "Is he kidding? He doesn't know that Scotty is crazy about him?"

Hamilton didn't seem to hear her as he continued. "I thought beauty was so important. My whole career is about *beauty*. But that boy is bad. He's rotten to the core underneath those looks." He paused and then added with a hiss, "And his beauty will fade."

"Do you want to use my bedroom?" I asked him. "I mean, to get dressed."

He nodded with solemn dignity. "That is a fabulous idea."

As he headed for the stairs, leaving the dropped shoe behind, Peck called after him. "Scotty is going to be very happy to hear about this."

He'd gone up the first two steps and he turned to us. "You're not to say a word. He's coming out on the Jitney any minute now. Please don't tell him."

"*You* tell him," I said. "Tell him how you feel."

"God, no." He made a face. "Why would I do that?"

"Because I'm pretty sure he feels the same way," I said, surprised that he could not know this about the tiny Scotsman who'd been mooning around with an infatuated glaze to his eyes every time we saw them together.

Hamilton shook his head. "We're friends. He wants to get *married*. Good God, he says he wants children. Can you think of anything more horrifying than having *me* for a father? I'd never do it."

"Just tell him," Peck and I both said at the exact same time. "Jinx," she added. "Buy me a root beer."

After he went upstairs Peck stared out the window in the direction of the garage. She looked slightly confused, as though she were trying to figure out what it was doing there. "It sure was nice having a butler," she said, somewhat wistfully.

"I don't know how anyone lives without one," I said.

"Miles had a butler," she said, still gazing out the window. "A rather surly Dutchman. But he fired him."

A few minutes later Hamilton came back downstairs with his hair combed. He was wearing one shoe and he calmly picked up the other one and sat on the sofa to put it on. "He's been trying to sell it to a Russian," he said, gesturing to the empty spot above the mantel where the missing painting had hung before Biggsy took it off the wall. "I'm not sure he believes it's a Pollock. The fool, I mean. Not the Russian."

"Where is he keeping it?" I asked.

Hamilton shook his head, slowly lacing his shoe. "For that information I would have had to shag the boy. And that I couldn't do."

"So what's next?" Peck wanted to know. "You can't do anything until I get back from Paris."

"Our boy Biggsy, or Jonathan as he is apparently known in the art world, if he's known at all, is spending the weekend on someone's boat. So I arranged a meeting for next Tuesday. My house. He's bringing the painting."

"We'll be there," Peck cried out. She'd opened the silver cocktail shaker on the bar cart and pulled out Lydia's revolver. "And we'll be loaded for bear."

"There are no bullets in that thing," Hamilton said.

"But Biggsy doesn't know that," I pointed out while Peck held the gun high. Peck had told him it was loaded. At the time I thought it was just her need to make every scene in her life more dramatic where possible, even to the point of total fabrication. But now I wondered if she hadn't been planning ahead, anticipating a moment when the use of a gun thought to be filled with bullets might be necessary.

"We'll take the painting back and send the young man on his way. Making him leave Fool's House is revenge enough for that poor fool. It should all be very simple. Let's hope weapons won't be necessary," Hamilton said with a chuckle. "Although you do look rather fetching with a gun in your hand. Very Bonnie and Clyde on the lam."

"I'm not afraid to use this," Peck exclaimed, swinging it in my direction. "And I may have to if you insist on selling this place to those dreadful people."

"They're your boyfriend's friends," I reminded her, holding up my hands in protest.

"Miles has terrible taste," she said matter-of-factly. "Everybody knows that. In people and in everything. Just look at his house."

"When are you going to take me over there?" Hamilton wanted to know. "You've promised me a tour."

"You loved that place when we went there for the party," I pointed out. "You thought it was the most fabulous house you'd ever seen."

"You're not the only one who's grown this summer," she said. Her words reminded me of my mother, who always used to say I grew in the summer. It was a theory of hers that maturation was boosted when the sunshine and a change of scenery and routine led to more noticeable growth. I always thought this was just one of her wacky ideas, like making me take a spoonful of coconut oil with my cereal in the morning, but now her words rang in my ears. Peck had grown this summer and I had too.

Hamilton left to pick up Scotty at the Jitney and Peck and I decided to take Trimalchio for a walk on the beach before she went off to Paris for the weekend.

"You going to miss me?" she asked as we trudged through the soft sand.

"Not at all," I teased. "I need to rest. It's exhausting living with a glamorous diva."

She looked pleased at the use of the word *diva* and then she said, "I don't just mean this weekend. I'm talking about after the end of this month. Are you really going to just disappear back into the wilderness?"

I shook my head. "No, of course not. We'll visit each other."

"Literally," she said, taking my arm. "This is a tease. We're *sisters*. I can't go back to a few phone calls every once in a while."

"We'll have money," I reminded her. "We'll be able to travel."

"Ah yes," she said, shifting tone again. "That does change things a bit, doesn't it? I hadn't thought of that. Well, I'm coming to Switzerland for Columbus Day weekend. And of course, we'll have Thanksgiving in New York. You've never seen the Macy's parade."

"I'm not really a parade person," I said. "But I like the idea of Thanksgiving in New York, especially if you'll cook."

"Of course I'll cook." I could see her already starting to think of a menu, decor, and what she was going to wear.

"What about Christmas?" I asked.

"Switzerland, naturally," she said. "But in the mountains. A family ski vacation with our little family. No Mum. She can stay in Palm Springs. She doesn't like the cold. But I'm thinking Saint

Moritz. Or Gstaad. Or what's that other one? Verbier. I've always wanted to pull off vintage ski pants, the stretchy kind, with a chunky sweater and a faux fur hat."

"We'll eat fondue," I added, lost in the reverie.

"Finn's a big skier," she said. "He loves all that outdoor stuff. Just like you."

I looked over at her, startled. "Finn's not going to be there."

"Of course he is. When I said family I meant the six of us. Miles and me, Hamilton and Scotty, you and Finn."

"Don't be ridiculous," I said. "You told me Finn should stick with Laurie Poplin. Didn't you tell me that?"

"Shut your piehole," she said with a laugh "You're in love with him. You just don't know it."

I did know it, I realized as she spoke those words. I was in love with Finn.

16

As would probably always be the case, my glamorously eccentric sister and I were a study in contrasts that weekend. While Peck was eating foie gras "by the shovelful" and sipping champagne at the Ritz in Paris, I was at Yankee Stadium, my hair tucked under a cap in the steaming heat, happily eating hot dogs and drinking beer while Finn explained the subtleties of baseball to me. I surprised myself, and Finn, apparently, by enjoying the game, quickly learning the players and following the score intently. "You're becoming quite the American," Finn noted as I ordered a second hot dog.

"I'll take that as a compliment," I said with a smile. He was talking about my taste in food, but there was a broader truth to his statement that I couldn't help but acknowledge: I *had* grown louder and bolder and more assertive since I'd been in the States. As Peck had been exhorting me to do, I'd come out of my shell.

Later in the weekend he took me to a clambake on the beach with his friends. Tony, the host, a big bear of a man, told me he was a "real estate novelist, like the guy in the Billy Joel song." His wife, Cintra, a British fashion stylist with a red bob, hugged me and told me she'd never seen Finn so happy. "We want to *bottle* you," she said warmly, as though we were already friends. "You're a tonic."

She paused and looked at me. "You know, we've always been mad for Finn, of course. He's Tony's best friend. But you seem to be very good for him."

"I find that hard to believe," I said. "We're just friends." We hadn't kissed again since that night by the car, though we did seem to find a way to touch each other often; he'd put an arm around my shoulder to direct my line of sight to something happening in the outfield, or tap my thigh to get my attention. We'd high-fived a couple of times when things in the game were going well, teasingly fake-punched each other in response to a comment, patted a forearm to make a point. He'd wiped mustard from my cheek and dabbed napkins at my shorts when he knocked a beer into my lap.

Cintra arched one eyebrow dubiously. "All I know is he was very keen to tell us all about you before you arrived. And since then? The chap's been downright giddy. We finally insisted he bring you 'round."

A swirl of people of all ages was gathered on the beach that evening, standing and sitting around a blazing bonfire, with torches for light and to keep the bugs away. The ocean was calm and the sky was pink and blue, and children and dogs were running everywhere. It was quite a scene.

"Ignore the beasts," Tony said to me, as a small boy came too close, wielding an enormous stick, on the end of which was a flaming marshmallow he was intending to make into something called a s'more.

"It's a melted marshmallow squashed between two graham cracker biscuits and a slab of chocolate, so called because apparently rude children are always asking for s'more," Cintra explained. "It's an American thing. I don't pretend to understand."

She and Tony had met on an airplane, she told me. She thought he was the most annoying man she'd ever met. When they arrived in London, he asked for her number and she gave it to him with one digit off so he couldn't reach her.

"I'd had it up to here with American men by then," she said. "I'd already had one—a first husband—under my belt. Not that the ones back home were any better, believe me. All those repressed schoolboys making shag jokes like they were still in boarding school—no thank you. I was fancying an Italian at that time. I wasn't planning on marrying one, just a fancy, you know."

"I do know," I said, immediately taken by her. "I've had a few fancies for Italians myself."

Cintra laughed in a conspiratorial way. "You can't marry them, though. Can you? Americans, on the other hand? They make the best husbands."

The night she arrived in London, she went on to tell me, by co-incidence, she headed down to her sister's "local" and there was Tony, the bearish American from the plane. "He bought me a drink," she was saying, as bunches of children weaved around us with their bamboo sticks for toasting marshmallows and the sea air filled with wood smoke. "Don't mind them. It's *Lord of the Flies* at these things. As long as none of them end up in the ocean or the fire pit, we should be okay."

"So what made you change your mind?" I asked. "About Tony? How did you know he was the one?"

"Oh, I didn't at all," she said, laughing. "I had no idea. Still don't. But he makes me laugh. And that's all it took."

"I totally agree," I said, catching a glimpse of Finn, who was helping the little boy blow out his flaming marshmallow.

"Is that a reason to get married?" she asked with a laugh. "I dunno. To give up my job, my friends, my family. Well, the family, I was happy to give up, at least on a daily basis. But I moved across the pond for him. Didn't know him very well at the time either."

"Did you date long-distance?" I asked as her husband came by with fresh beers and handed them to us without interrupting, except to say, "Don't believe a word my wife tells you."

"We tried," she said, giving me a knowing smile. "But that wears thin. And then, at some point, you just have to hold your nose and dive in, you know? You can't be afraid to take that chance. You know what I mean?" She paused, as though she wanted to assess how her words were registering.

I nodded as Finn appeared at my side with a paper bowl of clams to offer me. We ate corn on the cob and biscuits and lobster dunked in butter. Finn made sure I met a good number of his friends. They were New Yorkers, though most of them seemed to have landed there from somewhere else. Everyone was a *character*, as though it were a requirement to be unusual and have a particular accent and a style of dress and passions, and they all seemed to live big, ambitious lives, filled with yearnings and obligations and precocious children. I found myself enthralled and the evening took on a feeling of momentousness, like it would stand out in sharp relief later when I retrieved it from my memory bank.

One of the Girls, Sasha, was there. I was mildly shocked to see her on her own. She had no context without Betts and Lucy and Peck and their collective opinion. It was like running into a teacher out of school. She greeted me with a shout and a warm hug and suddenly I felt that *I* had context, with a friend there of my own. She was with a date—a divorced dad with a four-year-old son who kept smearing chocolate all over himself—but he was busy keeping the boy from falling into the bonfire in his eagerness for more s'mores, so we hung out for a while and she filled me in on the backstories of the people she knew.

"He's a pretty special fellow," she said of Finn, her soft Indian inflection turning the words evocatively.

"So everyone keeps telling me," I joked.

She gestured at the firelit scene with the ocean and the vast sky. "Clever idea too, giving you a taste of what could be. This is quite a sales job."

"Don't be silly. What would he be selling me?" Finn was on the other side of the bonfire talking to Tony, his hair thick and wild from the salty air. He caught my eye as I noticed him, and he smiled.

"All of this," she said softly. "It's like a dream, isn't it?"

"Someone else's," I said. I knew what she meant, but I didn't think it applied to me. "Not mine."

At the end of the evening Tony wagged a finger at me. "Did you fall in love with me yet?"

"It's your wife I'm in love with," I told him as around us children were coming down from their sugar highs and the fire was getting low.

He groaned. "So *predictable*. She's the easy one to like. I'm the acquired taste."

"Was it a test?" I asked. "Or can I pick both of you?"

"It *was* a test," he said, reaching into the cooler to hand me another fresh beer. "But *we* were the ones being tested."

I took the beer and popped the cap while the parents with the younger children headed off, waving their good-byes. "So that explains why you're all being so nice to me."

"No. It doesn't explain anything," Tony said with a laugh. He'd taken a beer for himself and he clinked it against mine. "We were planning to terrorize you. We thought we'd get rid of you the easy way."

I didn't know what to say to that, but then Finn came up behind me and Tony was pulled away by people saying good-bye. "Let's hang out for a bit," he whispered, once they were out of earshot. The planes of his face caught the firelight and I almost couldn't resist reaching out and touching his smooth skin. "This is skinny-dipping weather."

"No, it's not," I said, as I zipped up my sweater in response to the chill that grew more noticeable as the fire died down.

"Look how calm the ocean is," he said, pointing. "Don't you want to be able to cross that one off the list?"

I shook my head. "I'm not in a hurry," I said as the breeze from the ocean picked up and it felt colder. "It's getting arctic out here."

As Tony and Cintra gathered their belongings and their children and headed off, Finn set about building up the fire, carefully piling several extra logs onto the coals.

"You're very resourceful," I said as I sat on a blanket and watched the flames quickly grow high. There was something achingly beautiful about the fragrant air, and the rhythmic sound of the ocean and the flickering firelight giving the scene a seductive glow.

"Didn't you say I was dexterous too? Resourceful and dexterous. I must be quite a catch," he said as he sat down next to me. We were alone on the beach now.

We chatted for a while, gazing at the fire, rather than at each other, and in no time he had me laughing so hard I could hardly breathe. I made him laugh too, sharing more stories of my peripatetic life with my mother and the summers I'd spent at Fool's House with Lydia in the company of a wacky half sister who wasn't sure she wanted to be related to me. I'd gotten so comfortable with him in the time we'd spent together, and I enjoyed how liberating it felt to talk freely about my family and the inconsistencies in my mother's stories. I even shared the anecdote about my name.

"It could have been worse," I said, repeating my mother's line with the kind of aplomb I'd learned to copy from Peck. I was no longer the timid, sad creature who'd tiptoed up the porch steps at the beginning of July with my little wheely suitcase. I felt like something had awakened deep inside me, like a switch that had been suddenly turned on. "They could've played 'Bertha.'"

Finn let out a soft laugh. "You're funny, kid."

"Glad you think so, Killian."

He leaned back on his elbow and turned his head toward me. "So, what do you think? Does the ocean beckon?"

"I told you, I *don't* skinny-dip." I sounded like Peck again, I thought, as I made this declaration with Peck's manner of emphasizing at least one word in every sentence.

"Just like you *don't* flirt?" His face glowed in the firelight as he grinned up at me. "Come on, we'll make it quick. Like ripping off a Band-Aid. One two three, in and out." I wondered how he could evoke a thrill of excitement and a feeling of total safety at the same time. "I promise, I won't look."

He stood and pulled his T-shirt over his head. "Let's go, fraidy-cat. You can do it. Face your fear." He reached down and grabbed my hand. "I'll be right by your side the whole time. We'll make a run for it. A quick dunk and we're out. But we can say we did it."

"Suddenly I was game. "Okay, then. What are you waiting for?"

"We'll never make it if we go slow," he said, unzipping his jeans. "We've got to run and go all the way."

"I thought you'd never done this before," I said as I slipped off my sweater.

"Never naked," he said. "Never with a beautiful woman."

"You promised you wouldn't look," I reminded him, although I couldn't help sneaking a glance at the very flat muscles of his stomach. His wasn't the sort of body that comes from hours at the gym or from endless miles logged on a bicycle while wearing spandex, but it was lean and sexy.

He covered his eyes with one hand, pulling at his jeans with the other. "It's kind of hard to get undressed like this."

I pulled my jeans off my hips and tossed them on the sand, shivering slightly, but not from the cold. I didn't even feel the chill in the air anymore.

He took my hand, carefully averting his eyes. "One. Two. Three." We ran toward the ocean together, hand in hand. The icy water was a shock, but we dived in. It took my breath away at first, but once we were in, it felt wonderful. We swam a bit in the moonlight, allowing the waves to pull us along.

I wanted to feel his arms around me, to entwine our legs together. I'd never felt that way about Jean-Paul, I recalled, not even when we first met. There was always something businesslike about our arrangement and—I didn't realize this until much later—I'd had to continually talk myself into believing it was right, even when I knew, of course I knew, it was wrong. I didn't blame him when it all came apart, though it stung to learn he'd been unfaithful. We were simply not at all suited to each other, and I was just as much at fault for ignoring the signs. But with Finn, despite how much I'd been trying to talk myself out of him, there was something so right about him. And all I wanted him to do was throw me on the sand and kiss me.

He must have read my mind, because that was exactly what he did once we ran back up the beach to the fire and the blanket. He pressed his long body against mine and when our lips met it felt like coming home.

"I'm terrified," he said with a smile, holding himself over me when we came up for air.

I don't know what I'd been expecting his next words to be, but those were not them. "What do you mean?"

"I can't be your friend, kid. I mean I can't be *just* your friend." His voice was gruff. "I'm in love with you, you know."

Warmth suffused my body, despite the chilly breeze. "You are?"

"I think I've been in love with you since I met you," he said.

"And that's terrifying?"

His eyes met mine and my heart seemed to skip a beat. "It is. Because you're going to leave in two weeks."

I pulled him down to me to whisper into his ear. "Is that why you were so weird that night you took me for dinner at the Four Seasons?" He nodded, and I said, "You have to face your fear, fraidy-cat."

He kissed me again and then we couldn't stop. Time seemed to stand still and we stayed on the beach for a long time afterward. Eventually even the embers of the fire were completely cold and we got dressed and headed back to Fool's House.

Before we even got to the stairs, he was kissing me again and his hands were all over me. We kissed all the way up the stairs to my room where, I was glad to see, I'd remembered to make the bed with its popcorn bedspread. The bed became quickly unmade as we fell on it and pulled at our clothes in another rush of passion. Afterward, our bodies fitted together like spoons under the old, soft sheet. We talked and laughed, and I thought I would never feel tired ever again, not in Finn's company, but we did fall asleep eventually as the pink-gray light of dawn began seeping in around the curtains.

Later, Peck would tell me, and anyone else who would listen, about her weekend with Miles. "Did you know," she would start by asking, "there's an F. Scott Fitzgerald suite at the Ritz?" Often the person hearing her tale did not know this and she would continue. On the occasion when someone would know, she would ask the follow-up question: "Well, have you ever stayed there?"

She has yet to encounter anyone who had actually been in the suite, allowing her to describe it in lengthy detail, going on about the extravagant upholstery and the wood paneling and the fireplace. "It's *impossibly* glamorous," she would say, fixing her listener with a steady gaze. "And there's a whiff of *history* in the air."

She would pause and light a cigarette, and the listener—me—would feel as though there wasn't any place in the world she'd rather be at that moment than there at the Ritz.

"History isn't the only scent," she'd continue. "The whole place smells spicy and mysteriously rich, like a perfume ad. I swear, they pump this fragrance into the air vents. And then it's also in the body lotion and this cologne in your bathroom, acres and acres of marble."

She'd go on about the special cocktails at the Hemingway bar until you were dying for one, and the thick peach terry-cloth robes and the pool with its spa and the club sandwiches. She would tell anyone who would listen about how if you're a writer you can get your mail at the Ritz. "The Fitzgerald suite is where you *must* stay. It's all red and gold, with brocade fabrics and overstuffed furniture and the most incredible high, fluffy bed you could sink into for *days* with hundreds of pillows on it. A mushy down-filled acre of silk and satin."

Miles didn't exactly ask her that weekend. To marry him, I mean. What he said was, "We could get married." In the same tone, Peck told me, he might have used to say, "We could have tuna sandwiches for lunch." Or "We should all get vaccinated." Or "We could go to Morocco." *Some day.*

"But I said, 'Yes. *Some day*,'" she would say, neatly wrapping up her story.

17

Peck came back from Paris with an enormous feathered hat she'd found at the flea market. "I'm afraid it may *have* fleas," she said of the thing, which she insisted on wearing over to Hamilton's house for our showdown with Biggsy three days later. "Or the avian flu. But isn't it *fabulous?*"

Hamilton and Scotty certainly thought so. "It's so risky," Scotty decreed. "And thus, *frisky*," Hamilton added.

We gathered Wednesday evening, the six of us—Peck, Miles, Scotty, Hamilton, Finn, and me—on the patio behind Hamilton's house. This was the first time Finn and I had been in the presence of another human being since our night at the beach. I felt as though I'd been drugged for those three days, so distracted was I by the intensity of my feelings for him. He said he felt the same way and called in sick to the office. Afterward he said, "I didn't lie, I *am* sick. I'm dizzy, weak, I can't think straight. What have you done to me?"

I didn't know that one could feel this way about another person. Romantic love had always seemed like an abstract concept to me, I realized, until these raw waves of emotion overtook me so strongly I felt like laughing and crying at the same time. I was taken by total surprise, not only by the feelings, but that Finn—Lydia's Finn was how I thought of him—was the source of them.

We sat together in one of the enormous wicker chairs with navy cushions pulled up to a low table on Hamilton's patio. The others all took their own seats but Finn pulled me down next to him with an arm around my shoulders, prompting Peck to comment that we should get a room. Hamilton had instructed Scotty on the proper preparation of the traditional Pimm's Cup, and they passed around tall frosted glasses garnished with fruit.

"Are we certain it's not still alive?" Finn asked, wrinkling his nose as he inspected Peck's hat. "I think it's *moving*."

"It's probably in horribly bad taste," she explained in the self-deprecating manner that she adopted when she knew she was wearing something truly fabulous. "But I'd rather have bad taste than no taste any day of the week."

"Oh, me too," Scotty cooed. He was enamored of Peck's outrageous fashion sense. "What does your beau think of it?"

"My beau?" she scoffed from under the mass of drooping feathers. "He *bought* it for me. And then he had to carry the thing on the plane. He almost had to buy it its own seat, didn't you, Miles?"

Miles nodded distractedly, scrolling on his BlackBerry as he shoveled potato chips into his mouth. He spoke through a spray of crumbs. "When is that punk going to show up?"

On cue, Biggsy appeared on the patio, shocked to see the six of us gathered there. He was dressed in a tight-fitting seersucker suit and he too wore a hat. His was a small porkpie with jaunty red trim, and he looked too young and good-looking for this role, like a heartthrob leading man trying unsuccessfully to play the part of the bad guy. We're used to crooks looking like rats, with beady eyes and bad shirts, and crazy people looking ugly and unkempt. But Biggsy was so beautiful, with those razor-sharp cheekbones and full lips, that in the movies he could only be cast as the love interest. Or possibly the villain who would then turn out to have been on the good side the whole time. It had been so easy for him to fool us. We'd been so willing to be fooled.

"Uh . . . hello," he stammered, stopped short by the sight of all of us. He'd only expected Hamilton and someone—Scotty—who looked like an art dealer, and he was shocked to see me, Peck, Finn, and Miles on the patio.

"Hello, young man," Hamilton boomed. "Won't you have a Pimm's?"

"Um . . . sure." Biggsy didn't move his feet. He was empty-handed, despite the plan set in motion by Hamilton for him to bring the painting to this meeting. "What's going on?"

"It's an intervention," Peck cried out, the feathers on her hat bobbing madly. "We've had a few of those this summer."

Biggsy looked flummoxed. "It was only a couple of joints. I have ADD. I take it to relax."

"Not drugs, you idiot. Art." Peck said, glancing over at me.

"We want the painting back," I explained, speaking as calmly as I could, even though I wanted to strangle the good-looking young guy who stood there trying to look wide-eyed and innocent. "And then we want you to take your stuff and leave."

His eyes darted nervously between Peck and me. "I live here. This is my *home*."

"Jonathan," I said firmly. "We know you stole from us. And we know you faked that letter from Lydia."

He paused for a second, calculating a next move. "I just wanted you to *like* me," he said with a pout, like he was trying to be cute about it. "Lydia loved me so much. I was just putting onto paper the words she herself used about me. And she encouraged me to do those pranks. She called it art."

At this, Miles let out a snort. "Art?"

"That was a mean thing to do." I sounded like a stern school-teacher. "You've been nothing but trouble since we got here."

"And then you let me believe Miles took it," Peck added, pointing a finger at him. "You almost fucked the whole thing up for me. I should've kicked you the hell out right then."

"I think of you as my *family*," he tried to explain. "We have no more living family, any of us. And I thought . . . you, me, Peck—"

"Peck's mother is alive and well and living in a condo in Palm Springs," I interjected, losing what little patience I might have had for this charade.

"Where she belongs," Peck said with a nod in my direction.

"And *we*, Peck and I, are sisters, related by blood," I continued as Peck beamed her approval at me. "You, on the other hand, are a freeloader we've tolerated for too long. So don't try to put yourself in any category with us."

He looked down at his feet. "I can't let you do it. You can't let Fool's House go." He looked up then with a vicious gleam in his eyes as he directed his words to me. "You think you're so fucking worldly, just because you live somewhere else. But you're *myopic*. You and your sister."

Finn had been watching calmly from the big wicker chair, but now he stood. "Hey. Just give them the painting."

"And the book," I interjected.

"And anything else you took," Finn continued. "And then move on. Show's over."

"What the hell do *you* know?" There was a rehearsed quality to the venom in his voice, like he'd been watching soap operas for techniques on how to play the villain, and it made me want to laugh. "You're a fucking architect."

Finn gave him a bemused look. "What's that supposed to mean?"

"Architects are all failed artists." Biggsy was still standing at the edge of the patio, staring in at the six of us, who formed a circle in the wicker chairs around the low table with its bowls of chips and other "nibbles," as Hamilton insisted on calling them.

I stood and folded my arms over my chest, glaring at Biggsy. "Where's the painting?"

He didn't answer me but took a step toward Scotty. The elfin Scotsman was perched on the edge of his huge cushioned chair like a child at a tennis match, head swiveling from side to side as he observed the action with delight. "Are you the art dealer?"

"The *dealer*?" I repeated as I realized that Biggsy still didn't seem to understand what was going on here.

"I'm not an art dealer," Scotty announced, pulling himself upright in his seat.

"But he plays one on TV," Peck added. "This time the prank's on you, Biggs. There's no dealer. There's only us. And we want our painting back."

"And the book," I repeated.

He swiveled to look at me. "What *book*?"

"Just give us back Lydia's painting," Peck said. "And then get the hell out of here."

Biggsy answered with a sneer. "You can have the damn painting," he said. "It's not worth shit."

We all seemed to speak at once. "How do you know?"

He put both hands on his hips before he spoke. "It's no Jackson Pollock, that's for fucking sure." He appeared to be almost enjoying himself, in full performance mode now that he felt he had command of his audience.

"So who painted it?" I asked him.

He shrugged. "Someone short on talent. There's a lot of them."

"We don't care," Peck cried out. "It has sentimental value and we want it back. And then you've got to get out."

"I'll get you the painting," he said. "But you can't make me leave Fool's House."

There was a brief pause when nobody spoke. All this time I'd had Lydia's revolver in my back pocket and I pulled it out now and pointed it at the young fool. "Yes, we can," I said, trying to hold the gun as steady as possible as I focused it right between his lovely blue eyes. I'd never pointed a gun at anyone. I'd never even held one in my hand until that morning, when I pulled it out of the cocktail shaker in preparation for this afternoon. It felt surprisingly natural, though, to bring out this extra little bit of force, even though the unloaded revolver wasn't anything more than a prop.

He looked startled. And then quickly his bravado returned. "You could never shoot that thing."

"Watch me," I said, willing my hand not to shake.

Finn was grinning at me as he said to Biggsy, "Just get them their stuff, dude. Nobody has to get hurt."

Biggsy lifted his hands in protest. "All right," he said. "Don't get your panties in a wad. The painting was at Fool's House all along." He turned and gestured that we should follow him.

We fell into a line behind him down the path that led around the house to the driveway. I went first with the gun and the others fell in after me in close succession, like we were in a conga line at a party. "Wait until you see where that painting is," Biggsy called out from his spot as the leader in front of us. "You'll be blown away."

I'm sure we must have looked ridiculous, like costumed inmates from an asylum being let out for a parade, to anyone on the street as we filed out of Hamilton's driveway. There was Biggsy in the lead in his shrunken suit and hat, and then me with a gun. Behind me was tall Finn and then shorter Miles, who somehow managed to be texting on his BlackBerry while he walked. Tiny Scotty, in a purple paisley shirt tucked into orange Bermuda shorts with a red ribbon belt, traipsed along behind him, stepping daintily on the gravel in his flimsy espadrilles. At the rear, looking like they were actually supposed to be in an Easter parade, were Peck and Hamilton, arm in arm, he in a blazer and tie and she in a shiny long dress with that enormous drooping hat.

When Biggsy got to the porch, he stopped and turned to face the rest of us, looking both sly and stupid at the same time. "I told you, it's in the house. Can you guess where?"

"I know, I know," Peck exclaimed as she drew close. "The bar cart."

Biggsy looked confused. "The bar cart? Where would I hide a framed oil painting in a bar cart?"

Peck shrugged. "I hid the gun in it. In Grandma Nonah's silver cocktail shaker."

Biggsy turned and opened the screen door and we followed him into the house one by one. Peck had to hold the sides of her hat down so she could fit through the doorway.

In the hall Biggsy pointed at the Pink Lady, the doll that had kept vigil from the top of the stairs since Lydia moved into the place. "She knows all," he intoned, and then he opened the door to the overstuffed closet under the stairs that Peck and I had not had a chance to clear out.

"We looked in there," I said.

"Not all the way in the back," he replied with a grin. "And I dropped so many *hints*."

We watched as he burrowed into the closet, tossing aside blankets, sweatshirts, and an old-fashioned wicker picnic basket before emerging, his porkpie hat askew as he held up the painting that had been missing for more than two weeks. He handed it to me without making eye contact.

"Why did you take it?" I asked him, still holding the gun.

He shrugged. "I knew the way Lydia felt about that painting. When you said a thing of utmost value, I knew it had to be that."

"Did you think it was a Jackson Pollock?" Peck wanted to know.

He shook his head. "I didn't know what it was. But I figured it was something." We all went quiet then, looking at the painting. It had seemed to have such power when we were trying to find it. Now it was once more just a canvas rather amateurishly covered with oil paint in abstract fashion. "I didn't steal it," he added, gazing at me with imploring eyes. "I never *stole* anything from you. I was just doing what Lydia had always wanted me to do. Entertain. And all I want now is to be able to stay here."

I still had the gun in one hand and I lifted it again. "Where's my book?"

"I don't know what you're talking about," he cried out, the picture of innocence. "Why would I take a book? I don't even *read*."

"Go get your things," I said, gesturing with the gun. "And get out."

"And if you ever come within fifteen feet of the two of them . . . or their shoes," Miles added, "I'll have you killed."

"He will too," Peck chimed in. "He has a phone number in his wallet for just that purpose."

Peck took the canvas from me, shoved the chair over to the fireplace so she could stand on it, and placed the painting back on its hook above the mantel. Then we all followed Biggsy out to the garage and up the stairs to the studio. His camera equipment and a couple of packed bags were piled neatly by the door, and the mess of papers and other junk in the second room had been cleared out.

"I thought you couldn't leave Fool's House," I said. "But it seems like you got yourself ready to go after your supposed meeting with the art dealer who was going to broker a deal for the painting you claimed to have for sale."

He didn't answer me as he lifted the camera and quickly switched it on before aiming the lens at the six of us crammed into the small space. "One more shot before I go?" he asked, but he was already filming.

"That's enough," Finn said to him. "Get moving."

Biggsy didn't listen to him. He kept the camera rolling as he approached Miles. "I'd still be interested in discussing my piece *A Fool and His Money.*"

"Get. The fuck. Out of here," Miles said. "Now. Or you'll wish you'd taken the easy way."

Biggsy turned the camera on Peck, "You could *be* somebody," he said, focusing a tight shot on her face.

"Honey," she said, mugging for the camera like an old-time movie queen, "I already *am* somebody."

I swung the gun into his line of vision and said, "Jonathan. It's time to go." He reluctantly switched the camera off. As he slung one of the bags over his shoulder something fell out of a side pocket and clattered loudly to the floor. It was Lydia's copy of *Gatsby.*

I reached down and picked it up. "I thought you said you never read."

He shrugged. "You said it was a first edition. It's not, by the way. I had it checked out."

I thought for a moment before responding. "How did you know about that?"

He shrugged. "As I always say, you have to pay attention."

"I've never heard you say that," Peck cried out indignantly. "That's *my* line."

We all started speaking at once then, insisting that he go. Finally he did, roaring off on his motorcycle, which was loaded down with all his belongings. We stood in the driveway to watch him leave.

18

With Biggsy gone, Fool's House seemed a different place, airier and happier. It wasn't so much to do with Biggsy, or even with the fact that the rooms themselves seemed lighter and larger once we removed all the paintings from the walls except the one above the mantel. I think it was just that I was so happy that the whole world seemed different, lit with a clear golden light.

Even the brief period—it lasted all of an afternoon—when Peck was technically not speaking to me did not alter my feelings. Perhaps that was because she kept talking to me all through it. "I'm not speaking to you until you come to your senses," she cried out, after arguing at length that we should still keep Fool's House, even though we had not, in fact, inherited a Jackson Pollock worth millions of dollars. We were having this conversation on the porch and she kept stomping her foot to make her points. Each time she did the rotted slabs of wood would rattle loosely. I explained again, at length, that I too did not wish to sell the house we both loved.

"Why are you so depressing?" She addressed these words to the sky, as though she might find an answer there. And then she declared again that she wasn't speaking to me.

"All evidence to the contrary," I pointed out cheerfully. At this she pounded the porch floor once more and turned on her heel.

I'd never had much patience with happy people. Positive thinking and idealism had never seemed as interesting as the darker view to me. But then I turned into one of them. The week that followed will always stand out in my memory as the most thrilling time in my relatively short and oddly complicated life. I experienced it as an adrenaline high, the kind of sky-diving buzz that comes from conquering a deeply held fear.

Finn, like me, had never taken more than a couple of days off in years. He'd been so busy for so long, building a bustling multi-office business, that he was used to operating at full tilt at all times. Now he took a vacation, shocking everyone who worked with him.

We did all the things visitors to the Hamptons do. We took long beach walks in the mornings and water-skied in the evenings. We biked to Montauk and rented a canoe and laughed ourselves silly trying to get the thing to move in a straight line. We played tennis and took afternoon naps in the hammock in the back yard. We went to Sag Harbor to wander through charming antique shops, and sailed to Shelter Island, where we had a late lunch at Sunset Beach drinking rosé for hours until the fat orange sun sank below the horizon with dramatic flair. We went to the farm stand near Finn's house and made a picnic to take to the beach, where we met Cintra and Tony and their kids to ride the waves. Finn tried to teach me how to surf. We ate steaks at the Palm in East Hampton and drove to Briermere Farm in Riverhead to buy pies. He even helped Peck and me go through some of Lydia's things, lending a hand as we organized boxes to give away, to keep, and to throw out, which was more fun than it sounds with the music cranked up loud and some great snacks. And the sex? Well, it's best not to talk about such things; suffice it to say I never knew it could be that good.

The afternoon when Peck did not speak to me ended when she walked into my room without knocking.

"I don't want to fight with you." She was wearing nothing but a skimpy towel and her hair was wet. "Look at me," she added. "I'm a wreck."

"I don't want to fight either," I said. "And you're right. We should do whatever we can to keep this place."

She looked startled. "But you don't want to."

"Of course I want to," I said. "I just don't have the money."

She sighed, perching on the end of my bed. She sat there for some time in silence and then stood, having made up her mind. "I don't either. All I have is credit card debt. And we should do what Lydia told us to do."

By the time she rushed out of the room to "do something about this mop on my head," we had agreed to accept the Bosleys' offer on the house. She'd decided it would be too awkward to let Miles buy the place from us and would turn her efforts to attempting to rid his house of "every element of tackiness," as she phrased it. "You know, he's horribly *vulgar.*" It was her goal, she explained that evening, wrapped in her towel, to turn the enormous place into her version of Yaddo, where creative people could gather. "Stella!" she exclaimed. "You could come there next summer and write."

Perhaps I could. But now it was almost time for me to go back. My return airline ticket was waiting, marked with the date that loomed as a deadline for the end of me and Finn. I was scheduled to fly home on Sunday, the day after our final Fool's Farewell. And as we walked on the beach that morning under a deep blue sky, the sunlight glinting off the ocean, I made a decision that seemed altogether practical, although I was no longer sure how I felt about calling Switzerland my home.

"When we say good-bye," I told Finn that morning as we walked with Trimalchio on the beach, "let's have it be for good."

He stopped walking. "What do you mean?"

We'd been holding hands as we walked and now I turned and

took his other one in mine as I faced him. "I can't help thinking I'd rather keep the memory of this perfect stretch of bliss just as it is, as a beautiful little gem that could become a touchstone in later years, than let it fizzle out with dribs and drabs of resentment over time, the way long-distance relationships always seem to do."

He shook his head. "That's not how it would work, not with us."

"What makes you so sure? The first few weeks of any relationship are always great."

"Not like this," he interjected. "Nothing like this."

"True," I said. "This was extraordinary. But in this setting . . ." I gestured at the powerful beauty of nature that surrounded us on the wide empty beach.

"It has nothing to do with setting," he said. "I'm willing to take a chance. I'll visit. You'll visit. We'll make an effort."

I let go of one hand and started walking again. He fell into step next to me and Trimalchio trotted along at my other side, tilting his head up toward me as though trying to understand what was going on.

"That's just it," I said. "Effort. It already sounds bad. And then it will get worse. At first we'll approach it with enthusiasm and all sorts of plans. But over time, it will start to seem too hard. And neither one of us will want to compromise. And then one weekend you'll cancel on me at the last minute. A flight won't work out, there'll be a hurricane that night or a work emergency and it will seem too difficult to come. And I'll get resentful and we'll both wonder who the other one is actually having dinner with . . ." My voice trailed off as he stopped and stared at me incredulously.

"Jesus Christ," he said with a laugh. "Have you done this before?"

"No," I said. "But I've seen friends try to have relationships with people from far-off countries and I've never seen it work."

"So we're just to say good-bye at the airport, is that it? And never speak again?"

"You're going to take me to the airport?" I asked, surprised.

"I was planning on it," he said. "And then I thought I'd get on a plane myself the following week. I have a potential client to visit in Zurich and could easily stop in Lausanne for a few days afterward. And then you could come back here for Labor Day weekend."

"Labor Day is not a holiday in Switzerland."

"So I'll go back there then," he added. "It's too soon to say good-bye for good. What if this is it? You're not going to throw that away just because we haven't lived in the same city until now."

"We haven't even lived on the same continent," I pointed out. "Ever."

In *my* younger and more vulnerable years, as Nick Carraway would say in the opening lines of *Gatsby*, my father was not around to give me advice. This was a defining theme, I believed, of the story of my life, and for years I told myself this was why I often made poor decisions. But now I believed I'd undertaken a rewrite. And I could no longer use the fact of my father's early death to rationalize the choices that had later proved to be bad ones. My decision to end this seemingly idyllic relationship before it had time to begin was made, I fully believed, in the most rational and carefully considered manner.

By the end of our walk, Finn agreed with me. "Perhaps you're right," he said, as we headed back on the path through the dunes that led to the parking lot. "It will be more sensible this way.

We were quiet for the walk back to Fool's House. I'd planned, even before the walk on the beach, to finish packing that afternoon while Finn paid a visit to one of the job sites from which he'd been getting increasingly frantic phone calls. That night, we were having paella for dinner with Peck, Miles, Hamilton, and Scotty over at Hamilton's house. It was to be our own personal last supper, what Peck called "family night" before the increasingly large Fool's Farewell, to which Peck had now invited more than three hundred people.

"You don't even know three hundred people," I said to her as I made an initial stab at packing my suitcase in preparation to leave. Somehow, though, my clothes had multiplied like the bunnies that were hopping all over our lawn—how? I didn't think I'd bought much, just the dresses and shoes the day I went shopping with Peck and the Girls, a couple of bathing suits, a T-shirt here and there—and I was never going to be able to fit it all into the one bag I'd brought with me.

"Miles does," Peck said with a proud nod. As I was trying to pack, she'd appeared in my room wearing a long white caftan with elaborate beading around the neck, and she leaned in the doorway elegantly smoking without offering to help. "He knows *everybody*." Through Miles Peck had met all sorts of people, including but not limited to celebrities, fashion designers, and people who could get a table at a place called the Waverly Inn. They were all invited to the Fool's Farewell.

We were selling the house mostly furnished, although Peck was keeping the bar cart and its accessories and I'd planned to take a box of books, including Lydia's copy of *The Great Gatsby*. We were each keeping one of our father's paintings, already bubble-wrapped and placed in the garage with the rest of the paintings and the boxes. We agreed that the Pink Lady, who'd been in the house since before it was Lydia's, should stay where she was. The Bosleys would have to decide about her when they moved in.

I was feeling increasingly nostalgic that afternoon as we puttered around the house. I remember hearing the Coldplay song

"Viva la Vida," the summer's anthem, for what seemed like the hundredth time, and Peck with her tin ear singing along at the top of her lungs, getting the words wrong.

"I just remembered something," she cried out suddenly as I decided not to even try to fit everything into the one suitcase. I would use one of the dusty old cases on the shelf in the garage.

Peck flicked her ash in the direction of the small ashtray she clutched in the other hand and missed. "Back in a flash," she cried out.

I thought we'd finished organizing the contents of the house but Peck came back to my room a few seconds later holding a large wicker laundry basket in two hands, the cigarette and ashtray having been deposited somewhere. "Remember that day I dumped everything out of the desk drawer and then Finn called to invite you to the Four Seasons?" She held out the basket so I could see what was inside. "This is all the stuff that was in that drawer. I completely forgot about it."

"Is there anything in it?" I asked.

"I have no earthly idea," she exclaimed, turning the basket over so the contents, papers and business cards and clippings from magazines, rained down onto the wood floor.

A slip of notepaper drifted to my feet and I picked it up. It had several holes at the top, as though it had once been pinned to a bulletin board. Across the top were four block letters that read SAFE and then underneath, in tiny handwriting that was still recognizably Lydia's: "Scott's birthday." "Here it is," I said, holding up the loose piece of paper. "If we'd found this right away, we would have been able to open the safe."

Peck glanced at the handwriting. "Scott," she said with a laugh. "As though he were her boyfriend."

Another item in the pile at my feet caught my eye and I reached down to pick it up. It was a postcard, and it too was pricked with holes along the top where it must have been pinned up. The front of the postcard was an image that was unmistakably recognizable as the painting that we had erroneously believed to be a missing Jackson Pollock. On the back was an invitation to an opening at a gallery in East Hampton containing the following words: "The Woman as Muse. Oil on Canvas. New Works by Julian Powell."

I held it out so Peck could see it. "Julian Powell," I read aloud. "How did we not make that connection?"

She shrugged. "We weren't looking for it."

"I'm glad we found it, though," I said, waving the postcard in my hand. "That explains why the painting meant so much to her."

Lydia's copy of *The Great Gatsby*, not a first edition but a version published later, was sitting on the bedside table where I'd left it when I reread the last few pages only that morning. *And so we beat on, boats against the current, borne back ceaselessly into the past.* I tucked the postcard inside the dust jacket flap and closed the book.

19

Traditionally, the Fool's Farewell had always taken place during the day at the cracked and crumbling tennis court. The bar cart, holding champagne and strawberries—"Just like at Wimbledon," explained Peck, who'd never been to the All-England Lawn Tennis Championships but was quite the expert on what one ate and drank and wore and did there—would be wheeled down the driveway and set up on the sidelines along with white folding chairs for the spectators. She may not have attended Wimbledon, but she had been to a few more Fool's Farewells than I had, so she viewed herself as the keeper of the tradition. This year, however, we made the decision to break from tradition—or she made it and I went along with it—and hold the party in the evening, with a deejay for dancing rather than tennis as the entertainment. Our decision was made after a lengthy discussion with Hamilton, who "did so love the sight of men's legs in tennis whites," but also thought it would be fitting that this year's event take on a different flavor, since it was the Final Farewell.

It was a warm Saturday afternoon at the very beginning of August, but there was a gentle breeze, carrying the sweet smell of freshly mown grass and salt, to keep the sun, high in the cloudless blue, from beating down too relentlessly.

The deejay we'd hired was a pudgy boy wearing what looked like pajamas who seemed buried behind a mountain of equipment and speakers on one end of the porch. We also enlisted the help of a caterer for some of the food, although Peck and I had made guacamole and lobster rolls and a few other specialties of hers. We rented tables and bought flowers and votives we'd planned to use to light the porch. The old plank floors seemed to sag even more under the extra weight, but Fool's House in the candlelight looked its most charming.

The first strains of an amped-up version of the old classic "Love Is in the Air" were blasting as the Girls gathered around the two of us, pecking at us like friendly birds.

"Let me see you," Lucy demanded, stepping back to admire my dress, the one we'd picked together. "You're *fabulous*," they decreed. "Isn't she fabulous?"

"*Et moi?*" Peck wanted to know, never one to miss an opportunity to fish for a compliment or use her French. She was wearing a long turquoise halter dress that matched her eyes, and she'd never looked prettier. The Girls voiced their admiration at length until she exhorted them to get cocktails "before the mad rush begins." The Girls tended to be obedient, especially when vodka was involved, and they moved toward the bar as the place quickly began to swarm with people.

I took a cocktail and wandered through the lawn, as evening fell, catching snippets of conversation. There seemed to be a reckless glamour to the people gathered under the lanterns among the trees and crowded together on the porch, as though anything could happen, anything at all. Or that may have just been my perspective as I catalogued the scene, committing it to memory. I stood out on the grass, looking up at the ramshackle house Lydia had loved for so many years, and I wondered how the Bosleys would fare there. Would they "get" the house as Peck and I did and fall in love with it? Would they make it their own, renaming it perhaps, and starting their own traditions? Or would the house "get" them, overwhelming them with responsibility and faulty plumbing and the desperate need for an expensive new roof and a dishwasher, at the very least, to update the kitchen?

As I gazed up at the house, I noticed Finn come through the door to the porch. I hadn't seen him since that morning, when he'd gotten up early after a somewhat somber dinner at Hamilton's. He'd stayed the night with me at Fool's House, but neither of us had been able to sleep much, and by six he'd headed off, leaving me to finish packing and get organized for the night's festivities. He was taller than almost everyone, so he was easy to spot, and my heart flipped over when I saw his head, wet hair gleaming.

What was I thinking? I realized with a jolt that I couldn't possibly say good-bye to him. How had I not understood that this was bigger than both of us? We would have to work something out, a long-distance relationship, a bicontinental affair, until something more permanent could be decided on. But the idea of a final goodbye when I headed to the airport? That was impossible.

I moved toward the porch with the intent to tell him I'd changed my mind. I thought I'd seen him going toward the bar at the far end of the porch, and I tried to catch another glimpse of him as I moved through what was now a very crowded lawn. There were hundreds of people, it seemed, spilling over the grass, and a whole group of boldly earnest dancers bopped about on the creaking slats of the porch. Hamilton saw me and waved me over to where he and Scotty were watching the dancers. "If you're looking for Finn, he left."

My heart immediately sank.

"Don't look so gloomy," Hamilton snapped. "Scotty, look at poor Stella; she's morose. She thinks he left her for good. No, no, my dear. He bought you a gift, he told us, but he forgot it. He's gone home to fetch it and he'll be right back."

The relief that flooded over me—a gift? he bought me a *present?*—must have been comical, because they both burst out laughing. "Look how sweet," Hamilton said, nudging Scotty. "Now she's beaming. He bought her a going-away present. I wonder what it is."

I was now so excited I could hardly stand still, a fact that Hamilton noticed. "You and Scotty should *dance*," he suggested.

I'd never been someone who danced. But the fragile creature who'd washed up on this shore a month ago was gone, and I was now able to casually contemplate a little of what Peck had been calling "booty back and forth, booty back and forth." I had Peck to thank for that, I suppose. I now grabbed Scotty by the hand to pull him into the middle of the sweating crowd hopping about vigorously on the old porch.

We danced for a while—the little Scotsman knew how to *move*—as the crowd around us grew louder and more raucous. Eventually there were so many people packed in on the porch between the deejay at one end and the tables and the bar at the other that we couldn't move laterally, only hop up and down, like in a mosh pit.

"I think I've had enough," I shouted at Scotty when there was no more air to breathe on the porch. Finn had not yet reappeared; I kept checking the driveway every five seconds. But I could see Peck at the far end of the lawn, with just the glow of her cigarette for company as she gazed up at Fool's House. She was standing in almost exactly the same position that I'd occupied a little earlier, and I thought I knew what was going through her mind. I kissed my dance partner on the cheek and headed down to find my sister.

It was unusual for her to be alone like this at a party, especially her own, and I expected her to be in a serious, reflective mood. But Peck didn't much care for serious or reflective.

"There must be two hundred people on the porch!" She propped one elbow in the other hand and gestured elegantly with the cigarette toward the porch so I would look and admire the scene. I did. There was a kind of beautiful madness to the swirling frenzy, with all the flickering candles in the darkness. We stood side by side, smoking, watching the kaleidoscope of people and movement and light as the party built to its inevitable crescendo and the moment imprinted itself on my brain with the permanence of a black-and-white photograph.

Suddenly there was a loud cracking sound. It was followed by an ominous sort of groan, and then slowly, almost gracefully, the entire middle of the porch fell in on itself. The dancers disappeared right before our very eyes. The deejay and his mountain of heavy equipment slid from view, and the music scratched to an abrupt halt. At first it was quiet. Anyone who wasn't on the porch was shocked and stunned silent in disbelief. We couldn't possibly have witnessed what we just saw.

Then chaos erupted and there were screams and muffled yelling for help and people on top of one another and others emerging from inside the house, caught with one foot on the stable floor in the doorway and one foot now suspended in mid-air. Peck and I ran toward them, racing up what was left of the teetering steps to the sunken porch. We looked down into the gaping hole where the pieces of the porch and a number of our guests had fallen. There were people piled on the ground and jagged pieces of wood jutting dangerously. The deejay was still standing and he gave us a bewildered look from behind his equipment, which seemed to have landed upright as well, as though he could just go right on cranking the music from this new space underneath where the porch was meant to be.

Nobody appeared to be hurt. They started gingerly standing up, turning their wrists and stepping on their ankles to see if they'd damaged any parts, gazing up through the hole where the porch had pulled away from the house and fallen in on itself. And then the noise picked up again as people asked one another if they were okay and called out, "That was crazy!" Someone laughed.

And then there was another shout. "The candles!" At the far end of the gaping hole one of the ragged porch planks suddenly sparked where a candle had dumped its flame onto the old wood. And then another one. And another one. The planks sparked and snapped like kindling, and in what seemed like seconds, the flames were jumping, erupting into a full-blown fire before our eyes.

"Everybody out," I yelled, as the fire seemed to engulf the porch instantly and then spread to the cedar shingles that covered the entire house. Immediately the people on what was left of the porch poured onto the lawn in a mad rush to escape, and Peck and I helped pull those who were caught in the hole in the middle to safety. The deejay was trying in vain to pull apart his equipment so he could get it out of the way.

"Leave it," Peck shouted at him as the flames jumped to the second floor windows in a matter of seconds.

"Call 911," I called to the crowd behind us on the lawn, watching as Peck and I made sure everyone was out of the way. I couldn't believe how fast the fire moved to take over the house. It was like a tinderbox, igniting instantly. "Was anyone still inside?"

"Trimalchio!" Peck suddenly screamed, dashing down the steps of the porch and around to the back of the house.

I followed her. We had to elbow our way around some of the guests, who were all staring, dumbfounded, at the leaping flames quickly turning Fool's House into an enormous bonfire. "Where would he be?"

"Check Lydia's room," she cried. "I'll look in mine."

We swung open the kitchen door and raced into the house. It was already thick with smoke and I quickly grabbed two dishtowels and ran them under the faucet. "Wait," I called after Peck as she ran up the stairs, "put this over your nose and mouth."

She didn't listen to me. "Check the dining room first," she called down. "Anyone in here?" We both shouted at the top of our lungs. I didn't have to check the dining room. Trimalchio was at my feet already.

I picked him up and yelled up to Peck, "I got him." She didn't answer me and I yelled again. "Peck, come on, I've got him. There's nobody else in here."

I ran the dog to the kitchen door and swung it open. "Go get help," I told him. He gave me a worried look. "She's going to be fine; go on."

I let the door swing shut and raced back to the stairs. The living room curtains had gone up in flames and the fire was quickly moving into the house. I took the steps two at a time, still clutching the two wet dishtowels. I held them over my nose but I was also trying to yell for Peck. She wasn't in Lydia's room or in either of the other two bedrooms, or in the bathroom.

I moved the dishtowel and shouted, "Peck!"

By now the fire was already raging inside the house and I could hear loud cracks as beams snapped. I ran back down the stairs into a pool of flames, beating them off me with the damp towels. The kitchen was already burning and I couldn't go back out that way. "Peck!" I screamed again, heading through the dining room toward a window that looked clear. I told myself I'd missed her. She must have gone out the front door while I took Trimalchio out the back. I pushed at the window, which probably hadn't been opened since the seventies. It was stuck fast. I could feel the heat behind me as I pushed as hard as I could, still shouting for Peck. The smoke was thick in my lungs. Just when I thought I was going to have to find another way out, the window gave way slightly. I pushed it open enough to fit through the frame and punched and shimmied my way into the bushes on that side of the house.

As I lay there, almost unconscious from the smoke, I knew. Peck was dead. Hadn't she predicted this very thing, at the beginning of the summer? She'd said they'd have to carry her out of there in a box.

The pain of grief overtook me and in that moment, just before it all went black, I understood what Lydia had meant when she wrote to us about what she hoped we would find in her house. It was us, Peck and me, the bond of sisterhood between us: that was the thing of utmost value Lydia wanted us to find.

I passed out.

When I opened my eyes, the first thing I saw was Finn's face looking worried. When he noticed I was coming around, he smiled. "Hey, kid."

"Peck," I tried to say. But all that came out was a croak.

"Shhhh," he said in a soothing voice. There was no better sound in the world than his voice. "Don't talk. I can hear the ambulance. You're going to be okay. Everything's going to be okay."

I opened my mouth again to ask about Peck. But nothing came out. I started to cry. "It's going to be okay," he kept repeating in that voice of his, deep and raspy and comforting. "Everything's going to be fine."

Behind us, the house was a bonfire. I could hear sirens and men shouting instructions and I pulled myself up onto my elbows to see what was going on. I needed to know about Peck.

"Don't try to get up," Finn said. "Here comes the ambulance."

I tried again to ask about Peck, but then the medics were there and I had an oxygen mask over my nose and mouth. I didn't feel I even needed to ask. I knew she was gone. I felt it. I just sat crying, holding the oxygen over my mouth with one hand as Finn held the other.

Time seemed to stand still. The house burned on and I sat there watching and sobbing in utter sadness, mesmerized by the leaping flames. I don't know how long we stayed there like that, but it seemed like hours.

Then there she was. Standing over me in her turquoise dress with a martini glass in one hand and a cigarette in the other, looking no different than she had before the porch fell in. I gaped at her. For a second or two, I thought she was a ghost. "Peck," I was finally able to say when I pulled aside the oxygen mask.

"Literally," she declared. "You scared me half to *death*."

"I thought—" I started to say, but I couldn't finish. The words just wouldn't come, so I pointed at her to indicate that she was the one I'd thought was missing, presumed dead.

"You thought *I* was dead? Me?" She gestured with her cigarette. "It's going to take more than a fire for you to get rid of me."

She stood back to look at me. "I like the charred look," she said, referring to the black smudges on my face I wouldn't see until later. "Very *Rescue Me*." I must have looked confused because she explained, "It's a TV show. About a hot mess of a fireman. Speaking of hot messes, I need to get back to Miles to tell him you're okay. Finn, look after my sister for me."

"Peck," I managed to call after her as she picked her way through the grass in her high heels, holding out the martini glass so it wouldn't spill on her. She turned and I said, "I love you, Peck."

She waved to acknowledge my words, not ones I'd ever spoken to her before. "Love you too, Stella."

Finn sat on the grass next to me and reached around to pull something from his pocket. It was a small box, exactly the size that might hold a piece of jewelry, wrapped in white tissue paper and tied with a raffia ribbon. I slowly untied the ribbon and pulled off the paper. I could feel him watching me. Inside the paper was a small cardboard box with a lid that I opened with great anticipation, expecting, beyond a shadow of a doubt, to find a velvet box inside. But instead what I found, nestled inside the cardboard box in a bed of more white tissue, was a fake *rock*. No, not a fake diamond. An actual rock. Well, an actual *fake* rock.

"Just what I've always wanted." I managed to deadpan. "A rock. For my collection."

He smiled. "You're funny, kid. Flip it over," he said. "It opens."

At the bottom of the fake rock was a panel that popped open, revealing a key. The key slid out onto my hand.

"It's the key to my house," he said, taking the rock from me and holding it up. "You hide it in this. It's a couple of steps trickier than leaving it under the welcome mat."

I held the key in my palm and closed my fingers over it as a wave of emotion ran through me. I'd never been a jewelry person anyway. "Whatever will they think of next?"

"When I designed that house," he said, almost like he'd practiced what he wanted to say, "I wanted it to become a home. I always planned to share it with someone, and eventually to share it with a bunch of little someones too. And somewhere in the back of my mind, I always thought of you as that someone."

My eyes filled with tears. He helped me up and we stood together, arms wrapped around each other as Fool's House burned.

Peck made her way back to us, with Miles in tow. He held up one hand to meet mine. "I'm glad you're okay," he said.

"Thanks," I said. "I'm glad you're okay too."

Finn still had one arm around my waist and Peck wrapped an arm around me on the other side. I hugged her with one arm, still holding the key to Finn's house clutched in my fist. Miles was on her other side, and then Hamilton and Scotty joined us and we stood together, the six of us, watching the firefighters attempt to get the fire under control.

"Literally," Peck said. "I think I prefer this ending."

The six of us stood together watching as Fool's House burned almost to the ground. Only the stone chimney didn't burn and, miraculously, the Julian Powell painting we'd erroneously believed to be a Jackson Pollock hanging above the fireplace survived, slightly smoke damaged, but otherwise intact.

Epilogue

by Pecksland Moriarty

Summer again, 2009

Pecksland Moriarty here with what *I* have to say about all this. Normally I loathe epilogues but right from the start—from the very first line—I take issue with my sister's version of this story. For one thing, hats are almost *never* a mistake. For another, they aren't anything like first husbands. I personally intend to have only one, one husband that is—a feat that is easily accomplished if one chooses well—so perhaps I'm not an authority. But that never stopped me from having an opinion. And hats are always chic.

I *never* insisted that my sister accompany me to the Gatsby party and I certainly never begged. If there's one thing I don't do, it's beg. Stella was *dying* to join me. She even said, "I'm dying to come," with absolutely no irony whatsoever, even though everything out of her mouth when she got to Fool's House just dripped with sarcasm. I don't start sentences with the word *literally*. That doesn't even make any sense. I also *never* said, "A literary fetish is the new black." And I certainly don't scream during sex. I don't know where she gets this stuff.

She twists the facts and puts words in people's mouths, and

when I complain, she says, "But it's fiction." She's even more prone to hyperbole than ever now that she's officially a writer. Plus, that's roughly the same excuse—"Hey, man, it's art," he'd say—used by Biggs.

She left out a lot of the best parts. I had some really good lines last summer that she simply cut from her manuscript. If you ask me, that's rude. And another thing: Miles says he truly didn't plan the Gatsby theme party with me in mind. I'm totally willing to suspend my disbelief on that, so I don't know what business my sister has constantly bringing it up. In fact, she'll probably mention it this evening at the wedding.

Yes, this story ends with a wedding, as so many of the good ones do. She wanted to just leave you hanging there, in the smoke and fire at the end of last summer. What kind of an ending was that? She may have said she learned a few things about telling a story from me, but she never paid close enough attention. It's not her fault; she has ADD. I'm sure I do too.

But this story can't end with a fire. Comedies must end with a wedding. The kind where the bride and groom act like there's never, ever been a wedding before, the kind where there are enormous tulle bows on the backs of the chairs and calligraphy on the invitations demanding that everyone wear white. And hats for the ladies, of course. Hamilton says that's very British. Oh, and sugared almonds in little bags. Those were Hamilton's idea too. It's the kind of wedding where there is only the finest champagne and the best man is a dog wearing a bow tie.

Not Hamilton and Scotty's wedding. Theirs took place on New Year's Eve in Switzerland. None of us are sure it was actually legal, but it was mad beautiful in the snow with both grooms in white tie. The six of us did, in fact, spend Christmas in the mountains, exactly as I predicted we would. We ate fondue until I couldn't even fit into my ski pants, but it didn't matter because Miles and I didn't spend much time on the slopes anyway.

We also spent Columbus Day weekend in Lausanne, where Finn was then designing a small museum for a client. Their life is all very glamorous and chaotic and involves a lot of air travel now as they've been dividing their time between Lausanne and New York, aka the greatest city in the world. Yes, Stella's become one of *those* New Yorkers.

Miles's house is still for sale—he couldn't give the place away now—so we're having the wedding there. Then I'm going to look into turning it into my version of Yaddo. Miles likes the idea. He says it's good to give back. Since he's lost almost all of his dough-re-mi, he's had some firsthand experience with this.

Stella comes into my room now. She's wearing the most fantastic dress, which I found for her. Vintage, of course, and there's no tag, but I'm pretty sure it's Geoffrey Beene. Or someone equally fabulous. You can't even tell she's two months pregnant.

"Here," she says, holding out a tall cocktail on ice garnished with mint. "I brought you a dressing drink."

I almost start to cry but I don't want to muss my makeup. "You're a very good sister."

She smiles. "So are you." She takes a sip. "You ready? They're waiting for you."

I fuss with my hat one more time, checking the mirror. It's another Philip Treacy, quite absolutely fabulous, if I may say so. "Is Miles down there?"

"He's a nervous wreck." She takes my hand. "You are, without a doubt, the most outrageously stylish bride."

Wait, you thought Stella was the bride? You think I was going to end with their wedding? God, no. For one thing, she still says she's not getting married, even though she and Finn are disgustingly in love. Apparently it's very chic and European to skip marriage and go straight to the babies. I, however, am a very American girl. And I'm not ashamed to admit I wanted a big wedding. Of course, it's not *comme il faut* to throw big lavish theme parties anymore. So ours is a small affair. Just the six of us and Mum. And Trimalchio, of course.

Acknowledgments

Acknowledgements in novels are problematic. When too short they appear terse and we read between the lines, seeing tension and ambiguity in the faint thanks. When too long, with endless lists of names and adjectives, they read like a high school yearbook page—*look how popular I am!* Some include celebrities—or, worse, famous writers who provided "inspiration"(!)—and sound horribly pretentious. Frankly, I wanted to skip the whole exercise. One, because I've been out of high school for a long time. Two, because I'm lazy and a procrastinator and just finishing the novel was hard enough. And three, because I'm terrified of offending anyone. Also, I don't personally know any celebrities. But it would be rude and inaccurate not to express my extreme heart-felt (see? The adjectives immediately start to pile up in a way that seems cloying) gratitude to my editor, Kendra Harpster, and the other brilliant (yes, really) women at Viking: Clare Ferraro, Molly Stern, Nancy Sheppard, Tricia Conley, Veronica Windholz, Tory Klose, Rachel Burd, and Amanda Brower, who worked on this book with me. Thank you so much. I feel very lucky to adore my agent (sorry, do you think that sounds smug? I do), Leigh Feldman, and I have to tell her and the team at Darhansoff, Verill, Feldman how much all their efforts on my behalf have been appreciated. While my family and friends are all a little tired of this whole *novelist* thing, I want to thank them for their patience, especially my son Harry, who read *Gatsby* this year (or so he tells me), to whom this book is dedicated and my two younger children, Nick and Zoe, who were less than pleased to see their older brother singled out for attention. (Your turns will come, we hope.) And of course, I have to acknowledge and thank the man I've loved all of my adult life, my first, and presumably only, husband, David, who is not, I repeat, NOT, a character in this story and was most definitely not a mistake. (He *has* read *Gatsby*, though, or so he tells me).

Also by Danielle Ganek

ISBN: 978-0-452-28954-3

On Sale Now

Available wherever books are sold.

Plume
A member of Penguin Group (USA) Inc.
www.penguin.com